RICO

GEORGE HATCHER

CasaHatcherPress

DEDICATION

Molly
You are my sun during the day and my moon at night.
Love forever, George

ACKNOWLEDGMENTS

Managing editor, Allie Bates, you are the best!

WARNING

Adult matter

This book is intended for adults. Violence and sexual antics are not intended for minors, sensitive readers, or people living in the current crazy world where there are sexually transmitted diseases which are incurable, and a pandemic which has chased us inside to solitary confinement in our houses.

All of the characters, organizations and events portrayed in this novel are figments of my imagination.

BOOKS BY GEORGE

ONE WILSHIRE
PRETTY FACE
ARABE
MARIO 1: WOMAN IN JEOPARDY
MARIO 2: COMING OF AGE
MARIO 3: RISKY BUSINESS
MARIO 4: FREE FALL
MARIO 5: AFIRE
MARIO 6: MARKED
MARIO 7: AFTERSHOCK
MARIO 8: CAPTIVATED
GABI 1
BILLION DOLLAR RAINMAKER 1
RICO 1

COMING SOON

GABI 2

MARIO 9

RICO 2

BILLION DOLLAR RAINMAKER 2

BILLION DOLLAR RAINMAKER 3

CHAPTER 1
RICO SANTOS

IN THE BEGINNING

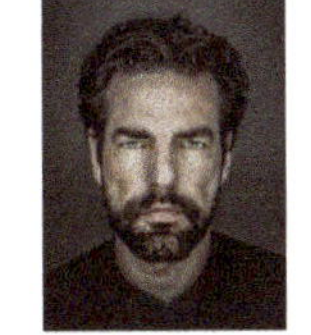

MY NAME IS Rico Hidalgo Santos. Hidalgo from my mother's last name, Santos from my father's last name. I was born on October 1, 1965. My father, a drug runner for my grandmother, died during a gunfight with a drug dealer who owed my grandmother money. My mother died after injecting herself with pure heroin. My grandmother, Magda Hidalgo Cordova, inherited her heroin business from Beto Hidalgo, her husband and my grandfather. After he died, she grew the business that made her the largest producer of heroin in Northern Mexico and became known as La Mala. My brother Victor is one year younger than me. My grandmother took charge of raising my brother and me after our parents died. We were infants, and the only parent we remember is my grandmother.

The only house I have ever known is the big house built by my grandfather, remodeled many times by my grandmother, where I live now with my brother. When I say big, I can't emphasize enough just how big it is.

The neighborhood is one of the worst in Juarez, Mexico. Before my time, my grandfather and grandmother ran the heroin business out of this house. I'm told the house was one third the size it is now when addicts would come to a side entrance, drop their pesos in a slot next to the door and were handed the powder for one injection.

After my parents died, my grandmother stopped her retail sales of heroin. My brother and I did not grow up in that environment. Many times, I caught my grandmother alone, crying for the passing of my mother, blaming my grandfather and herself for having heroin in easy reach of my mother. They didn't know my mother had become addicted. When she injected it, my mother didn't know it was pure. Pure heroin is deadly.

Before I was born, my grandmother bought all the neighboring properties and built a twenty-foot wall around the complex, so the house was not visible from outside the walls. The house and land occupy four acres surrounded by four streets. My grandmother could have built a dream home in a better part of the city, but this is where she's been all of her life. It is not merely her own neighborhood. She's created her own little world part of, but also apart from, Juarez.

"I love trees," my grandmother often said to Victor and me. We had more trees than any park in the city.

Sometimes big trucks brought more trees, grown trees, tall trees, unloaded and planted with the assistance of a crane. A wooden name-plate staked in the ground tagged each tree. Once I counted forty weeping willow trees. I love weeping willows.

My grandmother had two swimming pools built, one on the property for my brother and me, and the other, a big public swimming pool a short distance away from our house. From dawn till late at night all summer, three lifeguards and a manager were on duty at the public pool. Kids under eight years old had access to the pool from seven in the morning until noon. Adults and kids over nine years old had the pool for the rest of the day until closing at nine at night. When my brother and I went to the public pool we mingled with everyone, my grandmother encouraged us to do so but it didn't take much encouragement. Victor and I were loners for kids our age back at the house, getting outside the walls of the compound was like a vacation we had never taken yet.

Juarez is a border city, sister city to El Paso, Texas. For a long time, I did not know my brother and I were US citizens. My mother's doctor's practice was in El Paso. While expecting, she spent her last month of pregnancy in a hotel on the US side of the border. Both my brother and I were delivered in an El Paso hospital.

We grew up in the big house where construction seemed to always be going on. We had the run of the whole house and all the grounds, though there weren't any children around to play with on our side of the wall except on Sunday. My brother and me, we were close, and we knew we only had each other. Grandmother often told us that when we grew older, we could go outside the grounds and make friends with kids our age and not have to wait for Sunday to come around.

Every Sunday, children of men and women who worked inside the grounds came over to swim and play. Looking back, I don't know what method was used, if any, to select what kids came over. I remember they were children our age. There were always no less than eighty people doing something in the house, in and out. I know, I once went around and counted each one.

Yes, Sunday was a day to look forward to. It was a party. I asked my grandmother if we could have horses and she laughed and said she'd think about it. We settled for the swimming pool and all the great food and goodies that were prepared by the kitchen help. It was like an all-day picnic. I know about picnics because I see people in the movies, in the park with a blanket over the grass. Only our picnics were better because we had tables and chairs and at least two clowns making fun with us. Sometimes a magician doing magic. All this under the cover of big trees giving us beautiful shade. Juarez is very hot.

Now about the movies. My grandmother had two projectors and all the workers joined us outdoors to watch movies. Before the movie, we got to see two cartoons. I would learn later that this is how my grandmother gave us a movie theatre on the grounds.

If you want to know, workers put up tall white boards and joined them together to show the movie. I'd learn soon enough that was the screen. It was fun.

The kids that came over talked about going to school and my brother and I wondered what the heck was school anyway. We learned soon enough when James Baker moved inside the wall, and we began to sit in a classroom on the top floor of the house. Soon after, another schoolteacher joined us. Her name was Elena. I was about six and my brother was a year younger.

"Grandmother, why can't we go to school like the kids that come over on Sunday?" asked Victor during dinner one day.

"We don't have school near us that can give you the education that James will give you," she replied.

I didn't understand the education part, but my grandmother was not someone I argued with and neither did my brother. She never spanked me or my brother, never, but she did have a way about her that was scary. Her frowns.

"Okay," said Victor, looking over at James, who was sitting at the dinner table with us.

"I promise, learning will be a lot of fun," said James.

I clapped my hands and laughed at the fun promise.

CHAPTER 2
JAMES BAKER

I AM a Londoner born to Melissa and Robert Baker on January 17, 1917. My father owned and drove his own black Coventry-made taxi six days a week and earned good enough money to own the brownstone we called home in a nice area ten minutes from Heathrow Airport. Planes flew over our house, day and night, seven days a week. You get used to it. Pops always said that we could have never afforded the house we lived in if it was in another area of London.

I was a smart student, a loner who spent much time in the school library where I did my homework so I could have the evening free to watch television or read. I read all the time, a real bookworm.

I won a scholarship to attend Oxford University but had no idea what to major in. All I ever wanted was to graduate from high school, get a full-time job, save my money, and buy a Coventry taxi like my father. Before you become a taxi driver in London, you need to know the city, its shortcuts, its secrets, but I mastered that before Oxford.

I didn't have that many close friends. They thought the scholarship was out of sight. I got excited over the opportunity and decided to make the best of it. I moved out of my parents' home to Oxford, a sixty-mile drive from London. My counselor told me I would have many opportunities for employment with a psychology degree, especially with a master's degree. I became interested in languages, and I was pretty good with Italian, French, Spanish, and German.

My first job after I graduated was with the London Stock Exchange. I counseled human resources employees on hiring practices, interviewed new hires, and did a lot of consulting. When an employee was being fired, I would ensure a happy ending to the relationship. We didn't want disgruntled former employees with axes to grind. I made much more money than I could have made as a cabbie.

Without warning, my father had a heart attack at fifty. Within a few years, my mother sold his cab, sold the house, remarried, and moved with her new husband to Amsterdam. All of London made her sad, so I felt good about her moving on. The whole city was nothing but a memory of my father and her empty nest. I have no brothers and sisters.

I felt all alone in the world, or at least, all alone in London. I went from loving my job to finding it boring after ten years. I hooked up with a headhunter who found me a position with a giant stock brokerage for double the salary. I counseled the stockbrokers regularly, animating those who were getting sluggish or lazy without telling them they might get fired if they didn't straighten out. I didn't invest in the stock market where I worked, but I hooked up with a stockbroker, and paid attention, learned what stocks were good, what were hot, and what were sleepers. In a year, I invested fifty thousand British pounds. The investment grew to a hundred fifty thousand.

Sally, a lady janitor, worked at the brokerage house. She came in about an hour after everyone had gone home. I was always last to leave, a hangover from my school days. I still felt homework should be done before I got home. My homework at the brokerage was to sum up the day's work, tidy up the file of every person I counseled or met with that day, and prep my paperwork for the next day.

I ran into Sally every weeknight. She was a total cutie, eight years younger than I was, but she took an interest in me. The interest was mutual. A year after I met her, she quit her job. I married her and promised her she would never have to work again. Sally was adorable, and I loved her, thankful I had waited as long as I had to find the woman for me.

We rented an apartment in central London. It was expensive, but nice, and I could walk to work. I was making more money on the stock market than at my high-paying job with the brokerage firm. The stock market could plunge at any time, so I put away as much as I could, but I did reinvest. Reinvesting paid off.

Sally had female problems and could not bear children. I told her we could always adopt. I assured her we would be fine. We found the perfect flat for us in Knightsbridge, and it wasn't near the airport and the noise of planes. With no strain at all, I put down sixty percent of the sales price. Our mortgage payment was half of what our rent had been. Life was sweet.

I had not had a vacation in more than two years, so I took a month off from work. Sally and I flew to New York for a week, Los Angeles for a week, Miami for a week, Washington DC for two days, then flew home. My wife and I grew ever closer.

A month after our return to London, Sally went in for a routine checkup. The mammogram turned up cancer. Less than a year later, I lost Sally to breast cancer. Her family was devastated. I was crushed. The only family I had left was my mom in Amsterdam, who had never met Sally. She offered to come to the funeral, but I gave her a pass.

I asked the headhunter who had placed me at my job to find another psychologist, and he did. When I interviewed him, I found he was not from Oxford, but he was good enough. The COO of the company already knew I wanted to leave. I got the new man started and introduced him around. My friend who had taught me about stocks, also named James, was a trader. We went out and got so drunk at a tavern that I only recall the first half of the night. We promised to stay in touch with each other. A month after I buried Sally, I ditched the job. Somehow that broke my stiff British upper lip, and I was able to go home and grieve.

When I had no tears left to shed, I decided I would travel. Since Sally's parents lived in the same small, rented house where they had raised Sally and her two sisters, I gave Sally's parents the key to the house, and offered to let them move in and live rent free.

"Plan on me not selling the house for at least five years. I'm not going to be back to ask you to move. All the furniture is yours to keep. Give away the clothes I leave behind or do anything you want with them. I will not need them."

After I rented an apartment in Paris, I donated a full day of each week to a Catholic University that needed a psychologist to counsel troubled students on the path to expulsion or suspension. I spent a year in Paris, one in Venice, then a year in Rome. In Rome, I donated time to the Vatican, counseling priests and cardinals. I enjoyed my work and lived on the lavish ongoing proceeds of my stock market account. In Ethiopia, I taught two English classes a day in a public school, and I did the same in Nairobi. From country to country, I stayed in touch with Sally's father. The five-year mark came and went, and I told them to rest easy. I had no need to sell the house. By the time I arrived in Cairo, Egypt, I had been gone from London more than six years. A mild cardio event put me in the hospital for one day. The cardiologist who attended to me looked at my family history. He zeroed in on my father, dying of a heart attack at fifty years old.

I returned to Paris, rented an apartment again, and signed a one-year lease. Being a short distance from London made me happy. I preferred living in Paris for the time being. Two Parisian doctors told me to cool the drinking, maybe switch to wine, and to relax more. My family history haunted me and made me anxious. I found comfort in one-night stands, sometimes extending the one night to a week but seldom longer.

Sally's parents and one set of grandchildren were still living in my house, and that was perfectly fine with me. I had paid off the mortgage. Sometimes I would look at my investment account and think of gifting the house to Sally's parents. After all, half the house had belonged to Sally.

One morning, I got a call from Steve, Sally's father.

"James you had a call from Jeff Lewis. He left a number and wants you to call him."

My home phone was still at the house. There had been no reason to change it. Jeff Lewis was the head-hunter who had placed me at the brokerage firm many years ago and who had found my replacement after Sally died.

I called Jeff.

"You must be on the hunt for an unemployed psychologist."

"Where are you?"

"Living in Paris."

"You're so lucky," Jeff said. "I have an interesting inquiry. Do you have time to talk?"

"I'm retired. All I have is time."

Jeff told me he had a client from Mexico, an attorney, who represented a wealthy family in Juarez, Mexico.

"The family is looking for a teacher. Actually, more than a teacher, someone to live on the premises. They want a smart man like yourself."

"Jeff, I'm a psychologist, not a teacher."

"You're a graduate of Oxford with a master's. You can do anything."

"I don't want to live in Mexico."

"You haven't hung up on me. That means you are curious. Frankly, I'm curious too. The family will pay you fifty thousand dollars and fly you in a private jet to interview for two days with the lawyer and the family."

"Are you having a laugh? Are you barmy?"

"That's not all. I'm getting twenty thousand dollars if all you do is accept the interview, and a lot more if you accept the position."

"If I accept that interview, I'm your new best friend." I laughed. But then I had to be honest and make it clear to Jeff. "I have to take it easy. Three cardiologists in two different countries have convinced me that if I don't change my lifestyle, I'll be like my dad. He croaked it at fifty and I'm fifty-three. I am on borrowed time."

"Sounds like it's time to change doctors."

"Tell me more about these people. How well do you know them?"

The driver who had brought me from the airport drove me through the gates. Even expecting a mansion, I was surprised to see the huge estate behind the walls. A security guard greeted me by name and took me through a side door that led into the basement. That's where I first met Raul Robles, attorney for Magda, my boss. Raul gave me an informal tour of the basement, one of the areas he told me I could revamp as needed.

"I'll show you the rest of the house," he said, "but before you meet Magda, you should know some things." He told me about her husband and his reputation of being a monster drug dealer until he died. "The reputation has rubbed off on Magda," Raul said. "Everything derogatory you read or heard about her is a pack of lies."

Raul was lying through his teeth. He's a lawyer, after all, and protecting Magda's interests. I came to understand that her reputation was probably not a lie, but it was none of my business if I wanted the job.

"The basement is huge," I said. "I hope that I am not expected to live down here." I had not yet seen the living area upstairs.

Raul laughed. "Not at all. There are many rooms to choose from upstairs."

"I am sure they are fine. The thing is, in Paris I had a different woman every night if I wanted."

"Mariscal, the red zone, is three blocks from the house." Raul laughed with a suggestive edge to his voice. "You won't have to go on the hunt."

"I'm not sure how well that would go over if I am living upstairs," I said.

Raul mentioned a guest house on the grounds, but it needed work. Then he led me up to an elegant study where I spent many hours behind closed doors with Magda. After the meeting, I was certain she would not put her grandsons in harm's way by running a drug operation from her residence, and that was the only thing that mattered to me. If she had her fingers into something illegal somewhere in the world, it was none of my business.

After meeting Magda, Raul took me to see the guest house. I could see it had good bones, but it needed work. The subject came up at dinner that night. Raul was still there, and he suggested I might be more comfortable having my own separate quarters. Bachelor quarters, he called them.

"If that is what you want," Magda said. "I will make it a beautiful place by the time you move in."

My two-day interview lasted a week, and I lived it as a guest in the main house and spent hours with Rico and Victor. It was Rico and Victor themselves who cinched the deal for me. I liked the boys from the instant I met them. I felt right away that they were the sons I had never had. Sally and I had always dreamed of having children. I remembered how we tried.

I didn't know anything about the drug business. I saw a lot of cash being spent, not just feeding the employees on the premises, but jetting me to and from Paris, twice, and Magda handing me fifty thousand dollars, American, for the interview. In cash. I had never seen one-thousand-dollar bills before. She gave me fifty of them. The money had to come from somewhere.

On my return to Paris, I sublet my Paris rental, and two months later, I moved to Juarez, Mexico, to a guest cottage two hundred feet from the house. The gardeners had put in an English garden and a stone folly to make me feel at home. With all the trees, greenery, and flowers, my new home was hidden like one of Tolkien's hobbit houses. In the two months between my being hired and moving in, Magda had the guest house redone in record time.

When I settled in, Raul said that I would make all major decisions regarding how to teach the boys. I would be adding other activities.

"I will work it out with Mala, and you will have whatever you want."

"Mala?" I said. "She told me to call her Magda. Did I misunderstand?"

"Her friends call her Magda," he said. "Her name is Magda Hidalgo Cordova. Mala is a nickname, not always kindly meant. It's a little complicated."

I nodded, feeling sure I would understand the nuances of meaning soon.

My monthly salary would be twenty thousand US each month. I paid nothing for room and board. All my needs would be taken care of, including any female companionship I might choose. I didn't have to be told that until the boys were old enough to understand, what I did in my guest house stayed in my guest house.

Juarez was a rugged place. I had lived in rugged places before, but I told myself that I was going to spend most of my time behind the walls of the property. I had no reason to leave. The main house was enormous, and my guest house was beautiful.

This was a long-term commitment. I put it all out on the table. I soon was settled in my small house and anxious to get started teaching the boys. I was fifty-three when I started working for Magda.

CHAPTER 3
ELENA MUNOZ

I HAD FINISHED TEACHING my last class of the day at the university and was ready to leave for home when a man came to my classroom. He was much older than my students, and I did not recognize him. He introduced himself as Gusto and handed me a letter.

"Miss Elena, sorry to intrude, and please don't be alarmed. I was told to deliver this note to you."

I looked down at the envelope. Before I looked up, he was gone.

Dear Miss Elena Munoz,

I would like to discuss an important matter with you concerning two lads that I presently teach in a private setting. I am looking to employ a smart young teacher such as yourself to teach the boys a basic Spanish education, primary, junior high, and high school. I am teaching them English. I will explain why I came to you when you call me. Should you accept my offer, the compensation is three times what you presently earn, plus a 25,000-peso bonus on acceptance.

Sincerely,
James Baker
phone 45687 in Juarez.

. . .

Who was Gusto? I knew no one by that name. I stashed the note and envelope in my purse and left to catch the metro, wondering all the while what prankster might have sent me this. I knew nobody who would go to the trouble. I stopped at the corner drugstore to call the number on the note. A woman answered.

"Residencia Hidalgo."

Hidalgo is not an uncommon name, but I wondered that it was not Baker's residence.

"Is there a James Baker available to come to the line?"

"Yes, madam," the voice said. "One moment please."

I had no idea where James Baker was residing or who he might be.

"I've had two principals and one dean tell me that you are twenty-five and have experience teaching primary, junior, and high school. And you are currently teaching Spanish, history, and economics at the university."

"I'm flattered that you know all this. I read your note. Who exactly are you?"

I heard a chuckle.

"As I said in the note, I am a tutor in a private household."

"I am not looking for employment. How did I come to your attention?"

"I talked to a principal at a local junior high and she sent me to a principal at a high school, and eventually I ended up with the dean of the university where you teach."

"Seems like a lot of trouble."

"If you want to pass on this opportunity, it will break my heart, but I'll have to go back and keep searching. I think we should meet and talk."

"I read your note. I've been thinking this is a joke someone is pulling on me."

"Not a joke at all."

"In that case, it's an interesting proposal. Yes, we can meet. Where and when?"

• • •

My life is not the most exciting. The routine is predictable, day in, day out. Early hours in the classroom, office hours, the occasional mandatory after-hours teaching function, then home to spend half the night grading papers before bed. Occasionally, I exchange classroom war stories with another teacher and that can lead to dinner or dancing we can ill afford. If the chemistry is passable enough that we share a night of sex, I always regret it in the hard light of day. I can hardly wait to get rid of him, and then I dread running into him in the future.

My life is almost an open book. I have one secret I'll never tell.

One November, on a cold wintery evening, I was hurrying along the sidewalk, rushing to the bus stop around five. It was the time of year when five was already dark, and I remember pulling my coat tight against the chill. It was one of those bitter walks where all the people you pass are staring grimly down at the pavement and you all make your way through sheer determination till you get where you are going. I took that route every day at the same time, passing a park on one side and the street on the other. Sometimes it is not so bad, but this night it was bitter and uncomfortable. I glanced at the time. My bus was due in five minutes. If I was late, I'd have to wait thirty minutes for the next one. I picked up speed, but out of nowhere, someone slammed against me from behind.

I hit the pavement hard, then was forcibly rolled downhill into the park. I wasn't alone. Rolling with me, his arms around me, his body flush against my back, was a man.

Why didn't I think to scream? But it happened so fast. We were rolling in the darkness over grass and roots and rocks, crashing through bushes. I tried slowing down, but he was in control, and maneuvered us into anonymous black foliage at the foot of the hill, away from streetlamps and headlights. Both of us were breathing hard. One final roll, and he was on top of me. I felt cold steel against my neck. I could see his face in planes of shadow, but nothing made sense, nothing registered. I don't remember screaming. I smelled soap and sandalwood. This man was not a bum living on the street. I realized I was holding my breath in fear of the knife. I would survive sex, but not a knife.

"I'm not fighting you, not stupid. Put away the knife. You don't need it," I said in Spanish.

"Tell me that in English," he whispered in my ear. I detected no alcohol on his breath. He was lying flat on me. His accent was American. He was probably from across the border, El Paso, Texas.

I repeated the words in English.

"Good English. Let's see if you fuck as good as you talk. I'm only looking to get off. Don't want to hurt you."

His body lifted from mine, but not so that I could get away. One of his legs lay across mine, heavy, muscular.

Like me, he was wearing a long coat. He did something with the knife—I don't know what except that it disappeared—and one of his hands went up to his collar. His coat smelled of leather, sweat, sandalwood, and it creaked as he fumbled with the fastenings.

"Unbutton your coat," he said, unbuttoning his. I put up no fight. His hips rolled heavily against me. If I had a gun and shot him, I would be sent to prison. Rape is not justifiable homicide in Mexico.

I didn't make a move against him but did not help. His coat was open. He fumbled at my button-down shirt, jerked it open, spraying my buttons off into the dark. His hands on my flesh were surprisingly warm. My heart beat hard, and my lungs were full of a scream that died inside, locked in my throat. He tried kissing me. I turned my face to the side, eyes open. The intrusion went on and on, and the sounds he made circled in my head. I tried to focus on the noise from the street above. Horns, traffic. I could hear time passing.

Then he was done.

"You stay here five minutes," he said.

He got to his feet, pulled up his pants.

"I hope you enjoyed it. I did."

I could have cried. I could have screamed. I did none of those things. I don't know how long I waited. My shirt was wrecked. I tried straightening my collar and gave up and buttoned every button on my coat to hide the mess. I rolled to my hands and knees. My knees were bruised. I felt beaten up, but he'd never struck me. I shoved my torn panties in my coat pocket, then groped my way up the hill, hunting for one of my shoes. I found it with the low heel broken off. I put it on anyway. He didn't take my purse or my money. The bus I caught was a later one, but I didn't have to wait for long. No one said anything to me about the broken shoe. I limped up the public stairs in my building to the fireplace I'd never used. I burned my shoes, coat, everything I'd been wearing, then sat in a bathtub scrubbing myself and crying as the water turned to ice.

I never told anyone about what happened, but I think about it more than I should. Crazily, in my head, the whole thing replays, start to finish. The crazy part is that I end up on top and in charge.

Thank God there was no baby.

I am only twenty-five, and have indeed held positions teaching in grammar school, junior high, high school, and now am in my initial year of teaching at the university level. Perhaps I am young to have such a range of experience, but I crave a certain degree of challenge in my work. Once I have mastered a job, I find myself needing new challenges. Maybe I am just restless, still searching for my niche.

Two days later, I took a bus to the address James Baker had given me. I saw the wall around the premises. I remembered how the phone had been answered Hidalgo residence. I saw a guard at the gate. It was not the mansion of a well-to-do family who could afford a tutor; this guarded fortress was not at all what I'd been expecting. That's when I put two and two together, and realized I was standing at the gate of the infamous Mala Hidalgo. Mala was cloaked in mystery, but it was public knowledge that she was raising her grandsons. It was a name mentioned in newspapers and whispered on the street, shimmering in crime, mystery, power, and prestige. I had no idea how much was myth and how much was truth. Another woman would have kept walking and called Mr. Baker to tell him no thank you. As much as I liked my job, I was intrigued. I am not good at turning down a challenge. Were the Hidalgo children the ones James had mentioned in his letter? Was he teaching the grandkids of the mythical Mala Hidalgo?

I stood at the gate, paralyzed in indecision. It was hot under the beating sun, and I felt a trickle of sweat between my breasts, dampness under my arms, and the back of my neck burned where the direct sun was baking me alive. I felt like an insect under a magnifying glass. I met the guard's eyes. More than anything, I was curious. Just going inside was not a commitment. I could always change my mind. Maybe there was air conditioning inside. And ice.

"I'm here to see Mr. Baker," I told the guard behind the gate. "My name is Elena Munoz; he is expecting me."

The guard spoke into a phone set in a box in his station. I stood there for a few moments, hearing an approaching hum that turned out to be a second guard on a golf cart. I climbed up beside him. He navigated through a wonderland of trees I had not dreamed were hiding behind the walls. The house to our left was like the home of some American out of history, like some Williamsburg Colonial mansion that once housed a dead president, at least three or four stories of wine-red brick, balconies, stairs, verandas, topiary, but we did not go there. A metal cradle on the golf cart's dashboard held a walkie talkie, from which burst a brief shot of static with no recognizable words. We veered away from the house and followed a curving path through this unexpected forest, beautifully landscaped like some English garden, with a couple of wood and iron benches and a lovely iron and glass table inside a stone gazebo, like some English folly. Oh, I don't know if it was poured concrete or granite or some other stone, topped with a metal dome that was more air than iron. No doubt it was James Baker who stood up from a bench in that gazebo. He came down a couple of stairs to greet me. Under the trees, it was at least twenty degrees cooler than it had been on the sidewalk. All around the path the golf cart had taken was a fluffy riot of bright green foliage and wildflowers. The green was so bright it was breathtaking. I could not imagine how much water it would take to make dry Juarez so lush and tropical. The gardeners must be brilliant at their jobs. On the table beside where the man had been sitting, a book was face-down next to a large walkie talkie like the one the security guard had.

I stepped off the golf cart, shaking hands with James Baker, who introduced himself. We were almost the same height. He wasn't tall, but he was just tall enough. He wasn't fat, but he wasn't a skinny man either. His hair was dark gray, and his manner more outdoorsy than distinguished. I liked his cologne. He took my hand and led me up the stairs. I felt immediately attracted to him as we sat across from each other on polished wood benches. I'd never seen anything like the gazebo and looked straight up. There was no ceiling, just a latticework dome that looked like the Greek muses had woven it. The canopy above was so thick, I could not see the sky overhead, just trees.

"Amazing cupola, isn't it?" James said, also looking up at the tracery of tree branches, ivy, and wrought iron that rested on six iconic columns. "It's just like a folly you would find on a nobleman's estate at home in England. It was all the thing in the eighteenth century. It looks like it has been here a hundred years, doesn't it? Magda had it built just outside my cottage so that I wouldn't feel homesick. I don't know where she got the idea, but I love it."

All I could do is nod and breathe deep of the forest scent. It did not feel like we were in dry, dusty Juarez, but rather in some tropical garden. No sooner did the guard drive away than a second cart arrived driven by a woman with pitchers of ice and lemonade and a bowl of fruit on ice. I turned down the fruit. James peeled a thin-skinned orange, ate one section, and offered me a section in a way I felt I could not refuse.

"It's quite refreshing," he said with a smile.

After thirty minutes and two glasses of lemonade from the ice-filled crystal pitcher, James had told me more about the job. I told James I was interested. How could I not be interested in a signing bonus of twenty-five thousand pesos and a salary of three times what I made at the university? Their proposal was insane, and I would be insane not to accept it.

"Why is it necessary for me to live here?"

"The boys have lost their parents. I believe we can provide a family-type structure to their childhood just by being here and providing a nurturing environment. I believe it's good for the boys to grow fond of their teachers so that they eat up everything we teach them. Personally, I love it here. I hail from London, and I don't miss the city lights at all. I'm not imprisoned here, and neither will you be. There is also the savings of not having to pay room and board, no drive time to work, and everything you could possibly need will be provided."

"Everything?"

"You know that old adage, ask and you shall receive? It has been that way for me, and I am sure it will be the same for you. Weekends you're off. Whether you give up your apartment or keep it, you are free to come and go. Magda is easy about that. By the way, she's a very private person within these walls. I know you will never discuss anything about the family."

"Of course not."

"No matter what rumors you hear, nothing illegal happens on this property."

I nodded. "James, I'd like to meet the boys. Maybe they won't like me."

"They will like you. I already like you."

James picked the walkie talkie off the table and spoke into it.

"Send a driver."

I could see the house at a distance and wondered why we weren't just walking there.

"What if I get fired or quit?"

"If you get fired, I will give you one year pay."

"What about the bonus?"

"If you agree to the terms and if Magda agrees, you get the bonus today."

"Do I have to give the bonus back if I quit or get fired?"

James chuckled. The cart arrived. We got up.

"Hire on and the twenty-five thousand is yours for keeps."

"Why me?"

James put his hand out, and I got on the back of the golf cart. James climbed on next to me.

"You meet the criteria perfectly."

I patted him on the upper thigh twice like saying "roger that."

I climbed a lot of stairs to a playroom on the second floor where the boys were pushing around a wooden train on metal rails. Getting there, every room I walked through was large and spectacular with lots of wonderfully carved old furniture, richly made rugs of burgundy and gold, and more art than I had ever seen outside of a museum. There was a burgundy carpet runner running down the center of an elaborate mahogany staircase that looked like something out of an opera house. Even before James had told them my name, as soon as I poked my head in the playroom, the boys ran to me eagerly, and started showing me all of their toys, of which there were many. I was entirely charmed by Rico and Victor, beautiful boys with lovely manners and a fierce competition between them which would certainly help motivate them in a classroom. After my ten minutes with them, James left the boys with a young server named Mary who apparently played with them often. He took me to a parlor far down the hall on that same floor.

The study where I met with Senora Hidalgo was the most beautiful room I had ever been in. Before I'd been inside this house, I'd thought that the dean at the university had a beautiful office, but it could not compare. The wood paneling was exquisite, the ceiling frescoed like a church. I sat across from my potential employer at a partnership desk. I don't know furniture that well, but it was an ornately carved mahogany desk with griffin heads, cabriolet legs like the desk was genuflecting, and claw feet. It was like something out of my art history textbook back in college. Against the wall were bookcases and cabinets that belonged in a museum. In this setting, like some jewel in a tiara, to me, Magda Hidalgo was a queen.

"The most important human beings in my life are Rico and Victor," Senora Hidalgo said. "You must love them in order for this to work out. If at any time you think you can't handle the job, let me know and James will find someone to replace you. I don't want you here unless you are happy, and you won't know that unless you try it out."

I sat upright in my chair, my purse on my lap. I'd never minded my posture so perfectly. The senora sat with her wrinkled, delicate hands resting on the desktop. She wore no jewelry but was groomed like a woman forty years younger. Her fragrance, subtle, not sweet, was a scent I would have chosen for myself.

"Senora Hidalgo, thank you for the opportunity and for your confidence in me. I've met the boys. They are lovely. I would love to be their teacher. I accept the position."

"You are a beautiful young lady, Elena. Welcome to my home. You will never have to pay for anything as long as you live here. My workers will serve you like family, just as they serve James."

"I feel all choked up," I said, trying not to cry foolishly. I reached in my pocket to grab a handkerchief but did not want to use it in front of Senora Hidalgo.

Senora Hidalgo moved closer to her side of the desk and leaned toward me, though still a good distance away. "I will treat you like family, but you must never talk about me or anyone in this home when you are away from the house." Her demeanor did not change but her gaze delivered her message loud and clear.

"You will learn that I can be trusted Senora Hidalgo."

"Call me Magda from now on."

I smiled at her. I wanted to fit in. I wanted to live in this home. I would be able to save my money, live rent free in such an opulent setting. What a fantastic opportunity. I wondered how I got to be so lucky but didn't ask her. She dismissed me, and when I opened the door, I found James was waiting outside her study.

"Elena is hired," Magda said to James from her seat at the desk.

"Good news," James said, extending his hand for a shake.

I shook his hand then turned around to face Magda. She was up from her chair and walking toward us just outside the door to her study.

I extended my hand to her. She did a little wave to come close to her, and she gave me a little hug. For me, it was emotional. I thought of all the horrible stories I'd heard for years about this woman who had been nothing but lovely to me. I felt sure that every evil word spoken of her had to be a lie.

James walked me to the front door of the house. It wasn't dark yet, but it was after six. I'd been there for three hours. He handed me an envelope.

"Here is your twenty-five thousand pesos. I have a car and driver at the gate to take you home."

I put the envelope in my purse.

"James, thank you." My eyes were moist. "I need to give notice. When shall I start?"

"You don't need to give notice. I will arrange everything with the dean. He's on our side. Don't worry. You are not shutting a door there. I promise." He smiled at me.

There was no question in my mind that James had paid off the Dean.

"In that case, when do I start?"

"Is Monday too soon?"

"I'll be here Monday at the crack of dawn."

"Whenever you get here is fine," James said. "A room will be ready for you."

"Thank you, James."

I wanted to kiss him. I knew he liked me. He was at least twice my age, but he was still a hunk. I was even more attracted to him. I had the feeling he had gone out of his way to make me feel welcomed. I remembered when he'd peeled the orange and handed me a bit of it. For some reason, remembering that made me vibrate inside.

The doors of the sedan were thick, very wide. The driver was Gusto, the man who had delivered the note from James.

"So, Gusto, we meet again," I said.

"What a pleasure it is for me, Miss Elena."

He held open the back door of the car.

"The doors are so thick," I said.

"Yes ma'am," he said respectfully. "The car is entirely bulletproof."

I got in and sat back on the soft seat.

"Do you have the address?"

"Yes, Miss Elena, I have your apartment address. Do you wish to make a stop somewhere?"

"No. I just wondered."

"I will close the divider window. If you need something, please knock on the glass."

"I'm fine. Thank you, Gusto."

How long had Mala's people been watching me before James wrote me the note?

Did it matter?

I'm moving to a palace. I'll have no rent to pay, no utilities, nothing. I patted my purse lightly. I had never had this much money all at one time in my twenty-five years on this planet.

CHAPTER 4
RICO SANTOS

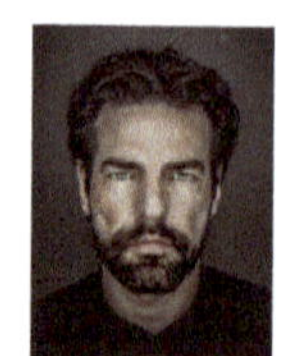

JAMES AND ELENA packed the school hours with learning mixed with games and explanations that made my brother and me laugh. We learned to sing the ABCs in English in no time at all. I was a year older, so things clicked faster than with Victor. If the pressure became too much, Victor cried, and James would call a recess. I want to say I never cried. Not that I can remember.

After school, James had activities for us. Most times he'd give us a choice of what we wanted to do. After our first trip to El Paso, Texas which is just across the border from Juarez, my brother and I always voted to go back there. Gusto would drive us in one of grandmother's big cars. We always hit an ice cream parlor for anything we wanted to order, and we visited parks and different historic sites. At first had no idea where we were, even after James explained. We were way ahead of our age and that was right from the beginning. Elena came along with us. To me, she was like a second mom, a beautiful mom.

James explained about the border and the states that made up the United States and Mexico where we lived. He showed us a map. My brother and I were just kiddos, but we soaked up the learning. He showed us the Rio Grande on the map and then when we crossed the border. "There isn't always a fence," he said to us.

"Why a fence at all?" Victor asked.

James said, "It's a good question. I suppose we need the fence just as we see on a map, a border around a state indicating what belongs to what side."

"Complicated," I said.

When we saw the uniformed cops at the crossing, we already knew why they were there inspecting the people coming across from Mexico.

James prepared us before our first trip. If the officer asked what nationality we were, we said, "American Citizen," in English. That's all you had to say back then. James said we spoke those two words perfectly without an accent. I wasn't sure what an accent was. I asked Elena, and she played around saying American Citizen in different ways. I understood accent after that.

Elena showed my brother and me a card with her picture on it. "I'm not a U.S. citizen. I need to show this to cross the border to go with you to El Paso or to shop and visit friends, but I am not allowed to work with this card," she told us. Back then I didn't understand about the ID card, but I did tell her how pretty she looked in the picture. My brother Victor nodded in agreement.

It's hard to pin down one role James played in my life. Tutor, mentor, father figure, friend. We loved him quick, Victor and me. Elena was easy to love, too. She was so pretty. She hugged and cuddled my brother and me all the time. She smelled so good.

"Grandmother," I'd say, "I love teacher Elena."

"Wonderful," she'd say, "and do you like James too?"

"You know I do," I'd say as I hugged her.

I was happy and had oodles to tell my friends on Sunday when they came over about our school at home and what we were learning and about our outings. Elena told us not to tell them everything because it might make the boys and girls feel bad and she explained that not everyone in school was lucky enough to have what my brother and I had. I would learn to understand this and as I grew older, I gave the kids money to buy a toy and ice cream or something they wanted. My grandmother has a great big room filled with money and my brother and I are in there a lot. We play in there. James calls it a vault. Elena calls it a *caja fuerte*. My brother and me learned about dollars and pesos early on. Grandmother taught us this. In El Paso, the preferred currency was U.S. dollars and in Juarez, Mexican pesos. We never went anywhere in Juarez. James and my grandmother told us we'd go out into the neighborhood soon enough after we got a little older.

James spoke Spanish, but from the beginning, he taught in English. Elena taught us in Spanish and talked to us in Spanish. "My job is to teach you as though you were in school in Mexico."

My brother and me, we knew that Juarez was in Mexico. I could locate the city we lived in on the map, in the state of Chihuahua.

James was like a shadow, always with us, except when we were sleeping. At night, he retired to a guest house, but he was always in the main house when we were awake.

My brother and me, we draw pretty good. We drew a make-believe picture of James's guest house that my grandmother fixed up for him. James said he loved it. I have to admit that Elena helped us. She draws better than us anytime.

I remember walking around the property with James. We went out the back door to where some of the biggest trees were growing. He was still new to us, because I could not have been more than six and Victor, five. It was a walk for an English lesson. James would say the English word and point out the thing. Tree. Rock. Dirt. Shrub. Flower. Grass. Leaves. So many things as we took the walk. It was an exotic door opening, and yet, just a game. We found a big bird and little bird, perhaps doves or partridges. I doubt he knew the local species, but he played the game. James said everyone had parents, even wild animals. He pointed out the baby bird, the papa bird, English and Spanish. But I didn't have parents, just my grandmother and Victor.

"Can I call you papa?" I asked. What I wanted, Victor wanted too, so we both asked him.

"Your grandmother may not like it," he said.

So, we called him James. Sometimes, teacher James. Mostly, James.

Elena, a university teacher, moved into our house to assist in teaching my brother and me the Juarez and El Paso curriculums. Thanks to agreements James finagled, the Juarez and El Paso school districts promised us diplomas for completing their courses of study. Our school days went like this: for three hours a day, Elena taught us in Spanish. Then, James taught us in English for three hours. The truth is that James never stopped teaching us after school hours. There was always something.

"I like when you are here on weekends," I told Elena.

"Why thank you, Rico. I like it too."

"Do you like the new bedroom?" My grandmother had done up one of the guest rooms and it was the only room in the house that had carpet that you couldn't move around. It was a beautiful green.

"I love my bedroom," Elena said. "It's beautiful."

I looked at her and smiled. "You are beautiful, too, Elena."

"Thank you, Rico."

There was no homework. I didn't even know what that was until James explained what it was.

"You have six hours of school a day. You don't need homework."

Did we miss going to school with other students? How can you miss what you've never known? We did fine.

James kept us busy. Good thing my brother and me are bigger than boys our age because the bow he taught us how to hold and use was quite large. I could barely pull the string back with the arrow. Eventually we got good at finding the mark.

I think I was four when I learned how to swim, and Victor was not far behind me in learning. James took us to a different level; he had a slide and a diving board installed on one side of our swimming pool. He didn't install it, but grandmother agreed with everything he presented to her. I heard Elena and James talking about how my grandmother gave him everything he suggested for us.

"Is there anything you can't do?" I asked James more than once.

Elena was there, and she replied before he did. "I think James can do anything."

I wondered often if Elena and James kissed like in the movies. I wanted to ask, but I didn't do it.

One of the funnest things my brother and I liked to do was camping. James put up a big tent for the three of us to get together in and learn how to tie different rope knots that James taught us and how to use a pocketknife for carving wood and cutting an apple then slicing it into smaller slices, and a bunch of other things. My brother and me, we put up a tent for the two of us and we slept on the ground in a sleeping bag. If it got too hot, we moved out of the tent without sleeping bags on the lawn. There were so many trees we couldn't really look up and see the stars, but James fixed that. He got us a telescope and the next time we camped out, we did it where there was a break of tree cover and that's when we learned about the planets. Juarez has clear skies most of the time. More than once my grandmother surprised us and came out to join us for a little while and she looked in the telescope while my brother and me explained what we were learning. James looked on and let us do the talking. James always smiled. He was a happy person. Elena always said that to him a lot.

Our house has three stories with many rooms on each floor, not counting the very big basement and the attic. As a kid, I figured out that the basement was much wider than the house. Of course, we asked my grandmother about it, and she said that our grandfather extended the walls. He wanted more room down there. I guess that was more room for his business. There were a lot of rooms down there, like the one with the incinerator that burned our trash, the laundry room, and other empty rooms that had no use at all.

James outfitted the classroom on the top floor with two desks for my brother and me, two teacher desks, and blackboards on the wall.

In the basement next to the laundry room, James set up a gym. A judo teacher from El Paso started coming to the house twice a week for one-hour classes when I was seven and my brother was six. James had books on judo and karate.

"I want to try karate," I told James.

"Too much bowing and discipline," Victor said after one lesson. "I'm sticking to judo."

James went across the border to El Paso and found a karate teacher who would come over twice a week to give me classes. My brother and I were tall husky kids, not a teaspoon of gracefulness between us. That didn't make us good students of judo or karate, but it was still a good start. We called our martial arts teachers Sensei. They only had access to the basement and were escorted from the front gate through a side entrance directly to the workout room.

Sometimes Elena came to the gym and exchanged bows with the sensei. She asked permission to enter, then sat in silence, watching. I'd sneak a look, and Sensei would give me his *don't do that* look. I enjoyed when she was watching.

She also looked in on Victor's judo lesson, but she watched me more. I liked that because I liked her. Victor complained to me and James that her watching made him nervous, and that made his judo like he had four left feet.

During class one day, Elena said, "I am fascinated by karate. Your grandmother gave me permission to take karate." She looked at me. "My class will be the hour after yours."

I pictured her dressed up like the sensei and smiled.

"Karate is not for girls," Victor said.

The next day, James brought in a couple of magazines full of karate girls. Some of them were written in Chinese, or Korean, or Japanese. One was in English, full of American girls in American competitions.

"Women around the world do martial arts," James said.

One day during dinner, "Grandma, Elena will be taking karate after my sensei finishes with me."

"If I was younger, I'd take lessons," she said. Grandma didn't joke around too much.

"Why, Grandma?" Victor asked. "You're a girl."

"I would want to know it for the same reason you want to know it. For self-defense."

"Grandma, you don't go out," I said. "And you have Gusto and many men guarding you."

"Women do not need to limit themselves," she said. "Most things, if a man can do it, so can a woman."

"I want to be able to defend myself," Elena said. "There won't always be someone there to come to the rescue. I should be able to feel safe even if I am by myself."

With all the guards we had, it seemed crazy she wanted to defend herself, but she was my teacher, so I didn't argue.

When I was done with my lesson, I was sweating hard like I always did. I hung around and watched Elena walk in the gym wearing shorts and a top that left her stomach bare. I wanted to stick around, but my sensei said I could not watch. I headed for the shower as I always did after working out.

Kiko, my sensei, started each session with two hundred sit-ups and two hundred pushups. It had not started off with that many, but eventually it was a breeze to do both. It took my brother longer, but he came through. His judo teacher was not as strict.

I asked Sensei if Elena had to do sit-ups and pushups like I did.

"You ask her," Kiko said.

So, I did. When there was a lull in our class the next day, I asked, "Elena, how many sit-ups and pushups does Kiko make you do?"

She closed the book she was reading, put it on her desk, and gave me a smile.

I loved her smile.

"Why do you want to know?"

"I think I do more than you do," I said. I rubbed my hand on the ridges of my abdomen, not showing off or anything. I was sitting behind a desk.

Her smile didn't change. "You think that because I'm a girl?" Her eyebrows raised a little.

"Yeah," I said.

"One day, let's do some sit-ups and pushups together."

"Deal," I said.

After two years in karate, I became interested in weightlifting. I paged through magazines that I bought on day trips to El Paso. James started buying the monthly issues. A basement wall was taken down to make the gym bigger. One of my favorite additions was the punching bag. The new four-station gym set included body building equipment. My brother and I took to the weights, though our teachers did not recommend weightlifting. Elena was getting good at karate and warned us not to get too muscular.

"You will get musclebound and stiff."

I was in the schoolroom putting some books on a shelf. Outside, I heard James and Elena walking back from lunch.

"The people outside the walls have no idea what goes on in here," James said.

"People think Mala packages dope in here," Elena said.

I scooted from the bookcase to the window and faced outside. They came in first, followed by Victor. I didn't ask about their conversation. I'm pretty sure they did not know I heard.

I wondered why people outside the walls would think that of my grandmother. It didn't make sense that anyone would keep rumors and gossip a secret from me, so I thought about it for a while, and eventually asked James.

"Why do people think my grandmother has anything to do with dope?"

"Listening at closed doors?" James asked.

"You and Elena were in the hall, talking. You said I could ask you anything."

"I'm sorry you heard that," he said. "When you get older, I will explain."

I let it go. Eventually, I figured it out for myself, but I didn't talk to Victor about it.

My grandmother set up a lot of rules regarding things like mealtime. Weekdays, we, including James and Elena, had dinner together. Weekends we would have lunch together, leaving dinner open. Elena was off on Saturday and Sunday but more often than not, she stuck around, spending time on the grounds. She used the pool, sat in the shade, read a book, or learned to cook from our chef in the kitchen. He had many recipes she wanted to learn. Elena was family, no question. I don't think she ever missed a movie night or the eating that went on Sunday during the day when the kids came over to visit.

Late one afternoon, I was in the yard alone while Victor was taking a nap, or maybe he had an earache from all the swimming. James and Elena were inside, probably with Victor. I was okay amusing myself, trying to hit a mark on a tree. I hunted for a pile of rocks, and then slung them, one by one at the mark on the tree. I kept practicing for a long time, just like I practiced with my sensei. I knew how important practice was. I got halfway through my pile of stones for the second time and suddenly had that neck-crawly feeling someone was watching. I turned around, and it took some time to find my grandmother looking at me from her bedroom. I waved at her like crazy hoping she would come down and throw rocks with me, but she turned away from the window. During dinner that night, as usual, my grandmother encouraged Elena and James to talk about our progress, Victor's and mine. James and Elena talked about math problems we'd done, books we were reading in Spanish and English, reports, geography, whatever the lessons had been that day.

"Are you lonely, Rico?" she asked me.

I hardly knew what loneliness was. I was hardly ever alone. "Not at all, Grandmother."

She turned to face James.

"Victor and Rico should go out to the neighborhood to meet kids their age. They can swim at the public swimming pool. I don't want them to be afraid of their own people," my grandmother said. "They've been waiting for this for a long time."

"Magda, they are both in martial arts. They are not afraid," James said. "I worry, but not that they will be afraid. I—"

"James don't worry. I don't want you or a guard to go out with them either."

My brother and me, we knew my grandmother liked James very much, and he liked her. He never argued with her. No one did. James was right about our martial arts. We could and would kick ass when needed. We were kiddos, but we were big kiddos.

And so, Victor and me, the next day, we left the grounds of the big house and for the first time, walked alone around outside of the big wall towering over our heads. Even though we seldom came out for anything, the kids knew who we were. We learned firsthand how much the people loved Mala.

Everyone, but everyone, knew us.

"Hey, you are Mala's grandsons."

I nodded at the kid who was with two other kids.

"My name is Tito."

Like grownups, we shook hands. I think I was nine.

Two kids were older. They wanted handshakes as well.

"Your grandmother was super to build the pool for us," Tito said.

"We were just going there," I said. "Come along?"

"Does Mala burn her enemies in the basement of the house?" one of the older kids asked.

My brother was first to laugh. There were two incinerators in the basement: one for the household garbage, and a heavy duty one for disposing of construction waste and things like that. It was crazy for anybody to think people were burned down there. I wasn't going to admit we were not allowed in the incinerator rooms! We kept walking. Tito and the other kid didn't laugh.

"Come to the house and you can ask my grandmother that question," I said.

Juarez is extremely hot in the summer. We had a big pool at home but after we swam in the public pool, we preferred it. It was exciting.

At our house, every room had air-conditioning. The trees on the grounds cast so much shade, we did not feel the heat as much as outside the walls.

In no time at all, Victor and me, we made a lot of friends. We made friends with boys and girls of all ages. Everyone wanted to be around us. We stuck around the pool and started giving lessons to some of the kids who didn't know how to swim. It's hard to do that when the pool is packed with kids and teens. We did it anyway.

"Hey," I yelled to one of the lifeguards. "Get off that seat and come down here and help my brother and me."

I got no argument. As a matter of fact, the two lifeguards I hadn't asked also dropped in the pool to help out. We rounded up all the non-swimmers and gave them lessons.

"Take a break," Victor said to those that didn't need lessons.

No one argued with my brother.

"For a little while," I said to some of the frowning faces who were getting out.

The pool is twice as big as the one at the house. But still, figure a hundred in the pool at one time, many kids.

At dinner that night, I told everyone at the table that we spent a couple of hours teaching swimming lessons.

"Magnificent," James said. "Good boys."

Elena had this big smile on her face.

"Tell us all about it," Elena said.

My grandmother didn't smile much, but she smiled a lot that night.

"I want to hear everything," Grandmother said. "This is very nice of you, my sons. You have to give back to the neighborhood. That's why I built the swimming pool."

"It feels good to teach," my brother said, managing to talk and keep spooning food into his face at the same time.

"Grandmother, the diving boards are out of bounds because the manager doesn't want anyone hurt. Too many kids in the pool. Can't dive." That's what I told her.

Victor didn't let her reply. "I think that the pool could be opened for those who can swim and want to dive from the boards for a couple hours a day and open after for others."

Lot of smiles at the table.

Grandmother nodded in agreement.

I said, "I think you should hire someone to teach diving, not just swim. James got Ernesto to teach us last year. Maybe him."

James looked at my grandmother.

"Good idea, son. I will speak with the manager, and James will see if Ernesto is available. If not, I'm certain we have many good divers and swimmers right here in the neighborhood who would like to have a job." She looked at Victor. "It's a good idea you have about limiting who is in the pool for several hours."

"See how easy that was?" Elena said. "You have the most generous grandmother in all the world." She exchanged smiles with Grandma.

"Gracias, Abuelita[1]."

I went over to where she was sitting and hugged her. She stopped eating, and I kissed her cheek. Victor saw what I was doing and rushed right there, kissing her other cheek. We were tall but no longer clumsy.

Another night that summer, Victor and I rushed in like we were going to fight to sit on the same chair, the one next to Elena. But then, one of us would sit by our grandmother so her feelings would not be hurt. We were giggling rather than fighting.

"What is so funny?" James asked.

"It's just like this afternoon when we went to the boys' bathroom. We ran in and tried to pee so fast, so we didn't have to smell the stink." Victor broke out into peals of laughter.

It was kind of funny when it happened, but not fun. Tito had been there too, running into the bathroom, except he ran so fast, he slipped and slid on the yucky floor, knocking over two peeing boys like a couple of bowling pins.

I said to Grandmother, "The toilets at the pool are filthy. No toilet paper, either. You should see it, Grandma. When I go pee there, I have to hold my breath."

"Grandmother, no lie. It is terrible."

"Why didn't you tell me before?"

"I thought it would get better," I said.

My grandmother was furious. I didn't think it was the right time to tell her about me and Victor and Tito running in the bathroom.

"Hand me the phone," Grandmother said to a server in the dining room with us.

The phone was on a long extension cord. The server brought the phone, and Grandmother slammed it on the dining table and dialed.

"Rincon, I am very mad at you, very mad." Her lips trembled.

We could only hear my grandmother's end of the conversation. No telling what the manager was saying to her, if anything. She ordered him to go that night and get that place cleaned up, to keep it that way or else. My brother and I stopped eating and watched my grandmother deal with this. The servers around the table froze in place, and the noise from the kitchen ceased. James and Elena, like us, stopped eating. It was like no one could move or speak again until my grandmother was happy.

When my grandmother hung up, she handed the phone to the server.

"Let's eat," she said. "I hope it's not cold."

"Grandmother, I'm sorry I upset you but I'm not sorry I told you," I said.

She put down her fork and looked at me.

"Next time, if this ever happens again, march in the manager's office and order him to get it cleaned up. That goes for you too." She looked at Victor. "I am not always going to be here."

Victor and I both nodded. It was just like when I told the lifeguard to help us teach the kids to swim.

I pictured Rincon being led to one of the furnaces in the basement. I thought about the kid that asked me if Mala burned her enemies. James said talk like that was dirty gossip and lies. I am very mad at you, Grandmother told Rincon! I hope she doesn't kill him.

---

1. Abuelita is Granny.

CHAPTER 5
MALA

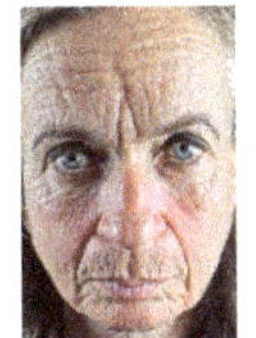

ACROSS THE STREET from the walled grounds of my home is a supermarket that never closes. I own the property and rent the building to a company that runs many markets. The store is large, busy, well-stocked, and carries many items imported from the United States. My chefs buy almost everything there. I feed my big house staff, runners, guards, and gardeners when they are on duty.

There's a locked storage room in the market and inside there is a long staircase that goes below ground level, a walkway that goes under the street in front of the market and ends with another staircase inside my walls. Years ago, I had this path built officially as a convenience for our workers to go to and from the market without passing through the main gate. The real reason I built it was to provide privacy. No one needs to know who comes and goes from my home.

The operators of my drug business are dropped off at the market and access the private walkway to my house. Once on my grounds, my guards escort them on foot or drive them in a golf cart. I have plenty of guards and spies inside and outside the walls.

My main business is no longer selling baggies. These days, sales are by the ton. Heroin, marijuana, and cocaine. I have managers and three bosses in charge of the product from the time it is grown, harvested, processed, stored, transported from South America and Mexico to the

United States, Europe, and several Asian cities. My managers collect the funds and turn it over to my chief in control of the money. Angel Montes, my accountant, channels the income to several corporations in Mexico, Switzerland, and Europe. Angel is a thin, slight, nervous-looking man with copious jet-black hair, a head for numbers, and a bad complexion. He has a beautiful, demanding, extravagant wife with a shopping habit that would have sent a lesser man to the poorhouse.

None of the companies bear my name. Bank accounts that matter to me are numbered accounts in all the right countries. These blankets of protection are costly but without such precautions, I would be vulnerable.

The architect of it all is my lawyer, Raul Robles, from Monterrey Nuevo León.

I told Raul Robles many years ago, "I never want to be guilty of a damn thing that is illegal."

It took a long time, but he fixed it. I am bulletproof, thanks to him. I believed him when he said I was bullet proof. Being bulletproof does not stop the gossip.

Raul Robles is not only my attorney. He handles the secret payments to officials throughout Mexico where my people are doing business. The payoffs go as high as governors, chiefs of police, and countless generals in the military.

The protection money is not to shield me. It shields the people who run my operations, the vulnerable ones. It guarantees safe passage of drugs when needed. There is no evidence against me. It's ironic that all the drug products that are sent to distributors are marked with a logo, BETO, my husband's name. When my husband ran the baggie business, he believed that having his name on the product was a guarantee that the product was high quality. My attorney wanted to drop the BETO logo, but I didn't agree. Let them stew over it. Millions of people are named Beto. It was his first name. The logo keeps my husband alive for me.

My chiefs and managers use the walkway when a meeting is necessary. No telephone calls are ever made to arrange a meeting. Runners deliver their messages in person. Sometimes a messenger travels a thousand miles or more.

I don't trust telephones.

A forest shields most of the main house from prying eyes from above and the tall walls are a good cover from the ground. I had them installed, tree by tree, the first ones providing the canopy that shades the house. Over the years, whenever the gardeners bring in a crane for planting grown trees to flesh out the forest, helicopters from local television stations are not far behind. The news stations are always looking for anything they can find, building up the myth that my home is the headquarters of my drug business. That myth is older than I am.

Once in a while, a news reporter gets a little nosy or a little mouthy, or flies one too many times above my house. If he crosses the line, he gets a visit. The smart reporters back off and live to report (on someone else) another day. Once in a while, some investigator is looking to earn a prize, or become a hero, or is just a little too impressed with the sound of his own voice. There's just a certain type of reporter who does not know when to keep his mouth shut, and when he's got the scent in his nose and fails to mind his own business, he fails to pay adequate attention when there is fair warning. There have been three who insisted on invading my privacy from above who must have believed the warning was a bluff.

Three fool reporters that have disappeared from the face of the earth.

These days, flyovers are rare as hen's teeth.

CHAPTER 6
IGNACIO

I DO it all for Mala. I'm a messenger, a chauffeur, a kidnapper, an assassin, an investigator. Mala knows all she has to do is name it, and it is as good as done. I work with two other men I trust with my life. They are loyal to the bone.

It was late in the evening when I arrived, not through the front entrance but the usual private way. The whole household goes to sleep early because of the children. Because it was late, Mala received me in a downstairs sitting room. It was a familiar room, small, posh, and quiet. There was a thick Persian rug underfoot. Red velvet curtains were pulled open showing a lit patio with orange trees growing in pots. The air conditioning was going full blast. Outside it was in the nineties even at this hour, but this room was in the mid-sixties.

I bowed to Mala as soon as I saw her. I kissed her hand which was adorned with many rings. My meetings with Mala are usually private, as we discuss things that no one else other than Gusto will ever hear. Tonight she had a visitor who worked for her.

"Ignacio, I wanted you to hear this for yourself," Mala said.

"A truck was short fifty kilos of product," the employee said. He was wearing a sleeveless t-shirt with sweat stains under the armpits and sweat was pouring off of him. "It's not the first time it was short. This is the second time."

"And who is responsible?" I asked quietly.

His eyes flicked from Mala to me and back to Mala. He seemed reluctant to speak.

"Were you responsible?" she asked.

"No, I would never…I am just a messenger. But…"

He stammered through a minute worth of apologies, denials, and praises of Mala, not coming to the point. It seemed obvious to me that he was reluctant to point the finger. His uneasiness made me uneasy. It was someone he feared naming, someone far up the food chain, which meant it might be someone I knew well.

"You have nothing to worry about," I said, glancing at Mala. I saw her nod slightly. "Who was responsible?"

"Gabriel," he whispered.

Mala sighed, and thanked him, and handed him a handful of pesos. He stammered his apologies and bowed a couple of times. One of Mala's house staff was waiting outside the door to escort him to the basement where security would get him on his way. I knew Gabriel. The suspected thief was an old-time lieutenant of hers that had too much seniority to be snuffed by one of Mala's bosses.

My team and I went out to collect Gabriel. He was easy to find, not at home with his family as he should have been, but out at a favorite cantina. We just waited till he was out in the gravel lot where his car was parked. No witnesses. A twin-engine Cessna brought us back to a private airfield in Juarez. We were entirely silent around him, leaving our prisoner untouched, and unenlightened about who had kidnapped him and why. He never saw us. Gabriel was gagged and cuffed, riding from the plane to the neighborhood in the back of a plumbing company truck that entered Mala's property through the main gate. It was twenty-four hours after my last interview with Mala, at two in the morning when Gabriel appeared in front of her. She awaited his arrival at an outbuilding on her property where equipment and tools were stored.

My men went back to the truck to wait on me, leaving Gabriel in the custody of Gusto and two other guards that worked at the residence. I would have joined my men, but Mala beckoned me to stay. I watched in silence.

Gabriel was shoved on a chair. The cuffs were removed, the hood taken from his head, the gag removed. He was pale as death and looked hungover and terrified.

"Tell me you did it, and I will spare your family," she said to Gabriel.

"Mala, I needed the money. Please forgive me. I will work for no pay to make it up to you. Mercy, Mala. I have been at your service for a long time."

"Was anyone else in on this with you? I must know. If you lie, your wife will die this night."

"I did it alone. Mala, please."

"Who did you sell the product to?"

"Mala, they will kill me."

"No, they won't kill you. You are already dead. This discussion is about the survival of your wife and family."

"It was Marco Santa Ana."

"You know I hate that man. How could you?" she shouted.

She slapped him. I was ready to leap forward to keep her from falling. Mala was not a young woman. She was fragile but neither fell nor came close to losing her balance. She slapped him again.

Gabriel cried in panic. He threw himself on the floor and crawled toward her.

"Forgive me, Mala. Forgive me. I have been at your service for years."

"If you needed money, you could have asked," she said to him. "Burn him," she told her guards.

They got on either side each taking an arm and pulling him upright, suspended between them.

"I curse you Mala," he screamed, "to die a painful death and that will not be enough for all the horror you have inflicted." He looked at Gusto at his right and Federico at his left. "In time she will kill you too, you Gusto, and you Federico. I curse you and your grandsons," he screamed.

From the floor, Gusto picked up the rag and wadding that had gagged Gabriel before, and in a moment, it was back on his face and the accusations ceased. I returned to my truck. Gabriel's noise was muffled as he was taken into the basement of the big house.

I never heard from him again. Before we drove the plumbing truck off the grounds, we smelled the stench of the crematorium. Gabriel was no more.

CHAPTER 7
MAURO ROBLES

IN 1975, **at twenty-three, I graduated from law school in Mexico City.** I'd had enough of the big city and headed back home to Monterrey, Nuevo León to become a partner in my father's prestigious and influential law firm, returning to my bachelor quarters at my parents' estate. My house was four hundred feet from the main house. The home was exactly the way I'd left it except that it had been refreshed with paint and decorator magic. My mother spared no expense to get it all done in grand style.

I had a close relationship with my parents. When I'd become a lawyer, my dad had been thrilled. It had been easy for me, nothing like the stories he told. I had been born with a silver spoon, thanks to all of his hard work. All my life, I'd heard stories of his struggle to make it. He had all but crawled his way through hell to earn his present station in life. It was the truth, but I had never experienced it. It took all the imagination I had to look at what the family was in my lifetime to have any concept of the rough times that my dad and mother had gone through.

My father represented Magda Hidalgo, the woman everyone knew as Mala. When I was a kid, I heard Beto Hidalgo's name bandied about. I heard how rich he was, what a good client he was of my father's law firm.

I would have had a perfect childhood, except that my best friend was Miguel Alvarado. Miguel's parents hated Mala and everything Hidalgo. Our friendship was not allowed. We could only be friends at boarding school. When we went home during a school break, there couldn't be communication between us, just because my father represented Beto Hidalgo once, and later, Mala.

By the time I graduated from law school, Beto Hidalgo had been dead for more than a decade. Mala was in charge. My father stayed on and represented Mala.

After I joined the firm, my dad drowned me in details of the work he did for Mala. I learned the ins and outs of paying off high government officials, police, military and even the governor so that Mala's doings had a veil of protection. My father's policy was always to grease the machinery if you wanted it to run. A little lubrication goes a long way, and a lot goes even further.

"There is no connection between her and the alleged drug business and no connection between me and any drug business. She is bullet-proof. Countless layers of protection between drugs and Magda Hidalgo. Important you understand this." My father said this.

"If you wanted to break away, could you? Would she have you and the family killed?"

"If you believe that, you are listening to the gossip. Her husband was a whole different story. I have done everything for her, from finding the grandsons' tutor to being the architect of the separation between herself and the drug business. Our family is worth millions because of the Hidalgo family. Why would I want to break up such a cozy and profitable arrangement?"

"You just said her alleged drug business. Now you say you were the architect to separate her from the drug business. I'm confused."

"Son, don't play lawyer with me."

"I have to think about it," I said. "I'm rattled to learn how deep in this you are. I knew you represented her, but I had no idea what you did."

"Did is past tense." He looked me straight in the eye. "If you can't handle it, find another place to practice law."

He got up from behind his desk, opened the door, and pointed down the hall to the fancy doors that led to the street.

I walked out of his office baffled, confused, furious.

My father bought me a new Ferrari. Red.

I got over my pique.

I went to see my dad in his office.

"I have no problem helping you with Mala's business," I said, "as long as it's not her drug business. Show me everything."

"Son, do you think I would be involved in drugs?"

I wanted to ask him if he ever had been. Instead, I shook my head. "I believe you, Papi." What I believed is that he had always done his best for me and Mama.

He walked around his desk and we hugged. He teared up.

"Mauro, there is no danger to us. She has a brilliant financial person that handles the money from the business and takes care of where it goes. She's totally hands off. It wasn't always that way, but it has been now for many years."

"What if things change? People move, retire. Change happens."

"It changes all the time. The outgoing gatekeeper fixes it so the incoming carries on as before. Not one of them would go along if they believed Mala was involved in the business."

"Papa, you are going to live to be two hundred, so I won't have to do the part I don't like about what I see. The payoffs."

"You need to be ready, son. If I thought this was bad, I would not pass it on to you. When dirty work needed to be done to insulate her, it was many years ago. Do you think I could have made the money I've made for this family practicing law in Monterrey, Nuevo Leon?"

"Miguel's father made his millions there and continues to make millions."

"He's a jealous fool," my father snapped.

I accompanied my father in his plane to Juarez. The pilot and co-pilot were guys that were like family. They had been with us for a very long time. No business was ever discussed around them. We were floating so high in the sky that I could see the plane's shadow on the clouds below us. Mala had a driver pick us up from the airport. The big bulletproof Lincoln he drove had a window divider for privacy.

"Why do they call her Mala?" I asked my father.

"I don't know the exact story when someone pegged the name on her, but it is because she's mean," he said in a low voice. "She inherited her husband's reputation of having no compassion. Two mayors died soon after speaking badly about her. It was commonly believed that she had them killed, but no one tried to prove it. Reporters have died or disappeared after writing a horrible story about her drug business or about her. There is no evidence she's connected. As her attorney I have to believe she is not connected. If I knew she was connected, I would have to defend her. I'm her lawyer."

"I hope she never gets mad at you or me," I said.

"She is loyal, but never lie to her or break a promise. I never have."

I nodded.

"She's fragile and elderly, but there's nothing fragile about her brain. She forgets nothing."

"I understand," I said.

My father had understated how frail Mala appeared. It was hard for me to believe anyone would fear her, though I knew she was powerful. She welcomed me warmly to her home and introduced her two grandsons to me. My father already knew Rico and Victor.

"You are buff," I said.

The young men smiled.

My father said, "You should see them practice their martial arts. I've seen them working out."

"Rico, are you into jujitsu?"

"My brother is," Rico said. "I'm into karate. I earned my first black belt at fourteen."

"Takes longer for me," Victor said. "Very few are masters."

I pulled out my handkerchief and waved it like a white flag. "I don't want to mess with either one of you," I said.

The boys laughed, shook hands with my father and me, and excused themselves.

"I would never be where I am without your father," Mala said after her grandsons left.

My father looked surprised.

"Magda, thank you but not true. You've done it all."

I saw Mala smile just a little.

I smiled back, shook her hand. Her eyes were penetrating.

"Don't believe everything you hear," she said, an eyebrow raised just a little.

"I hear nothing, see nothing," I said with a smile.

"Good boy," she said. We shook hands again. I know my father was happy.

We flew back in my dad's plane. It was too noisy to have much of a conversation, and, of course, we had two pilots with us. These pilots were like family because they'd been with Dad for so long, but they had ears. All they did is fly the plane. We never mentioned her name unless we were alone, though associates and lawyers who worked for the firm knew she was a client. Everyone knew my father represented her.

These days, all my father did was socializing and payoffs. There was no shady legal work to do. When she bought property, my father handled the transaction and paperwork. Everything was by the book.

"She has over four hundred rental properties in Juarez," Dad said. "That's not all. She has three hundred apartments that she gets no rental income from. If you are homeless or down and out, you can move in and pay no rent."

"I didn't know this," I said.

"Lot of things you don't know yet. She is the most charitable person you will ever know."

I was skeptical.

Even in a plane at twenty or thirty thousand feet in the air, and with no one around to hear, he still whispered near my ear, cautiously.

"The only evidence against Mala is gossip, and that's not evidence.

No one has anything criminal to pin on her. The woman is smart. She does nothing in public to make herself vulnerable to arrest, much less conviction of a crime."

"She can't be that smart," I said.

"She is. And she's ruthless."

"You don't need to defend Mala to me every time her name comes up," I told my father. "I've heard the gossip thing. I believe you."

She was smart, ruthless, and could not be connected to her drug business. He stopped short of saying she was innocent. It goes without saying that the innocent aren't ruthless. My father and I had some very tense moments, and they were always about Mala.

When I was in law school, I only came home for Christmas. Once I came home for my mother's birthday. Most of the girls I'd known had gotten married before I moved back. But there was always Mina. She was the only one who had kept in touch. We wrote letters back and forth and called each other at least once a month. Her family was very rich. Her father owned the largest meat plants in Northern Mexico. She knew when I was coming home and managed to smuggle herself into my bachelor pad as a welcome home present in my bed wearing nothing but a big red bow. Six months after I came home, we were married. It was a wedding to remember, with four hundred guests. Her wedding dress was white, but under her veil, her hair was tied back in a red bow, our little secret.

Within two years of our vows, Mina gave birth to twin girls, and a year later twins again, this time, two boys. My parents wanted us to move into the main house with them, but we stuck it out. My pad had four bedrooms and was just off the pool. Living there was no hardship.

But twins are twins, and they grow. After a couple of years, the boys were two, and kept each other awake at night. They each needed their own bedrooms. Right about the time Mina and I had decided to find a house outside my parents' property, my father unexpectedly died of a heart attack.

Mala reached out to me by phone. I was moved by her call. A month after my father's funeral, my mother died. I was heartbroken. It seemed like too much to bear. Mala called again and offered more compassion. It was so unexpected. I was still heartsick, though. I didn't go to the office for a month, but I talked to Mala by phone every week.

"Mrs. Hidalgo, it is a bad time for me, but please rest assured that I am ready to take care of anything you might need."

I knew that if she had pressing business, it would not be discussed on the phone. My father warned me about using the phone.

"You are a fine young man," she said. "I called to pay my respects. At the moment I don't need anything. I remember how agonized I felt when my Beto died. It will pass. Life goes on. You have a wife and four children. You have a lot of support."

Once my mom's funeral was over, Mina wasted no time pushing me to move us to the main house, my parents' three-story palace. A famous architect in Mexico City and a famous lady decorator from El Paso had put together the dream house that my mother and father kept adding on to. Every room was special, eclectic, and international. It was a fun house and Mina and I loved it.

I bought a new Learjet, had a hanger built, and sold my father's plane.

I offered to visit Mala once a month or anytime she wished with only a day notice. She took me up on that, but I think it was to get to know me more. I made the rounds to the designated persons that had money coming regularly. I didn't see the governor personally, but I took care of him through a trusted assistant, Bella.

On the first trip to see Mala after my parents were gone, I brought her a large, sealed envelope with the ledger my father had in his safe. She seemed impressed when she opened the bank accounts journal.

"I didn't know your father kept records like this," she said.

"I have never read anything in that envelope, but I know it was important because my father kept it in his personal safe." I had read it out of curiosity but not thoroughly.

"You are a fine young man, Mauro."

"Thank you, Mrs. Hidalgo."

"I've told you before to call me Mala or Magda. No need to be formal."

"Yes, Magda."

"I want you to find property along the beaches of Baja, California. I have seen many pictures of Ensenada, Cabo San Lucas, and other areas along the shoreline there. Hundreds of miles of undeveloped beach property. I will pay you a very nice commission on each property you bring me. I don't own property at all in Baja. I want to build up the portfolio of Rico and Victor. I know you know how that is. You have children, right?"

I reached for my wallet and showed her pictures of my children. She insisted I give the pictures to her. "Adorable children," she said. "The boys remind me of Rico and Victor."

I wondered if showing her the pictures had been wise. But then she started talking about her plans for the beach property she wanted me to find for her. I could not keep the smile off my face. It was an assignment that I'd love to take care of.

"I will find the best property and get it for the best prices," I said.

"I know you will, Mauro. One thing. I want to pay the seller in pesos. I have pesos that were never banked and I'm afraid they will disintegrate if I don't use them soon."

I thought she was kidding. I laughed.

She narrowed her eyes at me.

To cover up my gaffe, I said, "Magda, you have such a sense of humor."

She smiled, but there was no laughter in her eyes, just icy calculation.

I felt a chill straight through that smile.

I played it cool but could not leave that room fast enough. How had my father put up with her for so many years? Even though her husband Beto is always given credit, even by my late father, my guess is that Mala had always been in charge.

Isadora, my flight attendant, is stunning, desirable, and a flirt. It is difficult for me to be resolute. All the years I was a bachelor, I fooled around with woman after woman. It's hard to give it up entirely, even for my Mina. It can't hurt her if she doesn't know.

Right after wheels up, I got my glass of Louis XIII. After a dose of Mala, I needed just a taste. I liked to smell it, sip it slowly. It was too early in the day to get carried away. It was early enough that my kids would be up when I got home.

"You want me to work your temples?"

"Si, pero sientate aqui en mi regaso,"[1] I said.

A minute after her fine ass was on my lap, I got hard, pressing against the crotch of my suit pants. Her fingers worked my temples. A kiss came next. She adjusted her bottom against me.

"I'll give you anything you want," she said, her lips moving on mine.

On my flight back home, I wondered if I hadn't fucked up showing Mala pictures of my kids. By the time I landed, I was over it. Isadora was two handfuls. Thanks to her vigorous attention, I was able to shake off the pressure and stress of the meeting with Mala. I told myself that all I was feeling was my own anxiety. Mala had not been mean with me at all.

---

1. Yes but sit here on my lap

CHAPTER 8
MINA ROBLES

MONTHS after his mother and father passed away, Mauro started looking closely at his father's bank accounts and assets.

"I don't have to work a day in my life. You will not believe how much my father was worth."

I was surprised at what he showed me.

"Mauro, you are worth more than my father."

"The money is ours, and for our children."

Mauro didn't know how much my parents hated that he represented Mala. It was a frequent topic of our phone conversations.

"Tell Mauro to drop her. He doesn't need to represent that bitch. She's evil. Why didn't he walk away from the firm when his father died? It's embarrassing," my father said, every time we talked.

"Please don't mention that to Mauro," I begged my father. "His business is his business. Someone has to represent her."

Of course, my father didn't listen to me, and the next time we had dinner together, it was the first thing he brought up.

We'd all had a wonderful day making tamales as a family together, and my father had to ruin it as soon as we sat down at the table.

"Drop her as a client," my father said. "You don't need to represent that evil bitch."

"Her business with the firm is legitimate," Mauro said. "Give me hard evidence she's an evil bitch and I'll consider it. There is no evidence. All of it is gossip."

I knew he was lying. I had noticed strange moments when we went out to socialize with politicians. One day, I found a suitcase filled with money. I don't want to rattle a cage that may not need rattling. I trust Mauro. He would not do anything that would get us in trouble.

I have a lot of help here with the kids, but I don't believe in just sitting back and letting nannies raise my children. I have to be around the babies. I stay busy at home. I didn't give up my girlfriends from school. I socialize a lot during the day then rush back home to spend time with the babies.

My mother warned me about how men fool around. My girlfriends, all of them, are married now. Most of them suspect there is something going on with their husband and another woman.

I don't do laundry myself. I have help for that. I have access and I see spots on his underwear. No doubt it's Isadora. As long as he comes home at night and he loves me and my children, I don't plan to say anything. The venganza,[1] is that I will come across someone and I'll have my fun, too. That's what my mother did, and she never got caught. She could have caught my father, but she made no effort.

"Men will be men," she said to me. "What they do, we can do. Toss the standard in the toilet. That's what they do."

Still, my husband Mauro is the most wonderful man in the world.

---

1. Payback

CHAPTER 9
MAURO ROBLES

IN JUAREZ, in the paneled study, I waited patiently for Mala. I always met with her in this downstairs study. I thought of my grand house and compared it to what I'd seen of her house. Like the room I was in, most of it was dark-stained wood, and lots of ancient and heavy antiques. It was beautiful but not for Mina and me. Our house was fabulous.

Still, I would love to own Mala's ornate desk and chairs. I wondered where she got that partners desk.

I took out a thick folder from my alligator attaché case. The folder contained detailed information and numerous photographs of two large parcels of the beachfront property Mala had instructed me to purchase. The first parcel was two hundred acres in Ensenada. The second was two hundred acres in Cabo San Lucas, both in Baja California. The property in Ensenada would be deeded to Rico and the other to Victor.

Mala came into the room slowly, with the help of an ornate gold and ivory walking cane. I stood quickly and held the door open for her. If she died, I knew the gravy train would be over. Each step she took literally seemed an ordeal for her. I hated myself when I thought ill of her. My in-laws, not to mention my best friend, Miguel, had poisoned my brain. It was like they were on a mission to destroy Mala. Miguel's family, for sure, a mission that had been going on for years.

I waited till she took her seat before I accepted her thin outstretched hand into mine. I bowed and kissed her knuckles. I had done that before, and I had gotten a smile out of her. Today, she laughed.

"Tonto[1]," she said.

"Hello, Senora Hidalgo," I said softly and with respect.

"Te lo dije antes que no me llames Señora Hidalgo."[2]

She grunted.

"I'm sorry, Magda. It is difficult for me to speak to you so informally."

"Your father was a wise man. He was a man with great foresight. We talked about you before his death. He said I could trust you completely."

She squeezed that in at least one time during each visit.

"Si, Magda. I am at your service, and you can trust me just as you trusted my father."

"May he rest in peace," she said.

"May your husband Beto rest in peace as well," I said.

I saw a tiny smile. I placed the folders on the desk before her, open, and talked about each of the properties I had bought for her grandsons. She had questions about both. She was very happy with the properties. She looked at the pictures with a big smile on her face then put them away.

"These are perfect. I want to buy more property in Baja for my grandsons," she said. "Beachfront property is my first preference, and the seller must be willing to accept pesos or green dollars."

"Magda, sellers love cash. I will keep looking. I have two good brokers in Baja."

"Thank you, Mauro. I assume everyone that gets regular payments are getting them?"

"Yes, of course. Everything is covered."

"Who does the governor use to get his? And how often?" She probably had the governor spied on. I bet she knew the answer and was just testing me.

"Her name is Bella. Every three months."

"I bet she's only twenty. He loves young girls."

I nodded. "She told me she's twenty-four," I said.

"Mauro, I would like Rico and Victor to look at these properties we agreed on today. When can you take them?"

"You tell me, Magda. I will make the time, of course."

"I will have their tutor James get in touch with you. I'd like him to go along as well. Do you have room in your new plane?"

I chuckled. "Plenty of room, Magda. It will be my pleasure."

Mala stood up. I could tell it was time to leave.

"Your father used to say it takes buckets of grease to keep it all moving."

I had to smile again, but I made no comment.

Gusto and two strangers drove me back to my plane with cash packed in file boxes, thirty-five million pesos in various denominations to pay for the properties and my fees. I would have to leave the money on the plane in the hanger at my home. It was not the first time I had to deal with boxes of pesos. Briefcases or suitcases were used for dollars.

Two hours after I left Magda, my pilots were flying me home in my Learjet at thirty thousand feet. Isadora was feeding me caviar and keeping plenty of champagne in my glass. I drank a little more than before but was still sober enough when I got home. I gazed out of the window at the clouds. I don't know what it is about flying above the clouds, but there is just something peaceful about it. When I'm in the air, it's like all my problems are landbound, left behind.

I was feeling confident. It wasn't just the plane ride. It was the real estate deals. I would be able to find more properties. Easy money for me.

I looked forward to hosting her grandsons on a trip to Baja, California to fly over the properties I had purchased for them. Precious property, sandy beach, incredible property. If I was smart, I, too, would invest in land there. I would have to bring Mina one day to show her.

• • •

Mala's Mexican wealth was funneled into a trust in Luxemburg that administered a Panamanian corporation's bank account in Nassau. A Harvard banking graduate would surely smile at this money-laundering scheme that my father had set up for her over the years. Money bounced through a dozen countries and twice that many shell corporations. I emptied the champagne glass and smiled at the memory of my father. Bravo Papa. This was the dirty work you said you did for her.

Champagne makes me feel slightly drugged—such a pleasure to drink but dreadful after. No matter how expensive, all champagne affects me the same.

"Isadora, my temples, please."

I handed her the empty glass. She set it down, sat on my lap and her fingers began the soothing massage of my head.

"Kiss me," I said, my eyes closed.

"Two words that turn me on so," she said before her lips met mine, her fingers continuing the massage on my temples. "What else do you want me to do?"

---

1. Silly
2. I told you before not to call me Senora Hidalgo

CHAPTER 10
RICO SANTOS

JAMES and my grandmother decided that traveling would be part of our education. When I was fourteen and Victor thirteen, we started traveling with James. When I was fifteen, Victor and I pushed James to set us up in Paris with two hookers. It took some persuasion.

"I've already done it in Juarez," I said.

"You didn't," James said with surprise.

"I did it too," Victor spilled.

James laughed. "Where and when?"

I lit up with a grin. "I bring them back on the grounds and as you know there are many places out there."

Victor said nothing, he just laughed.

"Then why do you want a street walker?"

"Because we're in Paris," Victor said with a don't you know look.

Anyway, James got us two gorgeous vixens. We met them at James's suite down the hall from our rooms. Soon as I saw her, I knew who I wanted, and Victor's eyes were on the other girl anyway. My brother and I look older than our age and thanks to the education we're getting we can talk like mature intelligent students who are attending college. Our martial arts training shows in the way we stand, walk and look when our clothes are off.

Alizée was beautiful, tall, and I dug her color. We both laughed when she stumbled with her English, and I stumbled in French. The rest of the time, we made love. We fit perfect together, she was a stallion. I told James I wanted to stay in Paris longer just to be with her. The girls I brought back to the grounds to fool around with were older than me and the experience was dynamite, but this Parisian was a jewel.

Alizée

When Elena traveled with us, once to London and once to Rome, I assumed that she and James were sleeping together. Back at home, she lived in the house with all of us, while James lived in the guest house. It was hard to know for sure. My brother and I decided we'd ask James outright, but Victor left me alone to do it. We were in the café of the Paris hotel. As we had planned, Victor had chugged down his chocolat, grabbed a croissant from the basket and charged back up to the room. His girl was waiting, leaving James and me alone at the table. I picked up a croissant, looked at the balls of butter with the hotel logo, too pretty to touch, and put some purple marmalade on. It was the usual continental breakfast all the hotels offered, but in France the bread was out of this world. James had an English newspaper open in front of him. I forgot; James extended our stay in Paris by three days. Alizée was up in the room asleep.

"Hey, James, are you fucking Elena?"

His paper snapped down, folded instantly into a neat rectangle. He set it aside and looked at me mildly over the top of his reading glasses.

"What kind of question is that?"

"Come on, James, it's only me and you. If you have nothing going with her, then I won't feel bad about the dreams I have about her and me."

James didn't get mad. He was the calmest person I ever met. He laughed. A nervous laugh. In karate competition, sometimes I got an opponent who chuckled as we went at it. No, I wasn't going at it with James. I loved him.

"She's your teacher," James said. "You have to respect her."

I grinned. "I'm only joshing James. I love her, and I know she's my teacher. But tell me she's not the hottest teacher you've ever worked with."

James sipped his coffee; the waitress had just warmed it up.

"Come on James, agree she's hot."

James looked at me and smiled before he said, "She's hot, a beautiful woman." He changed the subject. "The young lady in your room is hot as well."

"No question," I agreed. I knew he didn't want to discuss Elena further, and I didn't push it. He was fucking Elena. I was sure of it.

The morning when I packed up to leave, I gave Alizée five hundred dollars.

She shook her head and said, "No, Rico. Mr. James pay me already."

My French was horrendous, but I did practice back home and on the plane. "Please take the money," I said in French. We were staring at each other. She smiled big. Her teeth were pretty.

"You speak good, baby," she said then kissed me.

She took the money and our phone number at the house in Juarez. I got her phone number too. "I will see you again," I promised. After a very wet kiss, I bent her over the bed, pulled down her shorts and panties and while she stepped out of them, I dropped my pants and underwear and took her from behind. Ten minutes later the doorbell rang and then it rang again, and again. There was knocking. I could hear Victor saying, "We're running late, Bozo, are you in there?"

We almost missed the plane.

We got back home and now James knew from our own lips that we were screwing neighborhood girls. "Here is a box of rubber protectors," he said to my brother and me, handing us two small packs. "You don't want to make any babies until you are ready. There is also the chance of catching a bad disease. Do I need to say more?"

"Read you loud and clear," I said.

"Those things take away the feeling," Victor complained, accepting the packet.

"Oh, so you tried them before?" James said.

"James, I'm fifteen and he's fourteen. I've tried them. I hate them."

CHAPTER 11
VICTOR SANTOS

THE FIRST GIRL I had in Paris kept rushing me and when I was on top of her, she told me to be careful and not squash her. I laughed it off. The next day I said to James, "I heard we're staying extra days. Eloise checked out this morning from my room. Don't forget me."

"What happened? You couldn't get it up, is that why she left?" my insane brother said, obviously making fun.

When we came from seeing the city on a tourist bus, there was a lady in the lobby waiting. James had private words with her then he introduced me, "her name is Yvonne. This is Victor." She was there for me. What a find. It was love at first sight. Kind of what Rico said about the girl he has in his room. "I love her already," I said to James. I kissed Yvonne lightly on the lips and headed to the elevator, holding hands.

Yvonne

CHAPTER 12
ELENA

JAMES WAS A GOOD LOVER. He could go once. Once for a longer time than a young one like I'd been with in the past. I knew about the women who were brought to him two or three times a week at night. The boys didn't know but I think everyone else knew. During a recess today, he was at his desk, and I was at mine in the classroom. He had finished his session and when the boys returned, it was my turn to do the next three hours. "I need a tune-up very bad," I said in a low voice, my eyes on his.

"I thought you'd never ask," he teased.

"You're horrible," I said with a giggle.

"I know, but I promise you a *Sacudida*[1] that might ruin your sleep tonight from the shaking."

"Shh, I said, my index finger at my lips." I had to be red.

We laughed.

Victor walked in before Rico. "What's so funny, guys?"

"School stuff," James said as he got up to leave.

Rico came in. "Were these two whispering again?"

After the promised *Sacudida* that night and lying-in bed with very little light coming in from the living room so that we could barely see each other, James told me about the Paris sex the boys had and the earlier conversation he had with them this morning when he handed them a package of protectors.

"They're too young," I said, almost in a protest.

James laughed. "I think Magda gave us the wrong ages of these kids. Fourteen going on twenty-one and thirteen going on twenty. That's why we extended the days in Paris."

"I'll be darned," I said in Spanish.

"Rico asked me if you and me are having sex?"

"What?" I sat on the bed.

"He's curious and holds nothing back. I handled it."

"Handled it?"

"I agreed with him that you are a hot lady."

"What?" I laughed but only a little. "He said that?"

"He did. It was only the two of us."

"Scandalous."

"No, not at all. Kids fall in love with their teachers."

I laid back down next to him and gave him a little shove.

"How do you know what teachers do? You never taught before." We laughed. I love the way James hugs me. Moments like this I realize how lonely I am after hours.

"Hold me," I said to him. "I promise to leave in fifteen minutes." I put my face on his chest. "Thank you, James."

"Please don't say that," he said in a soft voice.

"It was a great *Sacudida*. Got to thank you." I calmed down and joined him when he laughed. I kissed him, got out of bed, and dressed.

"Take a shower here, it's okay."

"I'll do it up in my room, thank you."

When I stepped out of his guest house, Gusto came out of the shadows and walked beside me to a back entrance of the main house where everyone was probably asleep. Five minutes later I was in my room, dropped my clothes to the floor and slipped into bed. I wanted the smell of sex to permeate the air I breathed.

---

1. Slang for a slamming fuck

CHAPTER 13
MALA HIDALGO

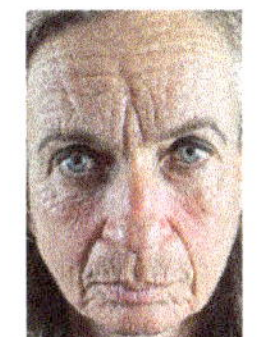

ALEJANDRO WAS one of my drug business bosses. "It's been eighteen months since I saw you," I said, my hand outstretched for him. He came around my desk, took my hand in his and kissed it, once, twice.

"Magda, we should meet more often."

He was back across my desk and stood there until I sat down.

"I trust you, no reason to take chances with meetings," I said.

He nodded in agreement.

"How about a drink?" I offered.

"Only if you drink with me," he said.

"Pour me a Presidente," I said and watched him get up and walk to the glass and brass cart that held different liquor bottles and crystal glasses.

I don't drink and didn't plan on starting now but I knew he wanted a drink.

He explained that cocaine was in big demand by the same suppliers we sold heroin to and also to the marijuana persons with whom we had done business for years.

"You have coke to sell them," I said, but I knew he wanted to move tons and not small amounts as was the case at the present time.

"Not nearly enough," he said.

"More coke means doing business with others we never did business with," I said. "We have our hands full with the products that have brought us here. Coke is a beginning fad that will come and go."

I had two other bosses that worked as a trio with Alejandro. A trio of men who were multi-millionaires from the fruits of our business and my extreme generosity to give back as much as I did to a non-partner. I had no partners.

After two hours Alejandro was ready to go.

"My friend," I said. "Let your two co-workers know we continue the coke flow at the same rate and not to do anything on the side that they would regret."

Alejandro turned red as a tomato. "You know we are with you until our death," he said, coming around my desk to take my hand again.

I know he meant until my death, but he was a good man and loyal as a man can be. He had proved it, time and time again.

When he opened my office door, Gusto was there to escort him back to the stairs and walkway that would take him to the market across the street.

When he was gone I sat at my desk and wondered again. What will become of my business when I die? Living and not knowing when the die date is, is almost as painful as knowing the date.

I don't want Rico and Victor in this business. They are a different generation and as smart as they are, they would not handle the pressure that comes with this business. The joke that it's a hands-off business is just that. I don't leave this house and I'm accused of running a drug business and they are right, but they can't prove it. If my boys were in the business, they might not be as careful. I would come back from my grave if the authorities were to take them prisoners. In the real world, if I'm dead, I can't protect them. They don't need the money; I've made sure of that.

Let the bosses take over the business?

Without me the trio would end up killing each other.

CHAPTER 14
RICO SANTOS

JAMES KEPT TELLING my brother and me, "Your grandmother wants you to stick around. She knows you need privacy to sow your wild oats. She has a surprise for you two."

Grandma had two guest houses built on the grounds, both a little larger than the guest house where James lived.

The contractor had twenty men divided in two teams. Ten men worked on each house. Victor's house was two hundred feet from mine, and James's place was on the opposite side. With the keys to the house, I got car keys. Victor was not supposed to get a car until a year later, but he convinced Grandma to let us have cars at the same time.

The houses were decorated a little differently, but the floor plans were identical. Victor and I, we sat down with decorators and picked colors we liked out of what they offered. My house had two bathrooms, a living room, kitchen, a room set up as a home office, large enough for a sofa, two soft chairs and a big television set. The bedrooms each had ensuite bathrooms with shower heads seven and a half feet above the floor. My brother and I were a little over six feet. My grandmother said we weren't finished growing but James told us we'd probably stay where we were. James was always right.

Florencia was assigned as my full-time housekeeper. She was only four years older than me, had two kids that her mother was raising, and the only other things I knew about her were that she could roll joints like a card-carrying pothead, and the man she never married had thrown her out of his apartment. I left out five lids of pot one time, and she rolled it all into joints.

If she was still working at the main house, she'd be wearing a uniform. Working for me, she gets to wear anything she wants.

I spend a lot of time in my house now and Florencia stays as late as I want. We enjoy each other with no commitment of her becoming my steady or anything. She is on my grandmother's payroll. I give her extra. Makes me feel good. We smoke together. We have sex. That's not why I give her extra.

"Your grandmother will burn me to dust if she knows this is what we do here." She was happy from the pot.

"You don't sound worried," I teased.

"Not worried," she said, taking a long drag. "Thank you for sharing yourself with me."

I released the smoke from my lungs. "On the contrary, I thank you."

Florencia

Elena was thirty-seven when I was seventeen and more beautiful than ever. It was no secret that I had always had the hots for her. James knew because I always told him I wanted her. My grandmother knew because she always knew everything. Elena knew it too. She was too smart not to know.

I had just turned seventeen, I was an adult in Mexico two years ago.

Up to that point, every girl I had sex with was older than me but that's only because I was so young. Even Florencia was four years older than me. The girls I brought home from outside were not much older than me, but still older. I didn't always ask their age. Elena was way older than me but that was perfectly fine with me.

I don't remember how long it took or what I said to get Elena in my bed.

"You are out of this world," I said to her in Spanish.

"I shouldn't be here, Rico. Your grandmother will kill me."

"Every girl I've ever been with except in Paris has said that to me. My grandmother will do no such thing. You're family. Besides, you're a senpai."

"Me being a senpai doesn't mean I can stop a bullet."

I laughed first. She blushed and laughed along.

"I think you are fast enough to dodge a bullet," I said.

"Yeah, right. Where is your housekeeper, I know you have something going on with her?"

"She went home and how do you know what I have going with her?" I was grinning as I spoke. I tickled her. She crunched, and I caressed her abs. I never had a woman with a body like Elena.

I was also a senpai. A man should reach that level in karate, especially after all the years I had practiced. Elena had as many years in training as I did. No one was surprised when she got her black belt the same year I did. To think that way back when she started I thought girls should not be taking karate lessons.

Earlier, Elena helped me undress, hurrying the process. We were steaming. We rolled around a little, then I got on top. She moaned loudly as I entered her and moaned again as I entered her deeper. In Spanish, she said I was monster sized, then said I was an animal, and she loved it.

Later we lay in the dark, facing each other. It was a different place in the dark. The blinds were open, the window cracked, and a breeze from the outside ruffled the curtains. Security lights outside gave enough light for me to see her face.

"I feel like I'm betraying James," I said.

I did not mention that a long time ago, I had asked James about the two of them.

Elena put her hand on my face.

"Why do you say that?"

She admitted they had done it but there was no commitment between them.

"James enjoys new encounters. For years, Gusto has had one of his men bring him women. I thought you knew that."

I sat up on the bed. This was interesting.

"Is that the truth?"

"Yes, but you can never tell him that you know or that I know."

"I'm not going to tell," I said.

I felt her touch me there, and I became hard again.

"I always wanted you," I said.

I heard Elena's soft laugh, felt her pull on my hardness. The next thing I knew I was facing her, our lips pressed together.

"I feel guilty. You are much younger than me. I've been your teacher for many years."

"You say this, but your hand is still holding me."

"I'm human," she whispered. "I'm also sex starved."

I felt a jolt when she said that. "Repeat sex starved," I said.

She didn't hesitate and repeated what I wanted to hear.

"I want you, Elena."

She let go, turning her back to me. I spooned her, grasped her breasts, and needed no guidance to find her wetness.

"I knew you would be good like this," I said. I remembered times I had watched her in the swimming pool or lying on a lounge chair in her bathing suit. When we traveled with James and she stopped dressing like a teacher and started dressing like a woman, I always stared, and she knew it. We had been living in close quarters for years now. I was mesmerized by her, no question. The scent of her now was ecstatic.

"Culeame,"[1] she said. Hearing this turned me on more. I fucked her for hours with only short breaks. I felt like Superman. My erection was hard like our abs. She went down on me. It was not my first time, but it was the first time I screamed with pleasure.

"Tell me not to feel guilty," she said later. "I totally overstepped."

"Don't feel guilty," I said. "You did no such thing. I'm not a kid anymore. It's not like we're blood relatives. We had a lesson on that, remember?" I chuckled a little to clear the tiny gloom that I felt from her. I heard her giggle, her lips pressing on my ear.

That year, Victor and I received our diplomas from the El Paso High School and the Juarez High School as James had originally arranged.

"You have three years of university study," Elena told Victor, James, and me. "James and I are going to try and get you credits from the university here in Juarez and from the Texas State College in El Paso."

"You were entitled to the high school diplomas three years ago, but you were too young," James said. "Your classes these three years were AP. Advanced Placement. That is, college level."

Victor said, "Get us whatever you can get us." He laughed. "I'm done with school."

"That's me," I agreed.

"I will be leaving soon," Elena said.

"My grandmother would love you to stay," Victor said.

"I would love you to stay," I said, without looking at James or Victor. It didn't matter to me if James and Victor might have picked up on my feelings. Again, I saw how beautiful she was. She had been trapped here on the premises for over ten years. She'd given up years of her youth to be here to teach us. This was the first time I ever thought of it that way. If she wasn't getting sex regularly from James as she said, where did she get her sex? She never left the compound. I wanted her again.

With our schooling finished, Elena moved away.

The night after Elena left, we sat at the table. Elena's seat was empty.

"You can stay here for as long as you want," my grandmother told

James. "I am saddened that Elena left us. I was so used to having her around. Don't be in a hurry to leave."

"Thank you, Magda," James said. "You have me living here like a king. You should charge me rent now that I am no longer teaching."

All of us at the table enjoyed watching my grandmother laugh at what James said.

James stayed. He had squirreled away his money somewhere. It had been years since he had needed cash. He liked his guest house, and my brother, and me. I think he loved everyone who worked inside the walls, and I know everyone loved him. I don't think he had anybody else in the world. Still, he was a happy person.

My grandmother rents out hundreds of apartments and houses, and in downtown Juarez, she has a block-long string of retail stores. In the heart of the tourist area in downtown Juarez, a restaurant that she rented out had been shut down by the mayor for serving liquor to minors and for allowing prostitution without a permit on the premises. It had been closed for more than a year. My brother and I planned to open a night club in that building. For a few hours, our grandmother objected to letting us open the business.

It was clear she didn't want us limited by having a night club in Juarez, but we all had a talk. At least my grandmother and Victor and I had a talk.

"You should be thinking bigger than a club."

"It will be a big club," I said. "We're thinking big. Maybe not as big as all the drugs in Mexico."

"No drugs," she snapped. "When I'm dead, let someone else have the drug business. You don't need it. Take what I have put away for you, invest in big business or disappoint me and become lazy rich heirs that will never be happy and die of boredom."

It was rare for grandmother to come that close to admitting she did have a drug business. My brother and I knew it but never asked questions. She became a little more open after James and Elena were done with our schooling.

"If we give up the drug business who will supply us with marijuana for our personal use?" I asked. My brother joined in laughing.

If my grandmother had a fly swatter at that moment, she would have nailed us with it as she sometimes did when we were kids. It's not like she didn't know we smoked weed.

She caved, finally letting us use the building, but it was probably because she saw our enthusiasm. In fact, she had us send James in to see her, because she had something to talk to him about. We wanted James with us, because we were picking his brains for our club plans, but you don't argue with Mala.

We had never worked before, never made a dime on our own. We were eager to put our ideas into motion. James had taught us about investing, making money, and I don't mean from a drug operation.

"Take the money you need as you need it from the vault," she told us.

We knew she had bigger ambitions for us than to own a night club, but it was a start, and it would get us some experience. We had ambitious plans for our first venture and called the new place the *Palacio,* and we intended to get it decorated like a palace.

James was as excited as Victor, and I were about the new business. Victor and I were caught up in that moment planning the club.

The next day, Mauro showed up in his plane in the morning, took us for a ride in his jet, and explained to Victor and me how the properties were held in trust. I listened to his spiel, but I was watching the stewardess, Isadora. She was real eye-candy. It was just James, Victor, Mauro, and me in the Learjet that took us over the coast. I hadn't been thinking about it. I knew we were going to get a look. I was just enjoying the novelty of a ride, and the beachfront property didn't seem really mine until I saw it. It was just a flyover, and we didn't even get out of the plane. We flew to the coast, to Baja, California. Mauro's pilots circled us over my beach and some amazing wild, unimproved land in Ensenada. It was crazy to realize that it was all mine. From there, we went to Cabo San Lucas and flew over Victor's property. We were excited, of course, but James seemed even more excited. What to do with the property was the topic of conversation for a very long time after that trip.

---

1. Fuck Me

CHAPTER 15
VICTOR SANTOS

YOU HAVEN'T HEARD much from me. Rico likes to do all the talking and always does. Let me tell you about the Palace Night Club we finally got open. It is the classiest spot in all of Juarez. The locals were on my brother and me from the start that we had put the club in the wrong part of the city.

Tourists from across the border and from many other cities do downtown Juarez, but not the locals. Tourists don't dress up; they don't wear sport jackets in a dusty city like Juarez. We knew that going in but the impact once we opened kicked our ass. Everything was fancy. Tourists didn't care about fancy. They wanted to eat, drink and to be served by pretty ladies. They expected to have a live show, danc-ing, and to hear American music. We had all of that. Business was outstanding from day one. But the dress code we expected never happened.

Rico and I, we were planning to make money off the rich locals. They came to us, loved the *Palacio*, but complained about having to venture into downtown. The club was popular, and the ritzy locals kept nagging us about building a *Palacio* twin in the outskirts. Rico found a vacant lot close to the money neighborhood where the families lived behind guarded gates. Though my grandmother is richer than all of them put together, we lived in the roughest neighborhood in the city. Except for the adventuring ones that hit the club, we didn't know any of these rich people that lived in the outskirts of Juarez in gated communities. They only knew us by reputation. As you can imagine, my grandmother was not social.

At the *Palacio*, we allowed smoking. Everybody everywhere allowed smoking—cigarettes, that is. Weed was a no-no, even though outside four vendors were selling it.

Sometimes we took our own cars, but as luck would have it, Gusto drove Rico and me to work, letting us off in the parking lot. I remember stopping to admire our hard work. It was dusk, and the lights we had added played well against the darkening sky. Even through the closed doors, the roar of music was lively and beckoning. The parking lot was already packed, mostly American cars with Texas plates. I saw a couple guys across the pavement and went over to talk to them. Fito and Chaparrito had the best weed around. I should know the quality because Rico and I got it for them.

I saw Rico was waiting by the door for me, so I said a quick hello and goodbye, and took the joint Fito handed over. Rico and I, we held off smoking it till the end of the night when we were closing. We really did work, and that meant different things every day. Sometimes we made a late run for supplies when something ran out or smoothed over situations between drunk patrons. The manager we'd hired was going to call someone to work the shift, but I volunteered. I hung out in the kitchen to replace a sous chef, not something I would want to do all the time, but I liked pinch-hitting for our regular guy whose wife was having a baby. Mostly, I chopped things with a very sharp knife and got in the way. I managed not to kill anyone with my cooking. Rico and I had been experimenting with different opening and closing times, and were talking about menu changes, gossiping about the barmaids, hookers, and American girls, and logging the proceeds.

Gusto was back at one a.m. to pick us up. Everyone was gone except the bouncer, Bruno, who was babysitting a drunk tourist till a cab came to pick him up. Rico got in first. I don't know what made me look, but I saw a heap against the wall where I'd seen Fito before. It was dark enough I couldn't make it out till I had Gusto stop.

"Hey, Jefe," Chaparrito said, sitting on the curb. He was a short, stocky guy, and looked smaller than usual, slumped over. In the glare of Gusto's headlights, I saw bruises and torn clothing. Chaparrito was smoking a cigarette, and he looked really messed up in the glow of the cigarette. Beside him was what looked like a pile of rags. It turned out to be Fito, who managed to sit up when he realized I was there. He didn't look too great either. Rico got out of the car. You know how he likes to talk. He took control of the situation and got them talking about what happened. It turned out Chaparrito and Fito had been beaten up pretty good. It hadn't taken long for an enforcer working for the distributor of weed, coke and heroin in that area to step up to our vendors.

"They got the weed," Fito said out of the side of his broken mouth. He'd lost some teeth.

Rico and I talked about taking the guys home, but they said they were okay to drive, and tottered off to their rusty Ford truck they parked around the corner because it's barely a car. We didn't want it in our lot.

My brother and I should have known that the cartel would take action. No one is more territorial. There are twenty or more cement walls between the Beto drug cartel and my grandmother, but I'm surprised they would dare. It's my grandmother's business. And she's scary.

In the morning, we were summoned from the breakfast table. As soon as we saw my grandmother pacing when we went in her study, it was clear Gusto had spilled the beans about last night.

"What is wrong with the two of you? Why are you selling weed on the street?"

Rico shrugged the way he does and sat down next to me. My grandmother was still pacing.

"Is that a problem?" Rico asked.

She slammed my brother's thigh with her cane, then poked me in the chest. She's not exactly a body builder, but she was angry, and it showed. There was no knowing what she might say. She wasn't against using her fists on us or against using something nearby, breaking a dish on someone's head or smashing a glass. Feisty she was.

The bottom line was that selling weed, coke, or heroin—pretty much anything—on the streets of Juarez was violating a territory that her bosses had assigned to a wholesale buyer that in turn had street dealers peddling the product.

"I will burn your club to the ground if I hear you have guys on the street selling anything. Anything at all. You understand me?"

I nodded my understanding. We were dismissed.

"Won't happen again," I said.

Rico was halfway out the door. He looked back, smiled, and said, "Te amo, Abuelita."

The words were barely out of his mouth when my granny threw her cane at him. He caught it in mid-air, smiled like only he could do, walked back and handed her the cane. He kissed her on both cheeks. And that was that.

Gusto drove us to the club.

"We don't need the money from weed sales," I said.

"Correct, we don't need the money."

The way this big car bounced over the potholes was like riding a carnival car.

"I'm going to let three vendors go and keep one with to sell coke baggies. Coke brings more money anyway, and she was only talking about weed today." Rico winked at me.

"You know damn well she was talking drugs, period. Why agitate her?"

"Let's concentrate on running the club and pushing to open the new one on time. What do you say?"

"I'll think about it," Rico said as we got out of the armored car.

Gusto heard everything. He left the car running and cornered the two of us before we got the club door open. He had been with the family long enough where he could do this and get away with it.

"Rico, Victor, don't sell drugs. It can bring heat down on your grandmother. Heat she doesn't need." He wagged his finger at us like we were little kids, and he was making a point. "You are her only family. You think the petty drug sales you propose won't lay blame on her?"

It took my brother a minute to reply. A siren blared in the distance. An unseen plane flew overhead. Car horns squawked. A truck close by bounced hard on potholes. Something blasted—a backfire or a gun. It was hard to tell which was which. Eventually Rico gave in.

"Okay, no drugs," Rico said.

"I promise," I said.

"I love you like my own sons. Do as I say. Your grandma is not as strong as you think."

A water truck was going by spraying for dust and hit the potholes just as Rico and I were hugging Gusto. Rico and I, we jumped up to the sidewalk and got out of the way. Gusto got wet and so did the car.

Gusto took off after the truck. It would have gotten away if there had not been a red light at the corner. He came to a halt. Gusto opened the driver's door and yanked the driver out of the truck and into the street. He slung him pretty far from the vehicle.

It was our turn to stop consequences that would get back to our granny.

We got to Gusto about the same time he picked up the screaming driver. It took both of us to pull him away.

"Go home, Gusto," I said, in as commanding a voice as I could manage.

The driver was tall but slight, a lightweight. He was terrified of Gusto until he looked at me and Rico. Then, if anything, he was twice as terrified. As for Gusto, he cussed out the driver and walked to the sedan.

"Sorry, Jefe," he said to both of us. "Asshole caught me off guard."

"Go home. Change clothes," I said. "You'll be fine."

The truck driver piled into his truck and high-tailed it for other dusty streets, his water trailing behind him.

I put my arm around my brother, waved goodbye to Gusto and we headed towards the Palace entrance with a little flourish. The street is lower by at least two feet so that heavy rains don't flood the stores. If you happen to be at the end of a block as we were, there are cement steps on the corner. My brother and I, we don't use the steps. We jump up and land on our feet. You should see us sometime. When the tourists see us, sometimes they make a fuss, especially if we're going the other way, down the steps, when we might try a flip like our sanseis were watching.

CHAPTER 16
ELENA

TWO MONTHS before I moved out of Mala's home, I was set for a life like I'd never imagined would happen to me. For all the years I lived there, I was paid once a month. Once a month, I would go to my bank to make a deposit, or I would take James up on letting him deposit my cash for me. I hardly ever touched the balance. Practically everything was provided for me.

My bank balance rose for the first three years of just putting the money in a checking account, but then I purchased certificates of deposit that at one point paid twenty percent annual interest.

Mala is one of a kind in her generosity. My monthly salary was equal to what the university paid in a semester. I knew James made more than I did, but his credentials were to die for, and he did everything in grand scale and style. He'd also been coaxed to live in a foreign country. He might be dedicating the rest of his life to Rico and Victor. I would never have known to do for the boys what James did. He's a wealth of knowledge and experience.

Before I sprang away from Mala's place, I had banked over ten million Mexican pesos, but that's not all. When I gave Mala notice that I would be leaving in two months, that night at dinner, I knew something was up because she had me switch seats with Victor, who usually sat at her left. After dinner, she had a surprise. We were all still sitting at the table. The dishes had just been cleared. She called Gusto in, and he handed her a cotton shopping bag and left. She rapped her cane on the floor because Rico was hamming it up when she wanted to talk. He turned, startled, and looked in her direction.

"Excuse me, Abuelita," he said, bowing his head jokingly.

"I am going to miss you," Mala said, her eyes on mine.

"All of us are going to miss you," James said.

"I will visit you no matter where you go," Rico said.

"So will I," Victor said.

I felt the tears gather in my eyes.

I reached over and touched Mala's hand.

She gave me a smile and handed me the zippered bag.

"Open it," Rico said.

Then everyone was chanting, "Open it!"

I looked in Mala's direction. She nodded.

I took the money out of the envelope and thumbed through it with shaking hands, shocked. It was two hundred thousand U.S. dollars. I cried like a baby.

Victor, Rico, and James, got up from their chairs and surrounded me, and I got hugs and kisses. Mala was smiling. I looked over to her and smiled back, tears streaming down my face.

In the limo, I went with James to El Paso because the first thing I wanted to get was a new car. I paid for my new Fiat in cash. It was hard to believe it was for real. I hadn't driven in years, but I guess you don't forget. Gusto drove the limo back home. I drove the Fiat with James in the passenger seat. All smiles.

That night I slept with James in his bungalow. It was not the first time. It would not be the last time, either.

He held me in the night, in the dark. The night was like a cocoon, holding us both.

"It's hard to believe that in two months, home will be somewhere else, some place I've never even been yet. Are you going home?" I asked.

"I am home," James said.

"I mean, England."

"I may take a trip to London. I have legalities I need to deal with. I'm thinking of going there to go over my will. If I do, want to come along?"

"I'd like to go, yes." No hesitation.

I had been working as the boys' teacher for about five years when I decided to apply for a green card to the United States. I already had a border crossing card that entitled me to cross over to El Paso to shop, visit, or whatever, but not to work.

I should have known better, but I asked Mala about the best way to get the green card. She may have thought I was planning to leave Mexico because she discouraged me. She said that I didn't need a green card. I assured her that I wasn't planning on going anywhere while the boys still needed me.

"Why would you want to live in the United States anyway?"

Mala was very negative about the idea.

One day, out of nowhere, Mala introduced me to her attorney who I had seen before coming or going. His name was Mauro Robles. A beautiful man. He was married. I saw the ring on his finger. He agreed to help me get the green card.

As negative as Mala was about the green card she made it happen.

"I'll bring you the paperwork later this month, and we can fill it out together," he said.

Mala, she was feigning a frown. I think she was. The attorney made his goodbyes and left.

"Thank you, Mala," I said. "You are so good to me. I love you."

The card took time, many hoops to jump through, much paperwork, much red tape. I had to go for two interviews at the U.S. Customs Office. Mauro went with me. Eventually, I got my green card. At the time, I didn't know what I would use it for. I was happy as could be to have it, even though the card just sat in my wallet gathering dust. If

Gusto had not been driving us, I would have fucked Mauro in the back seat of the big sedan. I knew he wanted me.

I still have the green card. Because I've got it, I'm thinking seriously of buying a house in El Paso instead of Juarez. I told Mala, and that made my indecision worse.

"Why would you want to leave Mexico to live in the United States? If you don't want to live in Juarez, move somewhere else in Mexico. Elena, invest in our country not in Gringo land."

James went with me to see a house, a brand new three-bedroom, three-bathroom house with a very large living room, kitchen, and a den as large as the living room. The house had central air-conditioning and heat. The yard was small. I'd never seen the neighborhood before. I realized how long I'd been behind the walls with Mala and family when I figured out that the whole neighborhood had sprung from bare land to a beautiful neighborhood while I'd been hidden. There were multiple neighborhoods with beautiful new houses behind gates. I wasn't interested in one area where the houses were mansions. I had lived in a rented apartment with nothing special when I took James up on the job he offered me.

I paid one million pesos for the three-bedroom house I saw with James. I paid cash, no mortgage. I had a monthly fee to pay for security and upkeep of the property. There were fifty-one homes. It was a beautiful, gated community of homes with street lighting, beautiful tress and manicured landscaping and lawns.

All my appliances such as refrigerator, washer, dryer and three television sets, I purchased in El Paso. Sure, I had fun driving around dusty Juarez shopping for furniture. Mala buys plenty on the U.S. side including television sets and appliances. She also has property in many foreign countries, but she wants me to invest only in Mexico. I do love her, but I didn't tell her where I got my appliances.

Two months from the time I gave notice, I spent my first night in my own home, alone. I had spent some time decorating in a whirlwind. You'd think I'd be anxious, but I had no fear. Since I'd been living in the compound, I had not worried about the bastard who had violated me. What had saved me at first were Mala's guards and walls, but now I was saved by karate. Thanks to martial arts, I had for years hoped the bastard would surface so I could defend myself. I knew karate gave me the power to kill him with a single blow.

I love my house.

Sitting in the living room having coffee during my first morning, I saw the patrol car cruise by every fifteen minutes. I had no time to get lonely. A phone call from the guard at one of the gates announced my first visitor.

Rico was here. He followed the security guard's pickup to my driveway. I opened the front door and waved. Rico was driving his convertible Porsche. It was flashy. I saw the Porsche and wondered why I had got a Fiat of all the cars in the world. I could have bought a Porsche for myself. I had the money.

Easy does it. No need to blow through my nest egg in one go.

Rico came through my front door. He shrugged off his shirt, tossed it on a chair, and flexed his muscles. I shivered at the sight.

"I've been wanting you bad," he said.

We were on each other like a couple of horny lemurs. I had already learned to block out knowing him as a child and being his teacher for all those years. This was not the first time and not the last.

· · ·

Rico brought marijuana joints neatly rolled up in a cigarette case. I had never smoked weed before I started having sex with him at his guest house. I didn't take too many hits, but I enjoyed the buzz. I had smelled it outside Mala's house. Her workers smoked it like regular cigarettes. It is possible I got a contact high on the smoke. I don't know. I smoked with him in my bedroom, both of us lying on the bed naked after a fifteen-minute round of sex.

"Not even a tour of the house. I needed it bad," I said with a little laugh.

Rico had a stormy laugh, loud.

I kissed him. Now that we were at my house, I didn't have the guilt or worry that Mala would incinerate me in her furnace for fooling around with Rico.

"You got anything left?" I asked, reaching for it.

Blame it on the pot. I took two hits, and I was feeling no pain. I kept hearing myself giggle. Weed does that to me. Rico was giggling, too. And he also got very creative with some chocolate syrup and whipped cream that were in the refrigerator.

"Who taught you all this?" I had to ask him.

"No one, it's original." He roared as he does.

We spent the day in bed. Or maybe I should say in beds. Rico did get his tour, and he tried out all the bedrooms. Some of the chairs allowed positions that I'd never imagined before. It was early evening when Rico left. I spent an hour in the bathtub. My nerves still remembered every single touch. In a way, I wished he hadn't come over. Now that he had gone, I missed him. His presence really filled a room.

It was a very hot evening. Rico had left me sated and restless. I took a walk. It was early enough that it wasn't fully dark yet. The streetlights had already come on. My neighborhood was so quiet that it was hard to believe I was only fifteen minutes away from dusty old central Juarez. It was like a completely different world. This neighborhood was brand new. All the sidewalks were in; each house I passed full grown lawns like my house and others were still not planted yet. The pavement was unbroken, graffiti-free, all perfect, unmarked, untouched. This would be a beautiful place to raise children. There was a park area for them to play in, the lines of the new sod still visible, like a patchwork quilt made of fresh grass. I don't know that I want to have children. I turned thirty-five, alone, no ring on my finger. No cars were driving along the street. The families were all inside. There were children in some of these homes. I saw toys, tricycles, trampolines. Children need a father, and I have no candidates. If the neighbors looked up from their late dinners or television sets, they would see me. They would wonder who the crazy lady is walking in the heat instead of being at home in wonderful, sensible, delicious air-conditioning.

I don't want to return to teaching. When I started, I moved up quickly because I was dedicated. I don't have that in me any longer. The challenge is gone. I can live right here on the interest I earn on my money at the bank. Mala spoiled me. All my needs are met. I'm content with what I have. I don't want to think I've become lazy, but I think that has something to do with how I feel tonight. I love my new life. It is so hot. I am still sore from Rico. I turn toward home. The air conditioning is calling my name.

Maybe I'm dreaming. How crushed I would be if I woke up and all this time with Victor, Rico, James, and Mala were nothing but a dream.

CHAPTER 17
RICO SANTOS

MY BROTHER and I often had the conversation: Why are we still living with granny?

It's really a moot point. It's not like the compound is built for one. There's a whole thriving community under one roof with dozens of servants, security, a whole machine that benefits Grandmother and Victor and me. But why not stay? I was all of nineteen, Victor was eighteen, and we had been successfully running the club for a year. We had independence in every way that mattered.

This is Victor's take on the subject: "I don't know about you, bro, but I'm fine where I am and until Granny passes on, I'm not moving. If we move, it will break her heart. Doesn't matter she doesn't see us every day. She knows we're there. She knows we're coming home."

I want to be there for her too, even though we don't have daily meals anymore. We work our club and lead our lives. We're not there all day. I see her for the first time in the morning when I make a deliberate run in to say hello before I leave.

So, when Victor brings it up, I usually tell him, "I'm not going anywhere. I am itching to go and…" Here the conversation branches off into whatever thing I want to do at the time. "…check out all the property I have in Baja and see what I can do there." Or maybe this:

"…jump in the hot cocaine business that's happening from Baja to the US of A."

"You serious about getting in the coke business?" Victor asked.

"Thinking about it."

"You keep saying that."

I smiled at my brother before I commented. "It's a much bigger commitment to go into the drug business than opening a restaurant."

"You got that right," Victor agreed.

Within that first year we ran the *Palacio*, we'd managed to open the new place, built from the ground up near where Elena lives. The *Palacio* was a popular, successful tourist trap. *Palacio II* became what my brother and I had dreamed of having downtown when we first opened. Patrons dressed up. They didn't come to the club only to drink booze. It was perfect for a five-star date with dinner and dancing in a plush ambiance. It was the most expensive place to eat on both sides of the border.

There's a lot of money in El Paso and my brother and I wanted some of it. In 1985 we opened our third club in El Paso, a block from the only five-star hotel in the city. The same contractor that built *Palacio II* renovated a beautiful old building that righteously looked like a palace.

Before the El Paso *Palacio* opened, a reporter wrote a wordy article on how Mala was using her grandsons to buy investment properties in El Paso to wash dirty money. When the article talked about the beautiful old building that we purchased for *the* El Paso *Palacio*, it failed to mention that the building had been on the market for three years. The article had a picture of me and Victor in very cool James Dean leather jackets and jeans in front of a couple of motorcycles with a couple of willowy biker chicks in an El Paso Park. Fortunately for our reputations, the picture was black and white, and didn't show that the Harleys were pink and belonged to the girls. I don't remember their names, but their capacity for beer should put them in the record books.

My grandmother summoned us to the house before two in the afternoon. I was at the El Paso club when a messenger came to give me a message and my brother was at the downtown *Palacio*. Gusto fetched him in the limo, and I drove my car.

"I warned you about opening a club in El Paso." Mala was not happy. She brushed off my attempt to hug her and did the same to Victor.

"We have nothing to hide," I said.

"I will personally look after the reporter who wrote this," Victor promised.

"Low profile, I told you both that a thousand times."

"Grandma, we are opening a landmark, how do we low profile that?"

"You build it here and not in El Paso."

"Grandma," Victor spoke up. "We have two restaurants already."

"Stay away from that side of the border," she insisted.

"Too late," I said. "You know that Grandma."

There was silence, but not for long. Grandma got up. We remained seated.

Grandma started pacing with her cane. We never knew when we'd get clubbed if we said the wrong thing. I smiled at her. It was funny, but it was sad. I didn't know that moment that she was worried.

"I have my hands full with Mauro's lifetime friend, the new governor. I don't need the bastard reporters in El Paso coming at me like this fool who wrote about you laundering money. Makes me sick."

I said, "grandmother, put everything on hold and take a vacation. I can't remember you ever taking a vacation before, you deserve a break."

"You have the villa in Spain," Victor said. "I'll drop everything here and go with you. In the meantime, we can plan how to take on this new governor."

"Kill the bastard," I said.

My grandmother's voice was not as loud when she said, "Mauro is trying to make a deal with him, but this fool-elect blames me for his brother's car crash twenty years ago under the influence of heroin."

"I never heard that story," I said.

"Nor me," Victor said.

Grandmother switched from the governor elect back to the restaurant." "Stop investing in El Paso," she shouted. "Burn the restaurant you built to the ground and let them write about that. We can blame the Mala haters for doing it."

"Grandma, Victor and I love this club. Please don't talk like that."

"You know I will do it," she said, pointing her cane at me then at Victor.

"Grandma, stop it," Victor said.

"I will handle this stupid reporter," I said as I got up.

"Rico, you can't do in El Paso what we can do here," Grandma said.

"I don't plan on getting caught," I said.

"Grandma, we will not buy anything new in El Paso," Victor said, also on his feet now. "Tell us you will not destroy what we worked so hard to build."

That got Victor a poke in the chest. "You didn't build it. Workers built it."

"Grandma, forget what they wrote in El Paso today. I promise there will be nothing more from this newspaper. Strategize on winning over the incoming governor."

We got no commitment of cooperation from her. As we walked out, Victor handed me the folded-up article, which I returned to my pocket.

I got in my car and Victor got in the Suburban, Gusto driving.

Two days after the meeting with Grandmother, the El Paso Police Department got a tip that an individual working for the El Paso *Dispatch* was supplying heroin to distributors in the city. The El Paso *Dispatch* published a story that their reporter Floyd Miles voluntarily allowed the police to search his car where two kilos of heroin were found stuffed under the back seats. Floyd was arrested on the spot for trafficking heroin. The reporter—not Floyd Miles—said that the *Dispatch* would not speculate until their reporter was tried before a jury of his peers. No follow-up article was published alleging that Miles had been set up.

It was early Friday evening, and I had come downtown to have a

Porterhouse Steak in the back office with Victor. We tended to rotate who handled the clubs, and then meet over dinner to touch base.

"Now the owners of that piece of shit paper have figured out we are not going to sit still when they write fucked up articles about grandmother. Bro, you did good," Victor said as he gave me a big hug.

"Me? I didn't do anything," I lied.

Victor started laughing. He was still chuckling after he finished his cheesecake and I got up from the table to head for *Palacio II*.

A couple of months after the reporter's arrest, a beautiful woman came running into the club in El Paso just as I walked inside. I stopped and held the door open for her. She had great legs. She stood in the opening while I was stuck being a gentleman and handed me her business card. Luciana Camacho was much too pretty to be a reporter, but that's what her business card said she was. She worked for the *Dispatch*.

"You work for the enemy," I said, staring at her. I let the door close. We were barely inside the club. As far as I was concerned, the *Dispatch* is the devil, and she was one of its minions. I did not want one of its reporters under any roof of mine.

Her hand went out to me. I looked at it like it was a pit viper, with noticeable hesitation. She kept it out there. We shook hands.

"I'm not the enemy," she said. "I only work there. Give me an interview, Mr. Santos, and I promise I will be fair. I will not speculate about anything."

I couldn't help staring at her. Her eyes, brows and hair were a deep brown. Her off-the shoulder cotton shirt revealed shoulders with a creamy quality that made my fingers itch to touch her.

"I like it the way it's been lately. *Dispatch* hasn't written anything about us. Why are you looking for an interview?"

"Can we sit and talk about it? All off the record."

I looked at my watch pretending Luciana wasn't attracting me like a magnet.

"I'm not sure I have time right now."

Brittany and Ashley, the hostesses at the front desk were looking at me. I had rules about where employees park, and stand, and socialize, and those rules included not blocking the patron's flow of traffic, which of course included the front foyer. Guests coming in were having to walk around us.

"I will meet you anywhere you want," she said. "I only need to know when."

"How about I call you?" I held up her business card that had her phone number.

Her smile reminded me of Elena's. "I look forward to the call. Have a good afternoon." She extended her hand for another handshake.

I looked at her hand and did not take it. I felt like using it to toss her over my shoulder and charge up to my office to interview my very long and wide sofa.

My brother and I were born in an El Paso hospital. As U.S. citizens, we had no fear of deportation. However, my brother and I are not fools. Grandmother is Mala, a name known everywhere. We don't drink and drive in El Paso. We don't smoke pot here. We are not providing cops any excuse to arrest us. Drunk driving and marijuana are both illegal in El Paso. As much as I love the El Paso *Palacio*, I do my drinking at the clubs in Juarez where I can do whatever I want, with no fear of arrest. Smoking pot in Juarez or any place in Mexico is a serious criminal offense but my brother and I don't worry about it. Not in Mexico, certainly not in Juarez.

CHAPTER 18
LUCIANA CAMACHO

1981 TO 1985

I MAJORED in journalism and graduated with a bachelor's degree in Tucson, Arizona where I was born. Getting an internship with a newspaper in Tucson wasn't going to happen, so I expanded my search to the rest of Arizona. When that didn't pan out, I went for Texas. The *Dispatch* in El Paso, Texas was the first opening I hooked. There wasn't much to my CV, but I included a four-page short story and three articles that I believed would showcase my writing. It worked with the El Paso *Dispatch*. The editor wanted to interview me. Juarez is right across the border from El Paso, reminding me of Arizona just as Nogales, Arizona is across the border from Nogales, Mexico. A job in the hand is worth two in the classifieds, I always say. Well, a journalist must start somewhere, right?

In some ways, the *Dispatch* was exactly what I had expected: a small, family-owned newspaper. The paper's circulation was greater than expected, and that gave them advertising income. I had not expected that the owners were rolling in big oil money. The small paper was not hurting for cash.

When I was hired, they gave me an impressive moving allowance, though my starting pay was small enough to be embarrassing. At least rent was cheap.

My supervisor was Floyd Miles. He was thirty-ish, and he liked to call himself an investigative reporter. The problem, though he really didn't see it, was that there wasn't all that much investigative reporting to do in El Paso. It was no Washington, D.C., or New York City.

Floyd was cocky, and I didn't take to him at first. My first assignment was to cover the illegals coming across the Rio Grande. I asked a lot of questions and found a possible entry point. I figured I'd take pictures of illegals swimming across the river or on row boats, and I got those pictures but that was not a story. It was old news. When I was spotted with my camera, I'd get waves from the people who should have been frightened of arrest or of not making it across the river and drowning. I didn't see any of that, and I was glad. That's why I was not surprised when Miles checked what I brought him, and said, "Did the boat capsize? That's a story. These pictures are nothing new."

A person who gets paid to smuggle an illegal is called a coyote. The real thing I should have been looking into is how illegal migrants came over with the help of coyotes.

Miles didn't push me to hurry the story. He told me to stay on it until I found a story to write about illegals. I'm sure the topic had been covered on the *Dispatch* hundreds of times before it was handed to me.

I started my search for the story in Juarez. I had no dress code for my job, and I didn't have to go in as long as I was in touch with Miles with progress updates. I wore jeans and felt like I was fitting in with the rest of the tourists. Being whistled at and getting cat calls from men as I walked past them was new to me. I mean, the crowds back home were so much more sedate. Juarez was a messy place but alive with vendors. To me, the people were exotic, incomparably more exciting than those in my hometown and those I'd met in El Paso.

I hunted for a person to speak to about the process of being smuggled over the border. The problem I encountered was suspicion. Too many figured out I was a fraud, probably an undercover cop from El Paso, or someone with border patrol.

Day after day I crossed the border to Juarez and burned daylight trying different strategies, looking for my break. Evening after evening, I crossed back to El Paso without success. I had been at it for almost a week. I tried yet again, this time approaching a vendor who sold photographs. It was early in the morning, my first try of the day.

"I have a boyfriend that I want to take across the border," I said and slipped him a ten-dollar bill.

His name was Jandro, and he told me to come back later. I did as he asked, though I had heard something like that before, and on my return, the prospect had cleared out and disappeared, as far as I could tell, off the face of the earth. I left and returned at two in the afternoon as he had requested. Jandro did not let me down. At least he was still there.

When I walked over to Jandro, he pointed out a new but very dusty blue van with a guy behind the wheel.

"His name is Pepe. Don't piss him off," Jandro said to me in Spanish.

On that encouraging note, I looked across the street. I could not see Pepe clearly through the tracks of the wiper blades through the streaky crud on the windows. I walked down some steps to street level where the car was and approached the window. He rolled it down. I extended my hand for a shake and felt the excellent air conditioning from the new car. The coyote, if that's who he was, ignored my hand.

"Get in and talk about the boyfriend you want smuggled across the border."

His English was good. Only the slightest accent. He looked Mexican. Clean shaven. Deep tan. Sunglasses. Khaki shirt. I went around the front of the truck, opened the door, and got in, about to say something complimentary about his unexpected but wonderful air conditioning. The instant I closed the door, we took off. Two strong hands from behind pulled me through the space between the bucket seats. I was slammed to the corrugated metal floor of the truck. A young man straddled me, his knees on either side of my waist. He smelled of beer. His hair was long, pitch black, and in a braid down his back.

"I don't believe you have a boyfriend wanting to be smuggled in. I believe you are border patrol. Yes?" He spoke in perfect Spanish.

He pulled out a pistol. I grew up with guns. My dad was a hunter. My mom was a sharpshooter. Even my childhood pet, a lab, was a gun dog. I looked at his pistol. Smith and Wesson. A .22 with a dirty barrel. The safety was on. I didn't mention it.

"I'm a newspaper reporter. This is my first assignment. I'm looking for a story," I said in Spanish. "If you were me, you'd have lied too."

"You aren't scared of the gun?"

I smiled at him. He looked more boyish than mannish. He was probably my age. Great cheekbones. If he'd asked me to the prom, I'd have said yes. Of course, these were entirely different circumstances. I ought to be terrified, but Pepe had dimples. "I prefer the new Glock to Smith & Wesson. No, I'm not scared of the gun. If I was in your line of work, I would have a gun at the ready too. More than one, and bigger than a twenty-two."

"Tomas, this Chica has a sense of humor."

Obviously, Tomas was the driver. The guy with the gun, Pepe.

The truck was in traffic and encountering a rough street. Pepe managed to surf a pothole on his knees, got off me and sat on the truck bed, practically hip to hip with me.

I sat up.

"Let me look in your purse," he said. It wasn't really a question. The question was a formality. He already had it open.

"Go for it," I said.

He pulled out the sixteen dollars cash that I had in my wallet. It made him laugh.

"You think this is enough to smuggle your boyfriend?" He laughed. "Tomas, she has sixteen dollars."

Through the now-closed window, I heard Tomas laugh as he drove down the noisy street we were on.

Pepe put the money back and tossed the purse to me.

"Which is it? You want to smuggle your boyfriend across the border, or you want to write a story?"

"There's no boyfriend. I'm working on a story about smuggling aliens to the United States."

Pepe laughed. "That's not news."

He had switched to English. No accent.

"I don't disagree, but that's my assignment. Can you help me?"

"Tomas, pull over," Pepe said.

Tomas pulled over. The truck stopped.

"We never saw each other," Pepe said.

"Wait," I pleaded. I wasn't too good at begging. I'd spent a week getting nowhere. I wasn't about to let my story drive away. "Can we talk about this? I'm only looking for a story. I don't want to make trouble. I don't have to disclose my source. You know this, Pepe. I will protect your privacy."

He'd put the gun somewhere. Pepe stood, hunched over a little to clear the top of the van. He pulled the latch to open the back door.

"Yes, I'm Pepe. Leave while you stand a chance," he said.

I picked up my purse and got to my feet. Like Pepe, I had to bend to avoid hitting my head.

"Guapo,"[1] I said as I passed him to get out of the van.

"Another time," he said in English.

"Are you saying we can meet and talk?" I asked, swinging my way to the ground.

We were both on pavement. I was a little taller.

"Hotel Cesar at noon tomorrow, room two-zero-one."

"Are you serious?"

Pepe grinned a little. Those dimples. "Come at me," he spoke in English again.

At noon, I knocked on the door of room 201 at the Hotel Cesar in Juarez. It was a nice room. Apparently being a coyote pays well.

There was no delay in getting it on with this stranger. "Business after," he said.

Pepe & Luciana

His idea was to let me cross over with everyone else.

"It's a ten percent chance the truck will be searched," he said. "If they find you, you've done nothing wrong." After a short pause and smile. "If I was writing a story like this I would want to be in on the action."

I didn't agree with his thinking that I would be looked on as an innocent because in a way I participated in the crime of smuggling.

Two weeks later, I paid him three hundred dollars, a sum equal to what he charged six people to smuggle them across the border to the United States. The money came from the newspaper. I joined fifteen men and women.

Everyone was anxious. Pepe grabbed my arm hard and pulled my head close to his mouth. In my ear, he whispered, "If you give me up, I will find you and kill you."

I heard myself say to him in a low voice, "Be sure you come with something better than the toy gun you carry around." He pulled at my hair. I showed him my teeth, a Pepsodent toothpaste smile. "You know damn well I won't give you up. Why the drama, macho man?"

"I'm serious," he said, his right index finger wagging at close range.

"I got the message," I said. "Chill out."

Frankly, I needed that drama to distract me from the stupid criminal act I was about to commit. No one saw this because the group was blindfolded. I was last to get the bandana wrapped around my face and eyes.

All of us remained blindfolded as we were driven to a secret location in Juarez.

When we arrived, the eye covers came off, and we got off the van. There were fifteen of us not counting the driver.

I got a chance to see the men and women around me. No children. Men and women, including me, were soaked with sweat. I tried hard to keep my cool. Mentally.

I saw the truck we were walking towards.

What the fuck? We'll die in there, no oxygen.

The fucking story is not worth dying for.

Be cool, I told myself, be cool.

I'll die with all these strangers.

Be cool. I kept walking with the others.

The man leading the way I had never seen before; he was not the driver of the van.

"How do we breathe?" I said in Spanish.

"You can breathe, now shut up."

We entered the tanker truck using a ladder to reach the top and through one of three hatches with metal covers.

"You must remain quiet," the man who led the way said as he stood by the truck while all of us climbed the ladder then a few feet on top of the tanker to reach the first opening. "Enter feet first and hold on to the edge of the hatch and let go. A few feet to the floor of the tube." He had a humorless laugh.

It was pitch dark inside the tanker. Every time a person dropped from the top, he or she had to move away so the next person didn't fall on them.

We all knew when everyone was inside when the fool we had followed dropped two flashlights down to us. "If you speak, you'll get caught and be arrested by the gringos. It's up to you." The laugh again before the hatch closed.

The truck started to move immediately after the hatch was closed. Two flashlights went on. All of us were close to each other. I took out the cash from the pocket of my Levi's and pulled out a bundle of tens. "Point the light over here," I told the man who was holding one of the small flashlights. I passed a ten to each one of them by having them pass the money down. "I want to take a picture. Put your bandana on your face."

I took pictures. It was part of the story. One was a group picture of everyone huddled together in the pitch-black space we were in. Once we started moving faster, it was hard to hold a camera and not get slammed around the tank. It got very quiet.

A middle-aged woman who could have been my mother was quietly sobbing. I hugged her, and she hugged me back. The flashlights were turned off.

Everyone was silent on the road, then the truck stopped. It stopped and started repeatedly. It felt like it took forever. Each jolt was terrifying to me.

Eventually the truck slowed down and was moving at a crawl. I figured we were in line to cross the border. Then eventually, it moved again normally, and I figured we were in El Paso. Still, everyone was quiet until we were out of the truck. The exit from the tank was not easy, easier for me than some of the others. The guy on top directing us to get out shoved me away when I tried to reach down to help the woman I had hugged during the trip. "Move," he said. "Move, go."

When the story was published, the newspaper used three pictures. In one, clearly you could see that everyone was inside a container but not necessarily a truck. The other was the group picture, it was dark, but you could see the huddled bodies clinging together. The third was a photo from the bottom of the tank with the hatch open.

The truck had the name of a dairy, real or fake, I would never know. Probably real. The truck delivered milk to Juarez then returned empty or with a load of souls arranged by a coyote.

I don't know why Pepe gave up so much for three hundred and a fuck. Don't misunderstand me, I'm not just a fuck. I'm a salivating fuck, but still. Miles and my editor Joe figured that the milk truck was not the only transport he used. I was never questioned about how I obtained the details of my story. In El Paso, people want out of the heat in the summer and out of the cold in the winter. They cared less about the illegals and their mode of transportation.

In a quiet moment with Miles, he said something he had already said to me a dozen times. "The risk of getting caught, what were you thinking? I thought you'd pay the coyote, and he'd give you something to publish. I had no idea you were being smuggled along with the others."

"It's done," I said. "I seriously doubt the story sold any extra newspapers."

"It didn't sell any extra," he agreed and laughed.

I kept thinking about the ordeal for many weeks after that.

When Miles stayed over one night at my apartment and we chitchatted as lovers do, he asked, "You fucked Pepe the smuggler?"

"I fucked him all afternoon one day, not only once. You wanted a story."

Miles looked me over and said, "You are very interesting."

As for Pepe, I never saw him again.

By the time I'd been with the *Dispatch* for two years, Miles and I were living together. We had an understanding, a sort of a relationship. It was a we-need-each-other relationship, not a love relationship. Still though, when Miles was arrested for trafficking heroin, it was like I got punched out. I landed on my sofa alone and silent for not sure how many hours.

Everyone at the *Dispatch* knew it was a set up. Mala in Juarez had to be responsible. It had to be revenge for the article Miles wrote. After Miles went to jail, instead of continuing to put pressure on Mala, the *Dispatch* stopped writing about the family all together.

Miles is scheduled to go to trial in a month. I said to a senior editor, "If her grandsons are clean as they appear to be, I could write a story about them, a laudatory story."

"What for?"

"It's a hunch I have that maybe I can win over the grandsons, and they can do something to free him."

"You'll never get either one to agree to an interview," said the editor. "Do you expect they will admit they had anything to do with sending Miles to jail?"

"Maybe," I said to Joe. "Can I give it a shot?"

There was silence and he seemed to study me from across his desk. I'd fucked him twice. My lips moved for him to read. "I will give you the most luscious blow job, ever."

He agreed. I went home early, and he was at my front door two hours later. Joe is forty something and a good friend of the newspaper owner's son, which probably had a lot to do with his senior position. He was already in that position when I was hired, and he turned me over to my supervisor Miles.

Three days without a word from Rico Santos. I can be patient, but enough is enough. I called the El Paso club.

"Rico Santos is expecting my call," I said to the lady that answered.

"Try Palacio in Juarez. He is not here today."

There were two Palacio Clubs in Juarez. I called one of them and was told he was not there. When I called the downtown club, I got the third degree. I hung up. The way the lady was screening the call, he was there. Had to be.

I parked my car in a public parking lot on the El Paso side and walked the short distance through Mexican customs then took a taxi to the club. As many trips to Juarez as I've made, I should be used to the bumpy car rides. My driver went over a pothole, and I came within an inch of my head bouncing off the inner ceiling of the car. I came bouncing down on the seat so angry I laughed. The driver checked me out in the rear-view mirror and started laughing too.

---

1. Guapo is handsome in Spanish

CHAPTER 19
RICO SANTOS

IF I WAS LOOKING for a good time, I hung around the club in downtown Juarez. When the floor show was about to start, I came out from my office to check it out as I often did. Thelma was ten minutes from finishing her fire pole exotic dance. By the end of the dance, all she had on was a pair of fire-red stilettos and a wig that in the spotlights looked like fire.

We had stopped the gourmet dining of our initial concept and fit the style to the crowds who patronized this location, down-scaling to finger food. We sold a lot of it, and the small menu was easier to manage. The tourists wanted to drink, watch a show on stage, and enjoy fantastic air-conditioning like no other place in the area. The night janitors kept the premises spotless. The tourists came in and daily trashed the place, but if the night janitors didn't do it up perfect, they were fired. There were plenty of potential janitors clamoring for the job. I could never accept a dirty joint like most clubs on the strip we are on. The place was immaculate, and it didn't smell like a sanitizer.

A customer would never get watered-down liquor from any of our places. And our finger food, the best around. Onion rings, French fries, cheese sticks, hot wings. Sometimes we'd have an extra specialty or two such as shrimp ceviche and lemon garlic shrimp. We don't have a cover charge to get in, but our drinks and food are not as cheap as our competition.

The bar at this location was the longest one a customer would ever see in Juarez or El Paso. Our club in El Paso had a beautiful bar, but only this place boasted a fifty-foot-long solid oak granite bar top. The cushy, beautiful black leather stools by the bar were mounted on brass posts with a circular brass ring for a footrest.

My dancer Thelma was in good form.

I spotted the reporter at the crowded bar, apparently waiting for a stool to free up. As the show had started, she would have a long wait. I walked through the crush of partying patrons, and I saw her hand go up, trying to get the attention of one of the bartenders.

I came up behind her.

CHAPTER 20
LUCIANA CAMACHO

I HAD NEVER BEEN to this club or the other one on the outskirts of Juarez. Gobs of people jammed up the place. It had good air conditioning and a fun vibe. Too bad Miles could not be here with me. I had told his dumb ass a hundred times to find someone else to write about, but did he listen to me? Stories were legend about reporters who disappeared in Juarez after writing something bad about that fucking family. Miles knew. He wouldn't listen. I don't know what he was trying to prove.

I was trying to get the attention of one of the five bartenders through a wall of thirsty clubbers waving dollar bills and pesos.

I felt lips on my right ear before I heard the voice.

"Luciana, welcome."

I turned and there he was. Rico Santos. I showed him a big smile.

"There you are," I said. "I never got the call you promised."

He feigned an I-don't-know-what-you-are-talking-about look and showed me teeth. Nice.

"I don't remember promising to call."

"You didn't promise. Can I buy you a drink?"

He grinned.

"Join me and allow me to buy you a drink."

He didn't give me a chance to say yes or no. I followed him to a table a short distance from the stage with four chairs. A waitress was on us the second we sat down. The servers were all in a black bustier, each different like snowflakes, and black shorts. Our waitress had little off the shoulder sleeves.

"I'm drinking Chivas rocks," he said. "Whatever you want, we have it."

"A glass of red wine, please."

"Can I call you Rico?"

"That's my name."

The day we talked at his El Paso club, I was not focused on him like I am now. He's adorable. His grin flashed. I had no idea where the show was going.

The stage was small with a lavish curtain. The lighting was excellent. I had never been to a club in Juarez before. Back when I was in college, I did go with girlfriends and once with a boyfriend to Nogales, a two-hour drive from Tucson. Nogales is tiny by comparison, both the U.S. side and the Mexico side. Drinking was a thing, and we got good and drunk. The shows were all vulgar stuff, and the crowds loved it.

Rico raised his glass to clink mine.

The stage was lit up in red depicting a house of prostitution. To one side of the stage was a bed. Six women were standing nude as a young man checked them out. The man was in jeans and a t-shirt with white tennis shoes. The madam was dressed in shiny black.

"This is my first time," the young man said into a microphone we couldn't see. The crowd responded with cat calls and whistles. After he picked a busty girl with a shapely figure, the other girls and the madam walked off stage. The bed was on a platform, high enough where they had to step up to it.

I won't go through all the motions of the girl undressing a dude pretending to be shy. His clothes came off. He jumped off the bed still pretending to be shy. She came after him, touched him and his dick expanded to what could have been a sixteen-inch water hose. She pretended to be surprised at his size.

Rico joined in the laughter that was blasting around us. He turned to watch me laughing. We clicked glasses again. By the time the two actors were fucking to workout music, I realized how long it had been since I had sex. Miles had been in jail almost two months.

My quick trick with editor Joe, I don't consider sex. He fucked me and was done in ten minutes then he wanted the blow job I promised. I tried for at least an hour to get him up. He didn't make it. "There's always next time," he said, and I nodded in agreement showing him a smile.

After the show, we walked through a bevy of people who were standing, dodging bar girls balancing trays.

"I apologize if the show struck you wrong," he said into my ear.

"That was totally boss," I said. "It didn't strike me wrong."

A guard let us through a black door that said "PRIVATE" in gold letters, and we went up a stairway. The noise followed us, only slightly muted. The walls were vibrating a little. A number of doors were at the landing. Rico opened the one with his name on it. When he shut the door, there was absolute silence. The office was modern with a huge, oval glass-top desk, a massive sofa, two pull up chairs, and the executive chair behind the desk. The floor was black granite with gold veins. There was Mexican art on the walls, all nudes, primitive watercolors, beautifully executed. I realized they were portraits of some of the girls I'd seen in the club.

"Luciana, take a seat. Tell me what you really want. I don't believe you want an interview."

I sat across from him at his desk.

I had a quick thought of how I'd had sex with Joe to get his okay. "I do want an interview. An interview of you, maybe your brother. I want you coming out. All the stories how you grew up in your grandmother's sanctuary."

"No interview for the newspaper," he said with finality. "Would you like a glass of wine?"

"I would. Thank you."

I could see this was not going to be easy.

I wonder if he knows I want to fuck him.

I didn't come to fuck him. I came here to get an interview.

Yes, I would fuck him to get the interview.

Yes, I would fuck him even if he didn't agree to an interview.

Rico picked up the phone. A few minutes later, a server knocked at the door, another knockout chick. Her black bustier had tiny red bows. Her tray held a glass of wine and scotch in a crystal glass. No ice.

There was no clinking of glasses.

"Luciana, here is what I know. Your boyfriend is the reporter who went to jail for being a drug trafficker. He was the author of a burning article about my family and me. It was a fantasy, a web of conjecture with no evidence to support anything. He did spell our names right."

I felt my eyebrows raise and couldn't keep from choking on the gulp of wine that went down the wrong way. Rico was quickly up and around his desk to hand me a linen napkin.

"Spit it out if you can," he said.

I shook my head. "It's okay," I choked. "I'm sorry, sorry."

I got up, still coughing.

"You can leave coughing and choking, or you can sit there and get your breath."

I put the linen napkin to my mouth and sat down. He was standing like a giant over me. I don't remember him being such a big man. Our eyes met. He was so manly. Adorable.

I don't know why I was surprised he had me checked out and connected Miles to me. I really wanted to leave having been caught in an entanglement I couldn't explain my way out of. But I was telling the truth about wanting an interview. I wanted to get a story approved by editor Joe that would put Mala's grandsons in a good light. I hoped by then I could ask for help for Miles. I didn't expect the grandsons to admit knowing about the heroin being planted in Miles's car. I was going to have to play it by ear.

I told Rico the truth about Miles, and that I wanted to do a real story. Not a bad one.

"I have no right to think that you or your family had anything to do with framing Miles. But, I'd be lying to you if I told you I didn't think your family framed Miles." I said it, fuck it.

"I should throw you out," he said with a roar of a laugh.

"No need to throw me out, I can leave on my own."

He stared at me. I stared back.

A short silence later, he said, "No interview for print but outside of you and me sharing a few drinks and maybe dinner, if you want to talk to me about your boyfriend, and how you envision me helping him, you need to remove all your clothes right here. I need to see if you are taping me."

I didn't do it right away, but I did take off my clothes. Once they were off, he frisked the seams of my jeans, went through the pockets, and then had the *cajones* to ask for my bra and panties.

"You are way too brazen," I said.

"When you go to jail, they make you squat and bend over," he said. "I saw it in a couple movies."

"Rico, this is not funny, and it's not a movie."

"You want to talk. I need to feel safe. I don't trust you. You lied to me."

"You wouldn't trust me anyway."

"Right, but I'd trust you more if I know you didn't come here to trick me into having a conversation. You just said you believe my family had something to do with getting your friend arrested. If you were a man, those are fighting words."

He didn't look me over when I handed him my panties, but he did check my panties.

"Rico, I am not wired like in a movie. How old are you anyway?"

"I'm old enough," he replied.

"You keep comparing this to a movie."

"I'm twenty, how old are you?"

"I'm twenty-four."

We were by his chairs. My clothes and shoes were on the floor. I felt the air conditioning chilling my hot skin.

"I'm not going to bend over, and I'm sure not going to squat," I said.

"You don't have to. I believe you," he said. "Put on your clothes."

"Just like that," I heard myself say.

He looked at me and smiled as he sat back in his chair behind his desk.

· · ·

There I was standing naked in front of him, and he said to put my clothes back on. I felt some kind of put down in there. I felt moist there. I got dressed as quickly as possible. I didn't aim to be sexy doing it, or even graceful. I just wanted them on, and fast. I sat down to slip into my shoes.

"I told Miles not to do the story, but he's stubborn."

"Are you in love with him?"

I stared at him. I don't know what love is. What kind of question was that? "I don't know what that means. We keep each other company. What else is there to do in a pitiful city like El Paso? I miss him."

Rico laughed.

As he was laughing, I wondered if he was really only twenty. Miles didn't mention their age, his and brother Victor. The reason he looked older was his size. The way he talked.

I was on the chair where I'd been earlier. He was back on his fancy tufted leather chair. He was smiling a lot. I was on my second glass of wine. He was on his second glass of Chivas.

"I think your boyfriend is guilty of the charges, and they just don't have enough evidence to convict him."

"Are you a lawyer?"

He laughed at that. "I am not a lawyer."

"I promise to do a story that will do you and your brother justice. I can talk about how you have broken out from the family and are out on your own, building fabulous clubs."

"My brother and I don't need that. My grandmother is our only family. I'm not going to hurt her with something like that."

"Rico, give me a story. I promise not to speculate. Consider it payback for helping Miles. I know you can help him."

He was wearing a long-sleeved shirt, the sleeves rolled up to his elbows, his three top buttons undone. He was so handsome. He looked chiseled out of granite.

He drained his glass and set it down.

"You can make the charges against Miles go away."

"Luciana, it is you that has been watching too many movies." He did a roar of laughs. "Why should I help a man that wrote such an article about my family?"

"Because you are above all that."

Silence.

"Assume for a moment I can help."

He put his finger on the top edge of the empty glass and moved his finger on it. It started to make the little hum. Crystal of course. It was a little mesmerizing.

"You told me you don't know what love is. Why this pressure?"

I shook my head. "I feel bad he's there for something he's not guilty of."

"And that's all?"

I shrugged a little. "He's a friend. We live together. We split the bills, we go out and most of the time we each pay our own bill. We go to the same theater sometimes and see a movie two nights in a row."

"You're in love with this man," he said lifting the glass to his lips for a drink.

"No, we're friends. Help him and tell me what you want. Did you like what you saw when you made me strip?" I wished immediately I had not said this.

"I didn't make you do anything." He shrugged.

It sure as hell wasn't my idea, but I wasn't going to argue that point. "You are correct. You didn't make me do it."

He smiled.

I asked him again if he liked what he saw.

"I was too busy looking for a bug."

"You asked what was in it for you." I pushed. "I'll do anything."

"The club is full of free pussy."

I was surprised. "Why so rude now?"

"Now you are willing to do anything for that *hijo de puta*."[1]

Rico Santos turned red as a beefsteak tomato. "Your scum boyfriend slandered my family. He wrote a lying article speculating about my grandmother, my brother and me. He spewed old garbage that's been written before, all lies, and for that *hijo de puta*, you will do anything."

"Rico. I'm sorry. I'm sorry he did that."

His chair was a high-backed style, not the kind where I could get behind the chair and touch him. I got up, got next to him, and swiveled him to face me.

My biggest worry was to be rejected like when he told me to get dressed. I knelt, the black granite cold and hard under my knees. I unzipped him and encountered no resistance as I got the cannon out. I'm not new to this but I'm far from an expert. I worried about the sharp edges of the zipper. I took him in my mouth.

I was doing it but wondering how to do it better. He put his hands on either side of my head and started directing my movement. I don't know if that meant I was doing something wrong or something so right he didn't want me to stop. I slowed for just a second and he pulled on my head.

"Wait," I said.

I grabbed the upholstery of his chair and swiveled the chair so that he was facing front again, and I moved under the desk. I looked up at him through the glass. He should have cum, but he didn't. I kept going.

The entire scenario was a turn on. I could feel myself getting wet as I worked him.

Rico Santos, big man that he is, was moaning. It was probably a good idea the room was soundproof.

I don't know how long the action had been going on when he released my head. He got up and pulled me to my feet. Our clothes flew in all directions. He finished inside of me on the leather couch.

He took my hand and led me to a door. I don't know what I was thinking he was showing me, but it turned out to be a luxury bathroom with the highest shower head I ever saw. I never saw so much marble, mirror, and glass outside of a magazine photo of Buckingham Palace.

"I will use my brother's shower in his office. He's at the other club tonight. Take your time."

The water was heavenly, and the shampoo that smelled like money was in a dispenser affixed to the wall. I used the shampoo on my hair and on my panties in the shower and dried them with the blow dryer after I dried my hair. I came out of the bathroom feeling good, tired, and hungry. Rico was at his desk with damp hair. He flashed his big smile when he saw me.

"Luciana, the bastard does not deserve you."

"No one deserves me, Rico," I kidded.

"You see, you agree with me. Let him stay in jail."

"Rico, please. I feel bad for him. If you can help, please."

He didn't hit me with a comeback. I met his eyes. I'm good at staring back, but he wasn't trying to stare me down. His expression was more thoughtful than that, but I didn't know him well enough to interpret it.

"Are you hungry?"

"I could eat twelve plates of those wings of yours."

"I think we can do a little better than that," he said.

His smile looked genuine. I felt like we had connected.

Ten minutes later, we were in front of the club.

"This kitchen is for tourists. We moved our real chefs to the *El Paso Palacio*."

We headed to El Paso, great for me as my car was parked on the El Paso side. He stopped at the private parking signs, first indicating a Suburban with a driver standing at the passenger door, and then a black Porsche.

"Your choice," he said.

Guess which one I picked.

He drove with the top down.

The roar of his car would have drowned out our voices, so we didn't talk. Our conversation were grins. The car's shocks were ok, but a Porsche is low to the ground. The condition of the pavement is abysmal.

I didn't ask about the Jeep that followed us. It was obvious they were on duty, following orders as they pulled out of the parking lot right behind us and followed close behind. He probably had security like that all the time. He didn't mention it. When we crossed over to the U.S. side, the road was no longer bumpy. The noise level dropped to a dull roar. The soldiers were no longer behind us, but a Suburban was. It was like a ballet how the military jeep fell back, and the unmarked Suburban took its place as soon as we crossed the border.

"Are the men in the car following us friendly?" I asked.

"I hope so. They work for the family."

"You always travel in a caravan?" I laughed. I started to say, "Paranoid much?" but I remembered Miles's article and bit my tongue.

He laughed. "I always have a ride if I get too drunk to drive. Still hungry?"

"Starving."

---

1. Motherfucker

CHAPTER 21
ELENA MUNOZ

RICO INTRODUCED ME TO LUCIANA, a beautiful young woman. When Rico introduces me, he spends five minutes bragging how great a teacher I was to him for more than a decade and then he switches to bragging about my karate expertise. He doesn't mention how we fuck like animals from time to time nor does he mention that I'm almost twenty years older than he is. Obviously, having been his teacher for more than a decade, I'm ancient.

I'm lucky. I look good for my age.

After I moved out of Mala's house, James visited me often. It was not unusual for him to spend the night. I liked his company. In bed, I could not tell how much older he was than me. He was a turn on.

James spent a lot of time at the downtown club that the boys opened first. He was smart, savvy about everything. I learned so much from him. So did the boys. He loved it when Rico and Victor auditioned dancers, singers, and actors, when they would pitch their acts. He sat with the bosses and gave them his input. When he came to my house, he would tell me about it.

"With all the sex you have going, why me?" I asked him.

"Sex with you is precious to me."

· · ·

During the years at Mala's house, I didn't have much of a sex life. James had been an infrequent event, made scarce by our healthy respect for Mala. It had been infrequent to meet with an old boyfriend for a few hours. In my new life in my new house, it was freer. It was a good thing James came around. Maybe he knew I needed it. James knew everything. Yes, James was a turn on. He was no ordinary fuck partner. James pushed it.

Never mind how rugged Rico and Victor are now. They recited poetry beautifully, sensitively; James was a fabulous teacher.

Sometimes after sex, James would recite poetry. It was always something that fit with the moment. Sometimes after sex, he spooned me from behind and recited in my ear.

One night, he started spouting limericks. He had me in stitches, making me giggle. He had just spent five minutes doing Edward Lear, and then mid-stanza, he went silent. I felt his body tremble against me.

"James?" I asked.

But he said nothing. I reached to my nightstand and turned on the lights. I was in a panic.

James had a heart attack, the kind that kills you right away.

I pressed the panic button.

The security team in my housing complex were at my door in minutes. James was dead. Two guards helped me dress him.

Everyone—probably including Mala—her grandsons, the entire household, the grounds staff, the security crew, everyone who knew us speculated that he had died while pumping away. It was a rumor that came to my ears, and not a very secret one. Without being graphic about it, I told Mala what happened. I told the boys about the poems.

I didn't feel as horrible as I would have if he had died during the act.

James left a will, two pages written in his beautiful handwriting. His signature had been witnessed by Mala's attorney, Mauro Robles. He wanted to be buried back home in London in the plot he owned next to his wife. His solicitor in London had been charged with carrying out the will on the British side of the pond. His assets in Mexico, aside from his clothes, two million US dollars in two banks, in a desk drawer, forty thousand U.S. dollars and several hundred thousand Mexican pesos were found. Like myself, we never had to pay for anything during the years we were there. Until recently, I didn't know how much he was being paid. "She paid me twenty thousand dollars a month from the time I started until we graduated the boys." That's what he told me one night.

His will was read outside on the grounds in the great stone gazebo Mala had constructed for him so he could look outside his little house and see something that reminded him of England. Mauro read the will aloud, and though his voice was unemotional, I was a basket case after the first few lines.

"...I ask my dearest friend Magda Rojas to take charge of my money and divide twenty-five percent of it equally among her employees who so magnificently managed the residence and grounds. I bequest ten percent of the remaining amount to Gusto who has been such a good friend to me. The remaining balance I leave for Elena Munoz. She's my rock star."

After the reading of the will, we adjourned to the big dining room where Mala had dinner served for the boys and me. She served fish and chips.

"This was one of James's favorite meals," Rico said. "He always said that it reminded him of home."

"We always teased him because it's so bland," Victor said, pouring a blistering pool of hot sauce on his plate.

"Gusto made sure one of our people went out three times a week and brought back a woman for James. I always worried about his heart. I wanted him around to finish schooling you." Mala said this to us.

"Grandmother," Victor said sadly.

"She's kidding," Rico said, looking at me.

•   •   •

It was a sad day when James died, but it led to my spending a week or so in my old room in Mala's home. We were all grieving. It took a few days for Mauro Robles to work through the red tape of repatriating our dear friend back to London.

It felt like we were having a funeral at the airfield when we were finally sending him home. Rico, Victor, and I met up with the funeral people outside of the plane. We were there to say goodbye, then they loaded the mahogany casket on the private jet. He had left me so much money. We were close. We had been lovers occasionally, but his bequest to me had been a complete surprise.

I wanted to pay for the jet that would take him home, but Mala would not hear of it.

After James was gone, I hunkered down at home for almost a month. My housekeeper did the grocery shopping and cooking. I sat around and watched television, at first, staring but not watching. It was on, and the noise was like an extra person in the house. Then one day about noon, Rico showed up.

"My brother and I want you to manage the *El Paso Palacio*. We know you don't need the money; we are hoping you will find it exciting to be the boss of a big operation. Ride with me. I want to show it to you."

I knew nothing about the restaurant, liquor, and entertainment business or about how to be a boss to ninety employees. That's not in my wheelhouse, but that didn't stop Rico.

Rico talked about the set up on our way to cross the border.

"If you approve her, your assistant manager is Gloria Quick. She knows everything there is to know about the business. She does the work; all you need to do is be the boss."

Rico was right, I did not need the money.

I accepted the position.

Rico and Victor worked out my monthly pay. I would have worked for free. I could certainly afford to take no pay.

· · ·

Gloria was a bright, big-eyed girl who really knew her way around running a restaurant. I was in awe of her expertise.

"Tell me I didn't block you from running this place on your own," I said to Gloria when we met.

"You didn't block me from running this place on my own. Elena, my pay is quite substantial. I look forward to working with you."

Gloria knew everything about a big operation like *Palacio*. She taught me the ins and outs of the business. It took a lot to run a bar with six bartenders, to manage the inventory, entertainment, and staff. Texas had laws about everything.

At first, I didn't put in the hours she did. I would drive back to Juarez to sleep. As time went by, my attachment to the club won me over. I put in more hours. I moved my housekeeper in and made her a live in. I didn't need a housekeeper but after living at Mala's all those years, I was spoiled. I knew many recipes gleaned from Mala's chefs, but I preferred sharing the recipe with Carmela and let her cook for me. Then I started eating dinner at the club. Yes, the club had taken me over.

We developed a schedule, both of us working seventy-hour weeks. We alternated who came in and opened, and who closed. Rico, Victor, and I all had offices. Gloria technically had an office, but she was never in it, being too busy managing things. I was glad of the work. It kept me from brooding about James and kept me engaged with Victor and Rico.

"Go get a life," I would kid Gloria.

"I got a life right here."

"Yeah, I'm afraid I have the same fever. If I don't hook up with someone soon, I'm in trouble."

I laughed, but it wasn't funny. I didn't make social time for myself.

"Elena, you are beautiful, and you know it."

Gloria had her own way of saying my name. It was funny. Only she could make it sound the way she did.

I laughed as I always did.

"You got nerve, youngster."

"You look the same age as me, baby."

We were tight. I wouldn't want the job if Gloria were not here.

I was the boss; I gave Gloria a bonus of five thousand dollars and a raise. She bought a house for her mother. I loved the neighborhood where Gloria owned her house so much, I bought a house across the street from her. It was a spec house, not behind gates like my other house but this house was two stories and gorgeous. I had a pool built and found myself spending more and more nights there than driving to Juarez to the other house.

"Chuck the Juarez house," Gloria teased.

"I can't do that; I love my house. My roots are in Mexico where I was born."

"With all the money you have, lady, you can afford a whole lot of homes." Gloria laughed with a mouth full of lovely teeth.

CHAPTER 22
GLORIA QUICK

"ARE you sure your last name is Quick?" Elena asked me a hundred times.

I laughed each time. It's my name. My daddy was Charlie Quick, and my mama is Nicole Quick. I'm kind of a typical African American made up of a bunch of nationalities and who knows what they are. My mother was adopted and raised by a big Mexican family in El Paso, and we don't know anything about her parentage except for her color which is my exact shade. My father's great grandfather (and the family name) came from around Devon, England, where the family name was Cowick. In old English, cu meant cow, and wic meant outlying settlement, so the family story goes that far back. We were dairy farmers. Anyway, at Ellis Island, my great grandfather said Cuwick, officials heard Quick, and Quicks we became. Great Grandpa Cuwick was white as milk, but when he moved into a Harlem brownstone in New York, he fell hard for the daughter of his downstairs neighbor, my grandmother, who was as black as he was white.

They didn't like the winters up there, so they came down to El Paso, where they were prolific and broke lots of anti-miscegenation laws that no one who mattered cared about. I have lots of cousins who are all kinds of shades, some Quick, some not. Through all my school years, my handle was my last name. Quick.

I waitressed part-time at the Buffalo Steakhouse & Grille while in high school. When I graduated, I was moved up to assistant manager. Melissa Wagner, who was sixteen years older than me, was the sole owner for more than five years since her husband died. Two hundred ten seats in BS&G, not counting two party rooms. Business boomed.

Melissa was very fond of men, but she took to jumping in the other direction. Which team she plays for does not matter to me now and never did. My pay was good, tips were great, and when I stepped up to assistant manager, no tips but more pay. I discovered I like the food, liquor, and entertainment business. Working alongside the boss lady taught me the food and beverage business better than any classes I could have taken in college. I dreamed of owning my own Buffalo Steakhouse Grille.

Someday.

"One day, I'll have a place like this, all mine."

"You run this joint like it's yours," Melissa said.

"You the best, baby." She liked me to call her baby.

When I turned twenty-one, my boss lady started taking off on vacation like she was playing catch up. I ran the entire operation. Melissa would come back from her trip and pump me full of compliments and generous bonuses.

I went from renting a nice apartment to buying a three-bedroom home in a pristine El Paso neighborhood. I even had a swimming pool that I used after work for a couple minutes, and on Sunday. The school district was to die for, not that I ever had kids. I did have a cleaning lady come in on Mondays. She spent the day cleaning everything even though I didn't use every room. She did my laundry, my ironing. It was like having a wife. I had it made.

I brought no one to my pad. When I connected with a fuck friend, I went to his place or a hotel. Then I met a tall, manly man named Victor Santos. He was young and beautiful in his white linen jacket over jeans and boots. His dinner date was a knockout. I came this close to playing waitress for them. It would have been a first.

While they were eating, I made rounds. Our hostesses are clearly hostesses; our waitresses are waitresses. I always make sure our diners are happy with the food and service. Call it quality control.

"Hi. They call me Quick. Just checking on you. Is everything to your satisfaction? Food, okay? Anything I can get you?"

The girl smiled and looked at Victor.

"Is your name really Quick?" he asked. He was beautiful.

"Gloria Quick," I said, putting my business card on the table. "Please call on me anytime for anything. If we're tight on reservations or you need catering, or, really, anything, don't hesitate to call."

I ran out of things to say but I got a good look at his left hand and his empty ring finger. The date didn't have a wedding ring, either.

"My name is Victor Santos, and this is Myra Lopez. Pleased to meet you, Gloria."

"The pleasure is mine," I said, and I got out of their way.

I worked the room back to the hostess station where Melissa was straightening the hostess's tuxedo tie.

"The lovely dude you were talking to earlier is La Mala's grandson."

Being born and raised in El Paso, of course I'd heard about the infamous La Mala. Everyone on both sides of the border knew who Mala was. She's a legend around here.

"How'd you know?"

"Luis told me."

Luis was one of our bartenders.

"He's gorgeous," I said to Melissa. "He didn't inherit the cloven hoof and horns."

He left the waitress a hundred-dollar tip. No one does that. We're a high-end operation but a hundred dollars is a big tip.

The next evening, Saturday, I got a call at the restaurant.

"I couldn't sleep," the voice said, "thinking about you."

"Who is this?" I asked, laughing. I recognized Victor's voice.

I gave Victor my address, and he came over on Sunday, my day off.

Like old friends, we fucked, swam, ate pizza, fucked, and swam some more.

It was just getting dark when I walked him out to the driveway where his Porsche convertible was parked. Before he got in the car, he gave me another hug and a very wet kiss. A turn on.

On Monday during the lunch rush, fifteen dozen red roses were carried in, an enormous arrangement in an enormous crystal vase.

Dear Quick,

Thank you for a wonderful Sunday.

Hugs,

Victor

After the flowers, I didn't hear another word from him.

If you give a guy everything the first time, there's no reason to come back.

It was a Friday night again when Victor returned to the restaurant. He had no reservations, and the hostess called for me. I went to the front and met up with Victor, his new female friend, and another couple. Victor was gorgeous, like a fantastic appetizer. The other man at the table had to be a relative. He was scrumptious, like the main course. Victor introduced him as his brother Rico. I should have guessed.

They wanted to be near the dance floor, so I had a table set up for them. I called the same waitress who had attended to Victor before. You can imagine she was easy to convince. She wasn't going to forget a hundred-dollar tipper.

About an hour after their arrival and just as they were finishing dinner, I walked up to the table to see how they were doing. I did not give up another business card.

Victor was nice enough, but Rico smiled big time and asked me to join them.

"I'm working or I'd be honored to sit with you," I said.

The girl with Rico smiled as though she was all for my sitting with them.

Saturday, I got a call from Rico. On Sunday, he came over to visit me. He didn't want to swim. We spent the day in bed. This man loved to fuck, and I loved fucking him. He had a half glass of wine, and I had the rest of the bottle. I can hold my liquor.

As though it was choreographed, Rico left about the same time Victor had left. I walked him out to his Porsche in my driveway. Rico picked me up, cradled me in his arms like I was a feather and devoured me with kisses. I giggled away. I couldn't figure out if he was the big bear or the bad fox in the fairy tale.

I got no flowers on Monday but on Tuesday, Rico called me at the restaurant.

CHAPTER 23
LUCIANA CAMACHO

MY LIVE-IN FRIEND Floyd Miles walked out of jail on bail the day after I was with Rico. A bail company posted the bond. I only heard one side of the conversation, but I understood that Rico's lawyer had arranged for Floyd's lawyer in El Paso. The lawyer hired for Floyd called Rico while I was there, and Rico had no idea who he was.

Rico and I had a big dinner at the *El Paso Palacio*. The pretty manager kept coming by to see if Rico needed anything. I could feel heat coming out her eyes at me. She was pretty. I wasn't clear what he meant when he said she had been his teacher for more than a decade. She didn't look old enough to be his teacher. I was fuzzy with the wine, which maybe had been the cause of my confusion. I'd been drinking a long time. My head start had been way before dinner.

He walked me out to the front of the restaurant.

"Your friend will be out tomorrow," Rico said.

I kissed him hard on the lips.

"You own me," I heard myself say.

"Remember," he said, his big hand on my chin.

I can't tell you how hot that exchange was.

The driver got out and opened the car door for me, then went back to his place behind the wheel. Rico sent me home in a Suburban like the one that had followed us from the border crossing. The driver was

Ignazio. I was silent during the ride, and so was he. I was preoccupied anyway, thinking about Miles.

I didn't love Miles more than a dear friend and coworker, but I felt horrible to know he had suffered in jail. So much had happened in the past twenty-four hours. I was convinced that Rico set Miles up as revenge for the article. I had started off suspecting Mala, but Rico was too smooth about the whole thing. I could tell that it was him. Stupid Miles. Stupid. Stupid.

I was tired like I couldn't remember when. It wasn't just the wine. I was emotionally drained. I dropped on the bed thinking I'd nap a few minutes then get up and undress. I went to sleep instantly and didn't open my eyes again until I heard a knocking on the front door.

CHAPTER 24
FLOYD MILES

A DEPUTY SHERIFF WOKE ME.

"Miles, you're going home."

It took a second to get my bearings. It wasn't like I felt rested. I always woke up tired. Jail is not the most restful place. The noise never quite stops, and even in your sleep, you can feel you're not alone. I'd slept in the jail's jump suit. I sat up in the bunk and started putting on my shoes.

"Hurry it up. Bring them with you."

I walked out of the cell. The clock across the corridor said it was 2:05. It's hard to tell in here if it's afternoon or early morning. No windows. I guessed that it was morning because I was half asleep.

"What do you mean I'm going home?"

Walking through the cell block, I heard cat calls. I ignored them.

"Shut the fuck up, trying to sleep."

"Hey, leave me your shoes mother fucker."

"Shoes are mine mother fucker," a third voice.

Then they started yelling at each other for yelling.

The deputy never answered my question. I was escorted through one gate then one to the receiving and release area, known as R&R. Three men were in a cell waiting to be booked.

"Sit on the bench there," the deputy said. "I'll get your property. Take off your jail clothes."

Then the deputy was rushing me to dress. He handed over my personal property, twenty-two dollars, my watch, lighter, and an open pack of cigarettes. I might as well quit. I hadn't had a smoke in the two months I'd been in this hellhole waiting for trial.

Two men were waiting for me in the jail's lobby. The burly one wore jeans, tennis shoes, and a pullover with the logo, "Ruth's Bail Bonds." He looked tough, shaggy, a muscular bouncer type. I wondered if the other guy was his partner, but they didn't exchange words even though they were practically shoulder to shoulder. The second guy was in a dark suit and had a better haircut.

"Your next court appearance is on March sixteenth. Be sure you are in court. Sign this."

I took the paper, a bail bond guarantee. Fifty-thousand dollars. I didn't have that kind of money. Ruth's Bail Bonds was charging $5,000 to post the bail.

"I don't have this five thousand."

The guy in the suit cleared his throat and put his hand out for me to shake. I moved the bail bond paperwork to under my arm and shook the guy's hand.

"I'm Gus Gomez," he said. "I'm your new lawyer if you want me. The five thousand has already been paid." He pulled the paper from under my elbow and put it back in my hand. "Sign the paper and I'll take you home."

I hadn't called either of these guys. Obviously, they had not appeared out of the clear blue sky. Someone had engaged them. I had no idea who had summoned them on my behalf. I'm a reporter. I'm inquisitive. I can be a pain in the ass about asking questions. I had a lot of questions.

I was no longer sleepy.

I signed the paper for the bail guy, and he left.

It's not like we had privacy in this dingy old building that had seen better days. This was the lobby of the jail. People were sitting around looking tired, irritated, discouraged, or asleep. The people who were waiting here were on the wrong side of the law or picking up family members on the wrong side of the law. These weren't people I wanted in earshot of a discussion of my private affairs.

"I'm confused," I said in a low voice.

He handed me a business card.

I looked over his shoulder at a group of shady looking people huddled in a corner. "Maybe we can talk outside?"

He took my cue, and we walked outside. It was good to be outdoors, even if it was predawn and the sidewalk in front of the El Paso jail, the inside of which I hoped I would never see again.

"I can guarantee that your case will be dismissed, or you will be found not guilty if we have to try the matter."

He turned toward one of the parking lots. I followed his lead. Mystery or not, he was the one with the car.

"Who is paying you and who paid the bail? Was it Luciana?"

"I don't know Luciana," he said. "Let me get you home. We can meet in a couple days and go over the case."

He opened the passenger door with a key and walked around to the driver side. The car was new.

I gave him directions as he drove the Lincoln Continental with me in the passenger seat.

"So, who exactly is my benefactor? Who paid you?"

It was clear that Gus was not going to tell me who was paying. I figured it had to be the *Dispatch*. But if that was the case, why now and not two months ago when I got arrested? He asked me a couple questions about the case probably to keep me from continually asking who hired him. I talked a little but didn't say much before we got to the apartment I shared with Luciana. He pulled into the driveway, and I got out.

I knocked. No answer. I rang the doorbell.

Luciana opened the door, and I walked in. It was good to see her. It was still dark out and she was fully dressed. I wondered if she was going in early but didn't ask. I had questions, but I was also dying for a shower to wash jail off of me.

She gave me a light kiss. I was expecting more. Luciana's passionate.

"When I got arrested, my car and keys were confiscated. Sorry I had to knock. My house key was on that ring."

"Miles, I'm beat. I was so tired I went to sleep in my clothes. We'll talk later."

"What happened that I got out?"

CHAPTER 25
RICO SANTOS

I DON'T WANT to rewind too far, but I need to tell you how Gloria Quick fits in the El Paso *Palacio* puzzle. Before we opened the place, my brother and I decided that Gloria was the perfect fit for a manager. Even though she was only the assistant manager of the Buffalo Steakhouse, she was the one in charge. She kicked ass. Our decision had nothing to do with our occasional Sunday sex.

I figured I could convince her easily. I first brought it up on a Sunday after a day spent in bed. Picture the red velvet bedspread crumpled on the ground, and the two of us lying on top of the sheets, a bottle of wine on the bedside table beside two glasses, and an empty bottle in the delicate little bin she used for trash in her bedroom. There was a white comforter, but it had been kicked to the foot of the bed. Our clothes were somewhere in her house, but neither of us were particularly modest. Frankly, her body is worth showing off.

"You can write your own deal," I said, playing with one of her curls.

"Rico, Melissa will go crazy if I quit."

She sat up in the bed and looked me straight in the eye or tried to. "My eyes are up here, Rico."

"I'll pay her to release you," I said. It was fascinating the way the curl always bounced back.

"She doesn't own me. I don't think she would stand in the way of any opportunity that came my way. But she does depend on me. I'd have to train a replacement, I think."

Maybe Gloria needed an additional inducement. "I was thinking I'd buy you a Cadillac. Any model you want."

"I would not want a Cadillac," she said, putting her chin on top of her fist in an exaggerated thinking position. "If I wanted a car, it would be a Mercedes."

Was she playing me? I did not think that she realized I was serious.

I nodded. "I agree, a Mercedes is more your speed."

"Are you kidding me?"

"I'm serious. I want you with us."

I'll cut to the chase. Gloria Quick joined our team.

At this point, we were in the final stages of construction. Gloria began working for us, spending hours with the interior contractor about changes. She had meetings with sellers of everything from China to flatware, kitchen appliances to linen services. She was working her ass off, delighted that she was going to be boss lady of the Palacio, and loving the hike in pay even before the restaurant was open.

Then we lost James. His passing was a blow to my brother and me. And even though she played at being tough, it was a blow to our grandmother. The final stages of construction on *Palacio* were slowed down because my brother and me were not available to make crucial decisions.

A month after James went to England in his casket, Victor and I learned that Elena was hunkering down at her new home, not even leaving to shop for daily needs. We decided to install Elena as the manager of the El Paso *Palacio,* and for Gloria to teach her the business and act as her assistant.

My brother and me, we met with Gloria and explained how close we were to Elena and that we wanted to help her. We didn't even know if Elena would accept the position.

"We're giving you twenty-thousand cash as a bonus if you agree to stay on with the title of assistant manager," I said.

"You going to give me twenty thousand in cash for a title change?" She put her hand on my head. "Do you have a fever?" she asked.

"I'm serious. If you don't want it, I'll give it to Carlos the dishwasher," I said.

"Not so fast." Gloria laughed, putting a hand on my forearm. "That wasn't a refusal. I'm not crazy."

"You want more?" Victor asked.

"It's okay, I'm fine. I only hope we get along. I don't need the twenty."

I exchanged a grin with my brother.

"You don't need it, but you'll take it? Si?"

Gloria grinned. "Is it really in cash?"

"It's green," Victor said.

"What's wrong?" I asked her. She got quiet and looked a little stunned.

"Where will I put it?"

"Spend it," Victor said fast.

CHAPTER 26
LUCIANA CAMACHO

I LET Floyd in the house and went to bed. I was restless and never really fell fully back to sleep. I kept glancing over at his side of the bed to see if I had been dreaming that he got out. The sun came up, and I rolled over to face my clock. I knew I would be taking the day off when I saw the time.

I heard the shower. It's a bummer to be alone and a bummer to share one bathroom especially when someone else is in the tub.

When you gotta go, you gotta go. I walked into the steamy bathroom.

"I got to pee. Sorry."

"Go for it. I'm staying in here until I run out of hot water."

"Welcome back," I said on my way out.

Thirty minutes later, a pan of biscuits was in the oven five from being just right. We both liked omelets, and that's what I had ready to go. Lunch was usually sandwiches. I always had cold cuts. Without him here, I lived on sandwiches. Actually, I'm a damn good cook, but sandwiches are easy.

When he came in the kitchen, the smell of his Boss cologne told me he was back. We kissed. I poured him a cup of coffee.

"Sit, Miles. Everything is ready."

"I am hungry for food and information."

"Food first," I said. I suspected what kind of information he wanted.

There was a wall phone in the kitchen. I dialed the *Dispatch*.

One of the secretaries answered.

"It's me," I said. "Is Dory available?"

"What you got for me?" Dory asked.

"I'm sick. Contagious flu or something."

Dory was my new supervisor. He had taken over Miles's job. I faked a cough and hung up, then Miles and I chowed down on everything: omelets, biscuits, and coffee.

Miles and I moved into the living room. Miles flopped down in the recliner, and I sat on the couch. Both of us vegged there like a couple of Thanksgiving turkeys, stuffed to the gills. Breakfast had been a killer. We both complained about overeating.

"I'm surprised Dory didn't ask me about you getting out," I said.

"Give him a couple hours when they get the arrests and releases. Did you forget I'm not working there anymore?"

"Yeah, I forgot." I frowned.

"How did you swing paying for my bail and getting me the lawyer who said the charges will be dropped?"

I was not sure whether to tell him the truth or a lie. Rico said no one was to know, but he meant the public.

I knew how to stall. "You want to fuck, or you want to talk about how I got you out? It's been two months."

"You know I know how long it's been. I am acquainted of every minute of the last two months. Of course, I want to fuck; I was ready to jump you last night, but you didn't undress."

"I was dead tired," I said. "What's it going to be?"

I got up from the couch and pulled off my shirt, figuring he'd want to let off some steam and give me a reprieve.

His eyes bugged out, but he wasn't distracted. I put the shirt back on and sat down on the couch again.

"Not so fast. Tell me what happened? The only fucking people who could have helped me, fired me instead."

"You can't tell anyone," I said.

"Okay already. What's the big mystery, anyway? The bondsman wouldn't say, the lawyer wouldn't say, and you're pussyfooting around. Who the hell got me out?"

"Rico Santos got you out, but you cannot tell that to anyone."

Floyd Miles turned white as a sheet.

"What the fuck are you talking about?"

"Hey, you sound angry. You should be happy. You could still be in jail."

I was leaning back on the sofa, a table between us. Miles was on a recliner across from me, but not reclining any more. His face was flushed. He hopped up like he was ready to fight, jumping around with fisted hands.

"How do you know Rico Santos?"

"Check the tone, Miles. You're out. Be happy."

"Why would that asshole get me out when his family put me in there?"

"Ask him."

He was pacing back and forth in my small living room that barely contained Miles's bristling energy. Back and forth, the walking, like watching a tennis match. His rage was like a personality in the room with us, a stranger.

"Luciana, what the fuck is going on?"

"Five hours ago, you got out and here you are. Be happy," I said it again.

Miles wouldn't stop. He pushed the reporter questions. I wondered if he would be stupid enough to push a story on the *Dispatch* about his release from jail. He would be shooting himself in both feet, but Miles is not a planner.

Finally, I had taken all the flack I could. He was furious and unappreciative. I jumped to my feet. He had a lot of nerve.

"You want the truth? Sit down and I'll tell you."

He sat back down on the recliner. It creaked on impact, maybe broke something.

"Well? I'm sitting. Talk," he said.

"I gave Rico a two-hour blow job while he sat at his desk. I sucked on his balls. He fucked me on his couch where he finally came like a bull—"

"Stop. Fucking stop. Whore."

I was pissed off beyond measure and pointed at him. "That's not what you said when I took on strangers to get a story that you took credit for." I remembered my very first story, the milk tanker truck ride with illegal aliens. I had fucked Pepe's brains out.

"There is something I don't get. You aren't such a good lay that he would spring me in exchange for sex."

A beautiful crystal vase was on the coffee table. My fingers itched to smash it across his skull, but my mom had given me that. As satisfying as that would be, I wasn't wasting an heirloom over that hypocrite.

"Miles, you have sixty seconds to get the fuck out of my house."

"I am leaving. I'll send for my clothes."

He wasn't moving fast enough. I started counting down.

The front door slammed.

I was out in front of the apartment in a flash, screaming at him.

"Give me the fucking key to the apartment, you selfish hypocritical asshole."

"I don't have it!" he shouted back. "It's on my keyring in some evidence locker!"

"Fine, then," I shouted. "Keep it. I'll change the locks."

I ran back to shelter in place while I sorted out what had just happened.

All the stress I'd gone through. All the worrying about him, worrying about his being in jail, unable to do anything for him. It was for Miles's sake that I went in hot pursuit after Rico in the blind, not even knowing what I wanted Rico to do. Acid burned in my stomach, but it wasn't from the coffee or the omelet.

CHAPTER 27
FLOYD MILES

I WALKED six blocks to a branch of Bank of Texas. It took me twenty minutes to withdraw three hundred dollars. All I had was my driver license. My checkbook was with my personal belongings at her house. I walked three more blocks to Casey's Bar. It opened at noon. Before I moved in with her, I used to come here two or three times a week. The food is good and not expensive unless you order one of their two-pound porterhouse steaks.

I started with a Bohemia Beer, an icon from Mexico. I'm not a heavy drinker. Two of these beers and I felt it. I switched to Beluga on the rocks, a Russian vodka. I'd had it before. It's a drink that a guy should sip and enjoy along with some conversation, but I wasn't in that kind of mood. Casey's was jammed now with the lunch crowd. Bar seats were taken by people waiting for a table. I had no one to converse with. The bartender and his helper were busy.

I stopped at the payphone and put in a long-distance call to my parents in Houston.

"Sorry to call collect, Dad. I'm on a payphone but I'm out of jail. I got a lawyer, and he says I'm going to beat this bullshit charge. For now, I'm out on bail."

My dad gave the phone to my mom, and I talked to her. She was crying.

"I'm out of jail, no more tears."

I didn't get much of a chance to use the phone in jail, but I got some access. All my calls from there were collect. I appreciated being able to use the phone without sucking up to some jail attendant.

I went back to the bar and thought of the blow up between Luciana and me over my getting out of jail. She was right when she said I should be happy about it.

She told me about sucking and fucking the bastard. I exploded like she did something wrong. I wasn't thinking. I don't believe Rico Santos got me out just for sex with her. There had to be more to it. The whole family of them, they're all conniving bastards.

I had another Beluga on the rocks and then another. I went back to the restroom and on my way back, I used a quarter and called Luciana. What the hell, right? I was full of liquid courage, or else I don't think I could have made that call.

"What the fuck you want?"

I could hear the fury in her voice. She was right to be angry. I'd been a heel.

"I'm sorry, Luciana. I'm fucked up. I'm sorry."

"You sound drunk."

"I had a few drinks. I thought it out. Thank you for getting me out. I'm sorry for being a selfish hypocritical asshole."

I could hear her breathing on the other side of the line, but she didn't say anything for almost a minute.

"Where are you?"

"I'm at Casey's."

"Want to come back?"

"I do. I shouldn't have called you a whore."

"I can come get you."

"I would like that."

"I'm coming now. I'll meet you in the parking lot."

"You don't have to drive in. Pull up to the bus stop. I'll be on the bench."

"Be right there."

. . .

I went back to the bar and settled out my bill. I gave the bartender a ten spot as a tip. I headed for the main door. After the near darkness of the bar, the sun was too bright to bear. Without sunglasses it was blinding. I was lurching a little, but that was the vodka. I had to cross the parking lot to reach the sidewalk where the bus stop was. I heard a thud, a loud thud. I swear I thought I had taken off and was flying. I saw myself crashing face down on the pavement, then…

CHAPTER 28
LUCIANA CAMACHO

I DIDN'T BOTHER PUTTING on a face or changing out of my sweats, just went straight to the car in my flip flops. The short drive to Casey's took longer than usual due to some snag in the traffic. I couldn't drive up to the bus stop bench either, since the traffic situation was due to two fire trucks that were parked in the way, taking up one lane of traffic in front of Casey's. I could see a paramedics truck in the parking lot, and I wondered if someone had had a heart attack in the restaurant. I figured Miles would tell me what was up whenever he bothered to come out. I could see that he wasn't at the bus stop. Eventually I got a heads up from one of the firemen waving me into the parking lot. Where the valet takes and delivers your car is where the action was, so I parked myself and got out of the car. As I got close to the entrance, I saw the gurney. A paramedic was holding an oxygen mask over the face of a man whose forehead was bloody. It couldn't be Miles.

I came closer. Caution tape was up. One of the paramedics blocked my way.

"I think I know him," I said, and then I got a good look at his face.

The first thing I thought when I recognized that it was him on the gurney was that Rico Santos or his family had come after him.

146

"Miles!" I didn't scream. "It's my roomie. I was coming here to give him a ride home."

The paramedic let go, and I sank to my knees. "What happened?"

He didn't answer, but the paramedic pointed out a caddy sitting perpendicular to the parking lot spaces. I felt a rush of relief that it wasn't Rico in that car but an elderly couple.

I left my car and rode with him to the hospital. Miles died on the way.

I gave the hospital the names of Miles's next of kin and called the paper. My boss at the *Dispatch* assigned me to cover the accident.

The car that hit him was a four door Cadillac sedan. A sixty-one-year-old man was driving his wife to lunch at Casey's. The police report said the driver thought the accelerator stuck. He came in too fast to the valet area and didn't see Miles until he was airborne.

Floyd Miles, former reporter for the *Dispatch*, was fatally struck by a car in the Casey's Restaurant parking lot in El Paso. The driver was in his sixties and could be facing charges once the investigation is completed. The driver was not arrested. The victim was out on bail and waiting for trial on a charge of drug trafficking.

Ten days from the date of his death, Floyd Miles's remains were on a plane headed to his hometown where his parents awaited his arrival. I talked to them twice by phone. I packed and shipped his personal belongings to them.

I was torn. I felt that it was my fault he had been struck by a car. I had been bitchy with him. I threw him out of the house. I had a lot of pent-up feelings as a result of his death and resolved them as best I could by writing a letter to Miles, even though he would never read it. I struggled how to begin it. Dear Miles? To my roommate? Floyd Miles all alone, without any endearment? I ended up leaving that part blank. I wrote about half a page of guilt-ridden tripe beginning with his phone call apology. Then I wrote word for word our last encounter, when he called me a whore.

I tore up the letter, burned it in an ash tray, and I didn't feel so guilty. He was the one who went to Casey's under his own steam. I was accustomed to his being gone. After all, he'd been in jail for two months. I was used to having my bed to myself now, and not having someone use up all of the hot water.

Four days after Miles died, I got a call from Rico at work. He had not read the article. Gus Gomez, the attorney for Miles told Rico about the accident.

"Is there anything I can do?"

"I got it," I said.

"If you think of anything, don't hesitate, call me."

"Thanks for all you did, Rico. I owe you."

"When all this is history and you are up to it, how about dinner?"

"I'm counting on it," I said.

"*Estoy muy atraido por ti.*"[1]

I pictured Rico as he said this to me and smiled.

The letter to Miles did not put me at ease. I still hear Miles's voice calling me a whore.

I use my body to get something done when I see no other way. Does that make me a whore? Miles used me more than I ever used him. When I brought him a good story, he put his name on it. My reward was that he kept me working at the *Dispatch*. That I had four years of college didn't matter, nor did it matter that he put his name on my stories. Dory had already given me more bylines in two months than Miles had in two years, and I hadn't slept with him once. He just likes my writing. Dory's boss, the editor, you know I've fucked him. Maybe he's the reason Dory is such a good boss to me. Fucking men.

RIP Miles.

---

1. I am very attracted to you

CHAPTER 29

ISADORA

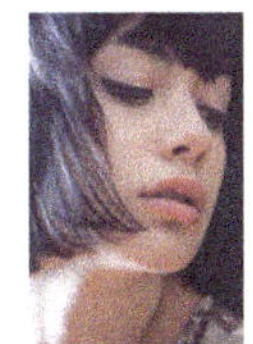

WHEN MAURO IS GETTING ENOUGH from his wife, he pays no attention to me. I recognize the look when he's not getting it. I understand exactly when to close the curtain so that the sitting area in the back of the plane is private. The two pilots who are flying the jet are busy in the cockpit.

Usually, the cabin only held Mauro and me.

The sofa was not wide enough to lie on, but the two individual seats are wide, plush, and comfortable. With some imagination, we went at it on one seat. It was so hot that the four closest windows get fogged. I might be exaggerating about the fog. Maybe it was just two windows. But the sex is fire hot. In those short moments of bliss, everything else burned away. I forgot everything else, even that I had a man at home who had a thicker and longer *Verga*[1] and could go twenty times longer than Mauro. The ambiance of being on a private plane makes it hotter, not to mention how handsome Mauro is. He is hot to watch, and I keep my eyes open. His are always closed. Doesn't matter. I know what to do when he's inside me to reach an orgasm, and I do it.

Before this flight, I had heard a loud knock at my door. I was in a hurry, ready for the flight, and answered the door while holding my carryon, wearing my cap and uniform. I opened the door thinking I was on the way out. The man at my door flashed a badge and shoved me backwards to push into my apartment. I would have fallen if there hadn't been a wall there. He was mean looking, a stocky middle-aged plainclothes policeman past his prime.

"Don't you look tempting?" He laughed nastily, stared at the short skirt of my uniform, and said that he wanted to get photographs of me and Mauro having sex on the plane. I had it in me to slap him. I saw in his face there was no room for me to be difficult. I listened to what he had to say because I had no choice.

"How do you know?"

"Tell me you don't fuck the boss and I'll punch you until you admit it?"

I was shaken. "Not on every flight," I managed to say, trying to keep my lips from trembling so I could speak.

He moved close to me, the heavy bulk of his belly pressing against me. I was backed up hard against the wall, suddenly scared to death of the bulky, sweaty cop. I felt his gun behind his belt buckle, and smelled the stench of his last meal, bitter coffee, rancid bacon. He stood there menacing me, then laughed harshly.

He stepped back, reached in his pocket, and pulled out a thousand-peso bill.

"If you tell your boss about this conversation, you are dead."

"I don't want the money. I swear, I will say nothing."

"You got no choice. Take the money. I will be in touch soon."

He left. I watched through the window as he got into a car parked on the curb, and I did not make a move until he had driven away. I ran out to hail a taxi to take me to Mauro's home like I always did. I couldn't stand myself for being so stupid. I wish I had not admitted there was sex between the Jefe and me. How had he known I was having sex with Mauro? Why did he want pictures? Where was this going? I waited more than a week before I started spending the thousand, he gave me, just in case he returned and wanted the money back.

· · ·

I thought nothing of it until one morning when we were preparing the plane for a trip to Mexico City. The first officer, Tomas, and I were alone inside the plane. The other pilot was doing his preflight check outside of the plane.

"If he wants action from you, how will I know?" Tomas asked.

Mauro had not yet arrived. I didn't know what Tomas was talking about. It took me a moment to get it. The cop had gotten to the pilot.

We moved into the galley, both of us speaking in low voices. I didn't answer immediately. A lot of things passed through my head. I could ignore him. I could pretend not to understand. I could refuse to cooperate. I could procrastinate. I considered a lot of choices, but I didn't consider telling Mauro. I didn't want to get dead.

I looked up at Tomas. I'd known him for a long time.

"The curtain will be drawn closed to the aft cabin where he likes to sit," I said. "I assume the fat guy talked to you."

He nodded.

"Don't stare at the curtain," he said. "If you have any say in it, take all clothes off."

"He likes it quick. I don't know about all clothes off," I said.

"This is a longer trip. Do what you can. The cop wants good pictures."

"Do you know this asshole cop?" I asked.

"No. And I don't know who he's working for."

"Be careful," I said. "It's a long way from the cockpit to the curtain."

"You do your thing, and I will do mine," he said quietly.

I nodded.

That day was the first time Tomas got pictures. The second time, I was turned on knowing that the pilot was behind the curtain looking at my ass, watching me fuck.

I never told that to anyone.

All of us on the plane knew that Mauro represented Magda Hidalgo, known as Mala, but we never sat around and chatted about it. Personally, I couldn't understand how anyone would want pictures of Mauro knowing he's Mala's lawyer. That would be suicide. Unless it was Mala who wanted the pictures.

. . .

When Mala's grandsons were aboard on the gig to Baja, California, we had more passengers aboard than ever before. They kept me hopping, but I didn't mind. They were young, but the older one, Rico, seemed to devour me with his eyes. He spent more time watching me than he did looking out the window when we were flying over his property. He didn't know it, but I would have devoured him.

The older guy, their tutor named James, was a handsome one. I would have said yes to him without too much coaxing.

Fantasy, I live in it.

We flew at least three trips to Juarez that month. The pilots and I hung out on the plane sometimes for two or three hours waiting for Mauro. We got paid each week no matter if we flew or not. In our business, that makes for a good job. Waiting for Mauro was part of the job.

About the pictures, I didn't talk about it with Tomas who was part it. I didn't talk to anybody about it, but I sure thought about it frequently. Who but Mala would have that kind of influence to make this happen? Who else would get a cop to approach me and the pilot with a demand instead of a proposal? I kept thinking she was behind the cop. Mauro was married with kids. Maybe she was planning for blackmail, or Mala wanted the pictures for leverage. Maybe I should have been more worried about my naked photos going to strangers. I had a life too. Naked pictures might or might not wreck my life, but there's not a whole lot to wreck.

When there were pictures, Tomas met up with the fat cop. On the next flight, Tomas had money for me. It became a routine. We split whatever the cop gave him. It was never less than two thousand pesos, that is, one thousand pesos each. I got used to the money. Getting paid for the sex I liked was another turn on for me. When we didn't have sex, I became upset. It was not just about the money either. I tried not to let it show. It didn't matter that I had someone at home who took care of my sexual needs, but I wasn't just looking to get laid. I wanted it on a private jet, with the boss.

. . .

We were going to Juarez. Mauro arrived. He greeted me with a smile and a kiss on the cheek. He shook hands with the pilots, walked to the back of the plane and sat in his favorite seat. There was a television back there, but it didn't work very well, so he seldom turned it on.

Once we were airborne, Mauro asked for wine. At first there was no hint that anything was going to happen, but half an hour out, after two glasses of wine, I drew the curtains shut.

"Can I take all this off? I'll be more comfortable."

Getting naked for sex was becoming routine even on short trips like going to and from Juarez. He liked me naked. Ever since I'd offered the first time, he'd taken me up on it.

Mauro smiled. "Good idea."

When my clothes were off, I moved to the small sofa and sat on it. He was on the seat facing me.

"Come get me," I said, licking my lips.

He hesitated for only a moment. I wrangled his shirt off, pulled his shorts down and took him in my mouth while he remained standing. I didn't see or hear, but I knew pictures were being taken. If Mauro turned to his left, he would be facing the curtain and might see the camera or the pilot. Mauro, even standing like he was, always had his eyes closed. I was always worried that he would see the pilot behind the curtain, but I still enjoyed him. He was adorable. Without his clothes on and with his dick in my mouth, I had control. I pulled him toward me, my hands on his bare ass. I laved him with my saliva, and he loved it. I did too.

We ended up on his favorite seat where we normally did it. I mounted him, my back to the curtain. I suffocated him with kisses as I rode him, his dick moving in and out of me. It never lasted very long, but it was always hot for me. I never got a look at the pictures. Neither did Tomas. He gave the cop the undeveloped roll of film.

Before the next flight, I was in the galley when Tomas came up to me between the coffee maker and the stack of sandwiches I was putting away.

"We have to stop meeting like this," I said. It was a bad joke, but Tomas laughed.

He handed me an envelope with five thousand pesos.

"Is this for me or are we splitting it? Why so much?"

"He likes the pictures. He told me this, that means he gets them developed. Could be he jacks off to them."

I poked Tomas in his chest.

"The five is yours," he said. "I got the same."

I was so happy I wanted to jump up and down.

"He wants as many sessions as possible."

"I'm all for it. We just need Jefe to want me."

"That won't be an issue," Tomas said. "You are very desirable."

He pawed my ass. I let him.

"I take all the risks," he said. "You should give me some of this." He squeezed my ass. He wasn't talking about a share of the money.

I can be a flirt. The five thousand I had just put in my purse made me very happy.

"Maybe one day when you drive me home," I said.

I touched him there, and he got all red. It's funny how a woman my size can weaken a big man like him with just a tiny rub against his zipper.

The next trip, we were in the galley again. He handed me more money.

"If Mauro sees the pictures, he will know it was a set up. Then what will we do?"

"I will deny having anything to do with it, and so will you."

"Okay." I put the money in my purse.

"He's our boss, not our friend. Don't feel bad."

At home, I didn't know where to hide the money. I was worried my boyfriend would come across it. At first, I hid it under the mattress. I'm the one who makes the bed. But I am not good at secrets. Finally, I told him. I didn't expect him to be jealous, and he wasn't. At least, he didn't seem to care at all. Together we stashed it in our mattress. Cut a slit on the surface and stuffed the money we didn't spend. The money I was getting was remarkable. It was enough to change my life. I hoped it would go on for a long time.

---

1. Cock

CHAPTER 30
MIGUEL ALVARADO

I GREW up best friends with Mauro Robles. From primary all the way through college and law school, we went to school together. My father is a lawyer and so is Mauro's father. They hated each other, but it wasn't always that way.

Once I had a brother named Jaime. He was born, lived, and died before I was born. At seventeen, he drove his birthday gift, a new Porsche, off a cliff to his death. An autopsy revealed that my brother had been under the influence of heroin when the accident occurred. He had nodded out, or maybe he was just too wasted to maintain control of the car. Jaime had needle marks on both arms, but he must have kept that hidden.

At the time of my brother's death, my father publicly called out Beto and Mala Hidalgo. They had murdered his son. They were the biggest heroin manufacturers in Mexico, and they were responsible. Mala's lawyer was Mauro's father. It is possible that our two families were among the richest in the entire state of Nuevo Leon. Our fathers were powerful, and it is obvious why they hated each other.

My father launched a discreet behind-the-scenes campaign to put Beto and Mala out of business. He received a lot of sympathy, but little support. He could not penetrate the protective veil the drug business had around it. It was frustrating for my parents, especially because my father was an influential attorney with widespread connections. His efforts against Beto and Mala proved fruitless. They were much too powerful.

As I grew up, my parents forbade me from associating with Mauro, but we were in school, then boarding school. It didn't matter not to see each other on the days we headed home for a weekend or a holiday. We saw each other regularly the rest of the time.

One year we shared a room in the school dorm. My father found out and demanded of the dean that we be split up. The dean wasn't going to be ordered to do anything, even though my parents were heavy financial supporters of the school. Mauro's parents were equally heavy supporters of the school as well.

"Our parents are crazy," I'd say to Mauro.

"They are," he replied. We laughed it off.

By the time we headed to college, I understood more about the evils of heroin. I felt the wound in my heart how addiction had stolen my brother's life. Older and more understanding of life, I sided with my parents and their reason to hate Mala as much as they did. By then, her husband Beto was dead. By then, word was she controlled the drug business in the entire Republic of Mexico. By then, the drug traffic she controlled was not only heroin. She was into everything.

I brought it up to Mauro.

"I have no way of knowing what the woman is into," Mauro would say. "My father is her lawyer, not her partner in crime."

"Your father helped Mala become who she is."

"Give me a break, bro."

We would have disagreements, but it never came down to anything.

Our families were very rich, and our fathers played at one-upmanship. Mauro's father would buy a new car. My father would go out and buy a bigger one, a faster one. His father would fly over my father's office in a new plane. My father would sell his plane and buy a new one.

They had to outdo each other in everything. I don't think Mauro's father knew how many cars he owned. It was crazy. My father always said that his own wealth came from his law practice and investments. Mauro's father's fortune came from drug money paid to him by Mala.

When we entered law school in Mexico City, we rented an apartment in a fabulous party complex with a big swimming pool and spacious guest parking. We were surrounded by beautiful women and money, living it up with all the gusto we had. We both got generous allowances and partied constantly with vigor. I don't know how we made time to study enough to graduate in the top ten percent of our class. After graduation, we both headed back to Monterrey, Nuevo Leon. Mauro joined his father's firm that represented Mala. I joined my father's firm who represented the biggest companies in the region. I had my eye on politics, but it was too early in life to think of that. Eventually Mauro married Mina. Eventually, I married Mina's sister. We were finally actually brothers.

My parents were elderly, twenty years older than Mauro's parents, but they still had trouble accepting the closeness of our two families. I began to hate Mala not only for her drug business, but for driving the wedge between our families. I no longer blamed my parents. I saw the pictures of my brother throughout the house, pictures I had been jealous of growing up, hence I'd ignored them. Every time I saw the picture of Jaime next to his Porsche wrapped with ribbon, I hated Mala more. Without Mala's distribution of heroin, my brother would not have had access to the drug, and he would be alive today. There was no one else to blame. There were many cartels, but it was Mala who controlled the heroin distribution throughout the country and that included our state.

Ten years after our graduation, I ran for governor of Chihuahua. My foe was the lieutenant governor in an administration that had the sitting governor in Mala's pocket. Everyone knew it, but no one bothered to try and prove it. I doubt the governor had ever met Mala, but she was behind every move he made, and behind every move past governors had made to keep her business protected.

Since I did not reside in the state of Chihuahua, I had to establish residency there in order to run for governor. I purchased a beautiful home on beautiful land, but it didn't compare to our home in Monterrey. Mala resided in Juarez; the capitol is Chihuahua. I wasn't looking just to become a governor, I wanted to become a governor of the state where I could cause Mala real damage and I went through the trouble and expense of establishing residency to do this. My wife was not happy but eventually she came around to accept my decision when I assured her she could go back and forth to our home in Monterrey when she pleased in our private plane.

After Mauro's father's death, Mauro took over his father's firm. The firm lived on and no doubt the payoffs to keep a veil of protection on Mala's drug business was taken over by Mauro but of course he was never going to admit that to me or anyone else.

I loved my brother-in-law. We saw each other regularly. My parents still wanted Mala destroyed. I too blamed her for killing my brother. Sometimes I let it slip to Mauro on casual occasions, like when we met for lunch. Sometimes we would be at his office, sometimes at mine, sometimes in public.

There was an English-style pub halfway between his office and mine where we sometimes went for lunch or dinner. Occasionally, we'd meet in one of the private rooms, but only when it was a serious meeting. Generally, we ate in the public rooms. We had gone there around four to have tea. It was technically tea, and they served tea in English style, but we went for Mexican chocolate and pan dulce, a buffet of spicey sweet treats like you get nowhere else. Often it devolved into eating hotter and hotter candied peppers or whatever else was in the menu. We tended to compete.

"I'm going to crush that old lady when I get elected. She killed my brother. Nothing personal, bro."

I picked out a pastry that had a habanero jam and handed it over.

Mauro bit into it, chewed and swallowed, with no other indication than a little sweat on his forehead.

Mauro is as cocky as I am, and, being a lawyer, as accustomed to argument. He handed me a piece of the same pastry. I matched his technique, not revealing I had swallowed pure fire. I moved on to the next treat.

"You have no evidence. The woman is at her home. She never leaves. How is she capable of running the enterprise you believe she owns?"

"You should be ashamed, brother. Drop the bitch. It's not like you need the money." I wanted to take a drink to cool my throat, but the argument was distracting me.

"Easy, bro. She's my client. You've got nothing on her. And if you make it to governor, you still won't have anything on her."

"You know damn well I'll be the next governor."

"I was kidding, I know you will win. She is not into drugs," Mauro insisted.

"In that case, maybe a stray bullet will hit its mark."

"Shame, bro," Mauro said. "I know you are making a joke. Killing her would be murder."

I disagreed with him, and as usual we got caught up in debate. Anyone listening would believe it was an argument. We'd been through half a dozen little treats. Not all of them were killer hot, but a few were pure lava.

"We both have kids to protect. Drugs are too easy for them to come by, thanks to her."

"Let's keep our kids out of it," Mauro said.

"I hear her grandsons are opening businesses. You know they were built on drug money and the businesses are laundromats for cleaning currencies."

Mauro laughed at me.

"Rico and Victor. Those are their names in case you don't know."

"I wonder how long before they overdose like their mother," I shot back.

From a pitcher, Mauro poured two glasses of the milky coconut drink that is the only thing that cools the fire. He pushed one glass in front of me. Moisture condensed on the sides. I resisted drinking it.

"That's dirty, Miguel."

"Drugs kill," I argued. "You know it. She controls the drug business in Mexico for sure and once I'm governor, it's over."

Mauro patted my back like a brother. "Bro, if Mala is in the drug business, you will never prove it. You know this. That's the only reason you now talk about a stray bullet."

"I hate her," I said.

"You hate her because you know you will never have the evidence to arrest her, much less convict her of any crime. The bad guy died when her husband passed away. That was years ago."

"You're a fool, Mauro."

"I've always been a fool of sorts."

"You said it."

We laughed.

"Te Amo," said Mauro. "I'm late, have to get going."

"I love you too," I said as we hugged. "Wait."

I picked up both cold drinks. We tapped our glasses and quenched our burning throats at the same time.

CHAPTER 31
RICO SANTOS

THE CONTRACTOR who undertook building the three *Palacio* clubs is Ron Vigil. He did a fabulous job, a resident of El Paso. He's a thin guy, one who looked like he would never indulge. I invited him for lunch so he could eat at the restaurant he had built. I gave him the full treatment. Anything he wanted was on the house. He'd seen it completed, and even dressed up and ready for service, but he'd never been pampered as a guest as only Gloria and Elena can do. He really tore into the aged porterhouse he ordered. I ordered a cheesecake for him for dessert, and espresso, which I remembered he had liked. He started on the steak, and I got rolling. He should be giving me the royal carpet treatment because I had him there to give him a big money job.

"I have property in Baja California that I want to build my house on. It's a beautiful spot on the coast on more than ten kilometers of beach property that extends inland across the highway. Are you the man I should give this huge project to?"

He nodded, swallowed, and said, "I can build anything. It will be an honor."

· · ·

Jerry, the architect I hired, was in Los Angeles, California. I had talked to him on the phone on a conference call with Ron and I told him I pictured a big house.

Then I said, "No, not a house, a castle."

"You can build a little city with that much land," said Jerry with a chuckle.

"For now, a castle, something grand."

I had bought a Learjet and had flown to Ensenada and drove to the property. I planned to build my own runway but there was a lot of work to do before that could happen. I traveled South to Acapulco, Mexico City, Guadalajara. Less frequently, I travelled North. I was in New York City four days and Chicago for two days. I spent a week in Miami, Florida. I checked in with Victor every day and with Elena. I called Quick frequently, especially if I wanted to laugh. She had a great sense of humor. I also called my grandmother, but with her, I was forbidden to discuss business. I asked how she was doing, and she asked how I was doing. I never mentioned where I was calling from. She hated phones. When I did go home, she said, "I don't trust little planes. Why did you buy a plane? Aren't you worried you might crash?"

"Grandma, it's not a little plane." I laughed.

She whacked me with her cane. Not hard.

I flew to Los Angeles in the Learjet with two pilots, two flight attendants and Luciana, whom I'd hired as an assistant. It wasn't hard to get her to quit her job at the newspaper. "Not fair if you fire me without notice," she said. "I put four years of college and kissing ass for years at the *Dispatch* to learn how to be a reporter and now you are whisking me away like Cinderella to who knows where. Just saying, don't let me have a hard landing when it's over." I had kissed her, grabbed her ass with both hands and said, "You're not going anywhere, ever. You're part of my team for as long as you want."

The Learjet was not as comfortable as in later years, but Luciana and I sat in the back with the compartment curtain closed and we fucked.

Ron Vigil, my contractor, was in Los Angeles for a week before we arrived.

Ron, Jerry, Luciana, and I had a meeting in an elaborate conference room three times larger than the dining room at Grandmother's house. Jerry Johnston was a partner in an influential company which was bagging most of the new high-rise buildings planned and under construction in downtown Los Angeles.

To get an idea of what I envisioned, Ron and Jerry provided me photos of European castles. Some of them were for sale. But I didn't want to buy a castle. I wanted to build one on the beach in Ensenada, Baja California.

"I suggest we pick a castle, and once we have a vision of your preferred style, we'll work the interior," Jerry said.

"You mean you will copy one of these?" Luciana said, eyes wide. She had a notepad out and was taking notes, not that I had asked her to. She had a lot of nervous energy, and was always doing something productive, independent, and useful.

"It's up to Rico, we can do anything." My contractor joined by nodding his approval.

After looking through a tall stack of photos, I found a favorite.

"I want this one," I said.

My contractor chuckled. "It's my favorite, too."

I didn't want to embarrass Ron. I didn't ask him if this was biting off more than he could chew. I knew he could build outlandish night clubs, but this was a castle.

Jerry Johnston would work on a survey of the land in Ensenada, Baja California.

"I hope you have some elevated land, a cliff over the water. Ron says he's seen the property and there are elevated areas."

"I have," Ron said. "He also has inland property across the highway. Plenty of room there too."

"On our way back home, I'll fly over and check for that," I said. "I didn't notice. I want the building on the beach side just like this picture. I love this house." I laughed. "I mean, castle."

"Rico, who will live there with you? It will be enormous. Are you planning to get married and have a dozen children?"

"Not so fast. I'm a youngster." I roared. When I let out a roar instead of a laugh, I do it for attention. I got the roar down to a science. It enhances laughter.

Luciana apparently ignored what I said. She had the picture in front of her and looked mesmerized. "It's beautiful," she agreed. On the round table where we were sitting, there was also a crude map of the property that did no credit to the look of the land. It only showed a few property lines.

"Wait till you see the property in person," I said to Luciana.

"We can do the engineering as well," Jerry said. "We've had projects in many parts of the world, but this will be my first in Mexico. I'm not sure about their building codes or restrictions regarding building something this massive along the coast. We may have to make changes to follow the local codes."

I grinned. "Jerry don't worry about codes or restrictions in Mexico. I have it covered."

"What are you going to do with the rest of the property?" Jerry asked. "The residence is taking up a fraction of what you have."

"I'm not sure yet. By the time my house is finished, we will know." I grinned to see him angling for the next build, whatever it might be.

We exchanged smiles and handshakes.

Our hired limousine was at curbside, the driver standing at the open door waiting for us. Ron and Jerry walked us out though they were going to continue conferring on the plans after Luciana and I were gone.

Luciana and I shook Ron's hand again.

"Don't let me down," I said. "Make it beautiful like the picture."

"More beautiful, I promise." He put his hand up with two fingers up and his other hand on his heart.

Two minutes later, Luciana and I were on our way to the Beverly Wilshire Hotel in Beverly Hills.

Luciana, as my assistant, was fabulous at organizing and helping me. Now that I had a plane, she received training from an agency about what a private jet owner needed to know and do, including but not limited to keeping a manifest for each flight and working with airports where a stop was planned for fuel or a layover. Lodging and transportation were handled by a travel agency in El Paso. Luciana told them what we wanted, and it was taken care of.

Victor had not traveled to his Baja properties. He was wrapped up in working the Palacios. He had a Porsche, a Ferrari and was thinking of buying a Lamborghini, but was uninterested in anything with wings. Victor was in no hurry to move from his cottage. I hadn't moved out either, but I had moved on.

Luciana and I got tight. We talked all the time. Sex was not what bonded us. "I don't plan to fall in love with you," she always said.

"Good to hear," I agreed.

CHAPTER 32
DIEGO SAN JUAN

I HAVE TWO SIBLINGS, a brother one year older than me and a sister one year younger.

My father, Ernesto San Juan, heads a cartel in Colombia that produces tons of cocaine a month. The cocaine is grown in Mexico, closer than Colombia to the United States border. I know all about my father's business, but we are hands off. Thousands of acres of our land in Colombia no longer have coca plants. Many years ago, my father made a deal with the Colombian president that he wanted to be left alone. In exchange, he demonstrated that he and his cartel partners were not producing the product. Colombia was only interested in shutting down the drug business in the country. Ever since that deal, my family no longer has to hide from law enforcement in Colombia. We live like the millionaires that we are, and no one fucks with us. We own many businesses in Colombia. We manufacture tires for automobiles and trucks, we own forty gasoline stations, two new car agencies, and many other businesses.

We run the drug business in Mexico through intermediaries, individuals disconnected from us in every discernible way. When things get hot in Mexico, the individuals at the helm send out attorneys to calm the storm with cash. The chain of command is hidden, as is the flow of cash. There is a network of offshore bank accounts in various countries, tied to a multitude of businesses outside of Colombia, like, for example, aviation. Among the family businesses are jet outlets in Mexico and Canada. My father called me when I was in Amsterdam for a week.

"Rico Santos wants to buy a Learjet," my father said. "Rico, one of her two grandsons." He paused long enough for me to figure out what HER he was referring to. "Rico found out there was a waiting list for the plane he wanted. He just tried to bully the manager at our Mexico City agency and when that failed, he offered the manager a million pesos for immediate delivery. He wants a Learjet and does not want to wait. The manager called me in Colombia, a first. A manager doesn't call me about a problem. I took an interest in the matter because this is her grandson pushing the manager with a million pesos. "

My father was being careful not to mention Mala's name. I thought that was funny. My father is normally not careful about telephone conversations, although we all should be.

"I see," I said. And I did understand. This Rico was probably the heir to the throne, so to speak. She wasn't going to live forever. People have been saying she's a hundred years old since I can remember.

"Diego, call the manager. Sell this young man the next plane we get from the factory. Don't take the million. Don't allow anyone to take a dime beyond payment for the plane. I figure he's about your age. You can become friends."

I understood what my father was after.

The Beto business that Mala owned handled very little cocaine. My father was looking to make a connection with the mysterious Mala, a woman my father had never met, and he'd been in the business for decades. Mala's grandson could be the key to a lucrative cocaine business relationship.

Several hours after he left the agency, I got in touch with Rico at the Ritz Hotel in Mexico City. I introduced myself.

"Out of respect to you and your family, I have ordered that the plane we have coming in next week is yours."

"Excellent," he said. "What did you say your name is?"

"Diego San Juan. I have instructed the manager not to accept any money from you other than the price of the plane."

"I promised the manager a million pesos."

"Rico, he will get fired if you give him the money or any part of it."

"Thank you, Diego. Your last name, San Juan. Are you from Colombia?"

I could practically hear the wheels in his brain as he placed my identity.

I laughed. "I live in Colombia, my friend. We must meet one day."

"Name the day," Rico said.

"It would be an honor to have you come visit me," I said.

He hesitated, but it was a short silence. "Diego, get me my plane and I will see you in Colombia very soon."

Rico got his plane. He called to thank me personally. We stayed in touch by phone. We scheduled a rendezvous, but things came up. Both of us put off scheduled meetings, then one day he called me.

"I'll be in Los Angeles this coming Friday through the weekend. Where are you?"

"I'm home. Colombia," I said.

"That's a long stretch for a couple days."

"Not at all. I will be there."

I have a Learjet but when I can, I borrow my father's plane, a Boeing 720. It once carried a hundred forty-nine passengers back and forth over Spain. When the airline went bust, my father bought the plane and had it converted to a flying luxury ride. Now it's like a flying party house. There's a bathroom for the crew, two bathrooms for us, plus a bedroom with a king-sized bed,

"I'm going to meet up with Rico," I said to my father.

"Take the plane. Impress him. By now I thought you two would be friends."

"We are friends." I laughed. "Telephone friends."

· · ·

It takes three in the cockpit to fly the 720: pilot, co-pilot, and flight engineer. When the flight is long range, I need a backup crew, but this time we were getting away with just the one crew. When I took off from Colombia, three men were in the cockpit to take care of the plane, one stunning stewardess to take care of the pilots, and two stunning stewardesses to take care of me. The three ladies were long-time employees of my father. If it had been up to my mother, they would have been fired long ago.

Valentina, Camila, and Clara. Any man would count himself lucky to be aboard a flight with these girls. If you have a plane, I don't have to tell you about sex at thirty-thousand feet flying at five hundred-plus miles per hour. I loved my Lear but there was no comparison to the 720.

The pilots had their layover at a hotel near the airport, on call till I needed them.

I was shown to my two-bedroom suite. Valentina, Camila, and Clara had the use of one of the bedrooms, at least technically. I certainly wouldn't beat them off with a stick if they wanted to stray into my room.

I dialed his room, and Rico and I connected.

"I have three *buenotas*[1] with me. Should I bring them?"

Rico had a resounding voice. I'd heard his boisterous laugh in past phone calls. It made me laugh too.

"The more the merrier," he said.

Rico's suite was on the top floor. I'd realized in the elevator on the way up that it would be bigger than mine, and it was. We shook hands, exchanging big grins. He was about my age, as my father had suspected. He was a big guy and seemed fit.

Right away, I could tell Rico liked the trio I had brought with me. I liked Luciana right off. She was blazing hot. Not a stewardess, though. He introduced her as his assistant. I am extremely curious about him, a close assistant like her might know many secrets.

• • •

The two days in Los Angeles were spent in our suites and in the hotel restaurant. Most of the time the women were with us, and we were all just being sociable. Rico and I only talked business in the sauna located at the hotel spa, alone.

Rico was extremely careful. I could respect that because I, too, am careful. He didn't say it, but he needed to be sure I didn't have a wire. I felt the same way. Both of us being naked in the sauna was good proof that we were both on the level. Neither of us mentioned the word cocaine until we were naked.

I gave him the price per ton on the Mexico side and a price on the U.S. side of the border and that's when I discovered he wasn't interested in buying cocaine.

"Diego, how many loads out of ten make it across the border?"

"I'm not sure but I can find out. I'd say we lose four out of ten."

"What if you could get ten out of ten across, guaranteed?"

"How you figure?"

"Give me a little time. I promise you will love what I'm doing."

The look on Rico's face was too energized for me to show him my disappointment that he wasn't interested in buying our product. "Rico, give me a hint, come on."

"I can't, it's top secret and when I let you in on it, you'll know why."

"Whatever it is, can we make money on it?"

"You bet, tons of money."

I lightened up. In the back of my mind, I thought of my dad. He would be the disappointed one, and he shouldn't be. We have a big business, big demand.

Whatever it was, Rico did give a hint. It must have something to do with getting our loads across the border with no loss. He must have a customs connection. We have them too, but we still have losses.

We shook sauna-sweaty hands.

"Diego, I will let you know when I'm ready to give you a proposal."

I chuckled. "I'm dying to hear," and thought about how this had turned around on me.

"I like you, Diego. I promise to let your family in on it. Until then, easy on the phone, no code, no questions."

We shook hands again.

"I hate phones," I said.

---

1. *buenotas* physically and sexually attractive, is a term that is used for reference is to a woman desired by a man.

CHAPTER 33
VALENTINA

WHEN DIEGO USES his father's plane, no matter where we go, it is a party. The three of us are never excluded. My partners Camila, Clara, and I love working for him.

This trip to Los Angeles was two days and nights of practically non-stop sex. We broke off to visit a restaurant somewhere in the hotel or for the arrival of room service who laid out a huge spread of food in the suite's private dining room. One time we went to the woman's spa on the lower floor of the hotel while Diego and Rico were on their own in the men's spa. Another time, we played around with Luciana on the bed. I think it was on the second day we were at the hotel. Me and my two girls consumed her at the same time. She went wild. We had just got back from the spa. It was trendy for women like us to frolic and play with each other alone or together with the opposite sex. Trendy or not, I know it was something new for Luciana. Diego and Rico had not returned to the suite from their second spa visit. They found us (in lingerie) asleep in a pile in one of the bedrooms. Missed the action just as we planned. This was for us.

The penthouse Rico was in had a master suite with a double king, and two other bedrooms. We used all three. At least once, I saw Diego leave Rico's suite with Luciana. When he was gone, the three of us took turns with Rico. Knowing he was Mala's grandson was an aphrodisiac for me. Mala was legendary. She was an evil woman that everyone knew and feared. They say she incinerates her enemies, and she can't be touched. Rico, however, can be touched, and he even touches back. If he's evil, then I want all I can get of him.

Before we were scheduled to leave for the airport, we had dinner in Rico's suite. All of us were in bath robes. I was having a great time. I think Camila was a little antsy. She likes her coke, but Diego told us that on the entire trip, there was no coke and no weed.

When we first met up with Rico and Luciana, Diego said to Rico, "My girls and I are not going to use anything while here, but I defer to you."

"I agree," Rico said. "I don't mess around in the states."

"I'm sure we'll find something to do," Diego said with a big grin, matched by Rico and laughter from Luciana and the girls and me.

Diego seldom traveled to the United States, at least not with his father's plane. Everywhere else we traveled with Diego, there was always plenty of cocaine and neatly rolled marijuana. Neatly rolled and labeled different weed types. Diego himself was into coke. I have worked for his father for years. His father won't touch product, but he's no angel. He smokes Marlboro, two packs a day, drinks tequila like it's going out of style, like it's water, and he likes his dick sucked. Diego is into blowjobs too.

I'm not into coke but sometimes it's necessary to snort a line with Diego. You don't say no when he hands over a rolled up hundred-dollar bill. Camila loves coke and Clara tolerates it if she has to take it. Same for having the white powder rubbed on our nipples or clits. I don't like it because it numbs it so I can't get off no matter what my fingers do to my clitoris. Without the additive I get off quick.

Diego treats me like an equal, not at all like an employee. He is generous, like his father. After a trip, we all get a cash bonus. The flight crews get paid no matter if we fly or not. The catch is that we are always on call, just as the pilots are and the backup pilots. We all live in Bogotá.

· · ·

When it was time to leave the hotel, the helicopter was waiting on the rooftop helipad. Rico's plane was at the Santa Monica airport and our plane was at LAX. Diego wanted to show off his big plane. Diego didn't have to twist Rico's arm; he didn't mind flying to LAX to check out Ernesto's plane.

"You will love it," Diego said.

"I've flown first class to Europe several times. I thought that the reclining seat was a big deal. But a bed. This I've got to see."

Rico grinned. Luciana matched Rico's grin. The engine started up. Our earmuffs went on, and all conversations ended.

With six of us and the pilot, it was tight. I sat with Rico and Luciana. Rico's big hand lay on my upper left thigh. His other hand was on Luciana's side, out of my line of sight.

I leaned forward and looked left to Luciana, and I said "fun" so she could read my lips.

I think she blushed a little, reminding me when the girls and I had our way with her. I gave her a suggestive wink, and yes, she blushed. I thought again that Luciana had never done it with a woman before. I could tell by the blush and smile she was fine with what we did to her. We bonded. Our secret.

CHAPTER 34
LUCIANA CAMACHO

RICO TOLD the helicopter pilot we'd be back on board in fifteen minutes. No such thing. An hour later we were still in Diego's father's plane. Rico fell in love with the luxury plane we toured, and he said so.

"Sell me the plane," Rico said.

"Can't. It's not mine. It's my father's," Diego said.

"Tell him to name the price."

Laughs.

I enjoyed going through it all. Diego explained every little thing. He showed us the cargo hold and pointed out the water tanks that provided the water for the showers.

The king-sized bed was marvelous. I pictured Rico and me making love on it, and then I pictured all of us on the bed. I have no idea what Rico thought about, but he had a wicked-ass grin as he checked out the bedroom with the connecting bathroom.

No less than ten times, Rico asked Diego to ask his father if he would sell the plane.

"Name your price. I want this."

Finally, we exchanged hugs and kisses and disembarked the big plane. We ran about forty feet to the waiting helicopter.

Rico kissed me as we took off. We were in the second seat at the back where we had been on the way there, only now we were alone.

176

The kiss lasted a long time. The pilot had his back to us, which was a good thing because Rico's hand was between my legs. His palm was hard, rubbing me through the fabric of my slacks and the friction was in the perfect spot. It took like half a second for me to go off like a bottle rocket. The whole helicopter was one giant vibration, and when I exploded, it was like my whole body was in on it. No such thing as too much sex.

Our teeth ground against each other. I know I moaned for half a minute. At least the noise of the helicopter covered it up. If it didn't, the pilot got a hell of an earful. Our earmuffs dulled out the engine noise. I tried to return the favor and did the best I could when Rico wouldn't let me undo his pants. I was for sure going to have my way with him as soon as we had some privacy.

I was soaked down there when we landed a few feet away from Rico's awaiting plane and crew.

CHAPTER 35
NOA

I'M TWENTY-THREE, a stewardess working for Rico full-time. I used to work for Ranna Airlines, an operator headquartered in Mexico City. The job and training I went through lasted nine months. I was fired after a supervisor saw me kissing a co-worker on the lips in public. I was told it wouldn't have mattered if we hadn't been wearing our uniforms and we had waited until we left the terminal. Victoria was also fired. She had worked there four months longer than me.

Munoz was the union representative, he interviewed us at the same time after Victoria and I filed an appeal. "Are you lesbians?"

"No, we're not lesbians," I said.

"What if we were?" Victoria was about to lose it.

"I'm on your side," Munoz said, his hands up for a second in surrender.

"If you're on our side, get us back our jobs," I said.

"The kiss was a so long kiss," Victoria said. "I was going out one exit, and she was going out another exit. I told Sifuentes that, but she fired us anyway."

Munoz says to us, "Why a wet kiss and in uniform and at the airport terminal?"

· · ·

We didn't get our job back, but Munoz gave us a phone number of a woman in Juarez, Mexico named Luciana. She was looking for two experienced stewardesses.

"My employer is getting delivery of a new Learjet soon. It's a dream job for the right two ladies," Luciana said to me on the phone. Victoria was right next to me.

It was strange in a way and Victoria and I discussed this. We are two hours plus by air between Mexico City and Juarez; how did Munoz know Luciana was looking for two stewardesses? Also strange, we were offered plane fare and expenses to fly north for an interview. Why us?

We met Luciana at a restaurant in downtown Juarez called the *Palacio*. We thought it was a lunch meeting until the hostess escorted us to an upper floor. Her office was modern and nice, and she was beautiful. We talked for about ten minutes. She handed us an application, a pen, and a clipboard. We sat across her desk and filled out the form. It was like we weren't across her desk. She made three phone calls.

"Both of you aren't married or have children?" asked Luciana.

"Correct," I said, Victoria nodding. We were still across the desk from Luciana, and she was looking over the applications.

"If you get hired, you'll get paid starting today. When Jefe is not flying anywhere you are on call, and you get paid for staying home. This is a full-time job; do you understand this?"

"Magnifico," said Victoria with a big smile.

Luciana smiled back and said, "If you get hired, you need to move here."

We both gave her a look of approval.

Luciana left us in her office and came back a few minutes later with this tall handsome young man. Victoria and I stood and faced the big one. We shook hands. His name was Rico Santos.

He hired us on the spot. Just like that.

· · ·

We left the *Palacio* with a full stomach and ten thousand pesos each for our moving expenses. "If you don't like the apartment we get for you, you can live where you wish as long as you run to the airport if I call you," said Luciana. Rico was already out of the office.

Victoria said, "We only need one apartment."

"Okay, we'll find you a two-bedroom, two bathrooms in a nice area here in Juarez."

"How much will it cost us?" I was shy about this question.

"It's part of the job. Mr. Santos's family owns many apartment buildings. By the time you return I will have something for you to look at."

I said rather rapidly, "Miss Luciana, we don't need to look at it, we already love it."

A few seconds later we all laughed.

What was nice was that Luciana came around her desk and gave us both a hug. "Welcome to our team," she said.

CHAPTER 36
VICTORIA

AFTER WE WERE HIRED, it took a month before Jefe Rico took delivery of his new plane. In the meantime, we settled into a boss apartment in a neighborhood where all the streets were paved. Everywhere you looked were apartment buildings. My understanding was that most of the complexes belonged to Mala. We knew about Mala in Mexico City. I often wondered if she was alive. I would never ask Rico or Luciana about it, for sure.

We got a cool pad, fresh paint, new carpets, and new furniture. It was hotel furniture, but it was boss, very nice.

Noa and I were fitted by a seamstress. We received a dozen uniforms, but they weren't really uniforms. Shorts, Short-shorts, short skirts, and short-short skirts. The tops were shirts we would wear in. No hat, beautiful shoes, flats, and heels. Luciana brought us a long coat for winter stops we might make: a short winter jacket and mink hats and earmuff. Real mink.

"You need to look good when you are out and about in a city, even if you don't know anyone. Eventually, the hotel clerks will know you are on Rico Santos's team and that necessitates what I just said. Understand?"

I did a salute and Noa did too.

Luciana saluted back.

The three of us laughed.

"I never asked you why you were let go from your job in Mexico City," said Luciana. "You don't need to tell me."

"You really don't know?"

I thought it was strange since it was the union guy that referred us.

"I don't know, and you don't need to tell me."

Noa spoke up and told her a two-minute short version. Before Luciana could say a word, I said, "We appealed to the union, but it did no good."

Luciana smiled and said, "What fools they are. Well, we lucked out because now you are working here."

And that was it.

When Luciana was gone, I said to Noa, "I bet she already knew."

"No question about it, she knew," Noa agreed.

We spent days at the *Palacio* on the outskirts of the city where the menu was to die for, and the clientele were wealthy locals and wealthy El Paso patrons. The wine steward pumped us with a whole lot of wine savvy in the short time we spent with him. The airline that fired us trained us in wine selections but no comparison to what we learned with Rico's man. When we were done, we were ready to serve an impressive selection of wines to Rico and his guests that came along with him. The steward selected the wines for the plane, so it was easier for us to understand the reds from the white elite wines. Apparently, Rico was really into wine and when he didn't drink wine, he drank Chivas Regal. Hard liquor we knew well. We had a session on that too.

The maiden flight was to Mexico City. Noa and I spent a weekend double-teaming the boss. "I didn't hire you to let me fuck you," he said in Spanish. "You don't have to do it; I promise I will not be upset."

Maybe he was kidding. He had that grin that he shows all the time.

"We want to fuck." I was the first one to say it.

Noa said, "I'm ready, Jefe."

"Call me Rico, not Jefe, not when we are having sex."

"Rico, fuck me already," I said, spreading wide. "Crush me. "

"I like crush too," said Noa with a don't-forget-me voice.

Without Rico there, I said to Noa, "I bet Luciana told him we were probably lesbians."

"So, what if he knows? You and me, we go either way."

"We do," I said. I was not in love with Noa, I don't think, but I wished we could be more open out in public with each other. It was trendy to roll around in bed with the opposite sex and same sex men and women, but it was not trendy for a same-sex couple to have an open relationship. In Mexico you could lose your life.

In New York, we left our sexy work clothes on the plane and put on civilian clothes to party with the boss. One night we went to eat at an elegant restaurant. The concierge told us to be dressy casual. Rico took us to a fancy store at the lobby of the Waldorf Hotel and bought us beautiful outfits to wear that night, including underwear and shoes. What he spent on us was more than four months' pay to each of us.

"Jefe, you are too generous," I said.

"Way too generous, Jefe."

"Are you happy or not?" His voice could be taken for angry, but his grin said no to that.

"Want me to show you how happy, Jefe?"

"He wants," Noa said. "Let's do him."

It was like Rico couldn't get enough of us. "I'm turned on by having you both at the same time as this," he said more than once. Even on the plane where we didn't have that much room and he was so big, we found a way to have sex. Noa and my laughter was genuine. I mean, we were happy with the attention Rico gave us and he allowed us to give him. It was like we'd known him all our life, seriously. It wasn't just the sex either. Yeah, the sex had lots to do with it, but it didn't seem that way. I said to Noa, "He's a man. The honeymoon will wear out and he'll park us, wait and see."

"I agree, but I'm hoping for a miracle," Noa replied.

"Yeah, right," I said.

"Don't be negative." Noa's voice was so laid back like she was high or something, but she wasn't high. That's just Noa.

It was in New York when without planning I kissed Noa on the mouth. A savory kiss. The three of us were on the bed. Rico sprang to a seat with a grin like you'd see on a pumpkin. Wide. The two of us went at each other. It was not new to us. We preferred a penis but there was chemistry between us. What we did came naturally. Rico became so excited he roared with gusto. Laughter.

"What's funny, Rico?" I dared to ask as I came up for air for a second.

"I love what you are doing to each other," he said. "Don't stop."

I doubt we were the first women he'd been up close to when they were on each other. He acted as though it was the first time. Maybe it was. Maybe the honeymoon would go for longer. I'm thinking this while Noa is working me over and I'm doing ongoing payback.

Rico was hooked on his plane. There was practically no down time. He kept wanting to fly here and there and everywhere. We got paid the same if we flew every day or if we didn't fly at all. No extra money for lots of travel but it was so much fun, and then, Luciana started traveling with us. She confiscated his full attention, and I can't blame him. She's a beautiful package. I kind of figured Rico would want all of us in a bed. That didn't happen.

"The honeymoon is over," Noa said to me.

"Yup. It was fun while it lasted."

In Miami, we were not invited. Noa and I were on our own. The plan was two nights and then we got a call to relax. We'd be there another two nights, maybe three. We were in a bitchin' hotel but living out of a suitcase for days is not fun.

"Let's hit it," said Noa. "We've been here on call like forever."

"I'm in," I said to Noa. "Need a man with a big bat."

"Oh, yeah," Noa agreed.

We arrived in Los Angeles for a weekend business trip and the crew, including us, were told by Luciana to relax because it was a sure thing we'd not be leaving until late Sunday. Noa and I were cut out of wherever Jefe was going to be with Luciana in Los Angeles.

"Honeymoon is over," Noa reminded me too many times to count.

"Fuck the honeymoon," I said. "It's not like we're ugly. Let's go party in Hollywood."

CHAPTER 37
RICO SANTOS

I FOLLOWED Luciana's succulent bobble up the plane stairs, unable to resist a grab. She squealed on contact, and stopped halfway up the stairs so abruptly, I bumped into her. I steadied us both with a hand on her shoulders. She looked at me, on different stairs but eye to eye.

"I'm too wet as it is," she whispered loudly.

Her color was high. Blushing? I took my hands off her shoulders and squeezed again, pulling her against me. Noa and Victoria were peeking out of the plane's open doorway, both grinning from ear to ear.

I had to bend a little to clear the door. I leaned towards Noa first and kissed her lips, then did the same to Victoria. Luciana gave them each a peck on the cheek.

"I feel guilty we didn't take you," I said to the girls. "On the other hand, I'm not sure you would have liked all the things we got into."

"Just try us," Victoria said with a giggle that made me laugh.

Noa nodded and asked, "What can I get you to drink?"

"Red wine," I said. "Two glasses."

"A Rothchild Bordeaux but you need to give me twenty minutes to let it breathe."

"Pour it in to a decanter," I said to Victoria.

"Got it, Jefe."

I took my window seat across from where Luciana would be sitting when she returned from the bathroom. The seats could be turned to different directions. That had been something I found a benefit until I had seen what was possible. I loved my plane, but the love affair came to a screeching halt after seeing Diego's father's plane.

I was sipping red wine when Luciana returned wearing grey joggers, socks, and no shoes. She sat down and reached for the bowl of cashews on the table between us.

"Rico, sweetheart, run and change. Get comfy like me before we take off."

It didn't matter that the plane was already pulling back. I walked to the back of the plane and did as she had suggested. I came back in sweats just as we went wheels up, and buckled in, taking in the outside view as we shot up and away. The noise and vibration were extreme.

The Learjet is not like an airliner that gradually climbs after taking off. Instead, it feels like we're in a rocket going straight up, then we level off at the altitude where the pilots have mapped us to be.

"I can't stop thinking about Diego's plane."

"I know you loved it. It was written all over your face."

We leaned forward and clinked our wine glasses. I tried not thinking of the over-the-top table and chairs in Diego's father's plane. I tried not thinking of the bed.

"It's the bedroom I can't get over."

"Diego said his father bought the plane from an airline and had it remodeled into an executive jet. You can do that."

"Probably. But I want his plane. I don't want to wait to have one redone."

Luciana laughed. "What business is he in?"

"Honey, how would I know that? He's never going to tell me."

"Sorry," she said.

"No reason for sorry. I know his family owns the agency where I got the plane and I heard they have many businesses."

We had already leveled off. Noa appeared.

"We have lots of food to choose from. Want to hear?"

"Too bad the flight is only two and a half hours," I said.

We were headed to El Paso. I considered holding off eating till we got home. I could practically taste one of those aged porterhouses we serve in El Paso.

Victoria heard and walked over. "You're the boss. Change course and make it longer."

"Why not?" Luciana asked.

Why not, indeed?

When we landed in El Paso, the plane was fueled. Pilots did their walk around the plane and waited for instructions.

Luciana and I used two pay phones at the terminal. I called my grandmother, asked how she was and told her I was fine, and I'd call her soon. I called my brother, Elena, and Quick. Luciana called my travel agent and booked us a suite, and rooms for the crew. We were headed to New York City.

CHAPTER 38
MAURO ROBLES

MY NEW PLANE IS A HAWKER. I've had it almost a year. My only wish is that I'd get more use out of it. My kids' days were filled with school activities. That kept my Mina very busy. For years, we had a nanny for each child and six housekeepers. Even so, Mina complained she was busy. We had no time to travel very much, at least not yet.

We had a full-time chef, a sous chef, two chauffeurs, a bodyguard for each child, two for Mina and one for me. We didn't have kidnapping in our state, but everyone we knew had security people. There were many kidnappings in Mexico City. It was just a matter of time before kidnapping would become a trend in smaller affluent cities like ours.

On my last trip to Chihuahua, I had made the last quarterly payment to the governor through his messenger, Bella. Even though Miguel was running against an incumbent lieutenant governor, we all knew that he would be elected. That's how it works.

"I have a message from him," Bella said after I handed her the envelope. "He says to advise your client to take a long vacation away from Mexico for a while."

"Thanks for the message and thank the governor for me as well. It's been a pleasure."

"I saw your plane," she said. "It is beautiful."

She was a lovely young woman. At twenty-four, she was leggy and slim, wore her straight dark hair long and loose, and seemed younger, like a college student. Unlike most of the governor's staff, she wore jeans, a short-sleeved hand-embroidered shirt like one you could get in the local street markets, and huge gold hoop earrings.

"I'd love to give you a trip anywhere you wish to go."

Bella smiled. "I'm going to take you up on that."

"I'll be waiting."

My father was right. Not everything about payoffs was as bad as I'd figured. I'd been doing his old job for ten years now. I was used to the grind. The governor was not being paid for protecting Mala. Instead, he was being paid, just as the governors before him, for protecting the Beto drug business. Beto was her deceased husband's name.

I should have been in a better mood, but I was about to see Mala. How was I going to explain to her that I had failed to reason with Miguel? I was delaying leaving the relative peace of my plane, seated in a plush leather seat gazing at the Baccarat Decanter Louis XIII. Outside, the big black Lincoln was waiting for me. My good friend was the new governor-elect of the state, and I was parked on a runway in Juarez. Mala owned this city from her mansion that was protected by tall walls.

"Ten years have gone by since your father's death. He was my poor dead husband's friend, and he was my friend. He protected us always. Mauro, you have done very well by me. I have never failed you. Now you must not fail me. Talk sense into that friend of yours. Offer him whatever is necessary. All I want is for him to stop publicly threatening me and promising his supporters that he's going to put me in prison. I'm not running a cartel; I never leave the house and there are no drugs in this house."

"Magda, I know all of this. I've told the fool this. I know you are hands off."

I should have not said this, fool that I am.

"Don't be stupid, Mauro. I'm not hands off. I have nothing to do with illegal drugs. The only businesses I have are in my name, and I pay taxes like everyone else. I don't have a drug business."

"I'm sorry, Magda. I know this. I didn't mean to say hands off, forgive me for that."

"If you know it, and he's the friend that I know he is to you, make him believe it. Tell him to do his best to put the so-called Mala drug business out of business. I don't care."

"I will tell him this. I plan to meet him again. I'm here because I wanted you to have an update, and I know you don't like telephones."

"You shouldn't like telephones either," she said.

"I hate phones," I said.

"This is the first real challenge I've put before you in ten years," she continued.

"I will do my utmost, my word on that."

"Then don't waste any time here, go do it."

The tiny fragile looking woman didn't stutter, her words were blasts erupting from her mouth. No, they were bullets, and her mouth was a machine gun. I dared not laugh in her presence, but my mood changed with my thoughts of her mouth being a machine gun.

I was driven back to the airport where my crew and Isadora were waiting in my plane. She offered more Cognac. I nodded and watched as she poured it in a Waterford glass.

I had been trying for more than a year to get Miguel to ease up his attitude on Mala. My head was pounding, and the tension was fierce. The plane was just taxiing, and the flight home was barely underway. It was dark out there, the runway lights brilliant against the dead black darkness beyond. Sans runway lights, the view of Juarez from the airport at ground level was like gazing into a bottomless pit. The contrast hurt my eyes.

"Close the curtain," I told her. I watched as she did what I told her to. I mentally compared lovely, compliant Isadora to stubborn old Mala, and shuddered.

"Sit on my lap while we take off."

"I thought you'd never ask."

She hugged me. We kissed as the plane made its turn to the main runway.

"I've always wanted you inside of me when we go wheels up," she said.

She got off my lap, unzipped me, and I came a minute after she mounted me. It was at least ten minutes before we released our grasp on each other. Loneliness clouded above me. Too much cognac depresses me. Mala depresses me.

At eleven the next morning, I was again in my plane, wheels up and on to the capital city of Chihuahua where Miguel was spending time before he was sworn in. He was moving his family into the governor's mansion there.

His home since birth had been in the state of Nuevo Leon, but two years ago, he'd bought a house in Chihuahua to establish residency. I had never been to the new house. I knew he looked forward to living in the governor's residence as had all other governors before him.

A driver and car drove up as I deplaned. The plan was to meet Miguel at our favorite restaurant, Mansion, in a private room where we would have lunch. Outside of the room where we were, the restaurant was all arches, cream-colored walls, cast-iron railings and hungry high-end diners enjoying good food. One of Miguel's bodyguards led me from the entrance where we had a massive table with two place settings, and stark white walls relieved only by a black and white Chihuahua map on the wall, and an installation of several black framed gold paintings, little more than post card size. They were too small to see what the paintings were meant to represent, if they were anything at all. But I did not have to waste time examining the room, because Miguel was waiting for me.

We started with a bottle of wine and light appetizers. I had a cup of creme de chile poblano soup that was very good. Three bodyguards who accompanied Miguel everywhere waited inside the restaurant, outside of our private room. The waiters walked past the hard-eyed guards like through a gauntlet to deliver our food.

I put down my soup spoon.

"I met with Mala yesterday. She said you should go after the businesses you believe are hers, and she wishes you good luck."

"We haven't even made a toast, and already you bring up that bitch."

I had to remedy that. I reached for my glass and toasted Miguel's health. We clinked glasses and smiled at each other.

"She's my client, bro. In the years I've done work for her, I have not seen a single indication of drugs. It's possible all that was buried with her husband Beto." *I knew there was a drug business because for years I had been making payments to government officials and others to protect the cartel, but it was true that I knew nothing that tied Mala to the cartel.*

"Listen to what you are saying," Miguel said. "She has you brainwashed."

"You know I'm not that easy," I reminded him.

"Since your father passed away, you have continued wining and dining all the important people that she needs to protect her business. Plying them with food, paying them off with cash, expensive meals, and champagne."

I felt a rush of anger. If I punched him, it wouldn't be the first time. If he punched me back, it wouldn't be the first time either.

I punched him. I didn't even get out of my chair. His eyes widened, but he didn't lose his seating.

He punched me back. I could have dodged it, but I let it hit me in the jaw.

We sat there looking at each other.

I was first to pick up my drink and make peace. I held my glass out for him to clink it.

He did.

"Good thing my bodyguards are outside," he said, not as my childhood friend but in his guise as the governor elect.

"Mine are out there as well," I said. "You talk like you have proof that I'm paying anyone off. My job is not paying people off," I lied. My job was broader than just paying people off, but my friend had it right. What made me angry is that I know he has zero proof.

"I have proof," he said then grinned.

"Asshole. You know she has businesses and property everywhere. That's what I do. I keep it flowing with trusted managers that work for her. There are no payoffs and there is no cartel that she can possibly be in control of. You should see her. She's fragile, she can barely move around." That was also a lie. She moved around real good with the help of her cane.

"I don't believe you."

"That's all you have to say?"

"I don't believe you. I don't expect you to disclose anything."

I sighed. "Brother, help me out. Let me tell her you have no interest in her personally, but you plan to go after all the drug operations in the state and shut them down and imprison her trusted people she has running the businesses."

Miguel smiled. "You see, you do know about her drug business."

"I swear I don't. I'm trying to find something I can tell her that aligns with what she told me to tell you, that you should go after the drug operations you think are hers."

Our silence was broken when three waiters appeared to serve our main dish, chicken in molé sauce. The corn tortillas were so hot that I burned my hand picking one up. Hot is the only way to appreciate their fresh deliciousness. I dipped the steaming tortilla in the molé, popped it in my mouth and savored it.

"You flew all the way here," Miguel said. "I don't have the heart to send you back empty-handed as when we met at El Cid."

Miguel, he could be serious, or he could be joking.

"Talk to me," I said.

"If she leaves Mexico, it's over. It's my intention to shut down all her drug operations in Mexico. Thanks for getting her permission for me to do that." He laughed. "I'll burn them to the ground."

"Go for it. Find where the businesses are and burn them down."

"Now it's you giving me permission."

"She's old but her hearing and eyesight are good. She heard what you said during your campaign, calling her out by name on radio, on television. You should be talking about opening up more schools and attending to the homeless. If the drug business was thriving here, these bums would be working. I know this is all for your brother. Miguel, let your brother rest in peace."

"My brother is not going to rest in peace until Mala dies."

"Please stop it."

"I want my state to stop hosting Mala's business."

"You sound like a broken record, bro."

"You sound like a brainwashed fool."

"If you go in with troops, you'll start a war in Juarez. Since I've been with her, I've learned the people fear her, but they love her at the same time. Don't be stupid."

"I'm giving your client a big break. She can get on a plane and go away by the time I am sworn in and there will be no reason for a war in Juarez. What part of this offer don't you understand?"

"She knows you have nothing on her. She will resist."

"Just because your father fixed it back in the day does not mean it will stay fixed."

"Leave my father out of it. He's not here any longer to defend himself," I said.

"And my brother is not here to defend himself," Miguel said quietly, staring into my eyes. "I take office in two weeks. All she has to do is leave Mexico."

"If she leaves, what happens?"

"Nothing. I will use every means at my disposal to kill her drug business. When I find them, whoever is running the businesses, they will be thrown under the bus. Simple."

"You have nothing on her to force her to leave. She's a business-woman who owns property throughout this state that you will govern. I can attest that everything she owns here is legally registered, and her taxes are current."

"If you don't want this generous deal I just gave you, tell me now."

"She's not going to like this deal. If it's not her idea, she won't like it. She's not making the decision to leave on her own."

"If she resists, she'll be shot."

"I don't believe you'd do that."

"You can tell her that I will request federal soldiers to run her out of the country or imprison her while we collect evidence of decades of atrocities that she's committed. If she is too much of an encumbrance, she will be shot."

"You mean the stray bullet you told me about before."

"Exactly."

"Miguel, come on. She's got to be ninety."

"By now, Jaime would be married. If she hadn't killed him with her heroin, I'd have nephews and nieces."

I'd had this conversation with Miguel too many times.

Miguel called a helicopter to deliver us to his Chihuahua home thirty miles from the capital. As we waited a few minutes for it to arrive, the same topic reared its familiar head.

"For you Mauro, and only for you, I'll settle for her leaving the state, but if she's not out when I take office, I'll exterminate her like a cockroach. I won't forget my brother died of an overdose. I hate that woman. My entire family is waiting for me to eradicate her and her business from the face of the earth. If they learn I have orchestrated a way out for her, they will not understand. I am doing it for you."

"When she's gone, someone will take her place," I said.

"I'll exterminate whoever takes her place. Our state is going to free itself of this curse we have been living with for decades."

It was in essence the same conversation we'd had at lunch.

I got off the helicopter with him to say hello to my wife's sister. I got a tour of the new house, an orange adobe and brick masterpiece. It did not measure up to the estate they had back home where they really domiciled.

"I can't believe you are going to leave this home to live at the governor's mansion in Chihuahua," I kidded my sister-in-law.

Miguel gave me a dirty look. He was being playful now; we were so much alike.

Mala was up to her eyeballs in the drug business, though I had never seen any indication of it. I made payoffs, but I was not in on what they were for, other to maintain the status quo. I was only a messenger who delivered money.

"I can't believe we are leaving for the governor's mansion," Melina said, putting her arm around his waist. She looked much like my wife Mina. They were sisters but not twins. "Five bedrooms, ten thousand square feet. We all but gutted this place. If we sell it while we're in the governor's mansion, we'll double our money."

"I like the courtyard, the outdoor Sala, and the rooftop living area outside of your bedroom. Don't send Mina pictures. If you do, I'll be remodeling the big house again."

"Too late," Melina said, giggling. "They're already in the mail."

With Melina around, Mala talk was off the table. Conversation delved no deeper than where they sourced turquoise bathroom tile, their trials finding an artist to carve the wooden deer's head in their bedroom, and how much ironwork was added to all the balconies they'd put in. Melina gave me the business card of the artist who had done a mosaic above one of their outdoor couches.

Eventually, the helicopter delivered me to the airport in Chihuahua where my crew and plane were waiting. Isadora was standing at the door as I came up the stairs. It was evening but where she stood was brightly lit, highlighting her assets, the long bangs she wore, and the blunt cut and gleam of her straight black hair. I wished the flight home was longer so I could spend more time with her. She lit a fire in me.

Passing the cockpit, I said, "Take me home."

Isadora rubbed my temples. My eyes closed. She moved from behind my seat where she was standing and sat on my lap, her legs over one side of the arm of the seat. My arms went around her. My mind wandered.

Monterrey was my home. As Miguel's main residence was, my house was fifty miles from Monterrey. My father would have never become a millionaire and tycoon if he had limited his law practice to

Monterrey, Nuevo Leon. The Hidalgos were behind my father's wealth going back decades, and behind my own for the last ten years. Even if I never admitted the truth to a soul, I knew that even the plane I was in had been purchased with drug money.

I was in this. I had to see it through. It would all be so much easier if Mala died of old age. She had to be ninety. If she were to die, that would solve my dilemma. Everyone—including me—was sick and tired of being terrified of her. I don't need her stress; I don't need her money. My father left me a wealthy man. I had an enormous amount of money and assets on top of my inheritance. It was greed and fear of her that drove me to stay on.

Looking back, I can see that it's been easy money. My father left arrangements so perfect that there was very little for me to do. It's not like acquiring property in her name was challenging. It was, in fact, a heady experience to handle that much money so freely. Miguel guessed that I pay off high ranking government officials. It is true. I wine and dine them and pass along money from Mala. He has no way of knowing this for sure.

If there is a change in the routine, such as the amount, the recipient, if someone dies or retires and no longer gets an envelope, Mala tells me in person. I've often wondered why she needs me to be the messenger, but that is a mystery to me.

When I got home, Mina was in our disco communing with our jukebox. The disco is what we call our huge party room with a flawless parquet dance floor where she was dancing barefoot to a song when I walked in. The kids were nowhere in sight, and the music was not loud. When we're in here together the music is loud. She was caught up in the music and got startled when I caught her hand and pulled her into the few steps of a jitterbug. I am not much of a dancer, but she is and being her husband, there were some things I'd had to master. It was almost the end of the song, so we did our favorite romantic embrace at the end. Then I picked her off her feet, set her on a bar stool, and kissed her till she cried uncle.

"Amor," I said. "I'm finally back. I stopped to see Melina."

"Amor," she said back, and we hugged. She remained on the bar stool, with her hands looped loosely over my shoulders. She smelled delicious.

"Yes, I talked to her by phone after you left."

"The kids couldn't wait up for Papi?"

"They're in their rooms. I doubt they are in bed. Go see them."

I kissed her. "I'll go check on them and be right back."

"Do you want something to eat?"

"I'm starved for tacos, beef and chicken."

"I'll call Marco."

I don't often count my blessings. I'm blessed with two beautiful daughters, two beautiful sons, and Mina of course. It doesn't matter how many women I come across. Mina is the only important woman in the world for me. I don't just love her. I adore her.

One of her bodyguards finks her out when she has lunch with girl-friends then meets up with Ricardo Lopez, a lawyer we have known for years. He is two years younger than I am and is a soccer player on the weekends. He's fit and looks younger than his age. I welcomed the news when I first heard it because it makes me feel less guilty. I hope she feels the same, that I'm the most important man in her life no matter who she beds.

Before I went back to the disco room, I summoned Mala's messenger. He had a place in the building where our live-in domestics stay.

"Let her know I will be there day after tomorrow at one in the afternoon. Await her reply."

"Right away, sir. I will leave for Juarez immediately."

Five minutes after I rejoined Mina, Marco placed a big plate of tacos in front of me.

"Plenty here for both of us," I said. "Buen Provecho[1], Amor."

I ate heartily. I fed her a taco, and she fed me one.

"Amor are you happy with me?" she asked softly.

I turned on my right to face her.

"I adore you, Amor. You and my children are the most important people in this world to me. The only important people."

She kissed my hand and smiled.

"I am feeling a little melancholy," she said. "I think you need to make love to me."

I got up and pulled her to her feet.

"Amor, finish eating."

"Later," I said, dipping my head to kiss away a morsel at the corner of her mouth. I walked with her to the back of the disco. Neon lights in many colors made the room festive. Three sofa seats were waiting for us. I dropped my pants, pulling her slacks off. Her legs went over my shoulders. I needed no help finding my way in deep.

"I love you, Mauro."

We went to our bedroom and had dessert—each other. We never stopped, but at some point, fell asleep entangled. With other women, sex is fast. I can't go long at all. With my wife, Mina, it's a different story. The two of us can keep going.

In the morning, the messenger confirmed Mala would be awaiting my arrival. Before the children took off for school, we actually had breakfast together. As Mina watched, I got an update from each about how their lives were going. It was a joyful morning, a rare day to be together like that. I spent the entire day at home. While Mina showered, I walked around the house that I knew so well. I didn't visit every room like I did that morning. Many of the rooms were still untouched from the décor of my childhood. Mina and I had redecorated many rooms, like the disco. Like Miguel's wife, Mina had a talent for decorating. We've had gatherings where a hundred people sat in this room and another fifty or more stood around.

I rehearsed how I would explain to Mala that leaving Mexico was not so bad. My father had always said that Mala and her husband knew that one day, their time in the drug business could come to an end. All the more reason to build a mountain of money that extended across Mexico and the seven seas to countries abroad. And she had done that.

.   .   .

We had breakfast together again on the day I was scheduled to see Mala. I gave each of my sons and daughters a special hug. When I was about to leave for Juarez, Mina walked me outside where a golf cart and driver awaited me. I gave Mina a big hug and a very wet kiss.

"I wish you had time for a quick one," she said.

"I promise to make up for it when I get back tonight."

"I'll be waiting," she said. "Good luck with Mala."

"I'll need it."

Mina's look turned to concern. "Is everything okay?"

I smiled. "Yes, I promise, all is okay," I lied with a big smile.

The driver pulled away and carted me to my airfield where my plane and crew were waiting for me to board.

Isadora was at the door when I entered the plane. I kissed her cheek. The cockpit door was open.

"Hola," I said. "Juarez, here we come."

"You're in good spirits, Jefe," Isadora said, following me to the back of the plane.

"I'm always in good spirits."

"Yes, you are," she said. "What can I get you?"

"Coffee, black."

"Nothing to eat?"

"I ate too much breakfast," I said. It was the truth. I stood up and loosened my belt.

I opened the Monterrey newspaper and scanned the headlines. I felt suddenly sleepy. When she brought me the coffee, I told her to take it back. I really didn't want anything. I reclined and closed my eyes. The plane roared along the runway, and we were wheels up. I dozed off. People insist that breakfast is the most important meal of the day. It only makes me sleepy.

My catnap was interrupted by my pilot's voice over the PA system. I looked at my watch. I had slept hard for two hours. Some catnap.

"Señor Robles, vamos llegando a Juárez."[2]

I fastened my seat belt. Isadora was there.

"Can I get you anything?" she asked.

"Ask me that when I come back from my meeting," I said, matching her smile.

"That's a date," she said.

She reached down to the buckle of the seat belt that was already snapped and rubbed her hand against me where it mattered. I smiled. She smiled. Then she went to the front of the plane.

I put my seat into the forward position, locked it in place, and looked out the window at the familiar outskirts of Juarez, Mala's city. Miguel would be sworn in in two weeks, by which time Mala had to leave the country. His offer was generous. I could not tell her it was generous. That wasn't something she'd be receptive to.

During the years I had been with her, this was the first time she had put so much pressure on me. She is networked and has eyes everywhere, one of the practices that make her so dangerous. She is a woman who knows everything. Mala knew that Miguel and I are like brothers. She didn't ask for compliance. She ordered me to get him to stop with the promises that he would destroy her when he was elected governor. She didn't seem to care about the promises to kill the drug trafficking. In her view, she was isolated from that. And now I should go convince Mala that she should leave. This was not something she was going to take well.

----

1. Bon Appetite
2. Mr. Robles, we are arriving in Juarez

CHAPTER 39
ISADORA

AFTER MAURO LEFT, the fuel was topped off, the pilots did an exterior inspection, then they took off to the terminal to kill time. They had a walkie talkie in case something came up and I needed to contact them. I took ten minutes to clean and buff the chrome in the galley before I sat near the doorway. It was already shining so I could see myself, but I kept on buffing. I had three magazines to go through, but I was saving those to keep my eyes open if Mauro dozed off. I was looking forward to the flight.

When the plane does a rhythmic one-two rock from side to side, it's because someone has stepped on the stairs. It was a bigger jolt than usual, so I thought it was both the pilots, but when I looked up, it was the fat cop that I hadn't seen since the first time he entered my life back home in Monterrey. This was Juarez. He wasn't supposed to be here. My heart jumped, and I stepped backward and fell into the seat.

He was as repugnant as I remembered. I remained seated.

"You're alone?" he asked.

That was not something I wanted to admit to him.

"I'm alone," I said.

He reached in a paper bag he was carrying. I had no clue what he was doing and cringed. Then, I saw the stack of pesos bound with a rubber band.

"Split this with the cameraman. I don't need any more pictures."

My heart was still racing from his unwanted arrival. How could I not smile at the bundle of cash? I smiled. My smile felt mechanical.

"You are very generous."

"It's not my money," he said.

I nodded my understanding. I didn't ask whose it was.

"When you land at his house, do not get off the plane before him or with him. Do you understand?"

"Yes, I understand."

He put his index finger up to his lips. He actually smiled, not a pretty sight. It was more of a leer.

"Tell only the photographer. Do you understand?"

"Yes."

His eyes flickered over me, not on my face. If you've ever seen the "undressing-me-with-his-eyes" look, you'd recognize it here. "You are a beautiful woman, Isadora."

I heard the implication in his words, and they floored me. He looked toward the back of the plane where I'd been naked on film with Mauro. He gave a nasty little laugh and looked back at me.

He looked me up and down again. He turned for the entrance and he could not see the expression on my face. He turned his back to me to face the exit, a broad back as wide as the door.

Still sitting, crumpled paper bag on my lap, I watched him leave.

A chill went through me. You needed to be me in that moment to understand how I felt. It's disturbing and contradictory to be frightened and get a hot sexual jolt at the same time.

I took the bills out, examined them, and put the bundle back in the paper bag. I went to the galley closet where I had my purse and stashed it inside. I returned to my seat and sat there in a sort of daze overwhelmed with revulsion and dread. Something terrible was going to happen, and I wasn't going to do anything about it. Mauro was not back yet. I didn't know what to think. The plane rocked a little, and a stab of terror popped me into the moment. My heart was racing in case it was the return of my new "admirer," the fat cop. I was glad to see the two pilots on the stairs. A cool wave of relief washed over me, not just because it wasn't the cop. I was glad to see Tomas. The captain went into the cockpit.

Tomas saw my wave.

The two of us retreated to the galley. I fooled with stacking and re-stacking an assortment of galley supplies as I told him about the visitor he had missed, and his order about not getting off the plane first. I told him that there weren't going to be more pictures.

Tomas asked no questions but looked through the window at the airfield as if there was a giant X out there, written in stone.

"Fats left something for us. You drive me home after we land, and we can handle it."

He nodded, turned around, and went to the cockpit as if everything were normal. A little later, both pilots came out. I served them refreshments and ham sandwiches on toasted *pan bolillo*. The plane's galley was stocked with several varieties of soft drinks, condiments, cheeses, cold cuts, and breads, but the last thing I was thinking about was building a sandwich.

Mauro had been gone about two hours. We never knew exactly when he was going to return, but he was rarely gone more than three hours from the time he left.

I was fidgety and nervous. I tried to look busy with a magazine while they ate across from each other across the aisle from me. I was open to somewhere in the middle, but it could have been written in Swahili. The words fell out of my mind like sand through a sieve. I avoided looking at Tomas.

CHAPTER 40
MAURO ROBLES

IT WASN'T long before I entered the study where Mala was waiting. Her white-streaked gray hair was pulled back into a bun. Her hands were clasped almost in prayer, elbows on the desk. On her, the look was slightly satanic, like some wicked witch out of a fairy tale. The skin of her hands fit loosely, translucent wrinkles over ropey blue veins, swollen knuckles, long red talons polished to perfection. She looked down, reached for a feathered quill, dipped it in ink, and began writing something on a sheet of paper. Only after a moment of writing, did she look up at me and motion for me to take a seat.

"I can tell you have bad news."

"I got him to agree not to pursue criminal action as long as you leave the country before he takes office."

"Do you consider that an accomplishment?"

"It's not an accomplishment, but it's an improvement on the message I delivered on my last visit. Mala, my father told me that you and your husband never knew how long your business would last. If this is true, why not consider moving on? Enjoy your life with your grandsons. You won, you outlived everyone who believed you would not last."

At best she seemed to be listening, but only for a minute.

"How can he pursue criminal action when I've done nothing criminal?"

"That is precisely what I told him. He wasn't listening. I got so mad I punched him in the face."

I didn't mention he punched me back. I didn't mention that we'd punched each other ever since we boxed in school.

"I don't want to hear you punched him in the face. That's not diplomatic."

"Well, I did. He's stubborn. His entire family is stubborn. A herd of mules, they are."

Mala was thoughtful.

"I will not be pushed out by a stupid politician who blames me for his brother's overdose years ago. I lost my own daughter that way. It's the person, not the heroin. It's ancient history."

"Mala, you know I'm on your side. Miguel will not budge. I told him a thousand times that I know of no drug business. I told him that after ten years representing you, if such a thing were true, I would know something."

"You should have killed him."

"You are angry. It breaks my heart to be here with this message. I know you take orders from no one. He's not saying you have to go, but if you stay, it will be war. The alternative will not be good, Mala. If you leave Juarez by the time his term begins, he will let you go. Better to leave and live to fight another day."

She didn't look happy, but she was listening. I figured I'd tell her Bella's message from the sitting governor.

"The outgoing governor's message to you was to take a vacation away from Mexico for a while. His assistant Bella told me this."

"Now that he's out of office and off the pay list, he's giving me advice to leave the country."

"I'm only delivering the message. Once he's out of office, he has no power to protect you. He's helpless to control the incoming governor. You don't have to leave for good. While you're gone, I can try and smooth things over. Everything cools off given enough time. Mala, please listen to me."

I thought she wasn't listening. She took a letter from the top of a stack on her desk. She ripped it in half her trembling hands betraying her age, then wadded it into a mass she tossed angrily into the trash.

She turned her eyes on me. I could see the rage there, in her eyes, in her contorted expression.

"You have failed me," she hissed, spraying me with saliva. "Your friend plans to destroy me. He must know that my businesses will not be so easy to destroy. He wants to come in here with soldiers, have me put up a fight, and kill me. That's what your friend wants. That will please his family. His father is alive only because he's waiting on revenge. He acts like I personally killed his son. He needs to face facts. His son was an addict."

"Mala, they are foolish. I tried."

"You are not strong like your father," she hissed. "He would not have quit with the job unfinished."

"He is giving you time to leave, Mala."

"Should I thank him and retire to Spain? I think not. Miguel will be the one who will be retired."

I thought of her villa in Spain which she had not even seen except in pictures. Two of this estate would fit on the acreage, and three of this old house would fit into the mansion there.

"You had to be thinking of retiring or you would not have bought the property in Madrid."

"You are right. I thought about picking up and moving there but it would have been my decision, not the governor-elect ordering me to leave my country with my tail between my legs like a whipped dog. I am the leader of the pack, and he is nothing."

"I don't blame you for being angry but please don't be angry with me."

"I am going to have that friend of yours blown away. Do you plan to warn him? Are you going to fly and tell him?"

She was fuming.

"Mala! Don't talk that way."

The blood rushed in my ears, pulsed at my throat, pounded in my chest.

"When your father was alive, he knew everything. He helped me in every way possible. For ten years, you've been doing easy work, raking in millions for finding and buying property for me and my grandsons. Wining and dining and delivering envelopes to the same people your father took care of. I am very disappointed in you, Mauro. Your father would be too."

She walked around her desk, opened a drawer, and took out a large envelope. She reached inside it and pulled out a bundle of photographs. Must have been a hundred of them sprawled across the desk. I could see Isadora and me in different positions. I could hear Mala's heavy breathing.

"You'd rather fuck this woman than give me the time I have paid for to get a job done. You are sidetracked by activities like these." She pointed down at the pictures. "You're a sex maniac. That's what you are." Her voice was harsh.

"You have no right invading my private life, Mala. I only saw Isadora in the plane going back and forth while doing your bidding. There was no interference with the work I did for you."

She pointed her right hand at me, the pointed red talon a perfect contrast to her shriveled witch's claw.

"You failed me!"

"Leaving the country could save your life. Listen to me, Mala. You can survive this."

Mala's narrowed eyes disappeared in wrinkles, and her mouth had pinched down to a hard point. Her color was high, an unflattering red flush almost the red of a turkey's wattle. I feared for her life, wondering if her old veins would give out in a burst of blood. Had her grandsons seen her in this ugly rage? We were alone in the study. If she just died, her reign of terror would be over. I thought of choking her. I made an unholy prayer: Let her have a heart attack this second, and it's over.

"Miguel plans on calling the president for federal soldiers. He will come looking for you. He has no evidence against you for anything. I warned him it would be a war because this is your city, and you are loved here."

"War it will be. I know," she snapped. "I know. I am La Mala of Mexico. I am not afraid of state governors. Who does he think he is? Who does he think he's dealing with?"

"Let's talk this out, Mala."

"You talked and got nothing done. The time for talk is done. Rico and Victor are in business now. Rico is expanding across Mexico and plans many big businesses that will pay taxes, enrich the government. Your fool friend, does he know this?"

"This has nothing to do with Rico and Victor," I said.

"How generous of this *bastardo* to single me out. I hate this man with a passion."

She snarled as she talked, her lips drawn back over her teeth, reminding me of a rabid dog. I never seen a rabid dog, but she looked rabid.

I wanted to shout and scream. I wanted to choke her. I pictured choking her, practically felt her fragile neck in my grasp. She would collapse where she stood, and I would have to flee. I'd never get out of the house alive. If I did, what would happen to me? How would I get out of the house with her lying dead across her desk? The only escape from my crazy thoughts was to leave Mala's house before I acted on impulse.

I got up from my chair and took a step backward.

"Where are you going?" she yelled as I walked out. "You cannot walk out! We are not done!"

I backed out of the room, stormed down the hall, out of Mala's house, out of her world. I was as doomed as if I had strangled her in fact, instead of leaving. Mina's face flashed in my brain. My kids' faces. I could only hope they were safe. Who should I blame? Who should I hate more, Mala for being the fanatical kingpin she was, or my best friend, Miguel for being so fucking stupid?

Even if Mala's heroin had killed Miguel's brother Jaime decades ago, it was Miguel's refusal to cooperate that would be the death of me. She had never threatened me. Even now, she had only offered intimidation not a direct threat to me or mine. Maybe I shouldn't have stormed out. But I kept walking.

She had been up to no good for some time. Assembling those photos had taken time and planning. What lunatic plans had she made for those pictures of Isadora and me?

. . .

I counted myself lucky that Gusto drove me to the airport without any interference from Mala. I could have hailed a taxi, but he had been waiting as usual. I was distracted. I got in and rode all the way while looking at the back of Gusto's head. We were almost at the airport. Maybe I should have taken a taxi. Would I even get to the airport? I felt a wave of terror. The odds of my survival were dropping. What did I need to do to protect my family and myself from Mala? Why was I thinking of this only now? Had my father had some kind of fail-safe so that she did not dispose of him on a whim?

Miraculously, Gusto left without incident, and I boarded the plane with a mix of relief at arriving intact.

I was at the steps of my plane when the question hit me like a ton of bricks.

How did the pictures get taken?

Isadora must have been involved but who took the photos? Did she know someone had been taking pictures? Who was the photographer? But no one had been aboard but me and the crew. I felt fury at my pilots and Isadora who must have all been complicit.

She greeted me at the door as always. I waited till the door was shut. One of the pilots announced wheels up in seven minutes.

She walked ahead of me to my usual seat.

I stopped.

"Sit down right there and tell me how it is that Magda Hidalgo has photographs of you and me having sex?"

Maybe it was a minor point when my life was on the line, but I needed an answer.

"You mean Mala?"

"Yes, Mala."

"I don't understand," Isadora said, her lip trembling.

"You're a liar."

"I'm not a liar. I know nothing about any pictures."

"If you value your life, get away from me," I said. I was still roiling in rage. My guts were knotted with it. I hadn't finished off Mala. I wanted to jump out of my seat and choke Isadora. For the second time today, I came close to committing unfathomable violence.

Isadora stood there just out of arms reach, tears streaming down her face. She made a pinched noise and ran to the jump seat where she sat down crying. To see her, I had to lean into the aisle and strain to see her hiding on the other side of the galley.

I would double my family's bodyguards. Mala was not the only person who had guns and men. Fuck Mala. I planned to talk to one of my current guards.

The wave of turbulence we hit was an unwelcome interruption to my mindset. I was busy planning. The plane shivered and bucked like it had a mind of its own. I was not moved by the jolts, only annoyed.

"Mr. Robles, very sorry about that. We will be above it in a few minutes," one of the pilots said over the loudspeaker. Was he the one who had taken the pictures, or had it been Tomas? Were they both in on it? All three? My whole crew, all of them backstabbers. Mala had paid them off. I wondered how much, how many pieces of gold it had taken.

From my seat, I could see all the way to the cockpit door. Isadora had moved from the jump seat to a front seat near the entry to the plane.

"Bring me something to drink," I ordered loud enough for her to hear me.

The engines were roaring. The plane bounced around as the pilots fought to get above the clouds. I saw Isadora get up. She wobbled as she made her way into the galley, the floor bucking beneath her. I saw her slam back and forth, into the cabinet opposite the oven, and against the galley itself.

I wished that the turbulence would toss the bitch on her face. She had sold out to Mala.

Isadora carried the bottle of Louis XIII in one hand and my Waterford glass in the other hand. No tray. It's not like anyone could have carried anything on a tray, intact. Walking was like on a trampoline. The plane bounced like it was on my side, trying to knock Isadora off her feet, but she made it to me without falling.

Her lip was no longer trembling. Her demeanor was the same as always.

"Sorry about the bumps, sir."

"Oh, now I'm sir. You betrayed me."

"You have always been sir," she said, holding her chin high.

Isadora handed me the glass.

"I don't know what you mean. I don't know what pictures you were shown. I don't know how anyone could get pictures of us."

I did not believe a word she said, and I still felt like strangling her. I could have unloaded my rage on her. It would have been a relief, but it would have been a luxury. I hadn't the time to waste. I had too much to sort out before we landed.

Isadora poured. "You want me to leave the bottle?"

"Don't be stupid. That bottle cost seven hundred dollars."

She took my words like the ice maiden she was. Not a trace of an expression crossed her face. Faithless bitch.

The plane was shaking like it was ready to crack but I knew turbulence wouldn't damage the plane. My father had died of a heart attack. I could feel my heart beating fast, hear it in my ears. Doctors had told me to slow it down, had given me a list of things to do and not to do. I had tossed it away. Drinking had been on the list, I think. Maybe I should turn over a new leaf when I got home. I drank from the glass. The wild action of the plane made waves in the cognac. The bitch was still standing there. I could not stand to look at her beautiful heartless face.

"Yes, sir. I will return when you want more. It was a stupid question."

I saw her walk toward the galley. The double-crossing whore knew how to handle turbulence. She was a hell of a playactor.

Finally, we were above the clouds. The plane stopped shaking. The ride became smooth.

The pilot came over the speaker.

"We're good all the way home, sir."

The fear I had felt during the car ride to the airport had vanished. The solution was to get more protection. Miguel's bullet would take her down. My life could go back to normal. I could create a new normal. It was stupid of me to keep pushing him to lay off the bitch. With her dead, I would retire. My kids weren't babies any longer. Mina and I could travel, buy a house in Beverly Hills near the shopping Mina loved, maybe another one in Switzerland near the slopes I love.

Miguel had been right all along. Mala had to go, and I didn't mean simply away from Mexico.

The cabin flashed and went dark. Only the emergency lights were on.

I called for the bottle. Isadora came in a rush. I held out the glass and did not look at her plastic face.

"Would you like a snack, sir?"

"Just pour. That's all I want right now."

CHAPTER 41
ISADORA

I HAD BEEN RIGHT; Mala was behind the photos. Something had happened that she showed him. I thought they were going to be leveraged, you know, against his wife finding out. What a mess. I have never seen him mad like this. He's never been mad at me or screamed at me. Tomas was right. He's not a friend. He's the boss. That's it. No doubt he will fire me.

I turned on the cabin lights as we made a fast descent to Mauro's airfield. The wheels touched ground so smoothly, you couldn't feel the transition. A perfect landing.

I wanted to run back to ask Mauro to forgive me, but he didn't call for me. I waited near the galley on my feet as the plane taxied to the private hanger, a five-minute walk to his home.

I sat at the seat nearest the entrance. I was dying with dread. What did fat cop know that he had not spelled out?

The plane came to a stop. The captain came over the PA and said to open the door and lower the stairs. I did that and walked toward the galley. Mauro was ten seconds away from the exit. I stepped in front of him. He stopped.

"I'm sorry about the pictures, Mauro. My life depended on following orders."

I heard the slap before I felt the burning of my face. It was no love slap. It knocked me off my feet.

"Puta. I don't ever want to see you again."

He shoved past me and went out the door carrying his briefcase.

The pilots were still in the cockpit. I sat down. I did not dare look out the window.

The runway lights were on. Tall park lights lined the streets of the property and illuminated everything. It was always so when we returned at night. With the door open, I could hear the outside noises. I heard the approach of the groundskeeper's golf cart, coming to save Mauro the walk home. All routine.

Then not so routine.

I heard shots. After the third shot, I put my hands up to my ears. I heard a helicopter, the loud noise of the main rotor turning fast. The wake of its flight rattled the tall doors of the hanger.

It was like things were happening in jerky slow motion.

The captain tore out of the cockpit fast, shoving me.

"Stay down," he said, and rushed out the door, the plane rocking as he scrambled down the stairs. Tomas paused with me but only a moment. I looked through the open door. Mauro was lying face down on the pavement at the foot of the stairs, a pool of blood spreading around him. I found an airbag and dry-heaved into it. There was nothing to come up. Tomas deplaned a minute before me and joined the captain standing over the body. I deplaned, stepping over his body without looking at him again except to see that one of his feet was still on the bottom stair.

No one saw the shooter or the shooting but when the groundskeeper was found unconscious in the ornamental bushes, it became clear that the assassin had assaulted him, snatched the golf cart and the keeper's cap, used the cart to ride to the plane, and shot Mauro. He had run on foot to the helicopter to escape. The grounds were immense and entirely walled as far as I knew.

It was a half hour before the police arrived, and two hours before the pilots and I were told we could leave. They didn't talk to me long.

"What happened to you?" he asked about my face.

I touched the cheek Mauro had slapped. "I walked into the galley door when I heard the gunshots. I didn't see anything. Then the pilot ran out and told me to get down."

I waited for Tomas, who was driving me home. I heard one of the policemen say, "Gunman got away in the helicopter."

I heard a lot of things. I heard that the governor-elect was flying in from Chihuahua. He had been Mauro's friend.

Mauro's helipad is maybe a hundred meters from the hanger.

When we were walking to Tomas's car parked near the hanger, a plane was approaching. We had been hours waiting to be allowed to leave, more than enough time for a flight from Chihuahua that only took an hour. I assumed it was the incoming governor of the state, Mauro's friend, Miguel. Mauro's own private airstrip didn't get a whole lot of traffic.

"I feel torn," I said to Tomas. "Let's go. I want to cry but I have no more tears."

As soon as we exited the manned security gate, Tomas said, "Tell me everything the fat man told you."

"He said to split this with you and that he did not need any more pictures."

Tomas nodded.

I left nothing out.

"I guess that the gravy train is over," he said.

We sat in the car outside my apartment, counted and split the bundle of money. Fifty thousand pesos in hundreds were in that paper bag.

"It doesn't make sense that Mauro knew about the photos. It sounded to me like it was Mala who showed him. He was pissed off. He knew I cooperated."

"It's over," Tomas said. "Mala spared our lives."

"I believe it." I touched my face. Mauro was dead. For that, I deserved more than a slap. I hadn't wanted him dead, but I hadn't done anything to stop it. I hadn't expected this to end in death. I just thought someone was going to shake him down, blackmail him. It made no sense.

. "I guess we're out of a job," I said.

"Someone has to pilot the plane. Let's see what his wife does."

"You're right," I said. "Did I mention that seconds before he exited, he fired me?"

"No one else knows that," Tomas said. "Buck up. We've still got our jobs, for now, anyway."

"Yeah, you're right."

I let myself out of the car, said good night, and walked to the front door of my apartment. At least I had my lazy live-in boyfriend Pepe to come home to on a night like this.

I called out to him. The television was off but the lights in the living room were on. The bedroom was dark.

"Pepe," I said again. The bathroom was dark.

I put my purse on a chair and turned on the light in the bedroom. The bed was made but badly rumpled. I snapped, walked to the bed, pulled the covers off and I saw the empty cavity in the mattress.

The money was gone. His closet was empty, his drawers empty. Pepe was gone, and the money with him, everything but what I'd been paid today.

At least he didn't get the cash in my purse.

I guess I was fooling myself that I was out of tears. I sat on the edge of the ruined bed and cried till I couldn't cry any more. Face down on the bed, I wiped my eyes and snotty nose with the top sheet. It left a streak of makeup, but I didn't care. When I got up, I felt totally defeated. I walked in the bathroom and washed my face. That's when I saw the horrible bruise on my face.

I took a hot bath. That can usually cure anything. It didn't. But I did feel marginally better. I put on a robe. I passed up the wrecked bed and shook out a sheet on the sofa in the living room. I turned on the TV. Pepe was normally sitting here when I came home from work. At least I had my sofa to myself and didn't have to share the remote control. I went to the front and back doors to double-check they were dead bolted and chained shut, put my purse with the bundle of money on the coffee table and went to the kitchen to get a beer.

I was angry at Pepe, not just for stealing the money.

I was angry because without him, I was alone again.

CHAPTER 42
MIGUEL ALVARADO

I HAVE no respect for the outgoing governor, but I have nothing to gain by being at odds with him now that I am the governor elect. There were two house phones on the table because we were multitasking, going over the transition in play for the past month by our teams. The governor had just hung up after talking to his chief of staff, and I had just finished a phone interview by a local reporter. We were dining at the Mansion restaurant in Chihuahua. My term begins in two weeks.

My phone rang. I smiled at the governor.

"This better be important," I said into the phone.

It was my wife. Her sister Mina had just called to tell her that my friend, the brother of my heart, had been shot as he exited his plane. I dropped the phone and put both of my palms flat on the table and stared at the tablecloth in front of me. I don't know how long I stared. I felt numb. It could not be happening. I could hear Melina's tearful voice coming from the phone. "Miguel? Miguel, are you there?"

The governor looked at me while I worked to get my head on straight. He handed me a glass of Chivas.

"Mauro Robles has been shot," I said to the governor sitting across from me. I accepted the Chivas. Gulped it down, in fact. "No doubt Mala."

I picked up the phone and tried to speak to my wife.

The governor mumbled something to me and got on the other phone. I don't know who he called. Melina was close to hysteria, and frankly, though I was trying to be calm, so was I. I told her to let Mina know I would be there as soon as I could.

I heard sirens. Then they got louder. I set the phone on the cradle and realized the governor was off the phone. I was furious at the governor. For all I knew, he knew this was in the works. I knew he was on the take with Mala. I controlled myself. What good would it do for me to freak out? I might need his help between now and the time I will take office in October.

The sirens that had been growing ever louder sounded like they were in the restaurant with us. Our private room where we were dining was suddenly full of uniformed police, and then men in military uniforms. I shook hands with the governor.

"Whatever you need, Mr. Governor-Elect, count on me. Anything," he said. His last words to me. Surrounded by men who guarded him, the governor left the room where we had been dining.

CHAPTER 43
PERRO

I HAD JUST FINISHED PUTTING the high-powered American-made rifle together and had locked in the scope when I heard the sirens of many cars arriving in front of the restaurant, blocking the street. A horde of men exited military jeeps and vans and ran into the restaurant's main entry.

I let the rifle point to the ground, realizing this was not going to happen tonight.

I realized that Ignacio, a shooter like me, must have gone after Mauro Robles. I would know soon if Ignacio's hit was successful. It would be all over the news. These men were here to protect the governor and governor elect.

I had no time to regroup. I dismantled the rifle, jammed it back in the bag and left the helipad area. Tomorrow would be another day. Another day, another opportunity. They could not guard him forever. Mala, forgive me. There is no way I can get to Miguel Alvarado. You should see what I am looking at down there. Mala can't hear me. I'm here and she's in Juarez.

CHAPTER 44
MIGUEL ALVARADO

I WAS ESCORTED out of the restaurant surrounded by my security team, a crew of police and a collection of state military soldiers.

A helicopter across the street from the restaurant took off with the governor. My armed escorts took me to the top floor of the building where my helicopter had just landed.

Soldiers headed out to the airport to secure the area where my plane was. My new security team lead said to hover until we got word to land. My pilot did that. The helicopter took me to my private plane for a flight to Mauro's residence in Monterey.

As my plane was readied for departure, my assistant Carlos gave me the hard details he had been given by the chief of police in Monterrey.

Mauro took five bullets to the head at close range before he got to the last stair of his plane stairway. He was dead before he hit the pavement. The two pilots and one flight attendant were still on the plane and were unhurt. One of Mauro's groundskeepers had been injured. The cap and cart taken from him had been used in Mauro's assassination.

That wasn't all Carlos had to disseminate.

At Mauro Robles law office, the first of three bombs exploded. As it was after work hours, only two individuals were in the building at the time. A night watchman and a janitor were killed by the blast. The three-story building collapsed to the ground. Fire ensued, made worse by two more blasts.

Carlos offered his opinion. "I think she blew up the building to destroy any records Mauro may have had there."

"No. Mala blew it up because she is a hateful, controlling bitch. Everything she touches ends in fire. Ends in death."

"No doubt you are right," Carlos said.

"You bet I'm right."

Flying to Mauro's home, I felt anxiety like I never had before. I wanted to scream in anger. I wanted to scream in sorrow. I wanted to fall asleep and awaken with all of this having been a dream. I couldn't stand the wait. The plane was not moving fast enough. I paced, running out of aisle space rapidly then making a U-turn. My security team were seated and didn't meet my lost gaze as I passed them. I was loco.

I am troubled by angles I never thought of before. Am I responsible for Mauro's death?

Could I have been more reasonable with him about Mala?

He stood up for her and this is how she paid him back. Killing him as he got off his plane, steps away from his wife and children. What kind of a person does that?

Even an animal is not so cruel.

Mala, you are dead.

One of my pilots spoke to me over the PA system.

"Senor Governador, I have a clear view of the runway. All the lights are on and it's clear. I don't need to do a fly by. Please fasten your seatbelt. We'll be landing in a few minutes."

I looked out the window. At first all I saw outside was pitch black, then I could see the lights at a distance. I had wanted to get here in the worst way and now that I was so close, I dreaded the thought of what I would find after we landed. My friend was now a corpse, his wife Mina now a widow. Hopefully, the children were in bed, not awake. It would be difficult for them to learn of their father's death. My father and mother-in-law had probably arrived already.

"She's not going to like this deal. If it's not her idea, she won't like it. She's not making the decision to leave on her own." Mauro told me this. Mala didn't like the message about leaving and she killed him. I know that's what happened. I know. I know.

Mala you are a heartless devil, and you are dead. Your death is not enough. I will start with that followed by destroying everything you left behind including your grandchildren.

The body was already in the hearse in a body bag. The coroner and two morticians were waiting for me, waiting to drive Mauro's remains to a mortuary.

I would be lying if I said I was not sickened. Five bullets to the head at close range. I wish I could unsee it so that my last vision of Mauro was that of a whole man and not this horror that will haunt me till the end of my days.

A security man drove the golf cart. I rode in the back seat. I tried hard to maintain my composure. I was barraged by such a mass of emotion: fury at Mala for doing this terrible thing; graphic horror at my last sight of Mauro burned into my brain; grief for the loss of my dear friend; sympathy for what Mina must be feeling. I felt not a trace of the composure I was doing my best to project. As the governor elect, I had to keep my cool under all circumstances. A dozen security men walked beside and behind the motorized cart enroute to Mauro and Mina's residence. My back stiffened as I saw local police around the house as we approached the back entrance to the residence. As the cart approached, one of the policemen saw me and scurried inside. I'd been here so many times but never under such disastrous circumstances.

. . .

I found all the adults in the main living room of the house. Intermittent wails reverberated in my body in sympathetic waves of grief. I focused on Mina sitting on a snuggle chair. Her mother and father had huddled around her, my parents not far away. I knelt in front of Mina. When she saw it was me, her cry became hysterical. She hugged me, and I hugged her back.

Immediately, Mina's father said, "Years ago, I told Mauro to stop representing that devil woman. He wouldn't listen. Miguel, you have to do something!"

My father had tried for decades to take Mala down and failed.

"First order of business when you get sworn in, you promised me, Miguel," my father said from across the room where he was sitting with my mother.

I didn't reply. I was still hugging Mina. At least here, I was able to cry with her out of the public eye, with only family in the room.

After a temporary calm ensued, tea was served. Mina's house staff came around with Cognac and Scotch for those of us who required something stronger. Mina finally spoke. I sat on an ottoman directly in front of her.

"Miguel don't listen to my parents or your parents. Leave Mala be. Do not go after her. You will not take her down. If by some miracle you managed to topple her, none of us will ever be safe. For the first time in my life, I fear for the life of my children." She looked around at everyone else. "I fear for the life of everyone in this room." She returned her gaze to me. "Promise me."

I choked up. I couldn't speak.

The room was deathly silent as Mina cleared her throat. She got to her feet. I tried to help her, but she did not want any assistance.

"Mauro never talked about her. He only mentioned real estate he had found, the buying trips where he bought property for her grand-children. There was only one time." She closed her eyes briefly, like she was remembering, maybe seeing the moment in her head. "Over breakfast one morning, he seemed troubled. I can see him now, playing at putting the huevos rancheros into tortillas, but just moving things around his plate as the children do. I asked what was wrong." Mina opened her eyes and looked at me. "He was having problems convincing *you* to ignore your campaign promises." The tone of her voice changed, mimicking the aggressive delivery of my campaign rhetoric. It was a startling change. "You are going to rid the state and the country of Mala." Then as quickly as the powerful mannerism had come, it left. She settled back into herself, into her small, quiet, hurting voice. "I'm never going to know for sure. I fear that my husband's death is an example, a sample of what is to come if you were to move against her."

My parents were watching. Her parents were watching. They were all waiting for my response.

"I can't promise you to let it go," I said. "Can't you see? She must pay for this."

"You will have more security than ever before," Mina's father said. "Don't worry about retaliation."

"Papa, stop the nonsense," Mina said, her eyes fixed on mine. "If you go after her, you are signing your death warrant. You are signing my death warrant, and that of my children. Will that fulfill your ambition? Is that what you want?" Her tears were gone, and with it, the beaten-down demeanor. This Mina was angry. This was not the downtrodden widow. This Mina was the lioness defending her cubs.

I opened my arms to her.

She stepped backwards, shouting, "Promise me!"

I should have kept quiet, but I didn't.

"I can't make that promise."

"Leave my house right now," she said. She pointed to the door.

Everyone came up close, crowding us. Her parents. Mine.

"You don't mean that *hija*," her mother said.

"I don't want you around. As far as I am concerned, you are the angel of death. It's your fault my husband is dead. Your words provoked Mala. I can see that now. You created an impossible situation for Mauro. He asked you to back off, and you refused. Get out, now!"

I tried again to get her in my arms.

She turned her back on me.

"We are family, Mina. I loved Mauro. We considered ourselves to be brothers."

I stared at her back. She turned to face me again. "If we are family, promise me."

I could not make that promise. She pointed to the door.

I walked to my parents and hugged them. I hugged my in-laws and walked out of the living room. Accompanied by the security I had come with, I headed to my plane.

I heard my head of security radio the pilots.

"Wheels up, soon as possible."

"Plane is fueled and ready."

I kept clearing my throat like I had something stuck there,

I coughed.

I pictured Mina when she ordered me out of the house.

I pictured Mina when she blamed me for Mauro's death. There was a finality in her voice, in her expression. I could only hope her stance would loosen with time.

I am not a drinker like I was in my school days. I don't drink alone. I don't drink to get drunk, but on the plane going home, I asked for a bottle of Herradura Tequila. I finished it. I have a vague memory of landing on the private airstrip, and my security crew helping me off the plane and on to the helicopter. When we made it to the helipad on my property, apparently my wife was there to greet me, but I was dead to the world. Halfway roused to consciousness, I was apparently something of a handful that my security detail didn't know what to do with.

I woke in the throes of a nightmare. The photos in my brain were blurred but clear enough to see what was left of Mauro's head. In my stupor I knew it was not a nightmare. It was real. Mauro was assassinated and the only person on earth that would do this to him is Mala.

The inside of the helicopter was dark but the security lights outside were plentiful. Through the window, I saw my security team standing guard through the night, though my heart was still racing from the visions of Mauro in my dreams. I focused on Melina. I bent my head and kissed her awake.

"Amor mío, Amor. Amor, wake up."

My wife opened her beautiful eyes.

"Amor," she said, "tell me all this is not real. I need you to tell me, please Amor."

I couldn't speak.

I stood. So did she. My legs were stiff and painful, my head a giant throbbing ache. Only the crew and Melina knew how long I'd been knocked out, drunk.

CHAPTER 45
MALA

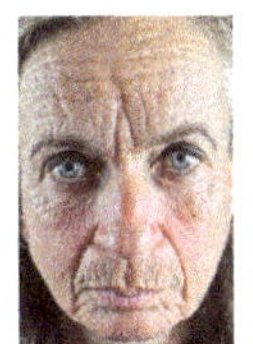

GENERAL GONZALES and I go back more than twenty years. I have trouble trusting, but if I had to trust one person not in my family, I would pick the general. I have never caught him in a lie. My attorneys have always paid all the other officials and politicians, but I deal with the general directly. He's stationed in Juarez, and his visits are always in secret. Outside of my closest staff, no one else sees him.

The general was across from me, his hair grayer than it had once been, but he'd held up pretty well. He was clean-shaven, short-haired, iron-jawed, and the buttons on his uniform were a little tight around the belly. I expect he put away more than his share of beer or tequila when he went home at night.

"I have not heard from anyone as of yet. Why do you think an attack on you is imminent?"

"The shooting of Mauro Robles is all over the news."

"I didn't hear your name mentioned. Have you?" he asked, making himself free of a cigar sitting in the humidor on my desk. He passed it under his nose, inhaled.

"No. I have heard nothing," I said. "Go ahead and light it if you wish. Mauro was here today. He told me that his friend the governor-elect expects me to leave Mexico before he's sworn in, or he will come here with soldiers."

The general stared at me quietly. He cut the cigar, swirled it in Crown Royal, and put it in his mouth, unlit. He rarely smoked in my presence, and never in my office. He sighed. "If he comes after you, I will know before it happens. What you need to worry about is not just a ground attack by soldiers. If the governor gets the backing of the president, they will come not just from the ground. Helicopters and small aircraft."

"How do you know this?"

He shrugged. "I know what works. If I knew anything for certain, I would be here to tell you immediately. We are friends, Mala."

I know he's being truthful with me. I nodded my head.

"I had nothing to do with my lawyer's death."

The general shrugged. "I believe anything you tell me."

I watched him take a small drink of the Royal Crown he favors.

"Here is what I'm afraid of. My lawyer Mauro is…was best friends with the governor- elect. You know the governor-elect's family hates me and has for decades blamed me for the overdose of one of their sons. After Mauro's death tonight, I am certain I will be blamed. That blame could be escalated into an attack here at my home."

"He's not governor yet." The general shrugged. "I wouldn't worry about it. I have a suggestion, however."

"Talk to me," I said.

"Consider leaving the country for a short time. Years ago, you showed me photographs of a villa you own in Spain. Why did you buy it if you don't plan to live there or visit?"

"I'll go to Spain if and when I'm ready, General. I'm not running away."

The general swirled the liquor in his glass. Without taking the cigar from his mouth, he had another drink.

"Magda, I am not telling you to leave. I am making a suggestion. If you decide to visit Spain for a month, a year, or a decade, no one will take over this property, I promise you."

"You are a good friend," I said.

"I treasure your friendship," he said.

I nodded my understanding.

I got up. We were done.

There was a briefcase on my desk at easy reach, reddish, crafted by a local artisan who excelled in such things. Diamonds of perfectly tanned alligator leather on the outside, several zippered pockets inside, holding enough money for him to finish his own villa if he so wished.

"There's a million pesos there. Take it with you, General."

"You are much too generous. Magda, you can count on me."

"More than ever before," I said.

He's never said but I believe he doesn't retire because he doesn't want to give up what I give him each month.

I knocked on my desk, summoning Gusto to escort the general out, and telling him to return. We were not yet done for the night.

Gusto has been my good right hand for a long time. Three reporters trespassed on the property here many years ago, on a night just like this, during one of the general's visits. I asked the general to leave before I cremated the intruders. The reporters had scaled the wall with an extension ladder, and guards caught them by the warehouse at midnight. By the time I was there, they were tied up in front of the furnace they planned to write about. They got to verify their story in person. Too bad they never got to write it. A lot of potential trouble has gone up in smoke in that chimney.

Gusto returned, reporting that the general left through the walkway under the street to the market, the same way he came on to the grounds.

I explained to Gusto my worry that the governor-elect's threats might escalate because of the assassination tonight.

"I'll call in our armed men right away," Gusto said.

That would be more than one hundred more to feed. "Let Maestro know, kitchen doesn't close down."

"I will take care of this," said Gusto, ready to run out.

"You are the best of the best," I said. "Have Angel come in, he's been waiting a long time."

• • •

I noticed when he came in that Angel Montes is not as thin a man as he used to be, but his skin hangs on him like it is a size too large. His mass of black hair has gray in it now, and he has to wear glasses when he is doing close work. He still has his massive beak of a nose and nervous mannerisms and often spends our meetings clicking the silver mechanical pencil I gave him years ago. Fortunately, the mechanical pencil is still in his pocket instead of in his long musician's fingers. I forget what instrument he plays.

"Angel, please sit down. I did not mean to keep you waiting."

He sat in the same chair the general occupied only minutes before.

"Mala, it is perfectly fine." Like the general, at times I'm Magda and other times, Mala.

Angel Montes is more than just an accountant. He is the treasurer of all my businesses. My late attorney, Raul Robles, worked with Angel perfecting the system that managed all my income. Angel gets one percent of every dollar he manages for me. He's made a fortune on that one percent.

"I don't know for sure, but it's possible that in the near future, I may be visiting my property in Spain. This new governor coming in is a crazy man determined to end me. While I am determined to defend myself and my property against anyone he sends, I cannot fight an attack from the air."

Angel, whose nervousness has always reminded me of a Chihuahua, jumped up, exclaiming his alarm.

"Sit," I said, shaking my head with impatience.

He sat.

"Yes, sorry to interrupt you," Angel said, his voice trembling. "I'm at your service."

There was a knock on the door. Angel didn't jump from that. His jumpiness is not that from fear, or he would never have lasted so long with me. He just has an excess of energy.

"Come in," I said.

The maid, Ricito, came in with two tall glasses of iced mineral water with twists of lime.

She put down coasters, placed the glasses in front of us, and hurried out into the hall.

"Listen carefully, Angel. If I leave, Gusto will be the person who will confirm I left. He will be in charge of the house. He will be me."

Angel nodded, verging on excitement. The mechanical pencil came out. He clicked it once, caught my glare, and stuck it back in his pocket.

"You will provide the money Gusto needs to run this house exactly as I have it right now. You know I pay everything with cash from the big safe here in the house. I want you to personally count the money in the safe and let me know how much is there. I want you to start tracking everything going out." I know it seems strange. I have never had the money counted. My husband, Beto, he always knew.

"You've always wanted to get the money counted," I said to Angel.

He smiled. The lines cut deep into his cheeks. I could tell he was happy.

"If I leave, I will send messengers to pick up information from you," I said. "And you will keep me abreast of everything with a messenger."

"Mala, I understand. I hope you don't have to leave." He sighed. "If you do, count on me as you always have."

I stared at him.

"Angel, I would be lost without you, but if you should ever cross the line, I will burn you. If I'm dead, someone else will cremate you and your family."

I saw color in his face. It was not the first time I had said this to him.

"I would never cross you," he said firmly. "You know this, Magda."

"You're a millionaire," I reminded him. "Your wealth grows as mine does."

"Mala, should you leave, I will miss you, but you can rest assured that your new money will be handled in the same way, and if there is a change, it will only be when you want to make a change."

"No change," I said.

Angel nodded. "Business as usual."

"How can you say business as usual? If I leave, I will be across an ocean?"

Angel jumped at the shrillness of my voice. "You know better. You have taught me well. I meant only that you don't need to worry."

"You know I hate telephones. Do not call me except to say hello. Cordial calls. I will do the same when I have sent a messenger to you. If there is anything business-related, or anything important, it goes through the messenger. Understand?"

"I understand, Mala."

I stood and Angel got up fast.

I followed Angel out of my office. Ricardo was sitting in a hardwood chair at the door to my study where normally Gusto would be waiting. He got up and escorted Angel out of the house and on to a golf cart that would take him to the front entrance of the property. Angel did not have to use the private walkway from the market across the street. Everyone knew he oversaw my properties all over the city.

Later that night, Gusto was back.

"What about Alberto, Rene, and Ramiro?"

Alberto, Rene, and Ramiro ran the drug operation. My generals. I paid for their protection every month and had not seen any of them for the last two years. By having that protection, they moved tons of product through Mexico to the United States and abroad.

"I sent messengers to see them," Gusto replied. "Our men are arriving now."

"Good work," I said. "Make sure they are comfortable and have plenty to eat and drink. No alcohol, you already know."

Gusto smiled and nodded an affirmative.

I walked to my bedroom.

On either side, Concha and Carmen walked beside me like they expected I was going to keel over any instant. They knew I would push them away if they tried to hold on to me. It infuriates me to be treated as if I am feeble, though it is true that moving around was becoming more difficult for me. I ran out of breath too easily, over nothing. Tea and coffee made my heart race and my throat burn with indigestion, but only I knew how I felt.

I went in my room alone and changed into pajamas. Even on steaming hot days, my house is kept cold. Air conditioning is worth it. Most of the pajamas are two pieces. My in-house seamstress makes them for me. Soft cotton with no buttons to poke me when I sleep. Light for summer, heavier flannel for winter. When I was young and married, things were different, but my husband has been six feet under for years now.

I sat on the side of my bed and turned off the light, but my mind did not stop.

Why had the general brought up an air attack? Why would he say that? Was he lying that he only guessed? Did he know something for certain? Damn him.

I pushed the bell button next to my bed. I heard a knock right away.

"Come in."

The door swung open, casting a stream of light from the hall, silhouetting Carmen.

"Have Gusto come see me."

Carmen looked puzzled. "Here?"

"Yes, here," I snapped. If it were somewhere else, I'd have said so. I could not help being impatient with Carmen being so slow on the uptake.

When Gusto came in my room, I was under the covers sitting up against three pillows, and I had switched on the bedside lamp again.

"I am taking advantage of you now that you moved in," I said.

"Not at all," Gusto said. "It is more efficient for me to be here."

"I've been thinking about the tunnel directly under the safe floor. If we get bombed, we're all going to die or be seriously injured. There's no sense having my money go up in smoke."

Gusto doesn't smile often, but he smiled then. "I understand. You want me to move it all?"

"All of it. It won't have the protection it has now but only for a short time."

The bigger bundles were wrapped in cellophane so strong a sharp blade was needed to tear it open.

"I will take care of it," Gusto said.

"Do not do it alone. You are too old for heavy lifting like that."

That got a laugh out of Gusto.

"Do not worry, Magda. I will have the bundles of cash relocated right away."

When he was gone, I moved the extra pillows.

So many people were dead. Vicente the tunnel builder was probably dead now. My husband, Beto, always had Vicente expanding the basement in different directions. The tunnel was built under the safe to hide money coming and going, not to protect it from bombs coming from above. It was built deep. Vicente always said it would be earthquake-proof. We don't have earthquakes in Juarez, so the tunnels had never been truly tested.

I hate second-guessing myself. Maybe I should not have had Mauro killed. It will be so inconvenient. Now I have to find someone to do the monthly rounds and payments.

I should have waited to have a replacement. It's too late now. Maybe I will let my generals worry about paying for their own protection starting tomorrow when I meet with them.

How stupid would that be of me?

Very stupid.

Too late to change anything that has happened. Mauro had been a fool, philandering with that woman on his plane and many others when he should have been concentrating on doing my business.

I clicked off the light, shutting myself in with the ghosts in my mind.

The bed could not be any more comfortable, but I could not find comfort. Sleep was elusive, even though it was dark and quiet. I was restless.

When you get as old as I am, you wonder if you will wake up in the morning. Sometimes I try to stay awake and not take a chance.

CHAPTER 46
MELINA ALVARADO

HIS PARENTS ARE MORE excited about Miguel being sworn in as governor than I am. His friends are excited too. My friends feel like I do. It's no big deal at all to be the first lady of the state. It's not even our state. We live on a gorgeous property and have purchased a beautiful home not far from the governor's mansion that Miguel wants us to occupy. The second house established our residency in the state so he would qualify to run for public office. I love him too much to tell him this drive of his (and his parents) to become governor has fucked up our lives. When I blow up at him, I tell him. This obsession of his turns me off at times, fills me with disgust and I get nauseous when I hear the same words over and over again about destroying Mala Hidalgo.

He has no political ambitions beyond his desire to destroy Mala. That ambition is the reason that my brother-in-law is dead, and my sister is a widow. She's scared that she and the children are next on Mala's list.

Miguel was drunk and sick. I've never seen him so drunk. The sight and smell of him in that condition made me ill. There was a moment when I felt us unlinking, but then…till death do us part. He had to be at rock bottom to need alcohol so badly. What could I do but be at his side to support him? Last night was rough. We made it to bed around six this morning. On the way, I roused my assistant Alessandra to make sure the nanny managed the girls so we could sleep. We slept until noon, something we never do as we are both early risers. I had planned to give him a piece of my mind, but he has to be conscious for that. What good is it if he isn't all there?

When he was out of the shower and before he dried off, I walked in the bathroom. I rejected his pass. We had issues to deal with.

"Mina told me she asked you to leave because you wouldn't promise her that your war with Mala is over."

"She just killed Mauro. How could it be over when she just put more fuel on the fire? More than ever, she needs to be stopped."

"You don't have enough protection from a woman like her."

"How do you know this? Do you know her personally? You and your sister are afraid of a ninety-year-old. What's wrong with you?"

"No, Miguel, what is wrong with you? You just said it. She's ninety. How much longer will she be around? Stop this mad pursuit. When she dies, this whole machine she has now will fall apart."

"I have a splitting headache. My throbbing head fills up this room. I can't take this. Leave the bathroom right now. Out, woman."

He made some effort to lighten his words, using his towel to snap at me. He winced dramatically, probably jostling his ailing head. Good. I stepped away from the towel which missed me, picked up a silver vase full of flowers and threw it at him. Didn't even come close to hitting him.

"*Imbecile!*" I shouted as the flowers and water scattered across the floor in his direction.

"Out. *Zorra.* Out."

I did as he said and headed out. But at the door, I stopped and shouted at him.

"I'm not moving with you to the governor's mansion. Shove your ego, your governorship, and your ambition to overthrow Mala. The kids and I are moving back home. Our real home."

I slammed the door.

• • •

We have three daughters, ten-year-old Rosa, nine-year-old Lucita, eight-year-old Bella. After Miguel left the property in his helicopter, my daughters, my assistant Alessandra, and I were aboard a rented helicopter on the way to the airport, just behind my security team. Mina sent Mauro's plane to take us home to Monterrey. It is Mina's plane now.

The helicopter landed near the awaiting plane. Isadora and two pilots whom I'd met many times before greeted us.

"You've been through a lot in the last forty-eight hours and here you are working to bring us home. Thank you very much."

"It is a pleasure, Senora Melina," Isadora replied.

Isadora had dark shadows under her eyes. She was still lovely, but I doubted she had been sleeping. I knew from Mina that Isadora had been fucking Mauro. I always figured Mina had been guessing because who would know? Did Mauro share that kind of thing with his wife? It didn't matter to me. Isadora would not have Mauro to take care of any longer.

My daughters were scuffling with each other competing for the seat they would be in for the ride home.

One of my security people, Federico approached. He said, "Your staff has been notified, and they are awaiting your arrival at home."

"Thank you," I said. "I plan to settle the girls in and go stay with Mina."

"As you wish," he said. "Are you in need of anything?"

"All good. Take a seat."

Isadora checked my daughters' seat belts and promised to get them refreshments after we took off.

"If you have coffee going, I need a mug of it. Black."

"Right away."

Isadora double stepped to the galley.

When my father called me on the night of the tragedy, he said the crew had heard but not seen who did the shooting. I wanted to mention something to Isadora but not now. I'd wait until we were in the air.

I feel so bad for Mauro. It is hard to believe he's dead.

On the phone, my father waited till Mina left the room, and told me there is nothing left of Mauro's face. He also said that he wouldn't let her see the body.

240

CHAPTER 47
ISADORA

ONE OF MINA'S security guards called me at home and asked if I felt up to working. He said Mrs. Robles wanted to send the plane to pick up her sister in Chihuahua and bring her to Monterrey. When the call came in, I had been trying to convince myself to leave for the supermarket because there was nothing in the house to eat. I mean, my pantry was entirely empty. The call to work was also a good sign that I was not getting fired. I was happy to get the call.

"Yes, give me the details. I will be wherever Mrs. Robles needs me."

In the shower, I first hummed a tune and by the time I was drying off, I was singing. Tomas had been right. If Mina keeps the plane, she needs a crew. The secret of the dirty pictures died with Mauro. The fat cop and Mala knew, but I didn't feel threatened by that.

I noticed that a security man was sitting in Mauro's favorite seat. If he only knew what we used to do on that seat. I should feel regret, but I had no control over what happened, and can't change anything I did. What I regret are my memories of the assassination: the horrible sounds of the shots as I realized what was happening; the horrible sight of Mauro at the foot of the plane steps in a pool of blood. This will be forever an imprint in my brain.

. . .

On many occasions, I had flown to Miguel's house. I was familiar with the outside of the Robles home estate. It has a landing field about the same size as Mauro's. Miguel has two helipads. Mauro has one. Miguel's Monterrey property had a hanger for two planes. Mauro's hanger was large but for one plane.

The pilot announced our impending arrival at Miguel and Melina's estate. I went around to make sure everyone was buckled in. It reminded me of when Mala's grandsons and their tutor came aboard to fly over the property in Baja California. Today, we had every seat filled. I felt like an airline stewardess again with this many people on board. The little girls were unnaturally polite, but I suppose that was drilled into them because their father had run for office. They were so cute and entertaining that I offered them too much in the way of snacks and drinks and escorted them so many times to the bathroom. They were fascinated by the bathroom. Bella, the youngest one, a dead ringer for her mother, asked if the potty emptied directly out into the sky.

As the plane touched down, I could see Melina was happy to be home. I wondered if she had left her husband. None of my business. It wasn't any of my business either how much Mina and Melina resembled each other. It was almost creepy, but only because Mina was so recently a widow to the dead man whose death was planted in my life like a big crossroads that I was doing my best to ignore.

This was not Mauro's airstrip where he had been killed. The proximity to the residence reminded me of Mauro's body lying at the foot of the stairs in a puddle of blood, within walking distance to his house where his wife Mina and children were.

CHAPTER 48
VICTOR

LESS THAN TWO hours after I got home at seven in the morning, Gusto was ringing the doorbell to let me know my grandmother and Rico were waiting for me.

Grandmother had messengered me to come home last night. At the time, I figured it could wait until morning. Well, the sun was up, and I wasn't. I put on jeans and sandals. As I walked out of my bedroom, I took a t-shirt from my closet.

My only two family members in this world were seated at the dining room table. I bolted through the big room, and before grandmother could say anything, I smothered her with kisses. My brother looked on with a big grin.

Grandma was at the head of the table. Rico and I were on her right and left sides, facing each other.

"You are up early," I said to Rico.

"I haven't been to bed yet."

"Enough small talk," Grandmother said. "My generals are arriving soon."

"I should have come right over," I said.

"I told grandmother I would have come right over," Rico said, "but Gusto couldn't find me." He laughed. One of his roars.

"Shut up," my grandmother said. "Enough."

I was hungry. "Can we order breakfast before we start talking?"

My grandmother stepped on the chime button, and two kitchen attendants joined us.

"Menudo," Rico said.

"Same," I said. I chugged two glasses of orange juice and worked on a cup of coffee. Grandmother was drinking tea. Rico was impatiently waiting for the food to be served.

"He had become worthless," my grandmother said of Mauro Robles.

"I liked him," Rico said.

"I did too," I said.

I had fond memories of the trip to Baja on his plane, and his patient explanation of my trust and Rico's.

"Do you have anyone to replace him?" Rico asked.

"I have lawyers if that's what you mean. You've met Luis from Mexico City but he's not going to give up what he has to become a Mauro for me. I also have another lawyer that represented the family of the past president of Mexico," Grandmother said impatiently. "I don't want to discuss that now."

"If my vote counts, it goes to Luis," I said. "What do you want to talk about?" I asked, hoping no one heard my stomach growling. The juice was gone as was the coffee.

"I have concerns that the incoming governor will make a move against me. He may come here with soldiers," Grandmother said, "or bomb this place from the air."

Rico laughed.

I didn't laugh. She wouldn't make stuff up out of the clear blue sky. Someone had given her the idea that bombing was a possibility. I wondered if it was a credible source or a troublemaker.

Grandmother's glare at Rico could have melted marble. She seemed furious at him.

"Sorry, Grandmother," Rico said. "Who suggested someone would bomb this place from above?"

"The general said it was possible. These are modern times."

The general was in a position to know. I would have felt easier if it had been almost anyone else.

"What do you want us to do?" Rico asked. I nodded, so she'd see I was in.

"This is not your fight. I want you to move out. I cannot risk you getting hurt or killed by this lunatic new governor's vendetta."

I heard this with misgiving, although I should have moved out a long time ago. I love it here. Rico looked puzzled, like he couldn't believe what she had just said.

"Grandmother, I'm taking you to Madrid. You have a beautiful home there," I said.

"If it had been my idea, I would go. His message to leave Mexico was a command. If I go, he wouldn't pursue any action against me, but it is still a command."

"Action. Against you in your own home? You never leave this house," Rico roared.

The food arrived, and we tore into it. Rico and I each had a huge bowl of menudo with steaming hot corn and flour tortillas. Grandmother's plain oatmeal and toast looked unappetizing to me. I like some flavor.

Grandmother looked at me accusingly.

"You eat menudo because you have hangovers!"

I didn't argue.

"I love menudo," Rico said, not denying the hangover, because he'd be lying.

We didn't drink together much, but we smoked a lot of weed, and drank every night. Menudo is a traditional hangover cure. It's also a hearty breakfast.

"I will go with you to Spain and stay," I said. "What do you say?"

"I'm not running away," she barked at me.

"If you decide to go, I don't want you to leave alone," I said.

Rico stopped eating. "I will handle this new governor." The servants probably heard his roar in the kitchen.

"You will not do anything of the kind," Grandmother said sharply.

"I'll do it," I said between bites.

Rico and I decided not to move. We had no place to go.

"I'm only here to sleep," I said.

"I'm traveling most of the time," Rico said. "I'm here maybe three nights out of the week."

"And I'm only here to sleep," I said again. "Grandma, let me hear you say you don't want us to move." Followed by, "Please, Grandma."

She didn't reply but for a second or two I thought she may throw her cane at me or at my brother. Of course, I understood that her wanting us to move was for our own protection because she believed something was going to happen.

Grandma, she loves her secrets. All my life, she's used messengers instead of the phone, and visitors we never saw came and went by way of a hidden passage that began at a staircase that began beneath Grandmother's market. This walkway was underground deep under the street and tiled top and bottom with recessed lighting. As kids we were not allowed to be there unless accompanied. The kitchen help brought groceries and supplies via the walkway.

CHAPTER 49
RICO

IGNACIO MAY BE A FORMER COP. I have never seen him not wearing a suit, or not groomed cop-style, with military-short hair. He still looks like a cop, but he's worked for my grandmother for many years. Before I went home for six much-needed hours of sleep, I told Gusto that I wanted to see Ignacio when I got up. It had been a long day. I walked to my cottage, threw off my clothes, and fell asleep naked.

Ignacio

Six hours later, Gusto and Ignacio waited for me in my living room as I showered. I came out in a robe to meet with them.

"I apologize for the wait," I said. I went right to business. "When does the new governor take office?"

"I don't know the exact date, but I heard it's in less than two weeks. I will find out right away," Ignacio said.

"The fourth of October," Gusto said. "I will double-check."

"Ignacio, my grandmother is your boss, but this is for me. You get it?"

"Yes," Ignacio said.

"I haven't decided yet, but here's what I need you to do. Put someone on Miguel Alvarado. I want a schedule of all his events between now and his swearing in."

Gusto's brow furrowed. Worry made him look his age. "Rico, if you want something done, just say so. Don't get in the mix."

Ignacio nodded.

"I haven't decided yet. For now, do as I say. Give me details twenty-four hours from now. Do it."

"I'll get what you need," Ignacio said.

Gusto remained quiet.

It was early afternoon. After they left, I crashed again for an hour, allegedly to sleep, but I spent it tossing, turning, and overthinking everything. I was determined to find a solution. Why should Grandmother be forced to leave?

I thought of letting Victor in on what I might do, but I saw no need for two of us to take a risk. With our mastery of martial arts, we were deadly weapons, but this politician would have an army protecting him. Army or not, I'm not going to permit anyone to come in with soldiers or aircraft. I will not allow this estate to become a battlefield.

Grandmother's friend, the general, predicted bombing from above. Stupid old man to worry her so. That's why my grandmother is worried. I can't believe she asked us to move out. She's worried about an impending attack. She has over a hundred men on the grounds right now armed better than any military people who would come in after her.

She's worried that she has no protection for an attack from above.

Grandmother should have just fired Mauro for his failure to get his friend to back off and taken out the governor elect. Granny. Granny. You were not thinking.

The next evening, Ignacio caught up to me at the downtown Juarez Palacio where I was in my office, looking over some paperwork. Ignacio was alone. We faced each other across my desk.

"He's not making appearances," Ignacio said. "I connected with a reporter in the governor-elect's press pool permitted full access wherever he is."

I was not surprised that Ignacio would get close.

"Does the pool know where and when?"

"Mauro's funeral is pending. There is no schedule. Everything calendared before his death has been scrubbed. The funeral is a sure date next week. The only other event is the rosary the night before."

I have never killed anyone before, but Miguel Alvarado has threatened to kill my grandmother if she doesn't leave Mexico. He can't get away with that.

James used to tell me that I was so good with a gun that I could shoot the ass off a gnat and that the military would want me as a sniper. Victor is not as good with a gun. He is deadly in martial arts. I can't get close enough to the governor elect to kill him with my hands. I must use a rifle.

"Ignacio, sorry. I was thinking."

I grinned at him. He grinned back.

"What else can I do for you?" Ignacio asked.

"Get me a rifle. We don't own the one I need."

His grin vanished. He looked perturbed. The corners of his mouth turned down, disappearing into a baked-in frown line.

"Please let me handle what you are considering."

He sounded like he was pleading. I doubted he ever pleaded with my grandmother regarding her orders. I ignored his comment and his exaggerated frown.

"I can't understand why my grandmother didn't go after Miguel Alvarado instead of Mauro."

"She might kill me if she discovers I told you."

"Didn't Gusto tell you about Perro?"

Perro worked for my grandmother, not around the house but he'd been around a long time. My brother and I both knew him.

"Know what about Perro? Tell me," I roared, standing up and slamming my palms on my desk.

Ignacio jumped at the sound and answered quickly.

"The night Mauro was killed, Miguel was having dinner at a restaurant with the outgoing governor. Perro was positioned to handle Miguel. After Mauro was shot, an alarm went off. Two armies of soldiers and police rushed to protect the governor, one converging around the governor-elect, and one converging around the governor who was at the restaurant with Miguel. Perro had to abort. I guess you'd have heard about it if it had been a successful hit."

Perro

That makes sense to me. My grandmother did go after the gover-nor-elect, the man who was the real target. Mauro was just inconvenient collateral damage.

"Glad you told me. Let me tell you what kind of rifle and scope I need."

He really wanted to take me out of the loop and go after Miguel himself, but he kept his mouth closed on the subject. That grimace was frozen on his face. We talked for another half hour and Ignacio did not ask me again to let him handle it. I'm sure he was torn, as he has been taking Grandmother's orders for so long. Grandmother would not want me doing anything risky. I gave him a list of what I needed. The rifle and scope were only a partial.

The next day, I told Ignacio that the rifle was out. I had rethought my plan and revised what he needed to get for me, an extensive list.

"Jefe, count on me," he said.

"You cannot imagine how I am counting on you," I said.

It doesn't happen often anymore, but yesterday I'd had breakfast with my grandmother. I planned on repeating the experience today, so I went to the big house. Victor was not there, and neither was my grandmother.

I saw Nana in passing. Nana works in the kitchen.

"I thought I might have breakfast with Grandmother today," I said.

"Too late, Jefe," she said, rushing to tell me that Victor wasn't here, and my grandmother had breakfasted earlier, and was out in the garden.

I figured Victor was still asleep in his cottage. It was just as well that I didn't run into him while I plotted the end of the governor elect. It was a one-man job. If something went wrong, only I was in jeopardy.

I was confident in my plans, but I'd never put Victor in a position to get hurt, killed, or captured by the force that protected Miguel. Ignacio was getting good information from his contact.

I started for the door.

"Going to catch up with my grandmother," I told Nana. I was out before she responded.

I would surprise her. Outside I circled the house, checking the gardens immediate to the residence, and enjoying all the beautiful trees I had grown up with. Though I lived here, I seldom walked around the property, enjoying it as I was doing now. I would ask the first gardener I saw where my grandmother was. They were always around, digging, pushing wheelbarrows, watering, hauling fertilizer. But as I walked, no gardener came into view.

Something seemed off. I stopped moving, listening to the peculiar silence. Usually there were forest noises, garden noises, frogs, birds, the distant thud of a hoe or shovel.

I could practically hear my sensei pushing me to use my sixth sense when sizing up my opponent. He said it was a gift. Believe in yourself. You can see trouble before it strikes.

What was going on? In this usually noisy garden, the sound of nothing is something. I spun around fast to assess my surroundings. I still saw no one. Where were the gardeners? Something was wrong. I walked rapidly, not as quietly as I should. I kicked off my Florsheim loafers at a run when I saw a man lying across the path a dozen yards ahead.

I closed the distance between us and found the gardener, Tacho, dead. He'd been an old, gentle man who used to catch butterflies to show me and then let them go. I knelt over his body, then stood, and yelled in rage. Then I was back on the path at a fast clip. On the other side of the walkway, two more bodies were sprawled, like Tacho, bloody with gunshot. A bolt of hot rage shot through me, like gasoline when it is lit. I was on fire with fury over this invasion of my family's sanctuary.

"Grandmother, where are you!" I roared. I could hear my voice echo, ringing off the walls. I was fifty feet from the back of the main house, a couple hundred feet from Victor's house.

"Rico, I'm here!"

I heard Victor's distant voice and aimed my voice in his direction, toward dense foliage.

"Grandmother is missing. Something is going on!"

I called for Victor at the top of my lungs, running headlong down the path toward him. He was somewhere out there, crashing toward me. I heard Victor again, many yards distant but sounding closer than he had been.

"Gusto, get out here now!" Victor yelled.

I heard carts. The guards were deployed, moving across the property grounds in golf carts. I was running. Victor and I finally converged, Gusto close behind and leading heavily armed men.

"I've looked everywhere except the mausoleum area," Victor said.

I expected the worst. I've seen at least nine dead groundskeepers on the south side of the property.

Mausoleum

I felt a chill hit me. It was like I did not need to see her body to know what had happened.

I took off at a run.

Victor delayed a second, calling out, "What is it, Rico?"

I stopped and faced him. "I don't know," I said. But the sick feeling inside was real. I knew.

I ran to the mausoleum with Victor close behind.

The mausoleum was built of marble in the style of the old Greek temples, four Doric columns, a carved frieze up above showing my grandfather and mother. They were the only people interred here, in two crypts. I knew before I reached the steps. I heard rapid-fire gunshots at a distance, chatter on walkie talkies. I heard Victor's feet on the steps. But it was all noise and nonsense. I could not comprehend anything but the bloody crumpled body in front of me on the marble before the mausoleum door.

Mala.

My grandmother.

She was on her back facing the sky, her forehead and cheeks torn by gunshots.

Victor and I knelt, her body between us. I felt such a huge wave of emotion, all of it at once: pain, grief, horror, fury. My emotions burst out of me in a huge unending roar. Victor had gone almost silent, his face resting on her chest. He was babbling, whispering, crying. I heard him apologizing for his failure to protect her, his begging her not to go. Blood was everywhere.

When I went silent, I heard a voice come over one of the walkie talkies. I turned my back to the mausoleum door to face Gusto and the men beside him, all of us listening to the voice on the walkie talkie.

"We shot six assailants attempting to scale the north wall."

I faced north. I had no thought, no motivation, no plan. I just found myself running full speed for the north wall. Behind me, the walkie talkie discussion continued.

"Where exactly on the north wall?" Gusto's voice was broken, panting, but I could make out his words. I was focused on getting there, negotiating the terrain, and had not realized Gusto and his men were running behind me, not until I heard him ask.

I waited for the answer, but all I heard was static.

"Jefe, near the stand of palm trees," Gusto gasped out.

We burst through the forest into the clearing where the palms grew close to the north wall. Four assassins lay motionless where they had fallen, all shot as they had been scaling the eighteen-foot wall. Lucky for me, unluckily for them, two were wounded and alive.

Gusto plucked something off one body, then another. He handed me a small metal shield while holding the other in his hand. I examined the badge.

"Jefe, these men are not soldiers. They are state guards. They are not the governor's men. Must be guards for the governor elect."

One man on the ground was moaning in pain. Gusto kicked him in the thigh, where he was bleeding, probably from a gunshot. He screamed, the harsh cry of a wounded animal.

"Don't kill him yet," I said to Gusto, more to frighten our trespasser than to inform Gusto.

I knelt beside him and grabbed his throat. One squeeze and he'd be dead. I needed him alive.

"Who sent you?"

He shook his head.

"We got our orders from our commandant, and he's over there," he choked out. "Ask him."

Gusto jostled the commandant with his foot. "He's dead."

"I'm just going to kill you." I was beyond angry, beyond thought.

Gusto put his palm on my wrist.

"Jefe, due respect. We need him and this other pig here."

He kicked the second guy lying on the ground. As we stood there, Loki, one of Gusto's men, cuffed the larger trespasser's hands behind his back.

"This one too, Loki," I said.

I released his throat; he took a deep breath. Loki jerked him face down, cuffed his hands behind his back, and rolled him over.

"Who sent you?"

He shook his head.

"Gusto, give me a knife."

I took the knife and stabbed him three times on the wounded thigh. He screamed in pain, a huge wail. I put the bloody knife up to his neck.

"Tell me no again," I said.

The blade was sharp enough to split a hair. I pushed the edge just enough to cut the skin.

"I told you. I'm not lying."

Gusto spat on him.

"How did you know where to find my grandmother?" I demanded, pushing the knife deeper. He was streaming blood from his neck, not long for this world.

"We didn't know. It was reconnaissance. We got to the residence and there she was, Mala. Out here, walking." He looked up at me, eyes pleading. He wanted desperately to live.

The guy was leaking blood from his leg and neck. He would be dead in a minute. I had to kill him soon before he died on his own. Had to. I'd never killed before.

"Mercy," he begged.

"Give me your gun," I said to Gusto.

"Sure," I said. "The same mercy you showed my grandmother."

I shot the bastard dead. Cheeks and forehead. Handed the gun back to Gusto.

I went for the second wounded guard. He was a big guy. He had a big head, bald, and his large, soft paunch strained his shirt. His shoulder had been hit. He was bleeding but not moaning. I kept seeing my grandmother's face. Bullet holes in her cheeks and forehead.

"Who gave you the order to come here?"

"Kill me now. I have nothing to say."

I stood over this beast, put one foot on the wounded shoulder. Put my weight on it.

He didn't make any noise but could not hide the pain.

"Gusto, the gun."

I put both feet on the ground, still standing over him. I reached for the gun. He made a move like he was going to try to bring me down. It almost made me laugh, except I was filled with a murderous rage and what came out of me did not sound like laughter. I sat down on him on his fat paunch and brought the gun to his mouth. He stirred but he couldn't do much. Loki had cuffed him.

"Okay," I said.

"Wait. Wait."

Gusto mocked him. "A change of heart."

"I tell you what I know, what happens to me?"

"You die fast," I said. "Gusto, hand me the knife."

"Slow or fast?" I traded the gun for the knife and slammed the blade in the wounded shoulder. I jumped off him to avoid a stream of bile that bubbled out of his mouth.

"Where was my grandmother when you saw her?"

The bastard talked.

"She was walking up the stairs of the mausoleum."

"Why did the men tending the grounds get killed?"

"They were in the way." His voice was barely audible. "They would have called for help."

"Who killed my grandmother?" My hand had a grip on his neck.

"Commandant."

"Who gave the order? Who commanded the commandant?"

"I do not know."

"Who commanded the commandant?"

"As far as I know, the commandant only took orders from the governor-elect."

"Gusto, give me the gun."

A shot in each cheek and one in the forehead.

I had killed two human beings and felt nothing from it.

I only pained for my grandmother. I hope she did not suffer.

The Juarez mortuary was huge. It had to be. The only undertaker in the city was here, and there were many deaths. My grandmother owned the buildings the mortuary occupied, and although I doubt the owner ever dealt directly with her, he certainly knew who she was. I called the owner, Martin Ponce, about the death in the family.

"I need you to come to the residence. My grandmother." It hurt to say it. "She's dead."

"Senor Hidalgo, my deepest condolences."

"Martin, you are dead if you mention one word about her death."

"Senor Hidalgo, I will attend to this myself."

"You can't do it alone. Warn your people that what they see is forgotten when they leave here."

"Si, Senor Hidalgo."

"You know we have our own mausoleum."

I wasn't sure how old this man was, if he had seen to my mother and my grandfather when they passed.

"Yes, I know, Senor. Do not worry about your grandmother. Everything will be perfect. I will get her the best solid mahogany casket from El Paso. Leave it to me, Senor."

"Don't fail me, Martin."

"Never, sir."

I had come in the house to make the call. I hung up and turned to face Gusto. The day's shock had carved new lines on his face. He looked ten years older than yesterday. There was something more. Yesterday he had been my advisor, always with his allegiance to my grandmother holding sway. Now instead of lecturing me, he was silent. I realized that he was waiting for orders. "I should kill you," I said, my eyes on his. "With all the men you have here, how is it possible that one entire section of the property was not guarded where the killers came over the wall?"

Gusto went on his knees.

"Jefe, I will take my own life, here and now, give the word. I have no excuse."

"Give me your gun," I ordered. "You have no say who kills you."

Gusto, still on his knees, handed me the gun. The same gun I used to kill two others.

The control I was trained to have in karate failed me. I was in a rage.

I held the hand and put it on the back of his bowed head.

I saw a flash of the past. Gusto was always there since I could remember.

I saw a flash of Grandma talking to Gusto. I knew. We all knew she loved him.

I saw James Baker. I heard him. "Spare him. Gusto is family."

I felt a hand on the gun I was holding on Gusto's head.

"Don't do it." It was my brother Victor.

My hand trembled.

I turned around and Victor hugged me.

A minute later, Victor spoke. "Gusto, get up. There is much to do."

"Wrap the assassins' bodies in burlap," I said. I was tempted to cremate them in the crematorium we had in the basement and the warehouse, but I wanted the governor-elect to know we were on to him. The bodies were loaded on the bed of a pickup truck, taken to the parking lot of the state building in downtown Juarez, and dumped. Once the officials realized the men were state security word would get to the capital and to Miguel Alvarado that he'd lost six of his men in Juarez.

"Send men to meet with the families of our deceased gardeners and your three security men," I said. "They died as heroes. Give each family fifty-thousand pesos with a promise of more."

Gusto nodded. "Yes, Jefe," he said.

The assassins' cadavers were gone by the time Martin the mortician and his ghouls arrived. When the undertaker arrived, Victor and I were sitting outside the mausoleum, our grandmother's body covered with a white sheet.

"I recommend you allow me to take your grandmother with me where I can attend to her. If we leave her here, we need dry ice and that will not be pleasant for your brother and yourself, sir," Martin spoke in a low, whispery voice that was unpleasant and rather creepy. I was glad that he hadn't been loud enough for Victor to hear. In person, he looked normal enough. Thinning hair, dark eyes, hair going gray, a little thin. You couldn't tell his profession at a glance, though it might have been my imagination that he smelled faintly of formalde-hyde. His obsequious mannerisms were more of a clue to his profession than his appearance. Truth is, I have no idea what formaldehyde smells like.

"No one must know she is in your mortuary," I said in a low firm voice.

"I promise," he said.

We walked down the mausoleum steps. Martin's ghouls had collected all the bodies of the groundkeepers and security guards and put them in one place on the path.

"Do you have room for all of my people?"

"I do, sir."

I turned from the view of the bodies laid out on the manicured grass and looked up the stairs of the mausoleum.

"When will my grandmother be ready to bring back?"

"As early as tomorrow, sir. I already ordered the casket from El Paso. It will be brought to me as soon as I confirm."

I patted Martin's shoulder. "Thank you," I said.

"Sir, your grandmother was good to me. She helped me grow the business. She expanded the premises as I needed more room. I only dealt with Angel, but she's the one who made the decisions. You owe me no thank you. I owe my thanks to you."

The mortician's ghouls pushed the gurney carrying my grandmother to the hearse. The whole morning seemed not quite real, and it was only eleven thirty. So much had happened since I'd tried and failed to have breakfast with Grandmother. Victor was as shaken as I was. His shirt and jeans were stained with Grandmother's blood.

"I've got to get a shower," Victor said. "I suppose you do too."

I looked down at myself and saw blood spattered on my own clothes. Blood from the men I'd killed today. Maybe some of my grand-mother's blood. Victor's hands and shirt were a bloody mess. It was even on his face.

"You're right. I'll do the same," I said. "I'll meet you at the house. Take your time."

Victor raised his hand as he continued to walk without looking back.

I thought of Grandmother's face as I had last seen it, and a cold chill went through my body. As soon as I was home, I went straight to the pot stash hidden in my top desk drawer. I took three deep drags of a killer joint, put it down, and called Elena at home.

"She's dead," I said.

Elena made an inarticulate sound.

"From what? How?"

She broke down into tears.

I was too choked up to talk.

"I'm on my way," Elena said.

When I was out of the shower, I tossed my bloodied clothes into the trash and sat on my bed to put on clean jeans, a button-down shirt, tennis shoes, no socks. I moved to the ash tray beside my living room sofa, picking up the abandoned joint. It took three tries to strike a match, but I lit it, took a hit, and dialed Luciana.

"I know who this is," she sang in her jolly morning voice.

"Luciana, my grandmother is dead."

"Where are you?" she said, her voice turning somber.

"Home," I said.

"Can I come over?"

"Yes."

"I'll be out of here in five minutes," she said. "Rico, I'm very sorry."

I finished the joint and tossed the roach into the ashtray. I ached to have Luciana and Elena around me. I closed my eyes and leaned into the couch. I sat up and reached for the gold cigarette holder on the coffee table and took out a neatly wrapped joint and reached for my gold Dunhill lighter. All I could see was my grandmother's face. I took a hit that fogged my brain, held out the joint and watched the edge burn, picturing Florencia, still my full-time housekeeper. She always made sure to roll joints for all my cigarette cases in the house. I didn't require her to use a uniform like at the main house. She was long-haired, lean, always dressed in jeans, midriff-baring shirts, looked like a centerfold, and was an obsessive cleaner.

Elena arrived at my cottage. I called Victor to join us. The three of us huddled together and cried for a very long time. We talked about how when James died, Grandmother would have entombed him in our family mausoleum except that he left instructions that he wanted to be sent back to London and be buried next to his wife. Elena and James were family. Grandmother had taken to both of them. My brother and I grew up with them around us, lived here with us. Yes, we were family.

"She didn't die of natural causes," I said.

She looked puzzled. I recounted everything that had happened that morning. I could see the pain in Victor as I retold the story. Elena made a fist, and it rested against her lips as she listened. Every detail brought new tears from Elena.

After Luciana arrived, Victor and I again told what had happened this morning. The three of us—Victor, Elena, and I—were a mess. Luciana came behind the sofa where I was sitting, bent over, and put her arms around my shoulders. Her forehead touched mine.

"My deepest condolences. I didn't know her, but I know how much you loved her."

She embraced Victor in the wing chair, whispered condolences in his ear, and then hugged Elena in the chair by him.

"I know you lived here for a very long time, and she was family to you," she told Elena. "My condolences. I'm very sorry for your loss."

The four of us walked over to the main house.

I couldn't remember seeing so many guards. Once again, it angered me that the intruders got to my grandmother without a fight.

"I was on the verge of killing Gusto," I confessed to Elena in the presence of Luciana and Victor.

"He's family," Elena said. "Your grandmother, she—"

"I know," I interrupted. "I know."

• • •

"Luciana, you're a reporter. Do you think we should let it out that my grandmother is dead?"

I could see that Victor snapped with my question.

Luciana said, "I'm not a reporter now but I get what you mean."

I held the door open for her, and we entered the screened-in porch. The guard in the porch opened the door for us, and we all went into the den at the back of the house.

"My on-the-fly reply is yes, let everyone know. You should write up an obituary and release it to the papers so that you have some control over what is said. I wouldn't release details about how she died. Whoever ordered this will wonder what is going on."

"We know who ordered it," Victor snapped.

I looked at Elena who had not shared an opinion but only listened.

"Victor, what do you think?" I asked.

"I agree that we don't give details."

"What if the governor-elect wants credit and does a press release that he had it done?" I said with a bitter taste in my mouth.

Elena looked at her watch. "I'm not an expert but if he wanted credit, he would have done it by now. It's been hours."

"Rico, you said all the intruders were stopped from fleeing the property. If no one got out, the person who sent them doesn't know what happened. He may not have released anything because he's in the dark."

"I hadn't thought about that," Victor said.

"Me neither," I admitted.

"That would explain the delay," Elena said.

"If we leak it out, he will figure the mission was accomplished. By now, he has to be aware that six of his men are dead."

Victor and I told Elena and Luciana about security exchanging fire with the assassins when they were fleeing back over the wall. I didn't mention that I had killed two of them. I wasn't ashamed nor was I looking for approval. I simply didn't mention it.

"We lost three security men and nine groundskeepers. They pretty much shot down everyone they saw," I said.

"What a tragedy," Elena said.

"Horrible," said Luciana.

"We lost Grandmother," Victor said in a low voice, killing the conversation

Luciana had only seen the residence from the outside and only the part of the house visible from my cottage. She had been to my cottage on the property but never to the main house. As much time as we spent together, I had been neglectful not to have introduced her to Grandmother. I would not have told Grandmother that Luciana had been a newspaper reporter before I hired her nor that her deceased boyfriend was the bastard that wrote the damn article when we opened the El Paso Palacio. It is possible that my grandmother knew all about Luciana and her dead boyfriend. If I had introduced her to Grandmother, it would have been a first. My grandmother never met any of my friends.

After a long walk through the house, we got to the dining room. Grandmother had always insisted that all chairs be left around the table. It had always been she who decided what end of the table we would use for a meal. Before we came in the dining room, the place settings were already out.

Nana greeted us as we came in the dining room, her eyes red and swollen. We sat around the right side of the table across from each other. Grandmother's seat, at the head of the table was conspicuously empty.

"The kitchen is staffed," Nana said. "Your grandmother would want you to eat."

"Please bring us four glasses and a red Rothschild, sixty or sixty-one."

"Right away, Señor Rico," Nana said.

"Nana is sweet to want to feed us," Elena said.

"She always wants us to eat," Victor said with a tiny smile. "It's her job."

"Give me your decision on whether we should leak to the press," I said to Victor.

He was directly across from me with Elena on his right. Luciana was by my side, facing Elena.

"I don't want to think about it, bro. You decide. I'm good with your decision."

"I'll ask Angel over. He needs to know what happened. He can orchestrate the leak or leaks to the press."

On the floor, there was a button on each end of the table that rang the staff. My grandmother had always used it. Using it now made me sad. Gusto was out there. I preferred to use my own voice.

"Gusto, if you're there come in here," I yelled.

He opened the door and joined us, immediately coming to my side.

"Send a runner to fetch Angel and have him come right over. Do not mention why."

"Very good, Jefe`," he said.

I saw curiosity in Luciana's face, but she did not ask.

"Angel is the don of finance for my grandmother," I told her. "A trusted friend for longer than my brother and I have been on this planet."

Elena said. "He's a very nice man."

Luciana nodded.

Nana brought the wine I'd requested. It was already opened, no fanfare. I thanked her and asked her to pour. She left right after. I raised my glass and so did Victor, Elena, and Luciana.

"To Grandmother who will always live in our hearts."

We talked about Pan Gratis bakery, one of my grandmother's projects. A block from Mala's estate a shop known as *Pan Gratis*, Free Bread, was open twenty-four hours a day. There was nowhere to sit. Bread was free, and so was coffee, milk and drinking water. People who could afford to pay put a donation in a tall glass jug. The money got passed out to families who came in with a baby, widows, and the like.

"All this talk of bread. Rico, I want some hot bread with this wine, please," Elena said.

I had no appetite, but I could stomach bread.

"Nana," I called out.

Ten minutes later, Nana brought in a large assortment of breads that had just come out of the oven. The scent was intoxicating. It was sad the reason we were sitting here.

My brother was first to lift the napkin and get a piece. I smiled, remembering how my grandmother loved her bread.

CHAPTER 50
LUCIANA

I HAD NEVER MET Magda the woman known as Mala. The reporter part of me would have given anything to get to know her if I could write about her. I don't know Elena that well but long enough and well enough to know she would not cry to impress Rico or Victor. She was desolate at Magda's death. Clearly, she loved the lady everyone feared. She seemed too young to have spent more than a decade in this house tutoring the boys.

I tried not to show how awestruck I was at the big house. I wondered if Rico and Victor knew the names of the architects, artists all of them, who had done the fabulous work in the residence located right in the middle of the worst neighborhood in Juarez.

I felt guilty over Floyd Miles's actions. He had pieced together an article from past stories and rumors about Mala. I would never fake an article just for the circulation. I would never do that. When Rico said that he trusts me without reservation, I was so touched. I got all choked up because I know he meant it. I know in his position, there are not many people that he trusts. I could never wrong him or his brother.

It is best that I didn't get a chance to write a story about Mala.

· · ·

Four bottles of wine are not a big deal when four people are drinking it and two of them are Rico and Victor. I'm guessing that Elena knew everything Rico and his brother talked about as we sat at that big table, drank wine, and ate bread. She participated in the stories as much as the brothers did. Not having met her, all I could do was listen.

"My grandmother has hundreds of homes and apartments for homeless families, homeless men, and women. They pay nothing for shelter. My grandmother has donated millions of pesos to the city for paving streets, for the infrastructure. The city coffers don't have the money. What people fear is the fable that my grandmother burns her enemies. Because of that myth, no one wants to be Mala's enemy. Don't ask me where that rumor started because I don't have the answer."

I have no tears of my own for Mala, but when I see Rico and Victor cry, when I see Elena cry, the emotion inside of me bursts and my tears flow. I feel the lump in my throat when I picture those two macho men, beautiful animals with huge deadly hands, crying like babies.

With all the tree cover of the grounds, I couldn't see if it was one or more helicopters that flew overhead. I was shown the mausoleum the day before the funeral. Elena said that the mausoleum was already there when she came to teach the boys. Rico pointed out the frieze in front where his mother's face had been carved. I'd never been in a mausoleum before. There was room for twenty-five people in the foyer. Downstairs with the crypts were a dozen chairs. A beautiful bronze lift like an elevator had been placed there to lower the casket. The ten crypts were built into the ground. Two of them were occupied when the guests arrived, and three when they left. Chilling. The marble work throughout the mausoleum was intricate and lovely. It must have taken a long time to build. I wanted to ask, but I didn't.

Less than forty-eight hours after she was murdered, Magda Hidalgo was entombed during a private ceremony. I was not inside, but I was nearby in the garden facing the mausoleum. I saw the backs of maybe a hundred workers, all wearing funereal black, all carrying a lit candle as the ceremony was going on inside. I knew that a Catholic priest officiated. Even though Rico's grandmother was very old and had outlived her generation, it was a very sad gathering. Inside only the nearest and dearest were gathered: Elena, Rico, Victor, Gusto, Ignacio, her accountant Angel Flores, a general, and the morticians.

Governor-Elect Miguel Alvarado did not hold a press conference. Just before she was laid to rest, a statement went public that a special task force had gone in to arrest Mala for the murder of Mauro Robles, that she resisted, shots were fired, and Mala was killed. The statement did not mention the losses from the government security force, nor did it mention the murder of nine gardeners and three security men.

Mala's estate is bordered by four streets. Soon after the governor-elect's statement was released by radio, television, and newspaper, the property was surrounded. This time, it wasn't armed assassins sneaking in. There were thousands of Mexican citizens gathered to pay their respects outside the walls of Mala's estate. From the inside where I was holed up with Rico, Victor, and Elena, you could hear them singing as they held their vigil. Streets were shut down to traffic. I saw some of the footage on the local news. The helicopters had gotten a lot of aerial footage of the crowds outside the walls.

Gusto's men coordinated handing out two thousand candles to the men, women and children who camped out since the announcement of her death. Gusto came back to tell Rico that they ran out of candles and had to get more.

"Do it," Rico said.

Gusto rushed off to do his bidding, and Rico's stern demeanor only lasted till Gusto was out of the door. Rico turned to me, and I held him for a moment. I could feel the tension in him, and when I let go of him, I could see the grief he was holding in.

"The people," he said. "They love her too."

The song that tumbled over the walls of the estate was *"La Despe-*

dida" (*The Farewell*). We could hear the lyrics then only humming. It was beautiful.

Rico and Victor went out to greet the people as they continued to sing holding candles that workers from inside the grounds were lighting for them. It was getting dark. Elena and I stood by outside the gates, but we didn't mingle. Later that night on the news in El Paso and Juarez, videos were shown to viewers about the ongoing vigil.

Portable toilets were installed around the property, on the four streets that were shut down to traffic. The streets that bordered Mala's tall walls bordering her property. Vendors hired by Rico and his brother served everyone with water, refreshments, and food. This went on, all night.

CHAPTER 51
MELINA ALVARADO

TODAY WE BURY my sister Mina's husband, Mauro Robles.

As if it wasn't bad enough that my stupid husband sent men to Mala's house to arrest her and they instead killed her and got themselves killed, he issued a statement taking credit for doing it. If he cared about the survival of his family, he should have aborted going after Mala. He had no proof that she had Mauro killed.

Mina is beside herself. She has not only suffered the loss of her husband, father of her children. Now she's sick with the fear of retaliation. I'm sick with fear too. The security men assigned to protect us don't make me feel any less afraid. Mina feels the same way.

After my husband's *declaración jodida*[1] to the press, Mina said, "I hate Miguel, Damn him to hell for bringing this shit storm down on us."

Days have gone by, and he hasn't even called. I had to hear from my lead security guy that Miguel is flying in for the funeral.

Mauro will be buried in the memorial park located on the family estate about a mile from the house. His mother and father are buried there.

We hear we should expect to have about three hundred people. Our parents have taken care of everything. They got the clergy, handled the staff, and hired the catering company which has a crew of eighty people to attend to the guests. A large tent has been set up with seating for more than three hundred guests. It is a big tent. The sky is overcast, as if it is threatening rain. I didn't even notice until one of the kids pointed out the clouds. It feels gray out there, whether or not it actually is. If there's any consolation, it is having family close by. My children and I have been here with Mina for days. I love my sister.

---

1. Fucked-up declaration

CHAPTER 52
MINA ROBLES

WHEN I TOLD her that I plan to get the hell out of Mexico after Mauro is buried, my sister thought I was having a temporary reaction, a moment that would pass. I don't need this huge estate, and neither do my kids. I have a plane and all the money my kids and I will ever need, but more than we need this plot of land, we need to be alive. I know my sister is also afraid. I almost believe that she will make this split with Miguel permanent. It's all because of his vindictive parents. They drove him to become governor to avenge the death of his brother. How stupid is that? An old woman, a hundred years old, and they still blame her for the addiction, their son's addiction, that got him killed decades ago.

A violinist in black was standing front and center at the gravesite, playing, stalling for time until my idiot brother-in-law arrived. Many of the guests had walked from the house where a massive tent was set up for feeding the guests after Mauro was laid to rest. Most of those who did not walk from the house were ferried by golf carts. The catering company provided two shuttles. Everyone had made it to the gravesite except for Miguel.

It was a picturesque little graveyard, with the marble stones of

Mauro's parents surrounded by green and lovely idyllic plantings. A paved path weaved here from the house, curving through flower gardens of sunflowers, orchids, red pineapple sage, orange Mexican honeysuckle, morning glory, yellow poppies, pink dahlia, and other varieties I did not recognize. My gardeners are horticultural geniuses.

My children and I sat on the front row facing the casket. Next to Melina and her children were our parents and Miguel's parents. Behind us, three hundred chairs were filled, and half again as many people were standing. The children were getting restless, and the violinist had started another repetition of his selections when my head of security let me know a radio call came in that Miguel's plane would be landing in five minutes.

The landing field at our house was a little over a mile from the residence, and probably a mile and a half from here as the crow flies. Our south-facing seats gave us a view of the airfield. We would be able to see Miguel's plane approach and land. While I was staring in that direction, I realized that Miguel would step out of his plane within feet of where my Mauro had stepped off his plane to be shot. It gave me a sick chill and an ironic sense of foreboding.

The violinist was playing Ave Maria again. Melina reached out and touched my wrist. We held hands for a moment. I tried to project strength in her direction. We would get through this.

Melina's daughters pointed toward the airfield to a speck in the sky I didn't yet see.

"Papa! Papa!"

I would not be surprised if he planned to arrive late to grandstand his best friend's funeral. I'd heard him plan such things back when he had been on the campaign trail. I'll never forgive him for the disgraceful act of murdering Mala. He wasn't even sworn in yet. And announcing responsibility for the killing of Mala so close to Mauro's funeral was disgusting. It's as disgraceful as it is careless of all of our lives, just for the chance to gloat, just for the chance to fulfill that murderous goal his vengeful parents planted in his head. It will be a cold day in hell when any of us ever forgive him.

Miguel's plane got close enough for me to see. It was descending fast, and we all watched it from where we were sitting.

"He knows how to make an entrance," Melina said sardonically. I wished I'd had the chairs set up facing some other way than south.

From a direction perpendicular to the plane, a helicopter appeared in an instant, looking as if it was going to fly into the path of the plane. The prospect between us and the landing field was a perfect vantage point for disaster. I heard one of the girls say, "Mama?" and found myself on my feet. The helicopter and plane flew close to each other; I expected a collision, not the horrible sound of gunfire. Bam! Bam! Bam! Rapid fire, the sound like firecrackers going off.

I was surrounded by hysterical people screaming, jumping, pointing. Chaos exploded around me as the plane erupted into a ball of fire. Miguel was in that plane. I heard Melina scream Miguel's name. My hands were fists, and I was screaming and screaming alongside my sister. The ball of fire burst into pieces on the runway, fire leaping and rebounding and springing off the runway like a live thing, a river of black smoke billowing into the sky. Melina folded in slow motion, fainting on the manicured turf. I sat on the ground cradling Melina's head on my lap, rubbing her hands, willing her conscious.

CHAPTER 53
ELENA MUNOZ

THE THREE TELEVISIONS at the bar are all set on different channels. I wasn't watching. I was in my office on the phone with our supplier telling him we needed one thousand new linen napkins. Mala had been buried three days ago, and I was back at work.

I heard Quick on the intercom calling me and I hung up with the linen guy.

"Keep your pants on, Quick," I said.

"Elena, come down and watch this. Hurry."

I heard the news jingle in the background on the intercom. Programs were interrupted for special news announcements, but she had hung up so fast I had no idea what I was going to watch. I ran from my office to the dining room. Many tables and chairs were unattended, full plates abandoned as customers had gathered around the bar, all standing. The crowd was thick enough I could not see the television screens until I squeezed through the crowd to see a news anchor and caught the tail end of what the announcer was saying.

"…when less than an hour ago, the governor-elect's plane was shot down as it was landing at the residence of the late Mauro Robles."

The news anchor continued, "The plane exploded before touchdown at the private landing field of the late Mauro Robles whose funeral was beginning. Hundreds of funeral guests—including the widows of Robles and Alvarado—witnessed gunfire coming from the helicopter which caused the plane to catch fire and crash."

The sensational story went on for hours, with details trickling out to the public as the day went on. Nine individuals, including the pilot, co-pilot, and the politician's security staff, were on the plane. Additional security personnel were on the airfield waiting to escort the governor-elect to the funeral. Their status was unconfirmed. The evening news had footage that panned from the tent by the residence to the wreckage on the airfield. The scorched bones of the crashed plane were scattered across the airfield like cattle bones ravaged by coyotes. My gut told me Mala's men were responsible. Were Rico and Victor consulted?

Later news coverage showed an aerial view of the unidentifiable blackened carcass of a helicopter crashed at a small landing strip in Monterrey some miles from the Robles' larger airfield. The hull's flickering image on the tv screen turned my stomach with apprehension. The news did not say if bodies were aboard. The burned-out chassis of the helicopter was all that was shown on the news, but it was fertile fodder for my anxiety. Rico and Victor would not have actively participated in this killing. They would not have been on the helicopter I was looking at. For hours I've wanted to call Rico and Victor, but I couldn't do it. I didn't want to know.

I tried to bury myself in work, but I was incapacitated with worry. In the evening, I broke down and called the downtown Palacio in Tijuana and reached Rico. He was chipper, upbeat.

"Did you hear the news about the shooting in Monterrey?" I asked him. I was so glad to hear his voice, I was choked up.

"I did. Someone saved me the trouble of doing it myself."

I wanted to explain how worried I had been about him and Victor, but it was like the ghost of Mala was sitting on my shoulder. I could not ask on the phone.

I asked if Victor was at the other Palacio. "Is he okay?"

"Why wouldn't he be okay?" Rico roared as he always does. "He called me a little while ago complaining that they've been busy all afternoon."

I immediately felt better. "Wonderful," I said. "I love you, Rico."

"Not as much as I love you."

The radio news reported a rumor that Mala had cursed the governor-elect just before she had been killed by his state security police. The next morning, newspapers were saying that Mala had killed Miguel Alvarado from her grave. The mourners who camped out around the entire property of Mala's estate since she was killed were said to chant approval of Mala's revenge from her tomb.

CHAPTER 54
RICO SANTOS

NOVEMBER 1986

OVER A MONTH HAD GONE by since the governor-elect's death and the calls from reporters to my brother and me kept on coming. Adults asking stupid questions about the curse on Miguel Alvarado by our grandmother. "Is it true, did she really place a curse on him moments before she died?"

"I wasn't there, fool," I barked.

Joaquin Perez from the *Dispatch* where Luciana had once worked wouldn't let up with conjecture about my grandmother's infamous run as the queen of heroin in Mexico. He stopped writing articles after he received a night visit at his home. The barrel of a 45-caliber pistol was pushed in Joaquin's mouth with a promise of another visit should he continue to write stories about Mala.

A Dallas reporter named Kota called me four times, and I finally took his call. "Mr. Santos, did you have anything to do with the assassination of the governor-elect and the many innocent souls who didn't go home that night?" I hung up on him.

The next morning, an article on the front page with Kota's name was published by the Dallas Herald. "…it makes perfect sense that the killings in Monterey, Nuevo Leon were a revenge massacre for the admitted killing of Magda (Mala) Hidalgo by State Police. Governor-Elect Miguel Alvarado issued a statement shortly after the death of the Drug Queen of Mexico stating that he had authorized the apprehension of the ninety-seven-year-old, dead or alive.

Two days after the article was published, Reporter Kota received a visit at the home of Lola Herrera's house. Lola was his mistress. Kota pulled a gun on the visitor but wasn't quick enough. He was killed. Lola was caught in the crossfire.

Days later a newspaper in Houston, Texas published a scathing story that the shooting of Kota was revenge for the story he had written. Two reporters wrote the story, Carlos Beltran, and Raul Castaneda.

I ordered a kill, but my brother Victor had already put the hit out.

My attorney Luis Campos called me. "We need to meet now," his voice stern.

Four hours later I waited on the tarmac of the Juarez Airport where he landed in his private jet. He deplaned, and we had a standup meeting between his plane and my car.

"You know I love you and your brother," he began.

I trust Luis and so does my brother. We respect him. He's smart and connected here and in the USA. His office is in Mexico City. His first language is Spanish, and he mastered English, French and Arabic. He reminded me of James Baker, our teacher, our friend who did a darn good job of teaching my brother and me foreign languages but not to the tune of our lawyer.

"We love you as well, Luis. What is so urgent you flew down here on four hours' notice?"

Luis moved up close to me and looked up. He poked my stomach with his finger, three times. "You stop this stupidity right now. You can't do this in the U.S. and get away with it. You are snuffing these people on U.S. ground. You can't do this, Rico!"

"Luis, I don't know what you are talking about."

"Rico, the homicides are not in Juarez. You get it? No one here to buy off."

"I get it. My brother and I had nothing to do with any of it."

Luis poked me in the stomach again. It was the poke that made me roar in laughter. I stopped short of lifting him up, so we'd be eye to eye.

"Rico, I'm not getting on the plane until you promise me this is over with the reporters."

I stopped laughing and paused a bit. "These stories are bad," I said.

"The stories will stop. I will be all over their ass if they mention you and your brother, I promise. I will hit them where it hurts, their bank account. They don't want to spend money litigating for the next five years."

Less than thirty minutes after Luis arrived, he was back on his plane, and I was back in my car, and we went our separate ways.

Later I met up with my brother Victor. "I promised Luis no more executions or violence. Luis says he will immediately sue the punk reporters and newspaper they work for if our name is mentioned."

"What about Grandma's name?"

I looked at my brother then gave him a hug. I was still hugging him when I said. "Let's move on and let Luis handle it. He has a string of lawyers here in Texas that need business."

"It's never going to stop," Victor said.

"I promise, it will stop when lawsuits are coming at them as fast as they publish crap."

Gusto sent the stretch Lincoln Continental for the trip to the El Paso airport where my plane and crew awaited. Menso was behind the wheel and Tapas stood by the open door waiting for me to get in.

"Why this?" I complained as I stepped into the car. "I should drive my car and you can follow me."

"Jefe, the other cars were blocked. Sorry, I know you hate this car."

By the time I replied, Tapas had shut the heavy bulletproof door and was settling into the front seat next to Menso.

"Okay, let's hit it," I said.

"Si, Jefe. Have you there in no time."

I pressed a button, and the glass partition went up.

I sat back in the comfortable leather seat and closed my eyes to see pictures of Grandma that my brain broadcasted. I smiled. I wonder if she ever rode in this car or any of the cars she owned. I tried to remember but no memory of her in a car. I thought of James and Elena. Victor and I were little ones jumping between this seat and the side seats while Gusto drove us on outings to El Paso a bunch of times. Elena didn't always come with us.

I looked out the window. Light rain caused droplets to appear and gradually be blown away as the car sped along the highway.

"Rico, I have a surprise for you. The architect has plans ready to show you. We can break ground right away. I need you in Los Angeles." That was yesterday, a call from my contractor. My dream castle on the beach in Ensenada.

My other dream was getting a plane with a big bed.

Menso stopped the car right up close to my plane, a moment later. Tapas had the door open. Just as I stepped out of the car, Miguel and Angel appeared all dressed up in suits.

"I told Gusto I'm not taking bouncers."

"Jefe, Gusto said we have to go," said Miguel.

I pointed my finger at Miguel and quickly at Angel. "Get in your car. Don't need security for this trip." I gently spread my arms and walked past them. I walked towards the plane stairs and looked up and there was Victoria and Noa, my flight attendants showing me beautiful teeth, my eyes on them. I thought how the rain had paused so I wouldn't get wet during the short walk from the car. I smiled to myself. I'm not religious but I believe in God. I figure nothing happens without him. Like pausing the rain. God did it for sure.

From afar I heard projectiles coming in my direction. I jumped away from the staircase and rolled on the tarmac.

A sudden burning sensation.

I could hear my sensei scolding me. "You moved too slow!"

Bullets ricocheting off the pavement. ---Screams. ---Darkness.

I can't remember feeling as tired as I feel now.

I can't remember having a headache before.

Someone is slamming my head with a bat. I can't move to defend myself.

My eyes won't open.

Not real.

… the bat not the person doing this to me.

"I will kill you," I hear myself say. It's not my voice. I hear a weak voice. A frightened voice. "Wake up." My voice is weak… I barely hear myself.

I see a floating vision above me, a face then another face.

"Grandmother, am I dead?"

"You are not dead. You must be strong."

"I am strong."

Another face—familiar, a photograph, an old photograph, framed in silver located in many rooms of the big house.

"Mama is that you?"

I felt an embrace.

"My son. You must live. You must survive."

"I will," I said, my voice stronger. "I will survive."

I'm spinning fast. I'm falling… flying… I spread my arms… My head is bursting with pain, my body is hot… I'm in a furnace… No… No… I don't want to be in hell… No… No…

I hear screaming. It's me… My mother is above me. Her hands touching my face, her eyes penetrating mine… I look away. I smell a horrible burning smell… Flames are all around me, my mother is no longer there… I'm ablaze. I scream very loud… The stench of burn flows into my nostrils. I cough. I can't stop coughing.

CHAPTER 55
ELENA MUNOZ

NOVEMBER 1986

I HEARD the news from Victor.

I said to Quick, "Rico has been shot. El Paso Hospital."

"I'm coming with you."

"Do a last call and don't let anyone else in. Come over when you close."

I didn't cry until I started my car and began the short drive to the hospital. I had to stop on the side of the road and tried hard to control the weeping that just kept coming. I started to cough. I'm a karate senpai, conditioned to be strong and calm under all circumstances, but at the moment that didn't matter at all. My grief was unbearable. My body trembled as chills engulfed it. I felt defenseless and vulnerable. Suddenly insecure. I had never felt like this before, not even when I was ambushed and raped.

CHAPTER 56
LUCIANA

NOVEMBER 1986

QUICK CALLED me and told me the terrible news. I had just gotten home. I hurried to get out of the house and in my car, headed to the hospital.

My head was filled with questions. I knew nothing. "He's been shot…" is what Quick said to me. "Soon as I can close I'll be there," she added.

About a hundred feet from the highway on-ramp I stopped the car, opened the door, and leaned out face down to the street while I remained seated and I vomited—no food, liquid foam. Dizzy, nauseous.

CHAPTER 57
VICTOR

NOVEMBER 1986

MENSO ACCOMPANIED by Tapas took Rico to the airport. Menso survived the slaughter, he was in the driver side of the bullet-proof car and he saw it all happen. Tapas never made it back to the passenger seat. Miguel and Angel who were supposed to travel with my brother as body guards were taken out by the sharp shooter. Stewardesses Victoria and Noa were shot dead and the two pilots in the cockpit were not expected to make it, shot through the cockpit windshield as they sat in their seats preparing for the trip to Los Angeles. I picture a tornado and I'm spinning in the cone of it. My teeth chatter from hate at the unknown person who ordered the hit against my brother.

My brother Rico is in surgery going on four hours.

The administrator of this hospital is a regular at the El Paso Palacio.

Elena and Quick know him well. His name is Paco Silva. He assured us that the surgeons were experts in their specialty. Three surgeons.

"I promise, your brother is in good hands. We attend to many victims of shootings from El Paso and Juarez."

I wanted to believe Paco. It was important the doctors were really experts. I felt better after hearing him tell us about the many victims. I didn't know there was so many shootings in El Paso. Maybe Paco is lying in an effort to make us feel better.

The administrator wanted to let us wait in his office but I declined. I wanted to be close to the surgery room, so we found seats in the waiting room. Quick, Elena, Luciana, Me and Gusto.

As time passed by I grew more uncomfortable. I asked myself, if the doctors are as good as Paco said, why are they wasting their time in El Paso?

Stay positive, I told myself.

Before surgery, doctors assessed the damage of the bullets. They were not certain, but it appeared that Rico got hit with four bullets. One bullet grazed a heart valve and exited through his back. Two bullets to upper torso, straight through. The fourth bullet scraped his temple and that may have caused him to pass out or it could have been why he fell head first on to the tarmac. If he had been himself, he would have rolled back on to his feet just as he does in karate or judo.

I'm stressing myself out by trying to figure it out. All I have to go by is what the driver told me. He was there in the bulletproof car; he saw everything. But he didn't see the shooter, wherever that bastard positioned himself to have such clear shots of my brother and all the others he put bullets into.

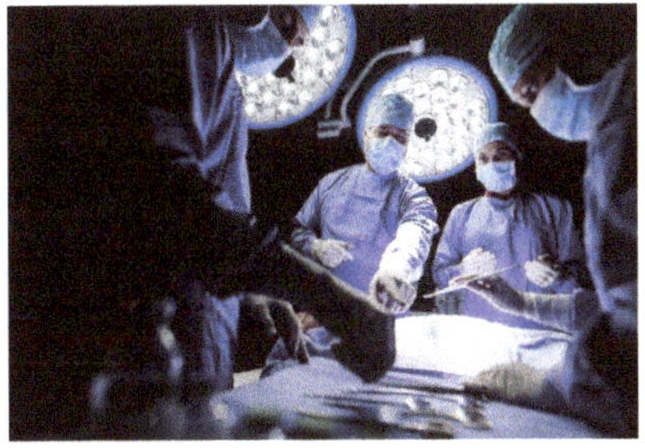

It seemed ten times longer, but it was five hours of surgery. Hospital Administrator Paco introduced us to one of the doctors. A Neuro surgeon. "He's fragile but I am very optimistic and so are my colleagues, Dr. Ramon and Dr. Fuentes. They will be out here soon. He's in a coma. We'll know more in twenty-four hours."

"Did you induce the coma?" I asked the doctor.

"No, we did not induce the coma."

I figured that was not good but Elena beat me with a question.

"What about the bullet to the heart?" asked Elena.

"Dr. Ramon will give you a better report. The heart valve was bruised not ruptured. Lots of blood from small vessels."

Luciana said, "Thank you, doctor, thank you."

"Yes," I said, extending my hand out again for another handshake.

Elena smiled, her eyes tearing. I saw her lips move, "Thank you, Doctor."

After meeting with the doctors I accepted Paco's invitation to use the conference room connected to his office. The cafeteria delivered coffee, pastries and sandwiches.

My brother was in the recovery room for two hours then moved to the intensive care unit. Paco arranged for us to visit him for five minutes. His head was bandaged up, and he looked peaceful as he slept. To the three of us, we would never know he was in a coma.

I went home to shower and change clothes. I convinced Elena and Luciana to get some sleep and if anything at all happened, I would call them immediately to come to the hospital. Less than half an hour after I returned to the hospital, Elena, Luciana and Quick showed up. We took over Paco's conference room and the four of us found comfort and sleep on recliner chairs that were moved in to the room while we were away.

Forty hours after my brother was taken to the intensive care unit he was still in a coma. I was in touch with our lawyer Luis in Mexico City. "Good news, Victor. I have a neurosurgeon from Mayo Clinic arriving first thing in the morning to check Rico. I chartered an executive jet and a ride from the airport and to stay with him as long as needed."

"Wonderful," I said. "Wonderful."

Earlier Luis had told me how prestigious the Mayo Clinic was. To hear Luis had a doctor from there coming to see Rico gave me a happy chill. I passed the good news to Elena and Luciana. I also brought Paco up to date with the news and asked him to let the doctors who were attending Rico know that a doctor was coming out to examine Rico and offer an opinion. Paco did not seem offended. That morning I gave him an envelope with five thousand dollars as a gift for the attention he had given us thus far. He refused to accept the money, but that only lasted sixty seconds. I felt much more comfortable accepting his hospitality at the hospital after giving him the envelope. You do for me, I do for you. That's me.

Luciana got away for a little while and visited the library and came back with two books about the Mayo Clinic. The three of us came away from our reads about Mayo extremely grateful, happy that Luis had accomplished this all from his Mexico City office.

Early in the evening after the news that the doctor from Mayo was arriving the next morning, Elena, Luciana and I took Paco's advice and went home to get a good night's sleep. He offered to give us sleeping pills to take with us in case we had difficulty falling asleep. We accepted the sleepers.

At the big house Gusto was there, and I met with him. "Hours are passing fast and no news on who did this to my brother."

"I have money out everywhere. Something will turn up, Jefe."

I would never know for sure if my brother would have killed Gusto had I not been there to dissuade him from doing it. I wanted to say something to Gusto. I forgive you or something but I couldn't do it. Too much going on. Gusto had to know we loved him. The fact that his army let him down was not entirely his fault, even though it cost my grandmother to be killed. Just like that.

I went straight to my bedroom, showered and crashed on my bed. I didn't need a sleeping pill. I was out. My marriage to marshal arts conditioned me so that I could awake fully alert no matter if I was in a deep sleep. I doubt that would hold true for the nine hours I zonked out. I was saturated with exhaustion, mentally and my entire body.

The neurosurgeon from Mayo was named Robert Johnson. His CV said he was fifty-eight, a doctor for half that many years. A neurosurgeon for twenty-years. He walked into the waiting room where I was with Elena and Luciana. He had spent two hours going over the medical record and examining my brother. Elena, Luciana and I wanted the doctors attending to my brother locally to attend the meeting with the Mayo surgeon but our lawyer Luis nixed that. Also nixed Paco attending. "Luis, we're using Paco's conference room since this happened. How can we ace Paco?" I forgot to mention that Luis arrived from Mexico City about the same time as the doctor arrived from The Mayo Clinic.

Dr. Johnson was not critical at all about the treatment Rico was receiving. "I would recommend a craniotomy to relieve the pressure on the brain. When the swelling goes down, we put back the skull."

"Doctor, no way!" I was on my feet.

Luis said, "Let the doctor finish Victor."

The doctor was ballsy. He was calm during my rise.

"Your brother is on medications to do the same thing but I would have recommended the procedure when he underwent the surgery for the other bullet wounds. Medications don't always work."

Luis said, "Are you saying that a craniotomy always works?"

"Nothing is a sure thing. Your brother seems strong, that's why its not too late to do a procedure to relieve that pressure and to take a better look at the bleeding."

Dr. Johnson made a long list of other recommendations, easier to accept than cutting my brother's skull out and putting the piece in a freezer until it was time to sew it back on. "When you are in a coma you are unconscious, however, we don't know for sure if the brain or part of the brain is functioning and if it is, talking to him, touching him, surrounding him with familiar scents, music he liked, his favorite singers…"

Elena asked if he would for certain come out of the coma.

"I can't tell you for sure, no."

Luciana sniffed, and I felt a chill only not a happy one.

An hour into the meeting, Luis sprang it on us. "I talked to the administrator at Mayo and if Dr. Johnson recommends admission it can happen."

Thanks to the books from the library, I knew Mayo was in Rochester, Minnesota. "Should we give him more time here instead of risking a move to Minnesota?" I asked.

"It is your call entirely," Dr. Johnson said. "You don't need to decide today."

"When are you going back?" asked Luciana.

Dr. Johnson stood. "Soon as this meeting is over."

Luis said, "A car is waiting for him out front and the plane is ready to roll."

"Can you stay for a couple days to monitor my brother?"

"If I could, I would. I have patients back at Mayo."

"What will you do at Mayo that he can't get here?" Luciana asked.

"For one thing, he'll have a dozen doctors working to get him out of the coma."

"You won't just cut his skull because you think it's the right thing to do?" Elena looked serious but I think she was kidding.

Dr. Johnson laughed. "No, I promise not to do that without consent.

He may improve and not need a procedure at all. Let's see what the medications do for him."

"One more question," I said, on my feet now. "If I had agreed to follow your recommendation about the procedure, would you have done it personally or were you thinking the doctors here would do it?"

"I would do it at Mayo."

Fifteen minutes later we were at the hospital parking lot seeing the doctor off in the hired car that Luis had arranged for him.

Gusto sent Vando with a big car to pick us up at the hospital to take us to the El Paso Palacio. Quick greeted us and we followed her to the private room where a table was set for the four of us. Luis, Elena, Luciana and me. Back at the hospital there were four licensed and armed body guards to keep Rico safe and just outside the door where we were, Juanita and Lolita stood guard. They worked for Luis. Somewhere in the restaurant there was security that Gusto had watching me twenty-four hours a day since my brother was shot.

We sat at a round table in a banquet room with moving walls to fit as many as five hundred people or as few as a private late lunch as we planned to have. "I know this is a bad time, but I am starved," I said. "All of you must be."

"I can eat," said Luis with a chuckle.

"Same here," Elena said placing the napkin on her lap.

"Rico would not want us to go without eating like we've been doing," Luciana said.

Quick was running the Palacio entirely since Elena was back and forth to the hospital and it was Quick who took our order while two waitresses quickly took care of the drink order. None of us had liquor. Instead we loaded up on Coca-Cola and coffee.

"Victor, please let me arrange everything and let me take Rico to Mayo in Minnesota." He changed how he said this but he said it at least seven times during our meal.

"Victor, what are you going to do?" Elena asked me. The plates had been cleared except for the coffee cups and an assortment of cake and sliced pie.

"What do you think I should do?" I looked at Elena and glanced at Luciana, but it was Elena who was family to my brother and me.

"It's your call," Elena said. "I took a good look at the introduction to Mayo book that Luis brought. No doubt, Mayo is way up there in national ratings."

"What did it cost to bring Dr. Johnson out here?" I asked Luis.

"I pledged twenty-five thousand dollars to their donations and provided the transportation."

"Good move, Luis. Thank you."

Luciana said, "Maybe you should ask Paco for an opinion and the doctors. They seem so dedicated to treating Rico."

Before I could say anything, Luis spoke. "Paco is the administrator of the hospital. He's not going to recommend you take Rico to Mayo or anywhere else. As for the doctors, they did a good job in surgery but did they mention the procedure as an option?"

"I already told you, no one mentioned the procedure and frankly I'm glad of it."

"I don't want to think that a piece of Rico's skull will be removed from him," Elena said.

"I won't permit that," I said. "Luis, how will you get him to Minnesota?"

"I promise it will be painless. Are you saying I can arrange it?"

I didn't hesitate. I trusted Luis, and I liked the seriousness that Dr. Johnson portrayed. "Yes, go ahead and do it."

Elena extended her hand to mine, a smile on her face.

I looked at Luciana and saw tears and a grin of approval.

CHAPTER 58
MIRASOL

NOVEMBER 1986

I WAS BORN in Mexico City on January 15, 1945, and baptized a Catholic when I was a few months old. My parents were schoolteachers who died in a taxi-bus collision when I was eight. No one in my family could afford another child, and so I ended up growing up in a Catholic orphanage.

The orphanage school was taught by teachers who went home after classes. The curriculum included writing, reading, history, geography, and math. Volunteers taught music, gymnastics, and English.

At ten, I started taking piano lessons. There were two guitars in class and one very old piano. One of my teachers, Margarita Lara, coached me in piano, guitar, and singing.

I felt comfortable with Margarita. I really had no one who belonged especially to me, and she felt like mine. The thing about her is that she believed that I had a gift, and she encouraged it.

"You're talented my dear. We're going to bring it out."

At the beginning of each music class, Margarita wrote a question on the board.

"What do you want to be when you grow up?"

Then, every time, she would go around the room, and we would all answer. Everybody's answers changed all the time, but not mine.

Every time it came to me, I would stand up by my desk and say, "I want to be a singer."

Then she would lock eyes with everyone, not just me, and say, "Now let's work real hard and make that happen."

It meant a lot that she had that much belief in me. Then, one day Margarita didn't show up to teach her class. No one told us why she did not come to class to teach us. Maybe the pastor heard from her. It was just a volunteer class, and since no one told us, we kids kept coming to class, day after day. That first day when there was no one to teach, we sat around and did nothing. The next day, when she was still a no-show, we started playing the guitars and piano, the last lessons we'd been taught. After that, we kept meeting and playing and singing together, and we all worked extra hard on whatever we wanted to do. We all sang and took turns on the instruments. There were two girls, Danna, and Josefa, both a little older than me and one boy named Juanillo.

I don't remember how old I was when Margarita returned. She hugged us and told us she had missed us.

"My husband passed away," she said. She had taken time off from her regular job and from coming to the orphanage.

"I missed you," I told Margarita.

She hugged me. "I missed you more my dear Mirasol."

She kissed my cheeks, and I went back to the dorm happy that she was back. She promised to show up every week like before.

I got curious about all the classes. I tried gymnastics, but I hurt my leg and didn't go back. The volunteer English teacher, Mr. German, came twice a week and pushed me to learn English. He was American, taught English at the University of Mexico City, and volunteered five hours a week at the orphanage. I was so lucky. There were usually about six students, sometimes a few more. We always had homework which I always did. I practiced with two friends in the class. I never became fluent at writing, but I did very well speaking and reading, according to Mr. German.

. . .

Mr. Enrique was said to be the biggest financial contributor to the home. He hired a full-time soccer coach and paid to clear a large area of the grounds and had a field built. Each year he did a little more. One year he installed bleachers with seating for a hundred, which was about how many kids were at the home at any given time.

Mr. Enrique never showed up at the home. At least I never saw him and no one I knew had ever seen him. We knew who he was because once a week all of us would group in the gym and watch one movie he was in, and a series of cartoons. We probably saw all of his movies. They were funny. Sometimes we saw cowboy movies from Hollywood.

The head of the school, Pastor Sifuentes always told us at Sunday services, "You are very lucky to be in this home. Most orphanages barely have enough to feed the orphans."

I knew I was lucky, but still I dreamed of what it might be like to not be in an orphanage. I dreamed of getting out. Boys could leave at fourteen. When I turned twelve, I helped out with the young children for two hours after school, then there was homework for an hour or more and when that was finished, I could have dinner. We all ate what we were served, lots of beans and rice, tortillas, and lots of stuff from the market in Mexico City because Pastor Sifuentes goes over there every market day with some of the teachers, and he walks around and the farmers always give him all their old fruits and vegetables because they are superstitious, and they are afraid if they don't, he might give them the evil eye, and it will rain forty days and forty nights or something.

The only time I had ever been outside the orphanage was with a group of kids going to the park escorted by two or three sisters that lived at the orphanage. We weren't Catholic, but the pastor required us to address our guardians as sister or brother. I knew nothing about the outside world, except for what I saw in movies.

We watched movies, and they gave me a tantalizing peek at the world. I ate up glimpses of homes and children with their parents, all dressed differently. It makes me wonder crazy things, like without uniforms, how do you know what clothes to put on every day?

The orphanage didn't recognize coming of age at twelve. Fifteen was the age accepted by the home. Boys could leave at fourteen if they could demonstrate they were ready to find a job and a place to live. The pastor did not press for anyone to leave, but almost everybody I knew wanted out, like me. It could seem scary though, because once you were out, you were out for good. I got a real good education. At fourteen, I finished with the classes. I could read and write Spanish and English, sing, and play the piano and guitar. Margarita offered to have me come to her home. I took her up on it.

Margarita said that until I decided what was next in my life, I could stay with her.

"I live alone in a small apartment. I have a good job at the university. You'll never have to miss a meal. I can't replace your mother, but I promise to love you like a mother would love a daughter. I love you, Mirasol. I always have," she said.

Pastor Sifuentes approved my departure. When I went out into the world, the pastor presented me five hundred pesos and some clothes. Like everyone before me, I wrote a thank-you letter to Mr. Enrique thanking him for his support and the going-away present.

I hugged my friends goodbye.

The orphanage gave me a small suitcase with underwear, two pairs of shoes, socks, two dresses and a beautiful warm coat like I'd never had while I was there. I was young, but I understood the value of five hundred pesos. It was a lot of money.

The pastor, Sister Mary Claude, Sister Mary Elizabeth, and two brothers—whose names I didn't know because they mostly took care of the boys—walked with Margarita and me to the awaiting taxi outside the front gates. I hugged and thanked them. I had been there seven years. I teared up. At fifteen, I wouldn't let on I was vulnerable like that.

"Pastor, when I become a famous singer and movie star, I promise to be back to help you save kids like me."

Then the cab driver opened the door, and Margarita and I got in, and she gave the cabbie her address.

The pastor blew me a kiss as the car moved away.

All those years that Margarita had asked what I wanted to be, I said I wanted to sing. It was true, but it was not all. The whole truth is that I wanted it all. I wanted to be a movie star.

. . .

The apartment building where Margarita lived was in Tacuba, a neighborhood in Mexico City. I could not remember being in a car before and the traffic was scary. I held on to Margarita's hand and kept a smile on my face. It seemed like an eternity before the car delivered us to our destination.

The building was three stories tall. The apartment was on the third floor. We walked up a lot of steps. The building was modern, and very different from the orphanage with its old worn-down steps, many dormitories, and public rooms. You could tell that the orphanage had once been a church. In the apartment building, there were lots of long narrow halls with lots of locked doors. Margarita stopped at one of those doors and unlocked it.

"Welcome home, Amor."

I walked in a place with many windows, giving a lot of light. Margarita showed me seven rooms, and one of them was mine. My bedroom was beautiful. I had slept in a dorm for so many years. I could not believe this wonderful room was mine alone. I took Margarita's hand and looked up at my friend.

"I love you, Señora Lara."

"Amor, call me Margarita or Mama."

I squeezed her hand. "What do you prefer I call you?"

We both sat on the edge of my bed and faced each other.

"It would be lovely if you called me Mama."

I smiled.

"Yes, Mama. Thank you for everything."

We hugged and cried.

When Margarita was teaching me to read music and play piano and guitar and later to sing, I had no idea that she could play many instruments by ear. She didn't tell me that, but I read it on her teacher bio. She taught three classes a day at the university, four days a week.

For all practical purposes I had gone as far as I could in school unless I enrolled in college, but I didn't think that could happen. I knew from my teachers back at the orphanage that college was not free, even though there were public colleges where it was affordable. The college Margarita taught in was very expensive.

"I talked to the dean. He said you can register in English class and music. All we have to pay for are your books. If you decide you want to take other classes and go for a degree, that is also possible."

"Mama, English and music would be wonderful."

The only music class at the college was taught by my mama, so I became a student. I took English in the morning and in the afternoon, I sometimes stayed for two of her classes. I was able to get used books cheap. There were bulletin boards in the university center building where students put up things for sale for cheap, like their last year's books, and furniture, and old musical instruments. I kept looking there for a guitar.

I knew Margarita could sing, but I had never heard her sing like she did in class. In no time at all, I fell in love with Mama Margarita. She had no kids. Her husband had a heart attack young. Margarita was forty-one, fit, and pretty.

"Get a boyfriend, Mama."

"What for?"

"You want babies, I know it."

"You are my daughter."

Two years later, when I was seventeen, when I was not in class, I was working at the Alameda Hotel located on the famous main street, La Reforma as a desk clerk. My English was very good. The classes at the university took me over the top.

The manager hired me for being bilingual, but he was looking for something else.

I didn't work weekends, and that was good because I hung around talent show spots on Saturday. The big one was on Sunday afternoon. I had practiced La Malagueña, an old-time song that everyone knew. I knew more songs though, because of the classes and because Mama Margarita never stopped teaching. Even a radio was a teaching moment.

It was big because it was shown on public television. The judges were cruel. When I wasn't trying to get picked to try out, I was home watching the program. Many times, the bell was rung on a contestant that had just started to sing.

I got on the Saturday show three times and the bell knocked me out of the box. There were cat calls from the audience when that happened, but I knew it was the guys who liked the way I looked up there. I finally got on the big show one Sunday when I was wearing my best dress.

I didn't get the bell rung on me, but I didn't win either. After the show I got three business cards from record company scouts. My mama said it didn't hurt to contact them, and I did. When I met them backstage, two proposed a lunch to get to know each other better and the third one wanted to take me dinner to talk about how he might be able to help me start a career in singing. My singing was not the top thing on their minds.

But it was a thrill. My colleagues at work had all seen me on television and everyone felt I had won. My mama was of a different opinion. She said I had a better voice, but the winner had more experience. It showed in her movement and the way she handled herself.

"Keep trying," Mama said.

I became friendly with a group of stewardesses who stayed overnight and sometimes for two nights depending on their schedules. Victoria was twenty-two and worked for American Airlines. We double-dated one night. She went out with a crew member, and I went out with one of her flight crew members, a guy named Danny.

"You are the perfect age to have a blast in this business," Victoria said. "Your English is perfect. Apply for a job."

I applied at Mexico Aereo. They hired me. Though the salary was less than what I made at the hotel, I grabbed the job. I gave notice at the hotel and started my training. If I flunked any part of the training, I would be out of a job. That wasn't going to happen. I dreamed of traveling.

Mama wasn't too happy at first, but she came around.

"You are such a brave girl. You've never even been on a plane. What if you become afraid?"

I shook my head, hugged my mama, and said, "I am not afraid. I want this."

. . .

For the past year, four of us have shared a two-bedroom, two-bathroom apartment in Mexico City, a very nice rental in a very safe neighborhood. We all went through the same training program and had the same amount of time with Mexico Aereo. All the other girls have families back home somewhere in Mexico. As far as anybody knows, Mama is my real mama. No one needs to know what my life was like until I was fifteen, anyway. The point is that I had money saved, picked out the apartment, and picked out the best roommates in our class. We are all best friends, like sisters. At least half of our flights, we work together. I wasn't scheduled to work for two more days but I got an early morning call from dispatch at the airport.

Samuel is head of special operations for our employer Aero Mexico Lindo. He handed me a copy of the manifest as he explained.

"Mirasol, you are the purser going and back." I did a playful salute that he ignored as he continued, "The medical passenger is Rico Hidalgo, a grandson of Magda Hidalgo who was killed not long ago as you may have heard."

My team uttered her name just as I did.

"Mala."

"Yes, Mala."

I made the sign of the cross. My team copied. Samuel didn't cross himself.

"Rico Hidalgo is in a coma. He's going from El Paso, Texas to Mayo Clinic in Rochester, Minnesota. You—."

I interrupted. "Samuel, why us and not an American carrier?"

"You are flying in Lopez's personal seven-twenty-seven, not a passenger airliner."

My team and I nodded our understanding like it mattered.

Lopez was our boss, CEO of Aero Mexico Lindo.

"Finally, we get to see the inside of his plane," said Thelma.

"I didn't know he chartered it out," Lupe added.

Maggie laughed. "Bet it's a Mafia thing, a favor thing."

I always say I don't listen to gossip, but the whispers say Lopez had grown quickly from two planes to a fleet of thirty because he's in the drug business. I'd never met my boss Lopez, and neither had my team. He's never around. We do see the TV commercials and billboards. He's gorgeous and the thought that he's a gangster makes him mysterious and all the more enticing. He's a hunk.

A couple hours ago, my team and I didn't know we'd be working this charter or working at all. Counting me, there are four of us: Thelma, Lupe, and Maggie. No matter where we fly together, we go all out to make the flight a happy and fun experience for the passengers. Management receives ongoing compliments about us. For almost a year, we've been working the same flights together. Return passengers cheer us on. Many who don't know us say they've heard about us. All nice, but we don't get paid extra for the popularity. However, working together is rewarding. Our overnight layovers are filled with fun. We make sure of it. Our team was off and not scheduled to work for two more days until Samuel called and offered us this special three-day work assignment. He needed the four of us. The extra money would be great. We accepted immediately, rushed to get ready and headed to the airport for this briefing by Samuel.

Samuel ignored our laughs. "Your first stop is El Paso where a medical team will be working with plane interior engineers to turn the master bedroom into a hospital room where Mr. Hidalgo will be lying on a hospital bed during the flight from El Paso. On your return from Minnesota there will be a stop in El Paso to convert the hospital room back to our boss's bedroom."

"I've never seen a bed on a plane before," I said.

"No one we know has."

My team and I are airline stewardesses, never worked on a charter before and only seen the boss's plane from a distance at the Mexico City airport. I felt excited that we were selected for this three-day trip on a mission that was different from our routine. Maggie, Thelma, and Lupe felt as I did.

CHAPTER 59
LUIS CAMPOS
NOVEMBER 1986

I AM Rico and Victor's lawyer. We took off from El Paso airport twenty minutes ago headed to the Mayo Clinic in Rochester, Minnesota. My friend's executive jet is a Boeing 727 with three engines mounted on the back. What a powerful feeling as we wheel upped. A plane made for 120 passengers and now there are twenty-five seats, one master bedroom suite presently converted to a medical suite and one smaller bedroom that is assigned to me. I've been on this plane once before on a trip with Lopez, the owner of this plane, to meet my friends who wanted to invest in Lopez's airline.

Rico is on a hospital bed in the medical suite cabin located near the aft of the plane. He's on oxygen so there is no worry about breathing recirculated air. I was bedside with him before we took off. The ambulance ride from El Paso Hospital to the plane doesn't show on him. He looks like he's sleeping. He has an oxygen mask, an IV receiving a steady flow of saline to keep him hydrated, and other gadgets to monitor his pulse and blood pressure. He's wired, ready for an EKG on doctor's orders.

Earlier when the plane arrived from Mexico City there were three teams waiting for it. The first team boarded the plane within minutes after it landed to dismantle my friend's personal bedroom and expertly pack everything including the king-sized mattress and box spring.

Within thirty minutes of boarding, the team removed everything from the bedroom on to a moving van.

The second team moved medical equipment, including a hospital bed on to the plane and into the bedroom that would now serve as an oversized hospital room. The carpet had been removed by the first team and the metal frame of the fuselage was exposed. The hospital bed and seven passenger seats were installed near the bed for the doctors and medical team who would be traveling with Rico, two doctors, a critical care nurse, a respiratory therapist, one nurse practitioner and two bedside assistants. The medical team also had assigned seats outside the medical suite where they could sit and eat and rest.

Squares of flooring were installed where the carpet had been. It looked like granite, but granite would have been too heavy. I didn't ask what it was, but it looked good. Less than two hours after team two started working, their work was done. The third team came on board to connect the medical equipment and sanitize the room completely.

No question I could have found a medical charter to transport Rico, but I wanted only the best for him and that's why I asked my friend to let me charter his jet. When that was in place, I conferred with a team at Mayo Clinic to source what was needed to convert the bedroom to hospital space.

Once I confirmed with Dr. Johnson at Mayo that Rico's brother had approved taking him to the facility in Rochester, plans were made quickly. I chartered a plane to fly the medical team from Mayo that would accompany Rico from El Paso to Mayo.

All the above took just under seventy-two hours to accomplish.

"May I get you something to drink, Mr. Campos?" I looked up and saw her for the second time, once when I came on board. There were four of them on the plane. Gorgeous.

"I'm impressed, you know my name," I spoke in Spanish.

"Of course, I know your name. You are the person in charge."

I returned her smile.

"I have a feeling you know everyone's name."

Her smile never left her pretty face. "I have the manifest," she said shyly.

"I think I'll have a Chivas on the rocks."

"Right away, Mr. Campos."

I read her name tag.

"Mirasol, what a lovely name. It fits you perfectly."

The smile again. "You are much too kind, Mr. Campos."

Mirasol appeared carrying a tray with a crystal glass filled with ice and a bottle of twelve-year-old Chivas Regal. She placed a cocktail napkin on the table, the glass on top and held the bottle. "Allow me, Mr. Campos."

I looked up at her and as my index finger pointed to the glass, she poured two fingers' worth of the killer scotch. Coffee was the hardest thing I drank today.

Mirasol placed the bottle back on the tray she was holding. "I'll be back the moment you need a refill, Mr. Campos."

"I have a better idea," I said. "Join me. You have plenty of help, take a break." I was prepared to tell her I'd put in a good word with her boss Lopez, or I could remind her that I chartered the plane. She looked at me long enough for my eyes to meet hers. I think she sighed. Maybe a nervous sigh. My wife tells me all the time that strangers who don't know me, fear me. That it's my look or something.

"Mr. Campos, I saw Mr. Hidalgo when he was brought on board by the medical personnel. He is very young. Is he going to be alright?"

I knew my answer but held it for a few seconds and smiled at her. I'm sitting and she's standing in the aisle looking down at me.

"Come sit with me and I'll explain why I think he's going to be just fine."

Mirasol brightened up when she heard this.

I smiled at her and pointed at the plane seat across from me.

"I'll be happy to join you. Allow me a minute to let my team know."

She took the bottle of Chivas from the tray and placed it on the table.

"I'll be back," she said.

CHAPTER 60
MIRASOL

NOVEMBER 1986

AS A STEWARDESS or purser on a scheduled passenger flight, I cannot sit and chat with a passenger, much less sit across from him with a bottle of Chivas Regal between us.

But this plane is not a scheduled airline flight, it's a charter. The person asking me to sit with him is listed as the person who chartered the plane. I can do it and I'm going to do it because I want to know more about Rico Hidalgo. My team and I were on hand when the medical team wheeled him in from the elevator lift. I led the way, the gurney and medical team walking behind me. I opened the medical suite door and stared at him, oxygen mask and all but I could see him. He was beautiful. A chill went from my face to my toes. It was love at first sight. I'd never been in love before so what do I know about love? Still, I feel close to him, and I don't even know him.

I get hit on by passengers often, and not just men. When that happens, I am the nicest person in the world, always with an excuse and asking for a rain check. Luis, the attorney for Mala's nephews, must be terribly rich to charter this plane and to arrange everything I've seen happen thus far. Exciting.

Lupe and Maggie were taking food orders from the bodyguards who were seated near the galley. Thelma was warming appetizers. "If you need me, find me with the man who chartered the plane. He wants to talk."

"You can't do that, and you know it," Thelma said to me with a gentle poke.

I chuckled. "Watch me." I walked towards Mr. Campos. He was the only person in the parlor area that was set up like a residence living room with plush airplane seats and four sofas. I could see the vacant seat across the table from him where I would be sitting. The pilot had said we'd have some bumps along the way but so far, no turbulence.

I looked at Campos and he gestured for me to sit. He'd barely touched his Chivas and I could tell he had not poured himself more.

"You are beautiful," he said.

I accepted what he said and simply smiled at him.

"Can I pour you a touch?" I asked in Spanish.

"I'm tempted but I must remain stone sober," he answered in English.

"I can get you something else to drink," I offered, starting to get up.

"No, no. This is fine. I will nip at it."

Just then, from behind, Maggie appeared and positioned herself so we could both look up to her. "Mr. Campos, can I get you something to eat?"

I kept a smile on my face. She had wasted no time coming by to snoop.

"I'll take you up on that a little later."

"Mirasol, how about something to drink, coffee maybe?"

"*Si café*, half a mug, black, *gracias*."

"I know how you like it," Maggie said sweetly and walked away.

"There are four lovely ladies on this flight. Lopez outdid himself."

I was going to tell him Samuel picked us, not Lopez. "We work together and we're roommates in Mexico City."

I figured Campos was getting to sixty. He was mysterious, making him interesting. He had a strong vibrant way about him. Scary in a way. He had a Jefe air, a person you called boss even if you didn't know him.

Campos grinned like I'd just given him good news. "Amazing," he said. "You live together in my hometown."

"I met your two assistants earlier," I said.

He chuckled. "They are bodyguards."

"I'm sorry. They introduced themselves as assistants."

"Bodyguards, assistants, same thing."

I figured he knew the two bodyguards were in his bedroom suite.

The conversation was controlled by him, inquisitive, wanting to know all about me and my roommates. He said he was married, four sons and two daughters, all of them off and married with children. His story was different from others I've heard. He didn't say he was living in an unhappy marriage. I felt allured by this important man. Happy I had been invited to sit with him and happy that I took him up on it.

Thelma, not Maggie, returned with my mug of black coffee. I introduced her to Campos. He didn't stand, but he took her extended hand and kissed the top of it. Maggie's smile was her only reaction. I didn't see a blush. Not a shy bone in her beautiful body.

I was halfway from finishing my second cup of coffee and Campos seemed to be enjoying the club sandwich Lupe had delivered to him when I said, "Can I ask you something about Mr. Hidalgo?"

"His name is Rico," he said. "Ask anything. You and I are friends."

"Will Rico recover?"

"The precise reason I'm taking him to Mayo Clinic. To recover."

I felt a chill. I smiled. I gazed into Campos's eyes.

"I will pray for him," I said, and he showed me a slight grin.

"Do you pray?"

I shrugged a little. "I will pray for him."

The orphanage flashed, a quicksilver stream of memories that made my knees ache. I saw the nuns who shepherded us. They led us in prayer. Before meals. After meals. On our knees at bedtime and again in the morning. And then, Sunday Mass. We prayed a lot.

"Rico and his brother Victor are family to me. I am also their *Abogado*."

I kept a smile on my face as Luis talked and talked. I kept thinking he'd bring up Mala. I wondered if he had been her lawyer. I would not ask him that. It was better to stay quiet. His conversation was fascinating to me. He said his home was in Polanco. Everyone in Mexico City knows about Polanco. A neighborhood with mansions for the very rich. His conversation infatuated me, but not about Campos.

My mind raced. I pretended, something I do. I got caught in the dream: I kissed Rico. He woke up from his coma and that bonded us, forever. I pretended Luis Campos asked his bodyguards to leave us alone in the bedroom suite where Rico seduced me. Luis droned on.

I'd never been to bed with a rich, powerful man. Bed powerful, yes, many times. Powerful in life, never. I had sex with two men who were quite older than me and I did it because I was curious and because I liked the way I was treated. I was charmed, conned, and I loved it. One-night stands.

When Luis eventually paused, I asked him about Rico. How old is he? Does he live in El Paso or in Mexico? Juarez? Is he married? Is he engaged?

After my questions, it was clear Luis was on to me. "You said you just today saw Rico and you have all these questions about him?"

I was embarrassed. I'm not sure I blushed.

"I'm sorry. Something happened when I looked at him today. You are correct, I don't even know him. I am worried about him."

"No need to be sorry. What else do you want to know?"

Luis was smiling and seconds later, I matched it. I reached across the table just as he gripped his glass, and I touched his hand.

As time passed, the conversation was plentiful. I realized that Luis was not after my body. He wanted me to sit across from him and listen to the stories he had to tell. I thought about his two female assistants, good lookers. I had only seen them twice: one time when they came on board and one time when they came by the galley for coffee not wanting to wait until we were airborne. Maybe they had heard all his stories, and he wanted someone new to talk to. They didn't look like bodyguards. The six men sitting mid-plane look like bodyguards, and I have them on the manifest as such. They are Rico's bodyguards.

"Are you sure you are flying back tonight?" Luis Campos asked four times in twenty minutes.

"As you know we are stopping in El Paso to have the team put the bedroom back and take out the hospital stuff. We are laying over there for twelve hours."

"Yes, it's too bad. I could take you and your friends to dinner."

"You are sweet," I said.

He handed me his business card and took another one and flipped it over on the table. "Write down your phone number. I will call you when I get back to Mexico City."

I took the pen he offered and wrote down the apartment number. I figured he'd never call.

"It will be nice to hear from you. If you get the recording, we are probably working."

"If there is anything I can ever do for you, call the number on my card. Someone answers that phone seven days a week, twenty-four hours a day."

I smiled. "Thank you."

. . .

Campos's assistants slept in the bedroom suite that was designated for Campos. It was small with a nice standard-sized bed. He spent the flight in the bucket seat across from me and I never saw him go inside the cabin. When the ladies came by to check on their boss, he introduced me to them. Juanita and Lolita.

"You are not missing out on anything here in Rochester," Juanita said. "I made the hotel reservations and got an earful about everything not available."

"Don't be so negative," Lolita said.

Campos smiled at the pretty girls then looked at me. "Never a dull moment with my two girls," he said.

"I hear Minneapolis is nice," I said.

"An hour drive," Lolita said.

"I need to go check on my boy," Campos said.

I braved it. Before I could stop myself, I asked, "Could see him once more?"

"Oh, you know him?" Lolita.

I smiled. "No, I don't know him. I saw him when the doctors brought him on board."

"He's beautiful," Juanita said.

"Come with me," Luis said, and started to the rear of the plane. I walked behind him.

My heart was racing.

How silly of me. I'm a fool for being enamored with a total stranger.

My thoughts didn't mess with my mood. I was on a high. As I passed the galley, I told Thelma, "Handle the plane door for me." As the purser, the door was my responsibility.

"You got it, *Jefa.*" She saluted showing me pretty teeth. Luis kept walking but I could hear his chuckle at Thelma's comment.

Luis opened the door and stepped aside to let me in first. I stepped in like I belonged. I stopped just long enough to whisper in his ear. "I will return the favor," I said.

The doctors looked at me like I was an intruder but when they saw Campos, they gestured that we could come close to the bed. Both wore masks. We didn't have a mask.

Rico looked pale and still on the sheets. Oxygen flowed into tubes in his nose. I wanted to move closer. I wanted to hold him. I wanted to kiss him. It was like I knew him. I stared at his face somehow so familiar to me, wrapped in my imaginings. Campo touched my shoulder and I looked up to discover a medical team had entered the room.

"They are from Mayo," Campos said. "Here to transport him to the hospital."

I followed Campos out to the aisle and away from the door that was now propped open. I wanted to be there when he was wheeled out, but Campos was headed toward his assistants. I rejoined my team.

I stuck by the galley and stole another look at Rico. It was fast. The transportation medics were all around the gurney. A lift was at the service door and in less than a minute the gurney was on it. We stood by a window and watched how quickly he was wheeled on to an awaiting ambulance. His bodyguards were all over the back of the ambulance then in two awaiting vans. Campos was gone. His assistants were gone. Not even a goodbye.

CHAPTER 61
FLORENCIA
1986

I HAVE BEEN Rico's maid for the longest time. He always flirted with me when I worked in the big house. When his grandmother built his bungalow, I worked full time for him. I kept his house neat as a pin. I could do the entire place from top to bottom in two hours, then what with the other hours I had to work?

I rolled his marijuana cigarettes and kept his two cigarette cases filled with the smokes. When he was home, we spent time together, listening to music and making love. He treated me like a girlfriend but we never went out or did anything to get attention outside his house. It wasn't him, it was me. I was scared to death that Mala would burn me in the furnace if she found out I was messing with her grandson.

Rico asked me more than once, "How do you know she burns people in the furnace?"

My answer was always the same. "Rico, I was teasing. I love your grandmother."

"Please, no kidding about her." He kissed me. Only I knew how stupid I felt.

"I'm sorry."

"Don't be sorry."

"I'm sorry." I was trembling.

Rico went through phases. First it was sex, then he wanted me to model for him. He asked me to pose for him in bathing suits, lingerie, or wearing something skimpy over my skinny body. The father of my two kids always said I was a sack of bones. Rico thought I was out of this world. I threw out the father of my kids before Rico was in the picture. Rico thought I was just right. When he drew me close and when we weren't together,I fantasized that we were more to each other.

Finding nice lingerie was not easy in Juarez, even with a purse full of Rico's money. I didn't have a border crossing card, and, without one I could not shop in El Paso, Texas. I bought what I could, and that wasn't much. When I tried to give him money back I didn't use, he insisted I keep it. He was too generous with me.

I'm an ordinary woman in the privacy of Rico's hideaway on the huge grounds of his grandmothers's sanctum, and I pranced around posing for the boss. I felt sensual. He made me feel beautiful with his compliments, whistles and cat calls that only the two of us could hear.

We didn't engage in the little games often because Rico was away a lot. When we did spend time together like this, going home was hard for me. I wanted to be with him all the time. I knew that was not going to happen. I dreamed; you would too. I never, never, made him feel uncomfortable. When I thanked him for his time and the extra money he gave me, he'd say, "I don't want to hear it." He has a beautiful smile. His teeth are perfect. With time on my hands when he wasn't there, I didn't send his laundry to the big house like I was supposed to. I took care of it. I even ironed his socks and underwear. He noticed!

The chief maid, Elba, works at the big house. She's my boss. Even when Mala was alive, Elba was in charge but all of us knew Mala commanded everything. When Rico arranged for me to work at his house, he didn't go to Elba. Of course, he went to his grandmother. She approved but a day before I started my new position, I was summoned to Mala's office.

"You must never become pregnant, you understand me?"

I was so scared I could have peed right there where I stood but was too petrified to do even that. "I promise," I said in a barely audible voice.

"I don't hear you," she said.

"I promise that will never happen."

When I left her office, I wondered why she thought I would get pregnant. Was she assuming Rico would have sex with me? I'm just a skinny runt, is what I thought. After that, I fantasized day and night. It didn't happen right away. When it did, Rico would say things like, "I don't have a lot of practice. I hope you don't mind."

I wanted to tell him I didn't have much practice either but more than he had.

It was fun.

Rico never played the macho part with me.

When he couldn't get it up after the first time, he said, "Don't ever tell anyone."

"Never worry about it," I said. I feasted on him and he'd come back up. He was a monster.

We became so used to each other. Rico could go and go. It had nothing to do with me teaching how to extend his pleasure. It was him. He was comfortable with me. I was in heaven with him.

After Mala died, Rico called the big house and asked Elba to come over to his house. I was in the kitchen but I could hear everything. I already knew what he wanted to tell her. Why were my legs shaking?

"From now on, Florencia will not wear a uniform. She can wear whatever she wishes and no one will make faces at her."

"Si, of course," Elba said.

"One more thing. She works for me and no longer reports to you or anyone else."

"Si, of course."

I don't consider myself an insecure person, then what was it that after Elba left, why were my legs still shaking?

We had a wild hour or two, then I lay on top of him, breathing hard.

I said it again."I'm sorry about my flat chest and skinny ass." It certainly wasn't the first time I said that. I wanted to hear him say it again.

"I love your ass and I love your tits. Just the way they are."

The slap on my butt with his big hand was loud. It never hurt. I loved it.

I loved wearing my own clothes. It took some time for me to get over the discomfort and awkwardness between me and my friends who still worked in the big house. One day, Rico gave me this huge candy sucker and said I had to sit there and eat it in front of him and I did. This man can keep a smile on his face for hours, or so it seems. His dimples and grin turn me on. I'm not the only woman. When he brings women to the house, I keep out of the way. I'm okay with anything I have no control over. As time went on, it did hurt, but I never showed it. I was hungry for any time at all he gave me, and appreciative when it happened. Sex was just that, it's not what I looked forward to.

Little by little I saw less and less of him. Just when I started to really miss him, he appeared. He teased me that he wanted me to go to Los Angeles with him. I reminded him I didn't have a tourist visa to travel to the USA, not even a day pass to cross the border.

"I will have my attorney fix that," he said. "I promise. I want to take you on my plane."

I was like a little girl. I could feel my cheeks get hot. "Really? Oh, I want to, Rico."

"I will have my lawyer come over and get your information and soon, you can go to the U.S. with me."

Rico left in a hurry. He had a meeting. He picked me up like he does, cradled me and kissed me. "You should sleep here any time you want."

"Oh, thank you, Rico, but I can't do that."

"You have two kids, I forget."

"No, my mother takes care of them. I can't stay in this house unless you are here."

He smiled, kissed me, and was gone.

Later that night, I heard the news that Rico had been shot just as he was boarding his plane. The radio and television stories said Rico's condition was not known. He had been taken to a hospital in El Paso. Two stewardesses on the plane were fatally shot as they stood by the door of the plane and the assassin didn't stop there. He shot both pilots in the cockpit, wounding them.

It was ten at night when I got to the big house where the entire staff was gathered. Everyone was there, including the day shift that had gone home like me and had returned. Elba saw me.

"You don't have to be here," she said in an even tone, but not mean.

"I want to be here," I said as she eyed me. "I have to be here, Elba."

I wanted to be there. I knew that news of Rico's condition would travel to the big house by reliable sources and not radio and television people guessing.

Elba shrugged. "Get a uniform and put it on if you want to be here."

"Yes, of course. Thank you, Elba."

I double timed it to the personnel room where men and women dress and use the bathroom facilities. I took a uniform my size from the clothes rack and five minutes later I was back in the kitchen where the staff was huddled.

I prayed silently to the Virgin that Rico is alive.

I joined over fifty workers outdoors in the garden to say the rosary. I didn't have to hide my tears because everyone was crying.

CHAPTER 62
RICO SANTOS

COMA

I CAN'T REMEMBER FEELING as tired as I feel now.

I can't remember having a headache.

Someone is slamming my head with a bat. I can't move to defend myself.

My eyes won't open.

This is not real.

I see the bat not the person doing this to me.

"I will kill you," I hear myself say. It's not my voice. I hear a trembling voice. A frightened voice. "Wake up." My voice is weak… I can barely hear myself.

I see a vision floating above me, a face, then another face.

"Grandmother, am I dead?"

"No, you are not dead. You must be strong."

"I'm not weak. Only tired, I am."

I looked at the other face. She looked familiar. I had seen her in a photograph, in many photographs, some framed in silver in many rooms of the big house.

"Mama, is that you?" She smiled. I felt her embrace.

"My son. You must live. You must survive."

"I will," I said, my voice stronger. "I will survive."

I'm spinning fast. I'm falling… flying… I spread my arms… My head is bursting with pain, my body is hot… I'm in a furnace… No… No… I don't want to be in hell… No… No…

I hear screaming. It's me. My mother is above me. Her hands are touching my face, her eyes penetrating mine. I look away. I smell a horrible burning stench. Flames are all around me. My mother is no longer there. I'm ablaze. I scream very loud. The burning stink flows into my nostrils, expands in my lungs. I cough. I can't stop coughing.

I must be dead. Everything is black. I don't hear anything. I know I was shot. When was it? How long have I been here? Where is here?

I must be dead.

I lose track.

I try to wake up.

Not dreaming.

My head has never hurt like this.

I feel pain.

I can't be dead if I feel this miserable pain.

I try to move.

Paralyzed?

Is anyone here?

There, I said it.

Is anyone here?

I want to wake up.

Can you hear me?

CHAPTER 63
VICTOR

MAYO CLINIC

THE HOSPITAL ROOM where my brother lay in a coma is a large suite. Glass doors stand between the medical area where Rico lay on a hospital bed at the center of everything, and the sitting area that surrounded the room. There were leather sectionals, two restrooms, a small kitchen with a refrigerator, coffee maker and a cabinet stocked with munchies.

When Rico arrived at Mayo, he was getting his fluids, nutrients and meds through a tiny plastic tube inserted in a vein. The team of doctors who attended him talked about changing this to a nasogastric tube that bypassed his mouth and esophagus, and went directly to his stomach, but that was on hold.

After a week at Mayo, my brother did not look as pale as before. His color was good, which the doctors said was an indication he was getting his nutrients and fluids. A team of registered nurses rotated so that there was always one of them in the room with him. There was one chair next to the bed where the nurse sat.

Elena, Luciana, and I took turns at his side, twelve hours each. We had plenty of room in the suite. I found myself standing and watching my brother through the glass, the nurse's back to me.

After the second week, the lead doctor tried talking us into going home. We compromised. Instead, two of us went home. One of us stayed at the hotel and walked two blocks to the hospital several times a day to spend three or four hours in his room. Every ten days, we rotated. I would come up or Elena would fly to Mayo to be with Rico.

Miguel left for Mexico City. He called several times a day for progress. He was also in touch with the doctors daily and so was I, even when I was back in Juarez.

When one of us talked or read to Rico, the nurse stepped out to give us privacy.

I would read till I got hoarse. When I paused my reading to him. I pleaded.

"Bro, wake up already," I said at least a thousand times. "The doctor says a scent could bring you back. I've thought about bringing you a hot pussy to sit on your face but I'm worried that a doctor might walk in." I laughed.

You've never heard the sound of loneliness until you've heard laughter echo in a coma suite. I needed to hear him laugh. I needed to hear anything from him, some assurance that he was still in there.

"Rico, please wake up. Please."

"A fragrance has been known to bring someone back from a coma. Music. The scent of a friend. A familiar voice. Conversation from someone he knows and loves and spent time with." The doctor hammered us with therapeutic suggestions. We all fit this template. Nothing worked. Rico slept on and on.

When I returned to Juarez, Florencia asked me about Rico. I could not help noticing what a beautiful girl she is. I wasn't sure if there was a personal relationship between Rico and her but probably so. My brother's personal maid. How is it possible he wouldn't have something going with her? I got an idea.

"Florencia let's go in my grandmother's office and have a talk. Let me explain what is going on with Rico."

CHAPTER 64
FLORENCIA

"RICO CAN'T SPEAK," explained Victor. We were in Mala's office. "There are times it seems he's trying to talk. His doctors insist he can't talk while in a coma. They are wrong. He said your name. I repeated it back to him, and he smiled."

I showed my excitement. I didn't believe Victor, but he didn't know that.

"Don Victor, really?"

"The doctor says there are things that may help him come out of the coma. Familiar voices talking to him. A fragrance. Please come with me and give it a try. I know I heard him utter your name. Not once. Four times."

Still didn't believe him. Still got a chill. "Of course," I said.

My mom would take care of my kids like she does every day when I'm working.

"Did you and my brother talk much? You go back a long time with him."

I know I blushed, but it didn't cloud my reply. "I am just a maid. But Don Rico never treated me like a maid. I mean. Yes, we talked a lot. He was always so friendly and kind to me."

Victor's grin went from subtle to blazing.

"You don't need to tell me, but I need to ask. Did you and my brother have a sexual relationship? If you did, he might recognize your scent."

I blushed again.

"Jefe, I will do whatever you want me to do." I didn't answer his question and he didn't ask again.

A movie played in my brain, scenes of Rico making love to me. I chilled all over.

The following morning, in Mala's office where we had met the day before, Victor introduced me to Juan Santiago, a lawyer I had never seen before.

"I told her to bring her birth certificate and Mexican passport," Victor told the attorney.

I handed my papers to Juan Santiago. I sat nervously watching him read.

"Is that all you need?" Victor asked him.

"I can do it with this. We need photos. We can do that across the street from the US Consulate Office. Are you ready?" He was looking at me.

"Yes sir," I said.

Next thing I knew, I was on a plane with Victor on my way to a distant place where Rico was hospitalized. It was my first time on a plane. It was my first time away from Juarez, period.

Everything happened in fast motion. Less than two hours after I took the visa photos, Victor's attorney had my U.S. Visa to travel. It wasn't a very good picture of me. I was too nervous when I took it, with the attorney's beady eyes on me the whole time. We got what we came for. The attorney delivered me back to Mala's house and Victor was waiting for me.

"Gusto will take you home to pack a few things. I will buy you everything you need once we get to Rochester. It is very cold there right now. Gusto will pick you up at six tomorrow morning, and I'll meet you at the airport."

"Yes, Jefe, I will be ready. I have warm clothes and this coat I'm wearing is very good in winter."

Victor grinned. "Pack light. I'm going to buy you everything you need."

Juarez is hell most of the year. Winters in Juarez are extremely cold. I'll see how cold it is where I'm going.

On the plane, I heard myself ask, "Did he really say my name?"

Victor looked right at me. "My brother has not said a word. I'm sorry for lying."

I smiled and raised my hand. "Please don't apologize."

Victor smiled. "I couldn't take a chance that you would say no."

"I'm honored," I said. "I wouldn't know how to say no."

His reply was a grin.

The plane bounced many times. One time, I must have looked scared. Victor got up from his seat, walked around a table that was between us and leaned over to hug me, plane bouncing all the time.

"Be careful, Jefe, don't fall." He laughed. He hugged me tighter.

"It's just turbulence," he said.

He reminded me of his brother, kind to the core.

The landing was bumpy, terrifying. I had my eyes squeezed shut and was holding my breath the whole time. As the plane slowed, Victor announced it was snowing. That's when I pried my eyes open and looked out the window next to me. The snow was coming down in a fluffy white shower. I'd never seen anything like it. I forgot everything but the wonder of what I was seeing. Maybe I even squealed in excitement. I looked from the window to Victor. Our eyes met. I could see Rico in his face, and my heart fell hard with the gravity of Rico's condition.

"You are beautiful."

"You are too kind, Jefe." I felt my cheeks burn with embarrassment as the plane came to a stop. I wanted to pinch myself to make sure I wasn't dreaming. I had been chosen by Rico's brother to come here. Such a high honor for me. I couldn't believe it.

· · ·

I felt horrible to see Rico lying there unconscious, but I didn't cry. Victor, Luciana, and Elena were around the bed. I'm just a servant. I couldn't cry in their presence. I remembered the women. I know them better than they realize.

"Hold his hand," Victor said. "Tell him you are here."

I felt the heat creep up my neck.

"Yes, of course," I said.

I remembered Luciana. Rico had her at his bungalow too many times to count. I stayed away when she was around. She was a screamer. I tried to not hear but even with his radio booming and his bedroom door shut, she yowled like a cat in heat. Elena, I've known for long long time. She was their teacher. I remember her at the bungalow but not too many times. Not a screamer. Always a class act.

I moved close to the hospital bed and put my hand on his index finger. His upper finger showed just a little bit of hair and as my fingers moved to his palm, I saw the other three fingers with a dust of hair but none on his thumb. I remembered asking about it. He didn't know why he had hair on his knuckles. We laughed over it. I became so wrapped up in the moment that I didn't care the others were there. I leaned over and kissed his big hand.

"Please wake up, Rico." My lips moved on his hand as I spoke in a low voice. I felt the tears spill out of my eyes and did nothing to wipe them away. I thought about his hands and fingers on my body. The man was never still. This was not the time to reminisce, but my heart felt squeezed like a washcloth, twisted, and wrung out.

"Please wake up, Jefe."

"I don't mind staying here at the hospital. I want to, if it is possible," I said for the third time. We had moved from the bed to the sitting area, and a nurse had taken ownership of the chair beside Rico's bed. "I can sleep on the sofa. It's so big, I fit easy." They laughed. It was good to hear them laugh. They didn't get along that well. They all had independent ideas, and none of them were great at compromise.

Elena said, "The hotel is three blocks away."

"I'll do whatever you say, but I don't mind staying here day and night." Victor told me about several cafeterias and eateries on the way to the hospital. I would be fine.

The group is difficult with each other. At one point they called Victor's lawyer Miguel. I never met him, but I listened to one side of the conversation. The group was looking for advice on whether I should stick around in place of them rotating turns like they were doing. I was quiet, smiled, and occasionally, picked up the coke bottle and took a sip. It was room temperature. I had been nursing it long time.

To cut to the chase, this is what happened. The lawyer Miguel arranged for the hospital to give me a room across the hall from Mario's suite. It was a very nice room with a large bathroom and a jacuzzi tub. The windows had drapes. I don't think it was a patient room. The bed was not a hospital bed. It was queen-sized and a comforter with all the colors of the rainbow. Before I fell asleep, I counted six pillows, hospital slippers and an assortment of toiletries. It was a better selection than what I had at home.

My last night in Juarez, I went to see a *Curandera*[1] who lives near my home. She's not a witch like many people call her. She's a healer. My two kids, my mother and myself, we rely on her when we are sick. I didn't tell her I was leaving to the United States. "I have a friend who is in a coma. Do you know what that is?"

"Yes, I know. Who is it?"

"It doesn't matter who it is. Do you have something to make him wake up?"

"Marijuana paste. I don't have the marijuana to make it for you."

I went back to Mala's home and came back to the healer with a small bag of the weed. Everyone has access to weed at the house.

Late that night, the healer gave me a small Pond's cream jar of paste and told me to rub it on him every day. "I have blessed it and made sacrifices," she said to me. Her look was a little wicked like she sometimes looks when she hams it up. Kind of funny but I wasn't going to laugh at her.

The ointment had no scent. I never thought if taking it across the border was legal or not. Marijuana is illegal in Juarez but no one that uses it seems to care. Rico smokes it all the time. His brother too.

I packed the jar with my toiletries and uniforms in my small suitcase.

On the plane with Victor, I considered telling him about it but I held back. It didn't seem important. Plus, the plane was overwhelming. I didn't want him to think me an old-fashioned peon for going to a *Curandera.*

"I don't mind wearing uniforms. Do I not look okay like I'm dressed?"

It was early morning, and I was already uniformed up, ready to sit by Rico's side, maybe see if I could use some of the cream without anyone yelling at me. A nurse was in the chair by Rico.

Elena and Victor exchanged a look. Elena put her arm around my shoulder and gave me no choice. She took me to a department store to buy clothes.

Victor had mentioned shopping. I wasn't really expecting clothes, but I wasn't surprised she was the one to take me to the stores. The department store was overwhelming. Rico had sent me off to buy lingerie before, but other than that, I never felt like clothes were that important. I mean, I had uniforms to work in, and that was most of the time. Who cares what I where at home? But I guess Elena cared. I'd known her for a long time, and she always was a class act. She had lived at the house for long time, long before I got hired as staff to work alongside my big sister. She was always kind to me. The only reason I can read a little is her insistence on helping me as I was growing up.

I asked her, "Why me?"

"Because you're special," she said. I was just a little girl, happy to be working with my sister at Mala's house. In Juarez, there was no better work to be had. You never go hungry and barefoot working on the estate. Even as a girl, I knew that work meant I had a future. That's how we begin if we're lucky enough to come from a family already working for Mala.

Elena insisted I stay in one of the outfits, and put my uniform into the shopping bag. I went back to the hospital with a wardrobe for ten days.

"Send everything to the cleaners, a block away," Elena instructed. "Victor is going to be so impressed. If Luciana is catty, don't be surprised."

Instead of my starched skirt, blouse, and apron, I had classy-looking slacks, sweaters, shirts, two beautiful warm coats, one light weight jacket, four pair of shoes, including snow boots, and a beautiful purse. As soon as I walked into Rico's suite, Victor whistled.

Elena said, "If you eat at any eatery here at the hospital, sign the bill and charge it to your room number—"

Victor put his right hand up to stop me, and with his left hand, gave me a handful of American money. I didn't count it till later, but it was one thousand U.S. dollars for expenses.

"—or simply pay cash," Victor added with a grin. "Cash always works."

"One of us can stay with you," Elena said. She patted my hand in a way that reminded me of my big sister.

The three of them had gone round and round about this many times in the last two days. Elena was worried about me alone in the big city. Victor was on the fence. Luciana was in a hurry, and I could tell she thought the others were too concerned about my feelings.

"I am looking forward to this," I said, a little worried they would start arguing again. "If you trust me, please go back."

"We trust you," Elena said with that beautiful smile she has.

"We will be in touch by phone," Victor said. "Anything at all changes, pick up the phone and call me or any of us."

"Jefe, of course."

"I'll call you here or in your room," Elena said.

"I'll be here," I said. "If I go out to eat, I will not be long."

Victor said. "Don't rush your meals. Thank you for being here for us."

I felt a flush. "It's a pleasure, Jefe."

When the nurse came into clean Rico up, I went into my room to put the new clothes in the wardrobe. Luciana cornered me in the hall, coming back. It was the first time she got me alone. I wasn't blindsided because I knew Luciana before, but Elena had read her right that she was going to show her true colors, all cat and jealous green-eyed monster.

"Puta is what you are. No matter what you wear, you're only a maid. He's never going to choose you. You are only a fuck to him. A skinny fuck."

I didn't show any surprise. In front of Victor and Elena, she had been pleasant for almost forty-eight hours since I arrived. I wasn't prepared for the words she spat at me. She was right, I am skinny. Models I see in magazines are skinny. Clothes look beautiful on them. I know, I'm not ugly.

I looked at her calmly, pretending I was classy, like Elena. I wanted to punch her in the face, but that was never going to happen. "Yes, Miss Luciana."

I remembered her screams when they were at it in the bungalow bedroom. Who was she to be calling me *puta*, anyway? No idea why she figured I was a threat to whatever she had going with Rico. I'm just a maid. I never forget I'm a servant dressed in these gorgeous clothes that Elena insisted I wear.

No matter what Luciana thought of me, at least I was giving them some relief. They knew I'd been with Rico at his home for long time. They knew I was his maid and could only guess about what went on between us. It was just sex. I'm fine with that.

When I was alone with him, I talked. When I wasn't talking, I thought about it. Rico, I need you to wake up.

A maid named Jackie spoke perfect Spanish. We got along. I gave her five dollars every day after she cleaned my room. In Juarez, that was a whole lot of money, but I wasn't in Juarez. Victor had given me a thousand dollars for expenses.

"You don't need to change my sheets every day."

"Everything gets changed," Jackie said with a smile. "All the rooms, even yours. Those are my orders."

"No argument from me."

On Jackie's day off, a lady named Lily was assigned to my room. I told her the same thing.

"Got to change everything, every day," she said in Spanish.

"It's just me," I said.

"Got to change everything, every day," she replied in English.

Most of my time awake was in Rico's suite and medical room. When I went into the room where Rico was, the attending nurse left to give me privacy with him.

I read to him in Spanish. I talked to him about everything. I sat next to the bed where the nurse normally sat but up close to the bed, so I could touch him. Normally I had held his hand. It was warm, seldom cold.

"Rico, my memories of you and me can fill a book of wonderful short stories. Funny, sensual, mysterious, loving and breath taking. Remember when you had me model for you? How difficult it was for me to find lingerie like you described because I couldn't cross the border to El Paso to shop. You should see the lingerie departments here! We don't have anything like it back in Juarez. Elena took me shopping. It was fun but not as much fun as you. You always ended up taking my clothes off. Remember, you had me prance around naked. You showed me how not to be shy and I got over the shy, did everything you wanted me to do. I never laughed so much in my entire life as I did when I was around you. I was never as happy. When I gave birth to my babies, I should have been happy, but I was sad because their father was a scum bag, and they would grow up without a father. But I don't want to talk about him. I want you to come back to us."

A nurse came in, fussed with some dials, wrote something down on her charts, and left. I held my tongue until we were alone again.

"Back to happy. I never said this to you before. I love you, Rico."

"Please wake up, Rico."

When a doctor came by to check on Rico, I left the medical area through the glass doors that divided the living room part of the suite. A television was always on there with the volume low or on mute. I had a television in my room and normally went to sleep with it on. When the station went off the air the screen went blank with snow and a persistent cracking sound. Most times it bothered me enough that I slid off the bed to turn it off.

The wing where Rico was had a cafeteria two floors below. Across the street from that part of the hospital was a delicatessen that was open twenty-four hours a day. On the same side of the street, a steak house opened at noon and closed at midnight. There was no shortage of options. It was all very interesting to me. America is different from my corner of Juarez.

I didn't eat big meals, but I ate at least five times a day. Hey, don't jump to conclusions. Look at me in the pictures. I'm still the same. I'm used to working all day. Here, there's no exercise, no walking to speak of except to the restaurants. I didn't do all that much of that when I was at the bungalow working for Rico unless I worked the main house. Those days were a workout for sure. When he was there and wanted me, the sex, that was sweet exercise.

When the lawyer Miguel came from Mexico City to visit Rico, he spent a good hour talking about how Rico got to Mayo. Miguel had been the one who arranged for Rico to be hospitalized at Mayo. He arranged for a private plane to bring him here. I told him that I had flown with Victor in a private plane too.

"I'm sure the plane you came in was nice. Now let me tell you about the plane I arranged for Rico to be brought in."

Miguel was fascinating. I liked him right away.

I must have looked like a dummy because I had a smile on my face the entire time he talked, and I listened. We were sitting on the sofa in the living room of Rico's suite.

Miguel checked my room and smiled approvingly. He said he wanted to be sure I was being taken care of.

Miguel was at the hotel where the group stayed, where I had stayed the first two nights until Victor, Elena, and Luciana decided I would be staying at the hospital.

Miguel returned late in the afternoon with three women. Two of them he introduced as assistants, probably his bodyguards. The third lady looked like a movie star. She was beautiful. Her name was Mirasol. The nurse was there by the bed, then she left the medical room. Miguel and Mirasol stood by the bed. I retreated to the sitting area behind the glass doors looking in with the assistants. I could only see the backs of Miguel and Mirasol. They stood there looking at Rico as he lay motionless,

This time when he left, it was evening. Miguel insisted I join them for dinner. I suggested the steak house across the street. It wasn't exactly my home away from home, but I'd been multiple times to all the eateries, and everyone knew me at all of them. When the three of us walked in, they greeted me, but everyone there remembered Miguel from when he had been there getting Rico settled in.

We ordered steaks, of course, and while we were waiting, exchanged small talk.

"Have you known Rico for a long time?" I asked Mirasol.

"Not even. I never met him. I was a stewardess on the flight that Miguel chartered to bring him here. When he was brought on to the plane by the medical team, I..."

The restaurant's lights weren't the brightest, but I could see a blush spreading across her face as Mirasol hesitated.

Miguel chuckled. "Mirasol says it is love at first sight."

"Really," I said.

I didn't laugh but Miguel, Mirasol and his two bodyguard ladies thought it was funny.

"Miguel was nice enough to invite me to join him on this trip." Mirasol said, "because he was coming to see Rico."

I wondered what Mirasol has done or will do for Miguel.

I have no business thinking that. Maybe I'm as big a cat as Luciana. Mirasol is beautiful.

I don't get the love at first sight. Maybe it's a joke between them?

She says she saw him on the plane and now she's here to watch him sleep.

I don't want to be like Luciana. I tell myself not to stress over nothing.

• • •

The morning after we had dinner, Miguel and his ladies' said goodbye. I enjoyed the break in routine. I liked Miguel, his bodyguard ladies and Mirasol. I wondered if Mirasol is going to become a regular in Mario's life when he wakes up. She told me she'd be back. Just like that. She didn't say she was coming back with Miguel either.

"Chow, Bonita," she said. "I see you again, soon."

I asked one of the doctors who saw Rico regularly if I could massage his feet. The doctor spoke good Spanish. "Good idea. I will have the nurse give you some oil."

"He likes lavender," I said. "I can go buy it."

"That's fine," the doctor said. "That way you get what you want."

I massaged his feet.

I read to Rico for hours at a time. I found a bookstore couple blocks away. Lucky for me they had many books and magazines in Spanish. I didn't bother with newspapers. The hospital had a wide selection but none in Spanish.

I talked to Elena on the phone almost nightly. "I'm getting good with my reading."

"You sound excited."

"I'll be more excited when Rico wakes up."

Elena sniffed. I heard. I thought maybe she'd been crying.

"He's going to wake up," I said. "I promise."

I heard another sniff.

"You have always been special," Elena said.

"Thank you for saying that."

Luciana seldom called. I certainly did not call her. When she did, she was very kind and nice. No doubt she was not alone when she called and was putting on for whomever was listening.

Victor called every day.

"Tell me when you get tired. I'll come up myself and relieve you."

Being sent away from Rico was the last thing I wanted. I assured Victor I was okay.

"I'm fine," I said. "Thanks to your kindness. I have everything I need."

"By the way, your mother said not to worry. The kids are fine," Victor said.

"Oh, thank you, Jefe."

My mother had no phone, but my sister still worked in the big house. She had called twice to let me know everything was fine with my babies. She'd told me Gusto or someone from the big house was making the daily rounds to check on my mother and my children and giving my mom money. I didn't know what I was getting paid for being here, but it wasn't important. I guessed it was the same as I got paid working for the Hidalgo family, but anything would have been okay. After all, Victor was paying for my room, had spent a year's salary on American clothes, and had handed me a thousand American, cash money.

Barbara had become one of my new American friends. She worked day shift for twelve hours and was chief nurse of the floor Rico was on. Her Spanish was as bad as my English.

"Is he your boyfriend?"

I thought I understood but I caught her meaning for sure after she put a pen to the back of a paper bag that was lying on the coffee table and sketched a man and woman kissing.

I shook my head.

"No, no boyfriend. Jefe, my Jefe."

One time I was leaning over Rico. I was not touching his body except that I put my lips to his ear. I whispered memories of one of the times we spent a night in bed together. My voice was low so no one could have overheard. I talked about a night we had been caught in the rain, showered together. It was the only time I ever showered with lingerie on, but it was a shower for the record books. I looked up and saw Barbara walk in. I know she didn't hear me, but she thought whatever she thought.

"Boyfriend, Si," she said with a little laugh and walked out.

I resumed my position and whispered to Rico, *"La Enfermera dice que somos novios.*[2]"

I giggled. "I wish that was true Rico but it's okay. I only want you wake up and be yourself again. Please Rico."

"I miss your *Gritos,*[3]. I miss your laughter."

I had been massaging his feet every night. It seemed to me he looked more peaceful while I was doing that, so I started massaging his feet twice a day. Of course, I had mixed the healer's marijuana creme with the lavender oil. It smelled heavenly. I love lavender.

The jar of creme was not very big. I only used a little, but I used it every time I massaged his feet with the oil. His skin was warm and fragrant to the touch. I had given him massages in the past, and the smell and feel of him revived vivid memories of times before. We would be lying around listening to music or watching television at his bungalow. He couldn't get enough.

I could not help the flood of memories that came rushing back every time. There was such a sense of intimacy, but it was so awful to be remembering this alone. I often became emotional, found myself rubbing his feet with tears pouring down my face. I would catch myself crying, and did my best to bury the emotion and find control over myself. The tears dried on my face. My hands were too oily to do anything about it.

I never missed a morning or night of doing his feet.

It was Sunday. The clock on the wall read 1:35PM. I had just finished working his right foot and was beginning on his left foot when I saw his toes move.

I pulled my hand back and stared at his foot, wondering if I'd imagined it. His foot jerked again. It happened so fast. I stared at his face, and it seemed I saw a trace of expression, a furrowed brow. I put my hands on his left foot, working it for all I am worth.

"Come back, Rico," I said aloud, my voice catching in my throat. His toes continued to move. Both feet moved. Just a little twitch, then his toes, one foot, both feet. His toes from both feet started moving. I bolted to the call button and jammed it with oily fingers. Seconds later, door opened and there was nurse Barbara.

I squawked some incomprehensible noise, then got the words out in English.

"Barbara, I think he's waking up, call the doctors!"

Barbara screamed!

I screamed!

---

1. Healer
2. The Nurse says we are lovers
3. Screams

ABOUT THE AUTHOR

George Hatcher is not simply an author. He is an avid world traveler, an entrepreneur with several businesses, and more. He's worn a lot of hats. If he's not flying off to some exotic location for work or pleasure, he's at home with his beloved Molly, the cats, and birds in Arcadia, California with his computer open to his latest work.

A longer bio is on his website at
http://georgehatcher.com/bio/bio.html